PIECES OF ME

BIJOU HUNTER
NOELLE ZANE

Dedication
To SaMiJaMaLu
My lovely betas—Carina, Cynthia, and Sarah
&
Judy's Proofreading

HOYT "RUIN" MACREADY

Ripping my club brother's dick off isn't my idea of a solid way to start the day. But Nash "Tomcat" Childs's cock has caused plenty of fucking problems over the years.

Plenty of women are happy to ride Nash's dick train. But climbing off leaves more than a few brokenhearted. *The latest weepy one was my assistant.*

Truth be told, I haven't had a decent one since my sister—Wynonna—got knocked up by her dumbass husband, Ralph. They're over the moon about their kids, and I'm fucking thrilled she found a man I didn't need to bury somewhere.

However, her happiness led me to one flaky assistant after another. The shitty ones never want to leave. The good ones get scared off by the club or Tomcat's apathy toward monogamy.

"For the love of God, stop fucking the help!" I yell at Tomcat as soon as I walk into Valley Gin Mill and find him sitting at a table with his feet up.

Our club's townie bar is located at the west end of a three-business complex next to McMurdo Gas and Go and Valley Homestyle Diner.

The Gin Mill is only open in the evenings. Most days, I use the place as an office. Despite renting an actual space at Valley Gorge Business Center, complete with a desk for my assistant and a waiting room, I'm rarely there.

A while back, I got a look at myself while walking into that place next to the suited types who also use the building. Couldn't shake the idea that I'd gone vanilla without noticing. So, most days, I work out of the Gin Mill.

Today, like most, Patrice Fuchs is behind the bar. Though the woman's got to be knee-deep into her seventies, she remains a beauty. Her long, wavy gray hair cascades down her shoulders and covers her impressive tits. She's part owner of the Gin Mill and like an aunt to me.

"What are you bitching about?" Patrice mutters while bringing my beer and a sandwich.

"Nash's dick scared off my latest assistant."

Studying me with her big brown eyes, she asks, "Does this job pay well?"

"Why, are you interested?"

"Fuck no," she says, wiping her hands on her towel before throwing it over her shoulder. "Spending all day following you around sounds like hell on earth. But I might know someone who could tolerate that shit. I planned to get her hooked up here as a waitress, but she has office experience."

"Wait, who is this?" I ask, and Tomcat's blue eyes widen in response to his next conquest.

"My granddaughters moved in with me. Selene worked in her husband's office. Don't know what kind."

Already on the hunt, Tomcat asks, "What granddaughters are these?"

"Mariah's kids. You know, my big-boobed daughter with a tiny brain."

"Did Selene inherit her mother's rack size?" Tomcat asks.

"Shut the fuck up!" I bark, but my cousin only chuckles and runs a hand through his short brown hair. "I'm more interested in if she's inherited her mom's tiny brain."

"I won't lie," Patrice says as her face pinches with irritation. "Selene's twitchy as fuck. Gets flustered a lot. Can't cook for shit. But she's not stupid."

Fingering my bottle's label, I'm aware I don't have many options. I've blown through all the local women willing to work for the club.

"Explain what you mean by 'twitchy.'"

"She isn't a meth head if that's what you're worried about. Selene had a shitty husband who

2

smacked her around. Her daddy was a rage monster. She recently suffered an injury. All that makes her glitchy when stressed."

"Maybe working for us wouldn't be the best for someone with her issues."

"Whatever," Patrice mutters, shrugging. "She'll just work here, then. Her sister's starting in a few days. Yazmin's weirder than Selene, but I need extra hands in here. Besides, I'm not running a homeless shelter in my house."

"Well, then, if she's gonna get corrupted by our scummy asses anyway, have her come around tomorrow at noon for an interview."

"Should she wear one of those dressy suit things?" Patrice asks, hiding her true feelings behind the unreadable face of a woman who fucks with people daily.

"Whatever she'd wear as a waitress, she can wear as my assistant."

"Good because her husband's being an ass about her shit. She arrived on my doorstep with barely any clothes."

"Who's this guy?" Tomcat asks.

"Just a rich piece of shit like her father. Don't you know women always want to marry their daddies?"

"Does that mean if I had a sister, she'd date assholes?" Tomcat asks.

He glances at where his dad—Glenn Childs—takes up an entire booth, having spread out his newspapers, laptop, and three phones across the table.

Always listening to our conversations, Glenn smirks. "Son, your artistry with words will be the end of you one day."

"He's a whiner," Tomcat tells Patrice, who shrugs and returns behind the bar.

Glenn's long nursed a crush on the local beauty. My uncle chased Patrice for years, even when he was married to Nash's mom. No matter his sales pitch, she always shot him down. He couldn't understand why until ten years ago when she returned from Vegas with her new wife.

"The love of my life has no use for cock," he told me after hearing the news. "Maybe karma's real."

I don't know if it is or not. What I am sure about is how I didn't appreciate Wynonna's skills until she was gone. Now, I'm forever scrambling to remember where I left shit and who I'm supposed to meet with today.

Because deep down, I'm not a fucking businessman in the real sense. I'm an outlaw who bought several legit places to launder money through.

Then, one day, I randomly got into a bitch fit with an uppity local businessman and ended up running for mayor as a "fuck you" to him. The next thing I knew, I had responsibilities beyond chilling with my bros—and our one biker chick member—and raising my daughter.

My life is filled with meetings, busy work, and crap no man like me needs to be worrying about. I dumped a lot of it on our accountants and lawyer. But I'm still stuck with more than I can keep track of.

I should have paid more attention in school. Or maybe they don't teach this shit in class. I wouldn't know since I fucked about until I was old enough to skip out.

Later after my early dinner at the Gin Mill, I sit on my massive front porch, listening to Joie scream on the phone at her bestie for smiling at a boy. My twelve-year-old daughter has taken a strong stance against dating. Apparently, Mikayla betrayed that oath.

Teenage girl shit is also something I never imagined I'd need to face. Joie's mom isn't in the picture. Considering Nicole had gone full hippie-dippy before I told her to get the fuck out, she isn't missed.

But now, I'm a single dad to a furious, hormonal teenage girl.

"Men are the worst," she announces after joining me on the porch. Her blonde hair is cut short and

4

layered. Her long legs hide behind camo pants. Her shirt has some internet character on the front. "Men are fucking scum."

"Sure, kid."

Smiling at me, she stares out at the pond in our front yard. Nicole insisted we build the house facing this way. I'd gone along with her ideas since I didn't give a shit either way.

Thinking of my ex-wife, I accept how none of my problems are created by others. Even the shit with Tomcat and my assistants happens because I won't rip off his dick.

I make poor choices every damn day. Anyone else would be in a world of pain by now. However, I was born under a lucky sign, meaning my stupid shit turns out golden.

Even the next day, when I oversleep, I don't miss a beat. My house manager, Tracey, already has Joie at school. I enjoy a late breakfast with Wynonna before meeting with my club sister, Lisa "Goose" Palmer. We ride around on our Fat Boy Harleys like we don't have a care in the world. But then, at nearly noon, I remember the interview with Patrice's granddaughter.

While I consider blowing it off and enjoying the warm afternoon, I can't fuck off each day. I need to work. To do that, I need an assistant.

I loop back toward downtown and the Gin Mill. Goose follows since she's bored and hoping I'll entertain her.

When I park my bike in the bar's mostly empty lot, I spot a woman at the front door.

"Holy hell," I mutter, yanking off my mirrored glasses and admiring the gorgeous thing fidgeting with her shirt sleeves.

"Whatcha bitching about?" Goose asks, already off her bike.

Never before has Goose offered me any pity for the dumb situations I find myself in. Today won't be any different.

5

"Please don't let that be Patrice's granddaughter," I say and throw my leg over my bike.

"Why?" Goose asks, frowning at the woman. "What's wrong with her?"

"Not a damn thing. That's why I don't want her to be my employee."

"Don't hire her, then."

"Patrice will hire her as a waitress."

Goose's blue eyes roll in response to my words. "You fuck the waitresses, Ruin."

"True," I say, wondering if there's a smooth way to shove this chick into a waitressing role without seeming like she's getting screwed.

I stroll to the front of Valley Gin Mill and take in the view of Selene up close. Her golden eyes widen at the sight of me. I can't tell if she's afraid or impressed. Maybe both.

Her face is a work of art. I can't believe this chick is real. Her thick brown hair is tugged into a loose ponytail with strands already flying free. She wears jeans and a shirt I've seen on Patrice.

Right then, I know if she wants the assistant job, I'll have no choice but to agree. With Selene focused on me, I can't imagine I'll have the power to tell her no about anything.

SELENE NORRIS GARRY

I don't know what I'm doing anymore. I've never run before. When afraid, I freeze and fawn. That's what my secret therapist told me before LeVoy found out and made me stop seeing her. My instinct is to become submissive and appease the person who frightens me.

But eventually, I had to embrace flight. Surviving meant leaving everything behind and moving into my grandmother's compact three-bedroom home in the picturesque town of McMurdo Valley.

Though unwilling to admit this fact out loud, I only ran to save Yazmin. Without my sister's life on the line, I never would have had the courage to walk away from LeVoy. Not even nearly dying could release me from my need to play the obedient wife.

With nowhere to go, we came to McMurdo Valley to stay with a woman we don't know. Patrice Fuchs was barely part of our life growing up. She didn't get along with my mother and was openly hostile toward my father. Carlos Norris isn't a man who tolerates such rudeness. As such, except for a single picture hidden behind others on the sunroom's piano, Patrice didn't exist in our life.

Yet, she opened her home to Yazmin and me when we begged her for sanctuary. Now, we're living in her tidy single-story house in McMurdo Valley.

Patrice and her wife, Cheryl, have several strict rules. 1) Never leave dirty dishes out. 2) Always check if a cat is around before opening an outside door. 3) Don't run the water while brushing your teeth. 4) The remote must be returned to the coffee table rather than left on the couch. *Apparently, a visitor misplaced a remote once and all hell broke loose.*

My grandmother and her wife have three cats with a room of their own. That means Yazmin and I must share the smallest bedroom with a queen-sized bed shoved inside.

"The cats need space for their toys," Patrice explained the first night we arrived wet, tired, and in pain. "Keeps them healthy."

I only nodded at her explanation. Before sending Yazmin and me to McMurdo Valley, my mother warned Patrice wouldn't like us.

"She's a specific kind of woman and doesn't like those who aren't like her," Mariah said, sounding sad as usual whenever her mother was mentioned.

I hoped Patrice might be different than my mom remembered. Yet, the night Yazmin and I arrived, my grandmother announced unprovoked, "I gave birth to tender-hearted, dimwitted daughters. Unfortunately, I never developed an appreciation for the soft or slow."

I knew instantly Yazmin and I were on borrowed time here.

We're not independent women like Patrice and Cheryl. We've never built anything. If we disappeared tomorrow, few would notice.

In contrast, joining Patrice at the store yesterday told me how much she means to the McMurdo Valley locals.

Respect isn't something I've often won from people. I ought to look up to my grandmother, but she overwhelms me.

On day one, she pushed for us to get jobs and pay rent. Then last night, she arrived home from the bar to find Yazmin, Cheryl, and I surrounded by cats while watching "Pam & Tommy."

"Selene, I got you a job interview with a local businessman," Patrice announced while tugging off her cowboy boots.

"What kind of job?" I asked as my stomach lurched.

"I won't bullshit you by cleaning up Macready's rep. I'm not your mommy with stars in her eyes. I'm a straight shooter, okay?" When I nodded, she leveled her mildly irritated gaze at me. "You know those bikers riding by this house all the time? Well, they're

8

the Steel Berserkers Motorcycle Club. They run legit stuff and stone-cold criminal crap."

A sleepy Yazmin frowned. "Why would you want Selene to work for them?"

"Who do you think owns the bar with me?" Patrice replied like we were halfwits. "They own lots of shit. Meaning they have plenty of money."

Tears bit at the back of my eyes. I'd just escaped one violent man. Now, my grandmother had tossed me toward another one.

How could I tell Patrice no? Her home was supposed to act as my sanctuary. If I crossed her, where could Yazmin and I go?

When Patrice patted the spot next to her on the couch, I joined her.

"Baby, your mama didn't get you ready for the world," Patrice explained as my gaze held Yazmin's. "Then, you married that monster. You've spent your life looking pretty and ducking punches. But those things won't help you now. You've got to make money to support yourself."

"But they're criminals," I mumbled, thinking about what I'd need to do to survive.

"Have any of those divorce lawyers you called gotten back to you?"

Shaking my head, I recalled how LeVoy always promised to ruin me if I left him.

"The club aren't good guys," Patrice explained in her most tender voice, "but they won't be the worst you've dealt with. So go to the interview. You'll mostly work for the club president, who cleans up well enough. Hoyt might scare the shit out of you, but he won't lay a hand on you. He'd fear I might slip something in his drink to immobilize him while I take my revenge on his nuts."

Yazmin and I laughed at the image of our seventy-four-year-old grandmother cutting off a biker's testicles. Her words calmed my fears. Hoyt couldn't be all that scary if Patrice was throwing around threats.

All night, I struggle to rest next to Yazmin. She's so quiet compared to LeVoy, who moved around all night. I'd lie next to him, pretending to sleep while he changed positions every few minutes until his pain medicine kicked in.

Around midnight, I watch Yazmin in the moonlit room. My thoughts return to how different she seemed after Robert got hold of her.

I can't imagine Yazmin waitressing in a loud bar. Maybe she ought to be the one to work for the club president while I waitress.

This morning, I consider suggesting the change. But Patrice isn't up by the time I need to leave. I think to ask Cheryl what she thinks. Except the auburn-haired beauty often exudes a weird vibe around me. She'll stare as if I'm an alien she's forced to cohabitate with.

Whenever I consider bailing on the interview, I remember how Patrice isn't helping us for free. We already owe our grandmother hundreds of dollars for clothes, food, and rent.

Those numbers roll around in my head when I take her car to the Valley Gin Mill to meet with the club president.

Administrative assistant feels like a grown-up job. If nothing violent or sexual is involved, I could handle office duties. I helped LeVoy with his business when he flopped hard after a few bad deals. We'd nearly lost our house. He fired his staff and had me and Yazmin help him.

"Your cunt sister already lives free at my house!" he yelled despite me immediately agreeing. "She eats my fucking food!"

I make myself remember how angry he got that night. LeVoy dragged me around all evening by my hair like it was the leash for his dog.

Even if I have to clean toilets, I can't afford to return to that man. I barely survived him the first time.

10

The Valley Gin Mill isn't open when I arrive. I admire the red siding and notice the lack of windows. Next door, people come and go at the gas station. The air is filled with rich meat odors from the nearby diner.

Waiting out front, I go over my answers to possible interview questions. Yazmin and I practiced at breakfast after looking online. Neither of us ever had a real job. We got internships and "daughter" positions in our late teens. Never did we need to hustle. Those jobs were no more than busy work until suitable men could secure us from our father.

LeVoy seemed soft when we were dating, yet he was a man prone to emotional outbursts and powerful fists.

In the twelve years I was married to LeVoy, I never found him sexy. He was mildly attractive with sharp features and a tall, thin build. Nothing about him felt impressive. Without his money, he was barely average.

The blond, bearded man walking toward me right now is jaw-droppingly sexy and very much impressive. His black T-shirt stretches across his wide shoulders and broad chest. His loose, shaggy hair blows in the wind, and a thick beard softens what is likely a rough face. I'd be intimidated by his tatted skin if he weren't so shockingly handsome in that special way rugged men can be.

My fatigue and fear fade as I drop into the clear blue warmth I discover in his eyes. This handsome man can't be the biker whose balls my grandmother will cut off if I'm done wrong.

I recall how Patrice explained Hoyt Macready's biker name was Ruin.

"He's ruined plenty of lives," she shared last night. "Bodies, too. Don't let his good looks fool you."

The words "good looks" don't do this man justice.

"Selene?" he asks, and my name sounds like magic in his husky voice.

11

Nodding, I can't form words. Feeling foolish, I wish I knew how to be cool and make a good impression.

No, that's wrong. I'm not aiming for a date. This is about a job. A paycheck allows me to repay my grandmother and move into a rental. Yazmin and I can get a car, too. Patrice said Hoyt was desperate for an assistant who'd stick around.

"He'll pay well," she explained. "You'll be out of my house and into a decent place of your own within two months. Won't need a dime from that asshole husband of yours."

Shoving aside my instant attraction to this insanely hot, dangerous man, I embrace Patrice's words. If I get this job, I have a chance at a proper second chance.

All I need to do is regain the ability to speak under the power of Hoyt Macready's penetrating gaze.

HOYT

Holy shit, I'm like a horny teen, fumbling over his dick as I try to get the damn door open. Selene's hazel eyes watch me struggle. Her expression seems so raw, unguarded, and terrified.

I remind myself how she's Patrice's granddaughter, has a shitty ex-husband, is suffering after a recent accident, and wants a job. She isn't jonesing to become my bed buddy. Just open the fucking door!

"There it goes," I say casually as if I wasn't ready to rip the thing off its hinges.

When our gazes meet, Selene still looks scared. Yet, fuck me, if she isn't the most beautiful woman I've ever laid eyes on. I've seen pictures of her parents. Logically, I know Selene should be hot. But this woman's something else.

Selene enters first and looks around like she's never seen a country bar before. *Hell, maybe she hasn't.* Patrice said her daughters married rich men. If Selene had herself a champagne upbringing, can she handle even a single day in my world?

"Let me get you a drink," I say, walking around the back of the shit-brown bar top.

Selene nods before shaking her head and then seeming unsure. She's trying to find the right answer. I bring her a water bottle and set it on a table in the middle of the room.

"Don't be nervous," I say, smiling as if I'm a nice guy with only the best intentions.

Despite Selene's nod, her raw fear fills the room. I can't imagine what she thinks when she sees me. *Am I why her hands are literally trembling?*

She shoves them onto her lap to hide their behavior. I remind myself how Patrice said her granddaughter was twitchy. That's all this is.

I need to stay focused on finding an assistant to help out. My mind shouldn't be on her fear, gorgeous face, or the curves barely hidden in her shirt and jeans.

"Patrice said you worked in an office before," I say while leaning back and trying to come off as easygoing.

"I worked for my hus— LeVoy," she stammers, stumbling over her words as if each one is an obstacle. "He was, is, he runs an investment firm. And I worked there. Not formerly."

Her inability to settle down forces me to take control. "Can you file?" I ask before she hurts herself with all her backtracking.

"Yes."

"Can you answer the phone and take messages?"

"Yes."

"Can you organize my schedule, so I know where to go each day?"

"I think so."

Running my hands through my hair, I consider how to make this job seem fun when it's really not.

"I don't sit in my office most days. I drive around and talk to people. Sometimes, I'll stay at a person's house for lunch. I meet and greet. But I find myself promising people shit and then forgetting once they're not in front of me. Can you write that stuff down so I don't need to?"

"Yes, but, um," she says, seeming to choke on air again. "I'll be with you for these outings?"

Imagining Selene at my side all day, I smile. "You'll go with me all day, yeah."

"On the motorcycle?" she asks, looking ready to cry.

"No, in my truck or SUV. We're not going on a date, Selene."

Though her cheeks burn red in response to my words, she also grins at my teasing. Finally, Selene stops acting like she might puke.

"I know you had some trouble in the past," I say, carefully picking my words. "Maybe you're not ready for this job. Some of the people we'll meet are bound to be rude. Others are downright hostile. As long as you can do most of the stuff, even if not all of it, I think we can find a compromise."

Selene's expression shifts over the next few seconds as if she's coming to a realization.

"I should be honest," she says, seeming so sad right now that I'm willing to offer this woman anything to see her pretty smile again. "I barely worked in his office. I also get flustered by stuff. I'm not super organized. I'm going to do a terrible job."

"How many job interviews have you been on in your life?"

"None."

"Sounds about right," I say, chuckling. "You're doing a terrible job selling yourself."

In her eyes, I see cold fear mixed with another warmer emotion. "I want to be honest. I'm worried if you hire me, I'll mess up your business."

"Or are you trying to get out of spending your days with a biker?"

Selene gives me the once-over like I'm a man she's considering riding. When her gaze meets mine, she offers a little smile.

"I thought you'd be scarier."

"I am," I say and rest my hands behind my head. "I'm a royal bastard to anyone who wrongs me. But you won't do that, will you?"

Selene's fear returns. "I'm not a good assistant."

"You're guessing with that answer. It's not like you know."

"No, and I really need this job."

"So, do you want it or not?"

"I do, but I'm afraid," she replies as her voice cracks. "What if I mess up and make things hard for you?"

I really wish she hadn't said "hard" since hearing the word slip from her sweet lips makes me fully erect. *How the fuck am I supposed to spend all day with this woman without constantly needing to wank it?*

"How about we give it a week? If it's not a good fit," I say, thinking of fitting in her sweet pussy and realizing I'll never be able to think straight around her, "I'll find you a job somewhere else. I own other businesses. That way, everyone's happy."

"You mean Patrice."

"No, I mean you."

"What did she tell you?" Selene asks, seeming smaller now as her shoulders fold inward. I swear she's trying to disappear.

"That you had a shitty husband and you needed a good job. Was there more?"

Selene shakes her head and reaches for the water. She sips the drink, fighting the urge to say something. By the time she finishes half the bottle, she's settled on keeping her mouth shut.

Against my better judgment, I ask, "This guy and you are over, correct?" Sipping her water again, she nods. "Officially?"

"Well, we're separated, but it's the permanent kind."

"When will it be official?"

Selene's expression flips to a sick kind of panic. I feel like her ex is currently in the room, ready to attack. I've rarely wanted to kill someone as badly as I do right now with this guy.

"If you need help with that, let me know."

"Help?" she asks breathlessly.

"With a lawyer or whatever."

Selene stares at her hands like she's reliving seriously dark shit. I don't know the right way to fix what's happening. I'm not a sensitive guy. I rarely offer advice. I'm never a shoulder to cry on. That's not me.

"Do you like burgers?" I ask, and she blinks a few times before nodding. "A perk of the job is free lunches. I get a lot of burgers. But the places I eat usually have more lady-oriented food."

"Lady-oriented?" she asks, fighting a grin. "Like salads or finger foods?"

Smirking, I shrug. "Chick stuff. Like chicken sandwiches or apple slices instead of fries."

Selene rewards me with a great smile. In the last few minutes, she's made my dick hard, my rage flare, and my heart race.

As we finish the interview with plans for me to pick her up tomorrow morning, I realize I've completely screwed myself here. I need an assistant who'll stick. Yet, there's zero fucking chance I'll keep things platonic with this sexy woman.

SELENE

Hoyt isn't at all what I was expecting. I figured a criminal biker would be an asshole.

LeVoy had illegal dealings, but he wrapped himself in an air of respectability. In contrast, I assumed Hoyt would be a brute. I still planned to tolerate him to make money.

But Hoyt was patient whenever I lost my train of thought. He clearly deserves a better assistant than me. I'll no doubt mess up his schedule or forget a call. He'll regret giving me a shot.

Exhausted and confused, I drive home in a daze. I park in the driveway of Patrice's dark blue-siding home. I sit in the car, wishing I could nap until my body felt like it did before the shooting.

Unprepared to go inside, I recall Hoyt's shirt tag sticking out. I'd wanted so badly to fix that for him. *What would my fingers find when they touched his bare skin?*

Hoyt's one of those effortlessly masculine men. He doesn't need to act tough. His size and quiet menace do the talking for him.

But his smile left me silly in a way I've never felt before. My dates as a teenager were chaperoned. The only man I've known in a real way was LeVoy. I'm unaccustomed to the lust swirling around in my stomach. The hot butterflies threaten to burn me up.

The sight of Yazmin at the side door, watching and waiting, rips me from my happy thoughts. My sister is so beautiful, yet her mind is tattered. I don't think she can see herself clearly.

Tomorrow, she's supposed to start working at the Valley Gin Mill. My tall, busty brunette sister will be surrounded by men making eyes at her. They won't be able to help themselves. Her golden eyes with flecks of green promise what her heart can never offer. Men have always been drawn to Yazmin. Yet, her one attempt at love ruined her.

Yazmin's survival has depended on me since she left the psychiatric hospital. LeVoy let her live in our guesthouse. Not out of empathy for my sister or me. Mostly, he wanted me to stay on our estate. Yazmin gave me a dependent friend to talk to. He couldn't chance I'd meet someone who might encourage me to stand up to him.

I climb out of Patrice's car and smile at my younger sister. She'll never be right in the head. I have to take care of her. My sister's survival offers me a goal. Pleasing Patrice does, too.

That's why I gasp and tear up when I reach the house. Yazmin hurries to my side.

"What's wrong? Did he not hire you? Was he mean?"

"I forgot to ask about salary," I mumble, crying now. "I got flustered and forgot to ask all that stuff we read about on the internet. Patrice will think I'm stupid."

"But you got the job, right?" she asks, wrapping me in her warm, familiar embrace.

"Yes."

"Was he rude?"

"No. He was really nice. That flustered me."

Yazmin looks at me and frowns. "Why would you be upset by him being nice?"

I glance around before whispering, "He's very handsome."

Yazmin doesn't react immediately. Her face freezes in that way it has since she got locked up. As if she slips into a part of her mind, hidden from the world. When she steps back into the now, Yazmin smiles.

"How handsome?"

"Exceedingly."

"But he's a biker," she whispers. "Like gruff and tattooed and dirty."

"Not dirty or gruff."

"But tattooed?" she asks, cocking an eyebrow.

"Yes, I noticed a few."

"And he was nice to you?"

"He really needs an assistant."

"You'll do a good job."

"No, probably not. I wasn't great at LeVoy's office."

"He was an asshole barking at you. His real employees didn't like him, either."

I open my mouth before snapping it shut as Patrice appears at the side door.

"Well?"

"He said I start tomorrow."

"How much are you getting paid?"

Feeling the tears returning, I lower my gaze and shrug. Patrice grunts her disapproval before disappearing inside.

"It's okay. Any money is better than none," Yazmin says in her melodic voice. "You did well today."

I look into her eyes, saying what words can't express. Basically, I'm drowning in fear.

My body hurts, feeling like it no longer belongs to me.

I'm afraid of dying yet scared of living.

A target remains on my back. Everyone around me could be in danger. I ought to return to LeVoy and let him finish what he started. At least Yazmin, Patrice, and Cheryl would be safe.

Instead, I selfishly hold on to hope for a second chance at life.

"I'm proud of you," Yazmin says and hugs me.

Her words pull me from the darkness, reminding me how we're a team. She needs me to survive. *I can't give up.*

So rather than worry about salary, I'll focus on succeeding on my first day as Hoyt Macready's assistant.

HOYT

The Valley Gin Mill is dead tonight. Most of the Steel Berserkers are partying at the Pigsty—the clubhouse where a majority of the members call home.

I'd normally be there, talking up my people and finding a warm pussy to enjoy.

Instead, I've got Selene on my mind. Now, I can't imagine any other woman hitting the right spot as long as I struggle with this itch for my assistant.

Patrice stands behind the bar, ignoring Nash, me, and her two other customers.

"Why are you here?" I ask my cousin.

His blue eyes light up. "I like when you pay attention to me."

"Idiot," I mutter. "No, really, why are you here when you could be plowing your way through the wild girls at the Pigsty? Don't tell me you broke your dick on my last assistant."

"Maybe I'm saving it for your new one. I heard she's a real stunner," he says, batting his eyes.

Patrice grunts out of nowhere. "I should have gotten Yazmin to start tonight when the place is dead. Give her a chance to learn shit before she has to keep up with you dumbasses."

Nash grins before leaning back in his chair and tempting gravity.

"Dana's going to be around the Pigsty," he explains, ignoring Patrice's comment. "I'm waiting until she finds a dick to ride before I show up and enjoy someone better."

"What's her deal with you?" I ask, opening a fresh beer. "She can't be stupid enough to think you'll love her."

"Dana has a goal to get double-plugged by you and me."

"Well, that's a dream she'll never realize. No way am I slapping balls with you."

"Insecure," he murmurs, making Patrice snicker.

I hear my uncle chuckle from his corner spot. Feeling restless with them all thinking of Nash and me bouncing balls with the same woman, I choose to hound Patrice.

"What did Selene say about today?"

"That you have a big dick, and she's going lesbian. Nothing else came up," she taunts before frowning. "What are you planning to pay her? Or is your star power meant to pay her bills?"

"Yeah, I guess we skipped that part," I say, rubbing my beard and thinking of Selene across from me. She's a damn fine-looking woman. I can be forgiven for losing my train of thought with such beauty within reach. "I'll pay a thousand a week. Half in cash, half nice and legal. Sound good?"

"Start her lower," Patrice replies, making me frown. "That way, if it doesn't work out, she won't feel like she screwed herself out of a good job. Then, give her a raise when she doesn't fuck up after a week or two. It'll be good for her self-esteem."

"Well, shit, Patrice, is there anything else you got to tell me?"

"Get a haircut and trim your beard. I'm not interested in looking at your sasquatch ass all night."

While my uncle chuckles at her taunting, I ask, "What's the deal with Selene's hubby? When you say he smacked her around, how bad are we talking?"

"Seems like a topic you ought to ask her."

Rolling my eyes at Patrice playing private when we all know she's a gossip, I mutter, "I'm not looking to make her feel awkward."

"So, you put it on me, then?"

"Come on, Patrice. What kind of kid gloves should I use with her?"

"Leave me alone," she insists and snaps her towel at me. When I offer my best smile, she only rolls her eyes. "Save your charm. It doesn't work on me."

"No, this might not," I say and grab my junk. "But you're still susceptible to a country boy's charm. I've seen how my dad gets under your skin."

"Under the skin, maybe," Nash says and adds while smirking at his father, "But never between her folds."

Patrice gives my cousin her sternest side-eye. "I don't know any details about her husband. Just that he was abusive."

"Then, what's the story about her accident?"

"Why do you need to know?"

"She's jumpy."

Bugging her big brown eyes at me, Patrice grumbles, "I told you she would be."

"But I need to know how much of that is just her being a goofy chick and what stuff I need to be careful about."

"Just be careful about it all," Patrice replies before grinning at her own suggestion. "I'll tell you, but you can't go all ape-shit caveman on me. I've got a headache, and your man-struation won't help."

I smile at her utter disdain for the even slightest emotions from men.

"I'll be a rock. Not a single tear will fall."

"I was more worried about you flipping out and seeking revenge."

I lose my smile. "Spill it."

"It wasn't an accident," Patrice says and shrugs. "As much as it was a man broke into her fancy house and shot her six times."

"Holy shit," Nash mutters. "How is she alive?"

"Almost wasn't. Mariah called me crying after she hadn't spared me a single thought in years. Suddenly, my daughter remembered my number, just so she could dump the news of Selene's impending death."

Patrice fists her wash towel and scowls. "I got hold of Yazmin, who sent a picture of her sister looking fucked up in a hospital bed. Then, I heard nothing until those two showed up in town."

"Why are they here?" I ask when I can't express what I'm really thinking.

"Mariah couldn't keep them at her house. Their father wanted Selene to go back to her husband."

"Did he hire the shooter?" Nash asks.

"Of course," she growls at him as if he's a moron. "A man like him pays someone to break into his house while he's out of town. You know, to create an alibi."

"That's what Selene told you?"

"Not exactly. You see how she gets when rattled. Getting info out of her is nearly impossible. But I know her father wouldn't let her stay. Mariah gave them enough cash to get them here."

Patrice shakes her head. "My girls married these rich men, thinking they'd never have to struggle. But that money is the leash their men use to tie them down. Mariah loves her daughters, but she won't walk away with nothing."

Nash strolls over to the bar top and drops onto one of the stools. "Why can't Selene get a lawyer to take some of her rich man's shit? With a good divorce settlement, she could quit her job and let Hoyt fuck her."

While I shove my cousin hard enough for him to frown at the pain, Patrice ignores our roughhousing.

"Selene's called a bunch of Louisiana lawyers. They're real interested when they hear her hubby is rich. Then, they look into shit and lose her number. I don't know what her man does for a living. I doubt Selene does, either. Doesn't matter, I guess. No way would she agree to be poor if she weren't sure he sent the gunman."

Sighing, I mutter, "This guy needs to die."

"No caveman shit," Patrice growls and pokes her finger at me. "You promised."

"Did I?" I ask and look at Nash, who shakes his head. "I feel like I just swore I wouldn't cry."

"Right now, that asshole is leaving her alone," Patrice grumbles, holding my gaze. "He gets to keep

25

his money and punish her. Eventually, I figure he'll give her a deal with a skimpy payout. Then, he can get the cheap divorce he figured the gunman would provide him."

Patrice pokes her finger in my face again. "But if you go sniffing around that asshole, he might decide to send someone else. Selene's poor body can't handle more trauma. Don't even get me started on her fragile fucking brain. The other day, Cheryl found her and Yazmin hiding in the closet after the doorbell rang."

"What's the other one's problem?" Nash asks, sounding overly curious.

Snarling at my cousin, I say, "Don't fuck her."

"I already promised Patrice I wouldn't."

"You said the same thing about my last assistant. Why would you keep your word to Patrice but not to me?" I bark at Nash, who smiles like I already know the answer.

Patrice sighs loudly. "Both of them are fucked in the head. Just let them do their jobs and make enough money to get out of my house."

"Is Selene ready for a job if she's suffered all that trauma?"

"I don't know. She was in the hospital for months. Yazmin lived there with her. Once she was released, they went to Mariah's place. I would assume Selene is healthy enough to live her life if she's not seeing a doctor."

"No roughhousing with the new assistant," Nash warns me and winks. "Maybe you should go to the Pigsty and find someone to take out your pent-up dick energy on."

Snarling at my cousin, I bark, "Why are you here again?"

"He's hiding from a club whore!" Uncle Glenn yells out and laughs at his son.

Nash struts over to his father's table, where they annoy each other. I look at Patrice, who watches me with irritated eyes.

"What?" I ask, feeling as innocent as the day I was born.

"I seem like a bitch, don't I? With those girls, I mean."

"You're letting them stay. Getting them jobs. Seems solid."

Patrice throws the rag down and rests her hands on the bar top.

"Mariah's husband claimed I was a bad influence on her. I never spent any time with her girls. Couldn't pick them out of a lineup most of their lives. When Selene got married, I was invited. Mariah called beforehand to insist I behave and avoid upsetting the big-shot groom. So why would I attend? They don't want me around. I don't know them. But now those two strangers show up, needing me to save them."

"They'll be in their own place soon," I say when she stares at the empty glass in front of me.

"Maybe I should be softer with them," she mumbles, seeming bothered in a way I've never seen her before. "They're fucked up. Not just ditzy like their mom. Mariah had some sense. I made sure of that. But these two are wired all wrong. Don't know if that's from their father or their men. Maybe both. Cheryl keeps saying they need patience. I know she's right. But I look at those women in my house and get so angry at how I don't know them."

One thing Patrice and I have in common is we don't do emotions. So seeing her struggling leaves me tongue-tied. I eventually spit out, "This shit might be good for you. It'll definitely help them out. Growing up with that ditz mom and their asshole dad left them missing fundamental ingredients in their makeup. You're a good example of how strong women act."

Patrice eyes me like I'm blowing smoke up her ass. "I'm an old woman, Hoyt. I can't raise those girls."

"They're not little kids."

"No, but they need supervision. I gotta get them ready for when I'm gone."

"Where are you going?"

"I'm seventy-four years old, fucker. I won't be around forever."

"It's only been a few weeks, right?"

"Less."

"And they have jobs now. Soon, they'll have a place to live. Beautiful women don't stay alone for long. In six months, you'll be living your life like before. Except maybe these two aren't ditzes like your daughters. Maybe you'll like having them around the Valley."

Patrice reaches across the bar top and grips my hand. She looks me in the eyes, real serious-like, as if we're making a blood pact.

"Don't hurt Selene."

"I won't."

"She isn't strong. Her father raised her to be a submissive bitch. She doesn't stand up for herself. She didn't even think to ask how much you'd pay her. That girl is weak, Hoyt. You could twist her up and make her your bitch so damn easy."

"Why would I do that? I'm never an asshole to just be one."

"She's beautiful," she spits out.

I cringe as if she's got my number. "So are a lot of women."

"Are you claiming you aren't interested?"

"Well, I wouldn't say that."

"Don't break her, Hoyt," she hisses, revealing the temper of a woman who's lived in a violent world for much of her life. "She's barely holding on. If you break her, I'll break you."

"Patrice, I've allowed you some leeway on account of us going way back and my uncle referring to you as the 'love of his life.' But you need to remember who you're talking to."

Patrice narrows her gaze. "I'm at the end of my life, Hoyt Macready. If you or your horny cousin fuck up my fragile idiot granddaughters, I'll kill you. What will I miss out on? A few extra years. Who gives a shit? You, though, are young enough to care about dying."

"Stop threatening to kill me."

"Joie will be fine with Wynonna."

"You're crossing lines!" I holler and pound on the bar top. "Don't talk about my baby!"

Patrice smirks. "You remember that ugly feeling you have right now. How you'd do anything to protect your girl. Then, you keep that feeling in mind when you consider fucking Selene. She isn't strong enough for your callous heart."

"Am I going to need to separate you two?" Glenn asks, walking over from his table as Patrice and I glare at each other.

"I'm done here," I say and stalk out of the club's bar.

The roar of my Fat Boy quiets the anger I feel at Patrice's poking. She might be right about Selene. Sure, I get why she's protective. I'd threaten anyone in the fucking world to protect my baby girl.

But that doesn't mean I like what Patrice has to say. I'm not a bad guy to people who matter. If I wanted Selene in a real way, I could be good to her.

Rather than ride to the Pigsty to blow off steam, I take the long way home so I can think.

I imagine winning Selene into my bed. Falling for her would be easy. She's gorgeous and delicate. She's already infected me with a heavy amount of lust. I could wrap her in my life and keep her safe.

But I'm not sure I have it in me to be with only one woman long term. Patrice is right about me being fickle.

And that's why I got so fucking angry at her. Not just bringing Joie into the discussion or Patrice threatening to end me. All that shit was her bravado.

My anger comes from her being right. No matter my best plans, I'll fuck up with Selene. That fragile woman will be ruined because of me.

Unwilling to have her suffering on my conscience, I'll force myself to keep things professional.

SELENE

My hair remains a sticking point as I prepare for my first day as Hoyt Macready's assistant. Up or down? Ponytail or half pulled up? I get through wardrobe selection quickly with Yazmin's help and my lack of options. My hair, though...

"Down is too sexy," Yazmin insists. "A ponytail makes you look too relaxed. Go halfway."

"He won't care about your damn hair," Patrice grumbles from the other door of the Jack and Jill bathroom. "You'll be in and out of his truck all day. Just wear comfortable shit."

After Patrice walks off to enjoy coffee with Cheryl on the back porch, I frown at Yazmin.

"I'm nervous."

"You'll do great."

"Probably not."

"You'll do your best."

"Maybe."

Yazmin cradles my face in her hands. "If you mess up, use the pity card. Just tell him you're in pain and mention your injuries. He'll be nicer that way."

"What if he thinks I'm a drama queen and fires me?"

"You'll come work with me at the Valley Gin Mill."

"He did say if this job didn't work out, he could find me something else. That's good, right?"

"Exactly."

I stare into her eyes and whisper, "I'm still really scared."

"You've suffered so much in the last year," Yazmin whispers back. "Today won't be anywhere near as terrifying as that. You said he's nice."

"He's a criminal."

"Yes, but he was nice."

"He probably kills people."

"He won't kill you."

31

"You don't know."

Yazmin glances in the direction of the back patio before whispering, "Patrice is scary. He won't want to make her angry."

We share a smile. "I know you have to start work today and will want to rest. However, will you stay close to your phone all day?"

"Of course. I have nothing to do until Patrice takes me into the bar."

"It's not a bad place. The bar is sort of retro cowboy."

Yazmin snorts at my description. "I don't know what that means."

"A lot of dark wood. Think 'Urban Cowboy.'"

"I've never seen that movie."

"Well," I say, sliding her thick brown hair from her shoulders and exhaling deeply, "once we have money from our jobs, we'll stream the movie. That way, you'll know what I mean."

"But I'll have seen the bar by then."

"Yes, but you won't know if I described it right."

Yazmin sees me getting teary-eyed and inhales deeply. We breathe together for several minutes before I get myself under control.

"If you embarrass yourself, it's okay," she tells me, and I nod. "If you don't know the answer, just be honest. If you're scared, tell him."

"What if he's the one scaring me and doesn't care?"

"Then run away and call for help."

"What if the police don't care here like they didn't in Bossier City?"

"Then call me," Patrice says, startling us. She rolls her eyes at how we flinch before adding, "Hoyt Macready is a bad man who does bad stuff. But he will not hurt you, Selene. He's a big idiot with women, letting them run wild since he can't pound on them. So stop fussing and get your ass outside. He's waiting."

Nodding, I move forward as if walking to my doom. Yazmin follows me until Patrice grabs her shirt and yanks her to a stop.

"Let her be."

I stand at the door and look back at my sister. We've survived a lot over the last few years. We're strong, sorta. I'm perfectly capable of working as the assistant to a dangerous man.

"I'll call later," I tell Yazmin before walking outside.

Cheryl appears behind me with my purse and phone. "You might need these."

Realizing I'm already messing up, I stare into her blue eyes and start panicking.

"He's a handsome guy," she says softly. "Go stare at his pretty face. It'll make the rest of the day easier."

Smiling at her advice, I turn to find Hoyt sitting in his large black four-door truck. I expected it to be run down like a work vehicle. While the truck is extremely dusty and the massive tires are caked with mud, the vehicle can't be more than a few years old.

Expecting him to honk soon, I get my feet moving until I reach the passenger door. I open it and realize I'll need to climb into this truck.

"Need me to get out and give you a push up?" he asks, smirking as he types into his phone.

"No, I just have to figure it out."

"Take your time. Your grandma said you'd been in the hospital recently. I should have brought something smaller, but I needed the four-wheel drive today."

Setting my bag on the passenger side floor and resting my phone on the seat, I reach for the assist grip. Height-wise, I'm slightly above average. Yet, I feel like a child as I lift my foot to the sidebar.

My first attempt doesn't go well. I wince in pain as the still healing torso muscles stretch. Hoyt stops playing on his phone and cocks an eyebrow.

"For serious now. Do you need help?"

"I have it."

"I feel like you don't."

"I'm just weak."

"Selene," he says in a voice demanding to be heard. "Let go of the handle."

I do what he says as my gaze holds his.

"Use the seat to get yourself up. Less stretching that way. If that doesn't work, I'll come around and give you a push up."

The thought of his hands on my ass breaks my brain. When I stare at him, Hoyt frowns and starts to get out.

"I've got it," I lie and slowly crawl into the passenger seat.

After more effort than necessary, I do get situated. Then, I nearly fall out of the truck while trying to reach for the door to tug it closed.

"This is on me," he says as I strap myself in before remembering I'm sitting on my phone. "I should have gotten you a stool to use."

"A stool?" I ask, wiping sweat from my face.

"Years back, Wynonna needed to go to the hospital, thinking she was in labor. It was just a false start. But I showed up to get her since her man was out of town. Imagine an eight-month pregnant woman climbing into a truck like this one. I finally got the step stool. Don't know why it never occurred to either of us to take her car. Guess we were just excited."

"Who's Wynonna?"

"Didn't Patrice give you any info on me?"

Like an idiot, I reply, "She said you won't kill me."

Hoyt flashes me a dark look. "She just blurted that out, huh?"

"No, well, I mean, she was, I mean…"

"Do I make you nervous?"

"Yes," I reply as we leave the residential neighborhood where Patrice and Cheryl live before heading toward the more rural area in McMurdo Valley. "But everyone makes me nervous."

34

"Because of your accident?" he asks, and I can tell he knows the details.

"I'm a nervous person. I cried a lot as a child."

"Well, don't cry today. I'm not good with tears."

"I'll do my best," I say, trying to sound casual. Quickly, I destroy the illusion by mumbling, "But it's my first day, and I'm stressed."

As the truck idles at a four-way stop sign, Hoyt flashes me a wonderful smile.

"We're going to have an easy day. Just driving around for a few hours. Eating lunch somewhere nice. Driving around more. Unless you get car sick, it ought to be fine."

"Okay."

"I forgot to mention salary," he says as we drive down a long stretch of nothing. "Are you okay with five hundred a week to start? If shit works out in a week or two, I'll give you a raise."

"That would be great."

Hoyt frowns at my enthusiasm. I honestly have no idea what anyone gets paid. Two thousand dollars a month combined with Yazmin's salary will allow us to buy more of our own stuff and stop mooching off our grandmother. In a few months, we'll be able to move out.

"Who's Wynonna?" I ask after we take a rough turn down another long quiet road.

"My little sister. She lives with her husband and kids in the Valley. Our dad does, too, with his latest wife. Our mom moved to Mexico."

"Why did she move?"

"She dreamed of working at a beach resort and made it happen."

"Do you see her?"

"I take my daughter to the Mexican resort once a year."

"How old is she?"

"Joie's twelve. Just hitting puberty. I'm not worried at all."

Smiling at his sarcastic tone, I feel calmer now. Hoyt is more than a scary criminal. He's an exceedingly handsome and warm man who just happens to be a criminal. For a biker president, he's less intimidating than my elderly grandmother.

"This first stop is nicknamed the Pigsty," Hoyt explains as we ride down a tree-lined road. "It's the clubhouse where most of our members are holed up. The former lodge feels like a frat house. I used to live there before Joie."

"What will we do there?" I ask, nervous about meeting more bikers.

"I need to look around and make sure the place isn't getting torn up. They really are a bunch of pigs," he says, chuckling. "I was supposed to come around yesterday when they were having a party, but I never got the time."

My nerves remain on edge. My body also hurts from climbing into the truck. Yet, despite those distractions, I sense Hoyt editing himself. His tone changes slightly when he's fibbing.

Is he taking me somewhere dangerous? Or is he just shining up the ugly truth like when he talked around the subject of my accident?

We arrive on a smoother road before it dips toward a large log-style building with a forest-green roof. The former lodge has a wide wraparound deck. I can imagine tourists visiting this place to enjoy the nature trails, lakes, and hills.

Hoyt parks the truck in a spot away from lined-up motorcycles. He tells me to wait. Though I assume I'm staying in the truck, he comes around to help me out. I end up sliding down his body like he's my personal ladder.

I shouldn't stare into his eyes for as long as I do. Despite knowing my gawking is turning this moment into something blatantly sexual, his masculine aura shorts out my common sense.

"I have an ulterior motive for bringing you here today," he says, stepping back when I stare for too long. "I figured the guys might see you around town and get overly friendly. You know," he mutters and struggles for the right words while rubbing the back of his neck. "You're an attractive new woman in town. Get it?"

"No," I mumble, thinking he wants me to date someone here or maybe even worse. *Are biker orgies a thing?*

"I figured I introduce you to the pigs during official business, so they won't get too friendly when you're around town."

"Oh," I say, realizing he's protecting me. "Okay."

When I smile too big, Hoyt goes overly still. I think I've offended him. His pretty blue eyes hide ugly secrets. When he gets tense like now, I almost see what lingers behind his easygoing vibe.

"Let's get this done," he mutters, seeming irritated now.

I follow him up the wide steps to the red double doors. He doesn't knock before entering. However, he does holler out, "Wynonna's in the house! Put your pants on!"

I hear some commotion inside while Hoyt blocks my view. After a minute, he moves aside so I can enter.

The foyer is grand with an antler chandelier that both enchants and horrifies me. I don't want to think of all those dead deer, but it's a beautiful piece nonetheless.

A large staircase leads to a walkway overlooking the foyer and a family room on the other side. Hoyt strolls through what was most likely a dining room but now acts as a game room, complete with a pool table.

We pass through the large kitchen with its shiny industrial-style appliances. Finally, we arrive in the massive family room overlooking an extended back deck, pool, and the sort of natural beauty anyone would pay to visit.

"Well, hello," mumbles a shaggy, dark-haired young man from his spot on the floor next to the couch. "Ruin brought a gift, Yagger."

The blond man on the couch opens his eyes to check me out. Men appear from different rooms until this one is filled with masculine energy.

Without thinking, I shuffle behind Hoyt.

"Don't be scared, baby," says another dark-haired biker from the back doors. "We're gentle and know how to wait our turn."

Hoyt clears his throat. "This is my new assistant, Selene."

"Good for you, man," announces a second blond biker, and I stop being able to see individuals. They become a living, breathing mass of muscles, tattoos, and smirks. "Does she do tricks?"

Smiling, Hoyt turns to me. "Wait for me on the porch, please."

I notice the men's demeanors shift. I don't know if I'm in trouble or they are. *Well, I think they are.* But I'm so used to worrying about messing up and getting punished that I still stress.

Hurrying out the front door, I breathe in the fresh pine-filled air and settle my anxiety. After fishing my phone out of my purse, I text Yazmin.

"Everything is okay."

Yazmin responds, "I nearly came outside and helped you get in that stupid truck."

"It's really big."

"I have a feeling you'll be saying that a lot around Hoyt Biker Man."

I reply with a laughing emoticon. Her humor keeps me sane, even as I hear loud voices inside the house. Something breaks, followed by more hollering. I back away from the front door as a stampede takes place inside.

Curiosity winning out over fear, I peek through a crack in the shades to find men running away from a threat. A beer bottle flies past one guy, barely missing his head.

Freaked out now, I leave the porch and wonder about escape routes. In horror movies, people who stand around always end up dead. The runners—aka cowards like me—sometimes survive. *Should I flee? Where would I go? Can I even run when my body hurts from earlier?*

The answer is no. I'm remaining right here and waiting for Hoyt. If a monster comes stalking outside after killing those muscle-bound bikers, well, then I'm screwed anyway.

Rather than a ferocious creature, Hoyt opens the door and steps outside. He stops to slide his hands through his messy blond hair and stroke down his beard. He reaches back inside and grabs something before shutting the door.

Flashing a casual smile, he walks past me and toward his truck. I'm so focused on how calm he is that I take a few seconds to realize he's carrying a step stool. I grin at how he fixed my problem.

"Thank you," I say, stepping up and into the truck with ease.

"This is going to work," he says, sounding like he's talking more to himself than me.

He shoves the step stool into the back seat and walks around the truck. I think to ask what happened. Did they attack him? Is one of the bikers crazy? I look back at the lodge to find it quiet. Whatever happened inside is over.

But I don't ask Hoyt questions. If he wanted me to know, he'd explain.

Settling into my seat, I text my sister to say I'm going on my second errand. She gives me a thumbs-up. I smile at Hoyt, who pulls the truck away from the lodge and heads down another long, quiet rural road.

HOYT

Selene is bound to make a fool of me. I feel myself already falling down that irrational hole.

She's too goddamn beautiful. Delicate too. I'm not used to such women. I don't know what the fuck to say to her. She leaves me tongue-tied with only a glance from her golden eyes.

When I think of her nearly dying, I want to burn down the world. The idea of her evil fucking husband still breathing offends me. I'm a man capable of truly fucked-up shit. I scared the crap out of my club brothers today when they were mouthing off in front of Selene.

They probably should have ganged up on me. But I'm a mean son of a bitch. I don't have a sense of humor about some things. If I'm challenged, I'll fuck them up. That's why I'm the president. My road name came from ruining assholes.

However, I don't hurt women. Okay, Nicole would claim I stole Joie from her. But the bitch went nuts with urine therapy and other wackadoodle shit. So fuck her rights. She needed to either reclaim her sanity or get the fuck out of our daughter's life. She chose crazy over her baby girl. *So, fuck Nicole.*

But I'm not a guy who hits women. I don't even fuck them rough. I like sex to feel good. Wrapping my hand around a chick's throat while I pound her hard doesn't do it for me. I prefer to separate my soft shit—like my family or fucking chicks—from my rough crap—like kicking ass and cutting throats.

Selene's piece-of-shit husband would likely piss himself if he ever faced a guy like me. Only a weak asshole would break a delicate creature like her.

My temper keeps simmering through our next outing to a local business owner's place. Todd Rogers is old as fuck, but he's got three big stupid sons. If Todd's unhappy, his idiot offspring break shit. If

Todd's happy, the dumb shits stay occupied on their stretch of land in McMurdo Valley's west end. That's why I prefer to keep Todd in a good mood.

Well, that's Mayor Hoyt Macready's goal, anyway. If Ruin gets pissed at those three dumb fucks, Todd will need to shuffle his old ass over to the funeral home to see what's left of his boys.

"You're Patrice's granddaughter, eh?" Todd asks, doing his deaf old-man routine. "She's a good-looking woman. I remember her daughter from way back in the day. Real pretty blonde with nice tits."

"That's my aunt," Selene says and eyeballs the ice tea foisted on her by Todd's nineteen-year-old gold-digger girlfriend.

The asshole frowns. "Is your mama ugly, then?"

"Yes," Selene says and sets down the drink when she sees me ignoring mine. "Face like a mule."

Though I don't know why she's lying, I enjoy watching Selene spit sass. She's such a passive, nervous creature. Even when she's perfectly still, I sense her panic.

Right now, she seems annoyed by the fan blowing right at her head. I have her switch places, so I block most of the breeze. She smiles at me like I'm a goddamn hero. *Hell, if her approval doesn't feel good.*

"I'm worried about those new people on the east side," Todd tells me. "They're building big houses and putting in little ones for their stupid city kids. I don't want this place overrun by urban dwellers."

"I met the Simpsons. They seem like seasonal visitors. We won't see them around much. Doubt you'll run into them at all."

"Is that what you're telling me?"

Holding his gaze, I mutter, "Yes, Todd, that's what I'm telling you."

"I swear people are getting soft these days. Right, Ashley?" he asks of his great-granddaughter-aged girlfriend.

"They sure are, Todd, baby. People today don't have any respect for tradition."

Todd nods at how the gold digger tells him what he wants to hear rather than speaking the truth.

"Well, the Valley doesn't say no to money," I explain to Todd. "If this place dries up, that's bad for many businesses, including mine."

Todd takes off his glasses and squints at me. He's hearing what I'm saying. My words don't belong to the mayor who kisses his ass. Right now, I'm speaking as the club president whose businesses rely on young people. Old fucks like him aren't the Berserkers' customers.

That's why if he interferes with the club's income, I'll bury him and every one of his shithead sons.

Glancing at the gold digger, I figure Ashley better get her name on a will soon if she wants to inherit anything. Todd's hatred of "new people" will interfere with his love of living.

"I trust you know what you're saying," Todd grumbles and returns his glasses to his face. "What happened to your old assistant?"

"She quit."

"Your dick too much for her?" he asks, chuckling.

Selene doesn't react to his words. I don't think she's paying attention. She's overly focused on the pictures on the wall behind the old man.

Todd likes to collect old photos of lynchings and other atrocities. At some point, he got old and rich enough for people to stop calling him out on being an evil fuck. That's why Todd puts his nasty shit out for everyone to see, just daring anyone to complain.

"Are you coming to the town meeting?" Todd asks me while I nudge Selene.

"It got canceled after Millie took a spill in the shower," I reply, thinking of the ancient biddies on the city council. "We'll organize a new meeting once she gets her new hip."

When I stand, Selene follows my lead. Todd frowns at how I don't stick around and listen to him bitch for an hour.

"We're not young men anymore," I tell Todd, who scowls darker. "Our time is nearly over. That might be a bitter pill to swallow, but the next generation needs their turn. McMurdo Valley will live or die based on their choices, not ours. Best to accept that now."

Todd figures he deserves to live forever because of his wealth. But he'll be dead sooner than he thinks if he keeps screwing with my expansion plans.

I'm only playing the "Mayor Hoyt" role with him for a while longer. Since there are downsides to setting Ruin loose on this evil family, I'll behave for now.

"He's a piece of shit," I say once Selene and I are in the truck, heading toward downtown. "But he's balls-deep in cash and power in this state."

"You scared him."

"Good," I say, smirking at her comment. "You never need to drink or eat anything they give you. I visit with a lot of showoffs and elderly people. They love to shove food and drink at me. I rarely touch any of it."

"Okay."

"Did he creep you out?"

"Yes. Those pictures on his wall…" she mumbles, seeming sad.

Before I can stop myself, I reply, "Doesn't your husband have money? Your family, too? I'm sure you've met nasty fuckers whose wealth made them weird and untouchable."

"Sure."

I take her short answer as a signal to shut the fuck up.

We end up on Main Street, where I stop at the post office. Selene takes notes on how to access my mailbox. I try and fail to view my world from her eyes.

Mostly, I can't picture her life before McMurdo Valley. Don't know a damn thing about her parents besides Mariah's a big-boobed ditz, and the father is a rich asshole. I haven't even got a glimpse of her sister.

When we stop at McMurdo Grill for lunch, I notice her hemming and hawing over the menu. I tap it to draw her golden eyes to me.

"Order whatever you want. The club owns a piece of this place. Costs me nearly nothing no matter what you ask for."

Selene holds my gaze long after the last word leaves my lips. I'm unsure if she is falling in love with me or worries I'll murder her. I can't be sure what her expression means when she watches me so intently.

"Where's Joie's mother?" she asks and then gulps hard as if I might freak out over her question.

"She married a Nashville chiropractor."

"Does she visit?"

"No. They talk a couple of times a month."

"Do you miss her?" Selene asks, and I get that "she's falling for me" vibe again.

"Never."

"Was she awful?"

"Hell yeah," I say, leaning back and chuckling at her expression. "I was younger and dumber when Nicole came up pregnant. I thought she was old lady material."

"Old lady."

"A biker's wife."

"Oh. Well, I'm glad you don't miss her. Life is easier without that baggage."

I think to ask if she misses her husband but stop myself from saying something so fucking stupid. I bet she misses his money, though.

She orders a steak before eyeing me to see if I'll complain. I'm proud of her for asking for what she wants. Then, she requests a side of steamed broccoli. *I don't even know what to do with that information.*

"Your sister lived with you in Bossier City, right?" I ask, and Selene flinches at the mention of her former home.

"In the guesthouse."

"Because you're close?" I ask when she looks ready to cry.

Blinking away tears, Selene surprises me with a smile. "Yes. We're less than two years apart. My father was angry when I was born. He insisted on trying immediately for a son. After Yazmin, he decided to do IVF to ensure he had a boy. Once Alex was born, my parents doted on him. Yazmin and I were often shuffled to the side together so my brother could shine. We've always been each other's support system."

"Patrice said you two were looking for an apartment together."

"We don't think we can handle a yard."

Grinning, I point out, "You could hire someone to mow for you. There are a couple of lawn care companies around the Valley. We own a piece of them."

"Oh," she says and then blinks a lot like she's adjusting to this knowledge. "Yazmin would like a dog. I hadn't thought about a house. How much would that cost?"

"Once you get that raise, you'll have no problem affording anything around here."

Selene's face lights up in reaction to my words. I feel like a fucking king when she offers such an unguarded smile. Even knowing I'm getting myself bent out of shape over a woman I ought to remain professional with, I still imagine her in my bed. Selene's hair looks soft, and her lips beg to be kissed.

"Can I ask a question?" she says, staring right into my eyes and gripping my heart.

"Shoot."

"Why are you called the Steel Berserkers?"

Grinning, I only shrug. "I'll answer that question if you do a good job for the next few days."

Selene isn't sure what to make of that answer. She might be worried she offended me. Her face is so damn expressive, yet I can't really read her. Mostly, Selene always looks on the verge of a panic attack. I bet she couldn't hide a damn thing from that monster she married.

My temper reawakens. That's how the rest of our day goes. I alternate between imagining her expression might be when we fuck and picturing myself killing her husband.

By the time I drop her off at Patrice's place, I'm horny, lovestruck, and pissed. I don't know how the hell I'm supposed to deal with this shit every damn day.

But firing Selene isn't an option. She needs the job, and I'm dying to see what she does next.

SELENE

Hoyt helps me exit the truck one last time for the day. We share an awkward moment that feels like the end of a date. *Will he kiss me? Fire me for being too much trouble?*

"I have a thing with my daughter in the morning, so I won't be around until eleven," he says while I struggle not to drop after a long day.

"Thank you," I say since I can't think of another response.

Hoyt only smirks, maybe sensing I want him to leave. *I really do want him to go.* Not because he isn't wonderful to look at and relaxing to be around. With my body feeling on fire, I need a hot shower followed by rest.

For a long minute, I wait for him to leave. Meanwhile, he waits for me to get inside safe. Though I appreciate Hoyt's protective nature, I don't want to limp in front of him. However, he won't go until I do, so I get my wobbly ass moving.

Once I'm in the house, Yazmin joins me at the front door. After Hoyt drives away, she focuses on my face.

"How did it go?"

"Good," I say, using the wall to remain standing.

"Felt invigorating to earn your keep, didn't it?" Patrice asks from her spot near the back windows. Cheryl and my grandmother work on a puzzle. Their cats sit on the table, considering whether to steal a piece. "Did Hoyt remember to talk salary?"

"Yes. Five hundred a week until I warrant a raise."

"Is that good?" Yazmin asks.

"Yes," I tell her and shrug since I don't know money. "I need to take medicine and get a hot shower. Then, I'll help you get ready for your first night."

"She isn't going," Patrice says without looking at us. "Turns out one of the local harlots is throwing herself a birthday party at the Gin Mill. I can't have Miss Flinchy over here start on such a wild night. She can come in on Monday when no one's around."

Yazmin stares at me with her "I'm a puppet having my strings pulled" look. I know that feeling. Limping to the bathroom, I strip out of my clothes. Yazmin hears me whimper and rushes to the bedroom to find pain meds.

When she returns, I explain, "I hurt myself getting into that truck. Right off the bat, I messed up. If I hadn't, I think I'd be mostly okay."

Yazmin turns on the shower. With her help, I peel off my sweaty clothes. My muscles remain damaged from the shooting. Physical therapy helped, but I had to stop when my father insisted I return to LeVoy.

"I wonder if I'll make enough money to get medical insurance," I whisper, not wanting Patrice to hear.

"I don't know how any of that works."

Nodding, I realize Yazmin and I are like children in the bodies of thirty-year-old women. We don't understand insurance or taxes. We've never lived alone. I'm not even sure how to rent a place. Can we both be on the lease?

The answers can likely be found on the internet. We just have to do research. Yet, I'm scared to learn something that'll stress me out. I'm nearly out of anxiety pills. Yazmin will run out in a month. Two days ago, I texted our mother to ask for more money, just for medicine.

She responded with, "I can't help you."

That's her code for she'll help once she isn't monitored. If she says she "won't" help, I know we're on our own.

It was the same way when I asked for help leaving LeVoy years ago. Yazmin and I came to visit. I showed my mom the bump on my head from when LeVoy shoved me into a wall.

"Please let us stay," I begged my mom.

She said she would talk to our father. When she returned, she said I needed to make my marriage work.

"If you leave him, I won't help you."

The entire time I recuperated at my parents' house after the shooting, I hoped they'd realize their choices led to me nearly dying. However, even after everything, my father insisted I return to LeVoy.

"He said the gunman was sent by his enemy to kill him," Carlos explained. "This person has been dealt with. You have no reason to deny your husband."

I stared into my father's cold eyes and realized he was scared of LeVoy. For years, I'd wondered why he picked a Louisiana trust fund loser for me to marry. I'd been sought out by many wealthy men back then. My father had options, yet he handed me off to LeVoy.

Yazmin assumed our father owed the asshole money. However, that day, when Carlos Norris told me to return to a man who hired a hitman to kill me, I knew he was scared.

My father rules the roost at our home. He's an important man in our town. But in the greater world, he was no one impressive. Neither is LeVoy, but my husband has connections to the slimy Louisiana underbelly.

"Do you think Hoyt is a bad man?" I ask Yazmin as I rest in bed after my shower.

"I don't know."

"He runs that biker gang. I kept forgetting that today."

"Patrice says he's safe."

I look into my sister's hazel eyes and remember when she smiled easier. Despite growing up squeezed under the boot of our father and paternal grandmother, I was mostly happy. I loved to take walks with Yazmin. We would talk about boys, fashion, and traveling the world.

Now, we're past the age when dreams can become reality. I recall how often LeVoy used the term "past your prime" to describe me.

"You aren't as beautiful as when we married," he'd randomly tell me.

LeVoy was never handsome. His long face, large mouth, and small eyes horrified me when we first met. Though I was repulsed, he acted sweet. Bought me lots of crap I didn't need and promised to treat me like a queen. I'd been twenty-one and trained to behave. I agreed to marry LeVoy for the same reason I did most things—telling a man no wasn't an option.

I hoped we would have children, even if they looked like him. I would love our babies like I couldn't love LeVoy. But I never got pregnant. Considering what came later, I should be thankful to be barren.

"I have a crush on Hoyt," I whisper to Yazmin, who smiles softly. "I've never met a man like him before. He's so effortlessly masculine and handsome. He constantly cusses, drives like he can't see the speed limit, and might have been violent today. He's clearly dangerous. But when he smiles at me, I feel like the world makes sense."

"That's good."

Tears prick my eyes. "No, it isn't. Because even if LeVoy doesn't kill me, I can't have a man like Hoyt."

"Why not?"

I look at her like she's crazy. "You've seen my body. It's destroyed. Scarred. Ugly."

"You're so beautiful, Selene."

"From the neck up, I look like me. I'm no longer in my prime, but I still make men curious. However, if they saw me naked, their interest would disappear."

Crying into the pillow, I'm ashamed to lust after Hoyt while knowing what hides under my clothes. As if I insult him to think he'd ever want me.

Calming down, I whisper, "I wish I could just work and get a home with you and be normal."

"We can."

Sighing, I know Yazmin doesn't believe her lies. I'll be dead in a year. LeVoy won't let me go. Living in poverty and pain isn't enough of a punishment. He wants me dead. Why not? My death costs him so little. He'd rather spend a few grand to kill me than let me leave him for free.

The medicine eventually soothes my physical pain. However, my heart remains heavy with regret and disappointment.

If I'd run away to Patrice's home years ago, I might have been able to seduce a handsome man like Hoyt. He would protect me. I could feel beautiful in his arms.

But it's too late for that now.

Besides, my focus shouldn't be on romance. What I need to do is please Hoyt to ensure I make as much money as possible. Every dollar will help Yazmin for when I'm gone. My sister is broken in a way I'm not. Some part of her didn't survive Robert or the psychiatric hospital.

However, I believe with Patrice's help and a little money stashed away, she can build something solid in McMurdo Valley.

That's my goal now. Not freeing myself from LeVoy's evil or winning the heart of a gorgeous man like Hoyt. Those dreams are for the old Selene, who died the night a gunman opened fire.

HOYT

Wynonna's husband is a working man. Ralph likes to get dirty, doesn't think hard or plan for the future, and has zero ambition. If my sister's survival were left to Ralph's salary, she would live in a dumpy house on the south side of town.

I've suffered through Wynonna's many shitty relationships over the years. That's why when she landed a man who stuck, I built them this house for the kids they planned on making.

My sister and I have always been tight. Wynonna was there for me when Nicole went bonkers, and I had to figure out how to be a single dad. My sister kept my office organized. Made sure I fed myself back when I was stressed. Cleaned my wounds after I kicked a few too many asses and nearly got owned.

I used to think Wynonna was the ideal woman. Then, I realized that was creepy. However, I still think she's got all the great ingredients for a perfect wife. She's soft but not weak. She works hard but likes to have fun. She's smart but never restless. Her dreams are small enough to come true. That's likely why Wynonna smiles so much.

Hell, she's grinning at the sight of me as I climb off my Fat Boy in her front drive. No reason for her to be so pleased to see me. She's just a happy gal.

"The town's buzzing," she says, waltzing around the porch of her two-story bright-white farmhouse-style home. Her wavy brown hair hangs loose and her nutmeg eyes shine. "Hoyt's got himself the prettiest assistant yet!"

Chuckling at her amusement, I step onto the porch, where Esther plays with her dolls. The two-year-old slams the toy down and reaches for me. I don't really want the pretty brunette slobbering on me, but I can't tell most ladies no. That's why I'm visiting Millie tomorrow despite knowing she'll whine the entire time about her busted hip.

"So, what's she like?" Wynonna asks.

I shrug like I don't have any view on Selene. My sister whips me in the ass with her dishtowel.

"You're full of shit. Typical Macready man, lying with the ease of breathing."

Once Esther rubs slobber all over my face, she wants down.

When I frown at her mother, Wynonna only shrugs.

"She's a gross little bugger," I grumble and use my shirt to wipe my face.

"Her father likes when she does that shit. Blame Ralph. What can I do when I'm surrounded by piglets?"

"But you're happy, aren't you?" I ask, wanting everything for my sister.

Wynonna's big brown eyes shine. Her thick hair is a mess. She smells like Pine-Sol and chocolate chip cookies. Of course, she's happy.

"Think this new girl will work out?" she asks after settling onto the front swing while Esther returns to slapping dolls together.

"I hope so."

"But you're not sure."

"She's had a hard time of it. Can't be sure she'll handle the job's rougher days."

"What kind of man shoots his woman that way," Wynonna mutters and shakes her head.

I sigh, wondering if it was my cousin or uncle who shared the gossip.

"Is she all gnarly?" Wynonna asks as I join her on the swing. "Filled with holes like Swiss cheese?"

"She's gorgeous."

"Uh-oh."

Chuckling at how she pokes me, I admit, "Yeah, Selene's gotten under my skin already."

"But she went through that traumatic experience. You should use that as an excuse to keep your hands to yourself."

"You say that because you don't know how hot she is."

"Like on a scale of one to ten, with ten being jizz-in-your-pants hot, where would you rate her?"

"I didn't jizz around her, but my dick was permanently hard."

"So, an eight?"

"No, she's a ten. Best looking gal I've ever seen."

"Good Lord, you're in trouble, Hoyt."

"Yeah, but she's real skittish like that stray cat Dad tried to coax into the house. Took him months to realize the animal wasn't interested."

"Think Selene's imagined you naked yet?" Wynonna taunts.

"No doubt."

"Then, she's not like that cat," Wynonna says and grins at my expression.

Chuckling, I remember how upset our dad was when he couldn't win that animal over. I'll be just as pissed if Selene shows up with a Joe Shmoe loser when she could have me.

"No way is this thing with Selene remaining platonic," I admit as my sister watches me with amused eyes. "But knowing her past ought to help me behave for a while. Once I fuck up our business relationship, I don't know what my next step will be. I was lucky to find another decent assistant."

"You probably need to hire a few people rather than expecting a chick to shadow you, take all the calls, and be your sounding board. It's too much for one person."

"You did it fine."

"Yes, but I never get distracted by dick, Hoyt."

Exhaling hard, I mutter, "Nash's dick is the problem."

"Think he'll make a move on Selene?"

"No, she's got too much drama going on. He can't stand that shit. I figure he'll behave around Patrice's granddaughters. If for no other reason than his fear of the woman's shotgun."

"Patrice does love the old 'asshole killer.'"

"Shooting that one guy gave her a taste for blood," I say, and Wynonna laughs. "Mind if I hang around? Joie is at her bestie's house. Tracey has her book club. If I go home, I'll be sitting alone all night."

"Poor thing. Unfortunately, you can't stay for dinner since I didn't make enough."

"I've seen you cook, Wynonna. You've never once made a dinner that didn't allow for leftovers."

"Ralph complained you're around too much."

"Fine, I'll fucking leave and not come back for a spell or two," I mutter, knowing she's fucking with me.

When I don't get up, Wynonna fixes my wayward hair. Our silence doesn't stick.

"I wish you could find a nice lady who didn't drink her own piss," Wynonna says, laughing at my ex's new age "healthy living." "Maybe then, my big brother could have a happy family like the one I've created."

Chuckling, I admit, "I wouldn't mind a woman. But Nicole felt like an anchor dragging me to my doom. I didn't know how to get rid of her. And that was before she went crunchy and used essential oils to fix everything. I always get restless in a relationship and want to hit the exit."

"Might be different with the right woman."

"Or it might be exactly the same shit. But instead of kicking out a weirdo like Nicole, I'd break the heart of a good woman."

"Like Selene?"

Shrugging, I mutter, "I don't know her deal yet."

"But what do you suspect?"

"Full disclosure?" I ask, lowering my voice despite us being alone out here on this quiet land.

"Don't hold back."

55

"I'm not sure if enough of Selene survived the last asshole. She's beautiful and sweet. No doubt about that. But she might be hollowed out. If I expect too much from her, she's bound to fail me. Soon, I'll bail on her. We'll both end up unhappy. Except I'll rebound. She probably won't. I'm afraid I'll ruin that poor woman."

Wynonna studies my face before wrapping her arms around my shoulders and cradling me like I'm one of her kids.

"Hoyt Macready, you're falling for this woman," she murmurs.

"I just said it wouldn't work out."

"Yeah, but if she wasn't special, you'd roll the dice and put yourself first. But you can't because she's already found her way into your heart."

"You're making me uncomfortable."

Wynonna strokes my head, forcing my hair into my face. I casually attempt to shove her off, but she knows my tactics and tightens her grip.

Laughing as I try to break free, she warns, "I'll pry your head right off."

"Crazy bitch," I grumble when she messes up my hair more before settling onto the bench.

"Dumb shit."

"Mama, don't use bad words," Ralph Junior says as he joins us on the porch. The four-year-old shakes his head at his mother. "Don't be sinning."

"Don't be pharisaic with me, child."

The boy throws his head back and laughs in that wild way his father does when he sees someone get a nut punch. Most days, I can't figure out why Wynonna fell for Ralph Nauls. He's a dumb redneck who calls her "mama" since she had his son.

"He makes me laugh," Wynonna says when she senses where my head has gone. "And his dick is huge."

"I've begged you to stop mentioning that."

"It's like a footlong from Subway," she taunts as I stand up and walk into her house. "Nothing breaks a dump loose faster than a wild porking by a mighty salami."

"I'm about ready to leave," I say before settling into a chair near where Ralph dozes.

My sister dances around in the kitchen, loving how she got me running scared. Ever since we were kids, her second-favorite hobby was forcing me to flee from her big mouth.

Decades later, she still high-fives herself over how I turn squeamish over something as natural as my baby sister taking a redneck's beef.

SELENE

Melancholy hangs over me. Every day, I spend time with a man I'm already crazy about. I have no practice at feeling this way. As a young woman, I went on sanctioned, chaperoned dates with men twice my age. None of them were anywhere near as sexy as Hoyt.

Sure, I've had crushes before. A college-aged tutor when I was in high school. A horse trainer when I was eighteen. They were handsome but not in that overpowering way Hoyt is without trying.

I try coping with these feelings. In my head every night, I prep for how Hoyt is my boss, not a potential boyfriend. I remind myself how my body is disgusting, and Hoyt is a ladies' man. *Well, that's what Patrice claimed about the bikers.*

So, in my head, I know nothing will happen. I need to stay focused.

Then, morning arrives, and he appears next to his truck to help me inside. I inhale his spicy cologne, and my heart flutters. Admiring his thick beard, I'm constantly struggling against the urge to touch it.

Whenever I stare into his blue eyes, I wish I was the old me. That woman might win over a man like Hoyt. I bet the fucking would be incredible.

I've never been with anyone except LeVoy. I haven't orgasmed with a man in my entire life. I can barely do it alone. My body used to look sexy, but it never felt that way.

With Hoyt's ability to make my nipples harden just by exhaling roughly, I imagine orgasms would be easy to reach with him as my lover.

He's doing his grumpy bull breathing today as we're joined by his cousin Nash during lunch. I smile at Hoyt's irritation. He's too sexy to be truly intimidating. I can't imagine him keeping these rowdy men in line. However, he's no doubt strong and seems larger than them. *Is that how being an alpha works?*

"Well, hello, Selene," Nash says after dropping into a chair across from me.

Hoyt pointed him out the other day while we were running errands. He didn't stop to say hello to his cousin. Rather than assuming he disliked the other man, I pretended Hoyt was protective of me and didn't want to share.

Watching each other, the cousins give off very different vibes. Nash exudes charm while Hoyt seethes a rage more intimidating on someone less sexy.

After I say hello to Nash, he asks me if Hoyt is running me ragged.

"No," I reply quickly since he's clearly taunting his cousin. "He's been very patient."

Hoyt allows a little smirk while he pretends to read the menu.

"Patrice said she's bringing your sister into work tonight," Nash announces in a way that makes me worry for Yazmin.

"Yes."

"So?" Hoyt grunts at his cousin.

"I'm supposed to keep our boys from showing up and getting rowdy. Only quiet regulars are allowed while Yazmin gets trained."

"That's good," I say, breathing easier. "Yazmin's never waitressed before. Patrice also seems very apprehensive."

"I'll be there, of course," Nash replies and smirks in a way that inspires a sexy snarl from Hoyt. "To ensure tranquility on Yazmin's first day."

"Selene, go powder your nose," Hoyt says without looking at me while he gets into a staring contest with his smirking cousin.

I hurry away from the table, wondering if I look like a mess. It's not like the cousins will come to blows at a family establishment.

The mirror shows I look similar to when I left the house this morning. I wipe smudges from around my eyes and use the restroom. After I've been gone a sufficient amount of time, I return to find Nash gone.

Looking smug, Hoyt stretches his long, thick arms in the air. As I drink in the sight of him, I wonder if my lust is palpable. No doubt Hoyt's accustomed to women admiring his gorgeous body. Several ladies in the restaurant haven't taken their eyes off him since we arrived.

When I return to my seat, Hoyt's gaze turns soft.

"Nash's road name is Tomcat."

Nodding, I recall how Hoyt's told me that information three times since I started working for him on Tuesday.

"He chases women," he adds when I just stare at him. "Obsessively."

"Why?"

Hoyt blinks rapidly as if he's never considered such a question. "Because women are soft and comforting."

Cocking an eyebrow, I wonder if those words are code for fucking.

"Do you chase women?" I ask after we put in our order, and I stare at my phone rather than his rugged face.

"From time to time," he says in a voice that draws my attention back to him. "Have you met anyone interesting since you arrived in McMurdo Valley?"

"Only the people you've introduced to me. I hide in my house when I'm not with you."

Hoyt doesn't ask about the "hide" part. I suspect Patrice told him all my sordid details. He rarely asks questions about my past.

Instead, we often fall into silence like now. Sometimes, I think we're hiding from what we want to share. Other times, we're in a comfortable mode like I have with Yazmin.

With Patrice, I feel like I need to project a certain image. With my sister, I can always be me. I love when I feel that way with Hoyt.

The waitress returns with our meals—ribs and potatoes for him and a chicken salad for me.

"Is that really what you wanted to order?" he asks, side-eyeing me like he often does.

"Yes. I like the chicken here."

Hoyt treats my words as if they're a coded message he must decipher.

"This isn't a healthy salad," I insist when he keeps watching me. "It has a lot of crap in it."

Grinning, Hoyt nods. "I just don't want you thinking you need to eat like a chick on a first date."

His words and that sexy damn smile leave me flustered. I want him to want me so badly. Yet, I go cold whenever I consider him touching me.

"Have I been doing a good job?" I ask after we've eaten for a few minutes, and I reply to a few texts on my work cell.

Hoyt taps the phone and shakes his head. "No work while you eat."

I swoon again at how he insists I enjoy breaks. Snapping out of my lusty thoughts, I ask my question again.

"Are you looking for that raise?" he replies.

"No, but you said you would tell me why your club is called the Steel Berserkers if I did a good job."

"Hasn't Patrice said anything?"

"No. We don't talk about you."

That's a lie. Patrice shared how Hoyt's ex-wife was a weirdo. However, I'm not telling Hoyt any of that.

Glancing around, my sexy boss shrugs. "It's not a big deal."

Despite his words, he doesn't explain. I figure he's nervous about sharing in public. I decide to change the subject.

"Can I have health insurance?"

Hoyt frowns. "Don't you already?"

"No. My parents cut me off, and my husband won't pay for anything."

Shaking his head, Hoyt explains, "No, I mean, from me. Shouldn't you be on the plan?"

"I don't know."

"Neither do I."

"Wait, is that something I'm in charge of?"

"I don't know," Hoyt says and scratches at his beard. "How did the other assistants get their insurance?"

"Maybe they didn't but were too afraid to ask."

"Afraid of me?" Hoyt asks like he just can't imagine such a thing.

"Yeah, I don't get that, either."

Hoyt grins at my meaning. "I think Wynonna is in charge of that. It's probably written down somewhere at my fancy office."

"I'm beginning to believe this fancy Valley Gorge office you speak of doesn't exist," I tease as he watches me struggle to fit a large cucumber slice in my mouth.

Tugging his focus from my food issues, Hoyt texts someone before setting down his phone. "Wynonna handles that. She already got you on the plan and will text the info to you this afternoon."

"That fast?" I ask, and he only nods since his mouth is full. "I need a local doctor for prescriptions."

Hoyt's gaze locks on to mine as if I've said too much. Looking at my food, I leave my words to hang between us.

"I'm going to Valley Gin Mill tonight for moral support," I mumble while staring too hard at my plate. "Yazmin is nervous about working with Patrice. She said I'm lucky my boss is so patient."

Hoyt gives me a half-smile. "Patrice is a ballbuster, but she had to be in this town. Her husband, well, your grandfather, was a royal asshole."

"Do you know how he died?" I ask, and his gaze locks on to mine again. "Patrice shuts down any conversation about him."

"He might not be dead. He just disappeared. Could have run off. No one knows."

Something about his tone makes me wonder if Hoyt knows where my grandfather is buried. Is it possible the biker president—who I pretend is super soft and sweet—killed him?

No, wait, the numbers are off. Hoyt is forty-two. My grandfather died thirty years ago.

I look at Hoyt and try to imagine him hurting someone. This is a man who drags that step stool around to make it easier for me to get in and out of his truck. He always ensures I have something to drink. When we're somewhere weird, he sits me away from the creepy person. Like with that Todd freak or the old lady who kept poking at us with her cane.

Hoyt Macready is simply the sweetest guy I've ever met. The men in my old life never did anything nice beyond buying women crap. They wouldn't suffer to protect their wives.

Of course, Hoyt isn't my man. As my employer, he obviously doesn't want me to quit. Yet, even if he acted selfishly or rude, I couldn't quit this job. Despite knowing I lack work options and won't complain, he's wonderful anyway.

Before we leave the restaurant, I clean up and look at my appearance. The woman looking back wants to kiss Hoyt Macready. She's crazy over the handsome, masculine biker. That Selene is very curious about the tattoos hiding under his tight shirts.

But that Selene is only an echo left over from the woman nearly killed back in Bossier City. The woman I am now will need to give up my big dream of enjoying the sexy biker.

Of course, I can't imagine there's any harm in fantasizing about what could have been.

HOYT

Lunch leaves me grumpy. Normally, I'd unleash my inner asshole, barking bullshit at people until I felt better.

Instead, I find myself hiding that side from Selene. So rather than drive around McMurdo Valley, searching for sacrifices to my temper, I end up at my sister's house.

Selene's eyes shine when she learns where we're going. I've noticed how curious she is about me. That's why she keeps asking about my club.

Yesterday, she peppered me with questions regarding my daughter. Selene wants to know more about the man she spends her day with, yet I have no choice except to hide myself.

That's why I pick Wynonna's house as our destination. When my brain doesn't behave, I turn to my sister for guidance.

"You haven't quit yet," Wynonna coos at Selene. "So brave."

Selene grins, seeming embarrassed by the praise. I don't know if she realizes my sister's a bullshitter.

Selene is a difficult woman to read. She looks scared, even when she's smiling. I can't tell what triggers her or if she has much of a sense of humor.

But she smiles at Wynonna's teasing and follows her inside the house. Hunkered in the family room, Esther and Ralph peel their gazes from "Bubble Guppies" to size up the newcomer.

Sensing Wynonna about to start trouble, I ask Selene, "Would it be rude to leave you here with them while I speak to my sister?"

"Since when do you give two shits about being rude?" Wynonna announces while I cock my eyebrow as a subtle "fuck off."

My sister responds with a very casual, slowly uplifted middle finger. Selene watches us like we're aliens, and she's supposed to do a report tomorrow on our bizarre culture. Her edgy curiosity makes me tense, so I ask my nephew and niece to babysit her.

"Don't let her run off," I tell them.

"I'm very responsible," Ralph replies while Esther shakes her head.

I leave the three of them on the couch and walk to Wynonna's office, which is as horrifyingly messy as mine.

"Oh, my, God!" Wynonna cries once the door shuts behind us. "Selene's gorgeous."

Frowning at how loud she's being, I mutter, "I said she was hot."

"Yeah, but she's old Hollywood hot, not titty bar hot."

"Why would you assume the stripper shit? You've seen Patrice's classy vibe."

"Yes, but I don't know anything about her husband or Mariah's man. Throw a few rednecks into the genetic cycle, and you get stripper hot."

"Well, I guess they didn't marry rednecks like our family did."

"I'm happy with what I see in the mirror."

Grinning, I shove her against the wall. "As you should be, princess. Now, pay attention to me."

Wynonna uses a chair to gain the height to tackle me. We end up on the floor, where she unleashes a slap-attack. I roll my eyes at her efforts.

"I need advice," I mutter when she hoots and hollers like she's riding a wild bull.

"Kicked your ass stupid," she says and flops to the ground next to me. We rest on our backs while Ralph sings a horrible song to Selene in the next room. "What did you need?"

"I want Selene."

"Well, fucking duh. If I batted for the ladies, I'd be trying to hump her leg, too."

Grinning at her amused snickers, I continue, "I tell myself how she just got out of a shitty marriage. She's vulnerable. Besides, I can't date my assistant."

"All good points."

"But I'm acting weird around her."

"Gross," she says, and we chuckle at her insinuation.

"I don't want her talking to Nash."

"Understandable. He will totally smooth-talk her into nudity. It's his gift."

"Yeah, but I'd have to kill him if he fucked Selene."

"Seems harsh. Just take one of his testicles and maybe an inch of dick," she says and then laughs. "Take the inch from the base. Then have them sew up the rest. Won't work right again."

"Are you stoned?"

"Oh, man, I wish," she says and rolls onto her side. "But seriously, just tell Nash that Selene requires a big strong man to save her. He'll stay away, then. He can't deal with woman drama."

"Yeah, but I'm hiding other stuff from Selene."

"Like Joie?"

"No," I grumble.

"Has your new assistant met your darling preteen daughter?"

"No."

"Because you're hiding Selene or Joie?"

"Once I'm sure Selene will work out, I'll introduce them."

"I totally believe that's your issue, liar."

"When Selene asked today about how we got the Steel Berserkers name, I blew off the question."

"Because she won't be impressed with your ability to tear through human bodies like they're made out of paper?"

"Exactly. She's not that kind of woman."

"You never know. She might want a man willing to remove her ex-husband's head."

"They're still married."

"Yeah, because he won't give her a divorce."

"How do you know so much?"

"Glenn came over for pie yesterday and gossiped his heart out. Patrice apparently told him Selene's life story. Turns out she doesn't know much."

"Well, I've also avoided bringing Selene to the Valley Gorge Business Center."

"Because you think she won't want to suck your dick if she sees how bad your filing skills are?"

Wynonna laughs at her own crap for so long that I consider leaving. Finally, she pats my stomach.

"So, what's the deal?"

"All those suited fucks there."

"So?"

"She comes from that life."

"And you think she's going to what? Flirt with those guys? Does she flirt with you?"

"She looks at me like I'm hot."

"You are. Why do you think you were prom king? Wasn't on account of your personality, bub."

"I want Selene to be mine," I mutter, realizing I don't know what happens afterward. "But I don't want a woman."

"Seems like you got scarred emotionally from that pee-pee lover you married years ago. Also seems like you need to get the fuck over that."

"What if I kiss Selene, and she likes it? Then, I take her to bed, and she likes that? Then, I make her my girlfriend and then my wife before it all falls apart? I told you already how I can't have this woman's misery on my shoulders."

"Then, don't be an asshole."

"So, I just change my whole fucking personality for Selene?"

Wynonna sits up and sighs. "Hoyt, it's only been a few days. She isn't going anywhere. If these feelings are real, you'll have them in a month. By then, you'll know her better."

She pauses to listen to her children in the next room.

"Maybe after a month, you'll realize she isn't right for you. So, you don't kiss her or take her to bed or make her your woman. Maybe you'll just be a good boss and help her out while she's a good assistant and helps you out. Why make everything complicated? That's not like you."

Exhaling deeply, I nod. "No, this isn't me. I feel out of sorts since I met Selene."

"She's gorgeous. That's bound to be distracting."

"It really fucking is," I admit, loving how I can tell Wynonna anything since she already thinks I'm a stinky shithead of an older brother. "And Selene smells really good. When we're in the truck, and the air conditioner brings her scent to me, my dick tents up like I'm a teenager."

"Awkward, but a totally normal response. Have you gotten laid since meeting her?"

"No."

"Yeah, you'll need to fuck someone. All that pent-up dick energy will make you insufferable. Respect Selene enough to fuck someone else."

Narrowing my eyes, I assume Wynonna's fucking with me. However, she's wearing her "supportive sister" expression.

"I'd feel like I was running around on her if I fucked someone else."

"But she's your assistant, not your girlfriend."

"With us spending all day together and eating meals and shit, it does feel like we're dating."

"I suggest you take a day off from that. Have her straighten up your office. You can run around without her. And get laid."

Irritated at her reasonable suggestion, I growl, "I don't want to fuck someone who isn't her."

"Yeah, maybe not yet. Soon, though, you'll be so horny that you'll have no other choice but to fuck someone. No one wants to deal with a horny Hoyt."

"Shut up."

"When you locked down your dick with Nicole, you became a tyrant."

"She wanted another kid. I wasn't doing that."

"Withholding sex in a relationship is evil."

Smirking, I ask, "Ralph's not giving you any, huh?"

"No, I'm the one who withholds it when I want to win an argument."

"You never did have any trouble being evil."

"I mean, I'd love to be a good person twenty-four seven, three hundred and sixty-five days a year. However, I love winning more."

Grinning, I sit up and rest against the wall. "Selene's had a rough life. I see her struggling. Her body and her mind need time to heal. I should back off. But she makes me crazy. Yesterday, she fixed my shirt collar, and I nearly tackled her."

"I gave you the answer. Just fuck someone else, so you don't ruin this good thing you've got with your new assistant."

"Remember when we visited our grandma growing up?"

"Sure."

"And she promised we could have McDonald's for dinner. But then she went home and made us eat that green bean bullshit?"

"I still have nightmares, yes."

"Well, that's how I feel right now. Selene is the food I'm craving, and any other woman will be that green bean bullshit. Just shoving my dick in someone else is like forcing garbage food down my throat. I won't be satisfied."

Wynonna's face pinches up as she considers my words. "I think she might be the one."

"No."

"Yes. Just because you wasted time with Nicole doesn't mean no other woman could make you happy. And you never got weird over Nicole like you are right now with Selene. I think you should be patient and let her fall in love with you."

"What if she doesn't?"

"Well, then, she's a moron. In that case, you're right to avoid taking her to bed."

Grinning, I picture Selene trapped with my nephew and niece. *As if she hasn't suffered enough in life already.*

Back in the living room, Selene sits between the warring children fighting over the remote in her lap. She stares wide-eyed at their battle, not saying a damn thing. Wynonna and I spy on them until the remote flips out of their hands and whacks Esther in the chin. The kid lets out a wail loud enough to wake the fucking dead.

Selene snaps out of her panicked lockdown mode and strokes the crying girl's head. Esther climbs on her lap and soaks in the attention. Ralph shakes his head.

"I done sinned," he announces and lifts his hands to the air. "Forgive me, Lord."

"You ought to be asking your sister for forgiveness," Wynonna announces as she enters and sits next to Selene. "God doesn't care if you roughhouse with your sister."

"Don't he, Mama?"

"No. If he cared, he would have provided you with two remotes."

Ralph senses something is off about his mom's logic, but the four-year-old can't put together just what. Selene looks at me as Esther switches laps.

"How about we call it quits for the day?" I suggest while admiring her lovely face. "You can get Yazmin ready for her first shift at the Gin Mill."

Selene unleashes a smile that wraps around my heart and squeezes until I'm lightheaded. Wynonna must see something on my face because she shakes her head.

My sister's right. I need to act like a man rather than a lovestruck boy. That means giving Selene space to breathe. She spent more than a decade with an abusive man. The last thing she needs is for me to fold her into my life and take control.

And that sensible advice sticks with me until I drop Selene off at Patrice's house. Watching her walk inside, I instantly feel deprived of something I want.

I'm a spoiled man. For twenty years, I've been the top dog in McMurdo Valley. I've probably gone soft. I sure feel weak as I drive away, nursing a need I can't quench.

SELENE

Yazmin doesn't reveal her fears in the way I do. She can seem empty. I notice Patrice doesn't warm up to her as much as she does me. My crazy makes more sense to our grandmother. Yazmin comes off vacant. I often think of her as an echo of the girl I knew growing up.

Today, I return home from work to find her sitting on our bed, staring into space. I can't imagine where her mind goes.

"How was your day?" she asks when I linger in the doorway.

"I met Hoyt's sister, niece, and nephew."

"What did you eat for lunch?"

"A salad," I reply and sit beside her on the bed. "Are you nervous about tonight?"

"No. I just want to make money so we can get our own place."

I don't share my fear of us moving to a rental, getting settled, and LeVoy finishing the job. *Can Yazmin survive on her own?* Maybe she could get a roommate. I can't imagine living with Patrice forever would be better. But that's mostly because our grandmother desperately wants us to leave.

If she weren't in such a hurry, I wouldn't mind remaining here longer. The house is comfortable. Sharing a bed with Yazmin is no biggie since I've gotten used to how quiet she sleeps. I even like all the cats. Plus, Cheryl taught us how to make cowboy casserole two nights ago.

Imposing on Patrice and Cheryl permanently isn't an option. So, we'll move somewhere modest. Maybe a rental cheap enough for Yazmin to survive on her own if I'm killed. She could still get a dog. One day, she might even find a man who can get past her trauma.

Or maybe not. I realize more every day how I'm not clued in to the way the world works. All my life,

I've watched people from afar as they lived their lives. I assumed the process was easy if LeVoy wasn't around to foul it up.

However, life is complicated. I can't even deal with the crush I'm nursing on Hoyt. Why can't I just turn off my feelings? Instead of being sensible, I find myself hoping he'll be at the Valley Gin Mill when we arrive.

It would be his style to show up on Yazmin's first night and leave a nice tip. Hoyt's very gracious with servers. LeVoy was dripping with money but always cheap with tipping. Most of his friends were the same way.

"Stingy tipper, stingy lover," one server whispered to her friend during a dinner years ago. I remember thinking she had a point.

Wouldn't that mean Hoyt would be a generous lover? I hate myself for even considering such a thing. I'm not on the market, and Hoyt deserves the best.

Rather than obsess over my boss, I focus on Yazmin. She wears her lush brown hair back in a ponytail. Her skin is makeup-free. I tried to get her to "freshen up" before we left, but she was trained to go barefaced by Robert. His programming remains locked inside her brain, despite therapy, pills, and time.

Yazmin and I follow Patrice around the bar as she explains the table numbers before describing the drinks. I don't really need to hear the instructions, but I still take notes.

I might want to grab a few shifts to save up for rent and a car. Earlier, Patrice smiled favorably when I mentioned this idea. She really approves of hard work.

Yet, at the Valley Gin Mill, Patrice finally turns to me and frowns. "Go sit somewhere and let Yazmin get her bearings."

I think to remind her of my plan to pick up shifts. Except Patrice isn't someone who loses arguments. Better to back down and do what she wants.

I look around the main room, unsure where to sit. I can already hear Patrice barking at me over picking a popular table.

In a corner, a blonde woman waves in my direction. Since I can't imagine she means me, I just stand there. The older man with her gestures to come over. I realize they are, in fact, engaging with me.

"Hello," I say, thinking maybe they want me to take their order.

"Sit down, Selene," the woman says. "I'm Callie. This is Hoyt's dad, Ed. We've been hoping to meet you."

I look into Ed's serene blue eyes and see the man I've fallen for over the last week. Though Ed's bald head and tanned face give him a rugged appearance, his eyes sparkle. Callie is his wife despite being considerably younger. I'd guess she was around Hoyt's age while Ed is closer to Patrice's.

Yesterday, Hoyt referred to Callie as "the gold digger" before chuckling. That's all I know about her.

She isn't flashy like I would expect. Her golden blonde hair hangs softly around her friendly face. Her blue eyes hold the same warmth as Ed's. They're both darkly tanned. I remember Hoyt saying his father liked boating.

"Is my boy treating you well?" Ed asks.

"Yes, he's a very good boss."

Callie and Ed share a grin. I can tell they've been gossiping. Their expressions mean something to them, but I don't know if I'm supposed to understand.

"We heard you're squirrely," Ed says, causing Callie to roll her eyes.

"Did Hoyt say that?"

"Oh, no," Callie reassures me. "Patrice did."

"She thinks I'm weird."

Enjoying his scotch, Ed nods. "Patrice is set in her ways. She's also got a lot of grudges against your mama. Some of that will no doubt sprinkle down upon you. No harm in it. Or in being squirrely. My first wife was always flinching and storing nuts for winter."

Callie laughs at his comment before I realize he isn't serious. Ed and Hoyt both have a way of joking that feels serious. I've never really understood the term "deadpan." However, I suspect that's what the men are.

"How many times have you been married?" I ask before realizing that's a terrible question.

"I'm his fourth wife," Callie answers and smiles. "He took forever to find the right one."

Ed chuckles. "In my defense, you were in diapers when I started looking."

"True," she says and winks at him.

Nervous about saying anything else stupid, I sit silently.

Ed grins at Callie and says, "She is squirrely."

Winking at him, Callie turns to me. "Selene, I heard your sister and you are looking for a decent rental."

"She's the top realtor in the Valley," Ed proudly announces.

"I could take you around to see a few places. Rentals don't last long in the Valley. With the women's college in the town over, off-campus housing is snapped up fast. So, you'll want to get all your ducks in a row for when that special place comes available."

"I don't have any money saved up."

Ed frowns. "Isn't my son treating you well?"

"I haven't gotten my first paycheck yet."

"How much is the cheap bastard paying?"

"I don't want to say," I blurt out. "I might get a raise if I do well."

Ed frowns. "Fess up, missy. I didn't raise a cheapskate. All Hoyt's life, I've told him how he can't take his riches with him. And I honestly never figured he'd reach forty. Best for him to spend freely and enjoy life."

"Why wouldn't he reach forty?" I ask, unable to stop myself.

I'm the same way with Hoyt, always blurting out nonsense. Ed and his son's beautiful blue eyes drawn me in until I forget to think before speaking.

Ed doesn't answer immediately. He glances at Callie, who gives him a warning frown.

Understanding her message, he just says, "His job isn't a picnic."

I know in theory how Hoyt is a biker. I've never seen him really ride a motorcycle, though. And his day is mostly spent engaging with the elderly and businesspeople.

Yesterday, we went to a brunch for the McMurdo Valley's Planning Committee. I ate strawberries while older women told Hoyt how everything was too noisy. Yet, they also couldn't hear anything he said in response. Somehow, they were deaf yet overwhelmed by noise.

That's what Hoyt does as mayor. I've never seen any biker stuff except for the Pigsty. I've convinced myself those younger guys created the chaos I heard inside. No way was Hoyt throwing things at them. He's too chill.

"Has Hoyt introduced you to Joie yet?" Callie asks.

"No."

They share a slight frown, followed by a silent conversation. I sense Hoyt keeping his daughter away from me is a bad sign. *Maybe they know I'm getting fired!*

No, wait, Ed wanted me to be paid well. Callie also offered to help me find a rental. They wouldn't say such things if they knew I was losing my job.

During my marriage with LeVoy, my main responsibility was standing silently and attractively at his side. I've forgotten how to share a normal conversation. The only person I've really talked to over the last ten years was Yazmin, who checked out mentally after Robert and the hospital.

"Joie's a great kid," Callie finally says. "She's more Hoyt than Nicole. I know you haven't met his ex, but trust me, when I say that no one needs more of her in the world."

Ed chuckles. "That's an understatement. Bitch is cracked."

"She tried to treat Joie's appendicitis with scented oils and chanting," Callie explains and then adds, "Oh, and sunlight. Hoyt returned from a ride with his bros to find his daughter nearly dead but with a nice outer glow."

"Smelled good, too," Ed mutters. "If she had killed that girl, well, yeah."

Callie smiles at me as if to say, "Don't think too hard about that part."

"How did the club get its name?" I ask since Hoyt won't tell me.

Ed smiles at Callie. "You can do the honors since my explanation will only make her squirrely again."

Callie smiles so wide as she turns to me. "Before the club was formed, Hoyt and the founding members did work for the Jordan family. These people ran the county. They were rude rednecks who would fuck women in the middle of the street and hunt down anyone who complained."

"Scumbags," Ed says, nodding. "I worked for them, too. They didn't pay shit. Cheapskates."

"Hoyt and his group acted as muscle, doing all the dirty work for peanuts. The Jordan family was huge with a few dozen men squeezing hard on people. The rumor was they took orders from the grandpa and grandma of the family. Those two jerks drove around looking like church people, all gussied up for the Lord. But they were sending their boys out and guys like Hoyt to break anyone who so much as looked at the family wrong."

Whatever Callie sees on my face, she pauses and pats my hand reassuringly.

"So, one day, several of the Jordan men were partying out by Dogwood Lake with a bunch of people. Hoyt, Nash, and a few other guys were there, too. One of the nastiest of the Jordan assholes was called Lil Danny. He was dating this little local girl named Pigeon."

"Tiny thing," Ed adds, and I realize all this stuff happened long before Callie arrived in McMurdo Valley. "Must have been five feet tall at that. Her people live in the hills. Mostly squatting in the abandoned Dearborn houses."

Callie smiles at how I can't possibly understand all the stuff he's saying since I don't know anything about the Valley.

"Lil Danny's girlfriend was very pregnant at the time. But he had her dragging a cooler to the party from their truck. She got pissed and started calling him a loser for not helping her. Lil Danny casually fired a bullet into her head."

When I gasp, Callie gets a weird look like she suddenly remembered something. She looks to Ed for reassurance, and he nods for her to continue.

"No one normally did anything when the Jordan family misbehaved. With their numbers and muscle, everyone was scared of them."

"McMurdo Valley, well, hell, the whole county was a lawless place back then," Ed clarifies and shakes his head. "We didn't even pretend to have cops."

"Well, after the gunshot, everyone scattered. To this day, people will claim they didn't see shit. You get me?"

Despite having no idea what she's saying, I nod. I used to do that a lot around LeVoy's friends. Just smile and nod. Nothing else was expected of me most days.

"The next day, Big Dave showed up to find out why Lil Danny wasn't picking up his phone," Callie says as her eyes glow. "When Big Dave arrived at the lake, the girlfriend's body was gone. Instead, he found the headless bodies of Lil Danny and Big Danny. They were propped up with beers in their hands. No one ever found their heads."

Ed grins at this comment, making me think he knows where those heads ended up.

"Well, Big Dave went nuts, obviously. He rode into town and started making threats. That's when Hoyt and his guys showed up and said they were taking over the county. Big Dave called his family for reinforcements. The Jordan family was going to war. But when his cousin Lil Dave showed up with the muscle, they found Big Dave's butchered body piled up on Main Street."

Ed chuckles at the memory while Callie grins at his amusement.

"Over the next few weeks, the male members of the Jordan family and their allies disappear. The rumor is parts of their bodies were dumped on the Jordan family's land. Each time, they would try to hunt down Hoyt and his people. But those boys and Goose know the land around here better than most. They only appeared long enough to take out another member of the Jordan family. Soon, the only ones left were Mama Anita and all the women and their kids. Not a single man remained alive, not even the great-grandpa who must have been seventy."

My mind rebels when imagining my gentle boss cutting off anyone's head. Hoyt is a guy who gave a sucker to a crying kid yesterday when we were walking down Main Street. No way did he hack people to death.

Callie leans back in her chair and smiles. "The rumor is when Pigeon's body hit the ground, Hoyt went berserk. He'd seen the Jordan family do fucked-up shit before. He wasn't a Boy Scout himself. But the girl dying like that set him off. And once he went berserker on Lil Danny, he refused to stop. His madness spread to the other members of his crew. They wanted blood. Only when they'd defeated their enemies could they stop seeing red."

"And no one did anything?"

"There was no law then," Ed replies. "Other organizations tried taking over the Valley after the Jordan family was finished off. This place is worth a lot. Plenty of people want to run it. But whenever anyone messed with the club, my boy and his friends went berserk. They got a rep for being fucking nuts. That's why they've run the Valley for two decades."

"I guess I understand why Hoyt didn't tell me," I mumble as Yazmin walks over in response to Ed's wave. "He doesn't know me well enough to share his story."

Ed and Callie exchange an unreadable look. I glance at my sister as they ask Yazmin for refills on their drinks and put in an order of jalapeño poppers.

I sit with them for a while before they head out to a movie. My heart is in a weird place after they leave. I sit in a corner spot and think about Hoyt.

The man I know is patient and kind. Whenever I looked into Ed's eyes, I saw Hoyt. My heart raced at the thought of my beautiful boss.

Except he's a criminal like LeVoy. Hoyt just rides in his Dodge Ram 3500 or on his motorcycle while my husband is driven around in his Lincoln Navigator.

Despite the cosmetic differences, they still make money through crime, destroying those in their way. My scarred body acts as a reminder of what it feels like to be a violent man's inconvenience.

Later, I rest in bed with a depressed Yazmin. I don't know what's bothering her. She was so easy to read when we were kids. But she changed a lot in the hospital. Or maybe it was just Robert. We were apart for years. The woman who returned to me isn't the sister I called my best friend.

In the dark room, I share the story behind the Steel Berserkers' name. She listens to me speak in hushed tones. When I finish, she doesn't reply for more than a minute. I wonder if she's fallen asleep.

"Hoyt's like a shield," she whispers. "A weapon, too. If he cares enough about you, Hoyt could protect you from LeVoy."

"He never shows his violent side. What if it's the real him, and I only see the cuddly façade he puts on?"

"One problem at a time," she replies, repeating what I told her many times when she'd get overwhelmed. "LeVoy is your main problem. Hoyt can fix that for you. Then, you can worry about your boss's hidden temper."

"I'm falling for him."

"I know."

"But it's not like I can seduce him into protecting me."

"No, but he needs an assistant, and you're doing a good job. Patrice said so. She blabs about everything. Hoyt is happy with you. Fucking him isn't necessary. Just be a good assistant, so he'll want to protect you."

Her words make sense. I've seen how Hoyt views the world. McMurdo Valley is *his* town. Those who do him right get treated well. People outside of town aren't his concern.

Right now, I'm part of his circle. Even after a week, he seems to care about me. If I keep working hard, I'll make myself important. When LeVoy starts shit, Hoyt could theoretically protect me. Or at least if I die, he'll protect Yazmin out of pity.

Either way, I choose to find his berserker past a positive thing. Better to have a violent man as my friend than as my enemy.

HOYT

Joie's Little League game keeps me from heading to the Gin Mill. She's the shortstop on the McMurdo Valley Vikings. My daughter has a solid throw and will hustle for every ball. But Joie can't bat for shit. She usually strikes out. Tonight is no different.

Pouting during the pizza party after the game, my tomboy remains in a bad mood when we get home. With our house manager, Tracey, at her art class, only our Chesapeake Bay retriever is around to greet us.

"I'm mad!" Joie screams when I ask if she's okay. "I don't like losing!"

"Because you think losing means you're a loser. But everyone loses."

There's no denying Joie has my temper. My baby girl gets wound up and can't come down without losing her shit.

Like usual, I take her to the gym in the back of our house. I hold the bag while her little gloved fists go to town. She screams and cries until she's tired and wants a hug.

"Why don't I get better?" she asks as I hold her against me and stroke her short blonde hair.

"You're not a good hitter." Though my honesty turns her beautiful face feral, I just shrug. "I couldn't hit for shit, either. I misjudged when to swing."

Deflating, she nods. "I always swing too soon."

"Some things you can improve on. Like the more you read, the better comprehension you get. The more you run, the better your endurance becomes. But swinging is about timing and concentration. And you and I lack something there."

"I should quit playing."

"If you hate playing, sure. But you're the fastest kid on the team. The Vikings would have lost by several more runs tonight if not for you."

Joie exhales the last part of her disappointment and frustration. She smiles at me.

"You're so much cooler than the other dads."

"Fuck yeah."

"They're all nerds and assholes. They yell or ignore the entire game. You're the only calm guy in the stands."

"You got lucky with me, kiddo."

Joie is a super chill kid when she's not flipping out. She gets that from me, too. The only thing she really inherited from Nicole was her snort-laugh and long eyelashes.

We sit on the dock, looking out over the pond as she throws balls to Wise Guy. The dog dives into the water to retrieve each one. Every time he returns, he shakes his coat and covers us with water.

Joie snort-laughs when the dog drenches her. My daughter drops next to me on the dock and dangles her bare feet into the water. Rubbing the moisture from her floppy blonde bangs, she ends up with a wacky faux mohawk. I grin at her and thank the universe for giving me a cool kid instead of a dud.

"How come you haven't brought your assistant around to meet me?"

"No reason."

"You brought the others around."

"It's only been a week."

"What's wrong with her?"

"Nothing."

"Is she weird?" Joie asks, nudging me with her elbow. "Ugly? Does she smell weird like that one with the poofy hair?"

"No."

"You said that one didn't smell weird, either. However, she stunk like a garden. Like dirt and plants and stuff."

"Selene smells like white chocolate," I say and smirk at how Joie frowns. "Remember when we went to that bakery, and they had the melted white chocolate on the cupcakes? That's what she smells like."

"Weird."

"No."

"Are you horny for her?" she asks and throws the ball out for Wise Guy. "Wynonna said you're on your best behavior with Selene. That means you're horny, right?"

"No, it means Selene is, um, delicate. I don't want to spook her and send her running."

"Delicate?" Joie asks, rolling her eyes. "That's code for a weenie."

"No," I reply, worried my daughter will come on too strong with Selene. "An asshole shot her a bunch of times. She gets to be delicate, okay?"

Joie's eyes widen. "How many?"

"Six, I guess. That's what I heard. I haven't asked Selene."

"Why not?"

"Do you like when people ask where Nicole is?"

"No, but if I got shot a bunch of times and didn't die, I'd be telling that to everyone. Like, it'd be proof I'm indestructible."

Grinning at her reaction, I muss up her hair. "Be nice to Selene. She's not a tough chick like you."

"When am I supposed to be nice to her? You're hiding her since she's all fragile. Apparently, I'm a wrecking ball."

"Well, then, I'll bring her to your dentist appointment this week."

A groaning Joie topples onto her back. "Like I haven't suffered enough."

"One day, you'll want a boy's attention and—"

"No."

"Or you'll want to get out of a ticket or win over a jury. That great smile will be very helpful."

Joie smiles at me, full of bright white teeth. "I look forward to meeting Selene and not discussing her superhero powers. I don't want you to have to get a new assistant."

"Thank you."

"Will she still work for you when she's your girlfriend?" Joie asks, snickering.

"Nash's the one who dates all my assistants."

"Yeah, but he has no taste. You make Selene sound yummy. Yeah, you'll want to get in her pants."

"Don't mention that when you meet her."

Snort-laughing, Joie mumbles, "Aw, you're shy."

"I'm about to dunk your ass into the water."

"Bring it," she taunts without attempting to escape my clutches.

Soon, we head back to the house with the dog still shaking water on us every few steps. I think about Yazmin's first night at the Gin Mill.

My father texted earlier to say they met my assistant, and she was "lovely." He added lots of hearts and winking emojis. I once again wish Callie hadn't taught Ed how to use his phone.

"What if I did start dating Selene?" I ask Joie after she changes into black boxers and her gray T-shirt with the printed words, "Fun Fact: I don't care."

We sit on the couch and pull up a streaming service to find something to watch. Newly home from her art class, Tracey looks ready to join us. Once she spots the old Kung Fu movie we're watching, she keeps on walking through the family room.

Joie snorts at Tracey's disinterest in violent movies. "I wouldn't care if you dated that delicate superhero."

"She'd be around."

"I don't know what that would be like since you've hidden her from me."

"Good point."

"Don't make any babies."

"You're almost an adult. I might need a new slobber monster to crap her pants and make me watch Disney shit."

"That was never me," Joie insists while getting comfy. "I was an angel."

"You used to shit your pants while I was holding you. One time, you shit right after I finished changing your diaper. Didn't have a bit of respect for me."

Joie's eyes light up as she throws her head back and laughs maniacally. "You hadn't earned my respect yet. Once you did, I potty trained myself."

I chuckle at her laughter. Though Nicole was a fucking anchor dragging me down, our kid is an unexpected treasure.

I find myself imagining what life would be like if Selene was mine. I can't picture her enjoying this movie. That's what life would be like with Selene around. I'd have to hide myself from her.

I'm even more certain of this fact when Goose and Tommy "Hobo" Clark arrive later with a half-dead fucker in their trunk. The club's only lady member has her short red hair slicked back tonight. In contrast, Hobo's wild blond hair makes him look like he stuck his finger in an electrical socket.

"He was lifting cars in town," Hobo explains as my road captain smiles down at the crying asshole.

"Did he know this was our territory?" I ask, and Goose nods. "Well, then there's no discussion. Chop the guy up and dump him somewhere. Without a body, his mama won't need to pay for a funeral."

I ignore the asshole's whining and close the trunk. Goose goes to sit in the driver's seat while Hobo swipes his crazy hair from his face. My club brother would likely send Selene running in the opposite direction. But Hobo and I aren't so different. He just looks like a berserk criminal while I clean up better.

And that's the reality of my situation. I'm always going to be me, even if I hide from Selene. For the last week, I've only introduced her to people I could control. Not Joie, who might give away I'm an asshole.

Unfortunately, Selene met Ed and Callie tonight. They likely offered details I wouldn't want shared with her.

After the thief is gone and I return to the quiet house, I accept how my feelings for Selene can't go anywhere. She's gorgeous and kind, but she'll never truly be mine.

SELENE

Hoyt starts off the day with a visit to his accountant's office. I remain in the car since "the guy's a perv." I admire Hoyt's build as he strolls toward the accountant's office located inside a 1970s-style ranch. I'm just as impressed when his large frame returns to me.

"Yeah, you wouldn't have enjoyed that encounter," he says once back in the truck. "Tomorrow, I want you to come along with me to Joie's dentist appointment."

Grinning, I admit, "I'm curious what a little girl version of you looks like."

"She isn't little anymore," Hoyt says, smirking at the thought of his daughter. "She's nearly a teenager. Already full of sass. She'll probably say something rude. Might want to prepare for that."

"I don't know much about kids."

"Never wanted any?" he asks as we head back toward the other side of McMurdo Valley.

"No, I did. It just wasn't in the cards," I mumble, looking out the open window. "How long were you married?"

"Five years."

"Did you like it?"

"No," he says in a tone that screams, "Drop this topic!"

"Marriage isn't for everyone," I reply and enjoy the sunlight on my face as we fly down back roads before turning onto more established ones. "Where are we going?"

"To my office."

I'm still unfamiliar enough with McMurdo Valley to be sure if we're close to the Valley Gin Mill. Rather than the bar, Hoyt pulls the truck into a parking lot belonging to the three-story Valley Gorge Business Center.

"Is this the mysterious office you often spoke of?"

Smirking at my tone, he shrugs. "I have an official office here. It's where I keep my legal crap."

"Do you have a meeting here?" I ask, checking the schedule to ensure I didn't miss anything.

"No, I'm just showing you where it is. That way, you can come here in the future to work if you want."

I only nod since Hoyt never mentioned me working in an office before. *Is he ditching me?* I wake up every morning, looking forward to spending the day with him. I'm not sure I can hide my disappointment if he starts dropping me off here regularly.

I stand next to Hoyt as he puts away the step stool. As usual, I admire him whenever he isn't looking. Occasionally, he'll catch me checking him out. His smug expression always makes me feel like an idiot.

However, my lust puts me in good company. At yesterday's lunch, three women—one of them married and with her husband—also got caught checking out his fine body.

As we reach the glass front doors, a few suited men in their thirties exit. They ignore Hoyt but hold the door open for me. I do the usual "thank you, have a good day" while they reply with the customary sleazy, "overly obvious checking out my tits" move. Hoyt stands at the elevator, glaring at them.

We're soon on the third floor, where his corner office is located. SBMC, LLC is printed across the glass door. Underneath in smaller black letters reads, "Mayor Hoyt Macready."

Inside is an empty desk and two waiting room chairs. To my left is the bathroom. Hoyt's office is at the back.

"So many windows," I mumble, admiring the gorgeous hill view behind the office building.

Hoyt stands in the doorway, watching me while wearing a furious frown. "Is that what your husband was like?"

"What?" I ask.

"The slick suits and fake smiles. Is that what you liked about him?"

Hiding from his gaze, I mumble, "He was chosen for me. I didn't like anything about LeVoy."

A frowning Hoyt crowds me. "I saw how you were with them. The way your demeanor changed. Is that what you want?"

"I don't want anyone," I lie, forcing myself to look into his sky-blue eyes. "I'll never be free of LeVoy, and my time with him left me..."

"What?"

"Ugly," I mumble as hot tears fill my eyes. "I didn't run away when I was young enough to start over. Now, it's too late."

"You're only thirty-four," he says as his fingers skim my lips. "And there's nothing ugly about you, Selene."

"You don't know."

"I know plenty," he grumbles, stepping back. "Those fucks out there might look slick. They might say the right things. But they're scum."

"I was being friendly."

"No."

Lowering my gaze submissively, I whisper, "You're wrong."

"I know women."

"I know myself."

"Whatever," he says and kicks a box out of his way. "Date the shitheads. What do I care?"

"I don't want to date anyway."

"Because you're ugly," he mutters in a mocking tone.

I force myself to hold his gaze and nod. "You don't know me."

"You don't know me, either."

"I ask questions, but you don't share."

"I'm not an open book."

"Neither am I. But you figure I'm easy to read because I'm a woman, and you know women."

"Don't make me the bad guy."

I hear the anger in his tone and shrink back instinctively. "Do you want me to leave?"

"Where would you go, Selene?"

"Home."

"How?"

Realizing I hadn't thought that far ahead, I stammer, "Walk or call my sister."

"What would be the point?"

"You're angry."

Hoyt opens his mouth several times, ready to speak. After battling the words in his head, he sighs.

"I don't want you around those men. That's why I didn't bring you here. They're always prowling around."

"Why not just say that instead of claiming I was flirting with them?"

"You were."

"I said hello and nodded."

"You smiled."

"Because they smiled at me."

"People smile at me all the fucking time. I never just throw smiles back." When I stare at him, wondering if he's nuts, he asks, "What?"

"You're you. Of course, you can choose how to react to people."

"What's that mean?"

"You're powerful and independent. How can you think we're the same? You're not even the same as your cousin Nash."

Hoyt stands at the window and glares outside. "I want you to file this shit."

Accustomed to being dismissed, I nod and look at the pile of papers.

"Stick them in that file cabinet. I'll be back."

I watch Hoyt disappear out the door. Through the window, I notice him walking to his truck, where he climbs in and drives off. After figuring he'll be gone for a while, I walk to the bathroom and cry.

I've had this idea of Hoyt in my head. He's kind and patient. However, today, he revealed the man underneath—an angry brute who views me as a thing to be bullied.

His behavior makes sense, of course. Hoyt's the boss. Not just of me but of the town—maybe the whole county—and his club. He doesn't need to care about scaring people. We bend, so he doesn't need to. And for over a week, he's put up with my nervous behavior. He's bound to get annoyed.

If I viewed him as my employer rather than a possible boyfriend, my feelings likely wouldn't be so bruised right now.

After cleaning up after my cry, I text Yazmin to tell her what he said. She doesn't respond right away. I think today she's helping Cheryl in the backyard.

After quickly filing the paperwork, I sit in Hoyt's impressive leather chair. I lean back and close my eyes, thinking of how the room still has his scent. Spicy and rich like a fine meal. I smile at the thought of tasting his lips.

"This is why you're so weird with him," I mutter to myself before looking around, paranoid someone's listening. The office is still empty. I check my phone to find a message from Yazmin.

"He's jealous of those men," she replies.

"Why?"

"He's insecure."

Snorting, I roll my eyes. "A powerful man like him does not suffer from insecurities."

"Everyone does. Even hot bikers with big dicks."

"How do you know about his, you know?"

"Educated guess. The rest of him is large, so…"

"He got so angry."

"Would you get jealous if you saw those very sexy girls they call 'club sluts' rubbing against him?"

"Yes, and then I'd get sad."

"Well, he got mad."

"He scared me."

"Good. If he was a weak biker, he might get dethroned. Then, you would be out of a job. A scary biker is better. Just ignore him."

"What do I say when he comes back?"

"Ask him if you can have steak at lunch."

"Why?"

"You said he likes it when you order expensive items from the menu. Distract him."

"Solid plan!"

Setting aside my phone, I go through his mail before worrying I might see something I'm not supposed to. I head to the bathroom and clean up. I rest again in his chair and wait. Thirty minutes later, I hear Hoyt's truck rumbling into the parking lot.

Trying to seem casual feels stupid, so I get up and walk to greet him at the front. Hoyt sees me through the glass and frowns at how I'm waiting for him.

I back up so he can enter. His expression turns frustrated at the sight of me.

"You were crying."

"No. I have allergies."

"Don't lie to me," he demands, and his grumbly, growly voice clenches at my gut.

"I was crying."

Stepping inside, he closes the door. Hoyt glances back. Maybe realizing people might see us, he gestures for me to go to the back office.

I stand next to the desk and stare at him. He rubs at his bare forearms and then looks over my head out the window. Finally, Hoyt levels his blue-eyed gaze on me.

"I get possessive of people."

"Okay."

"You're an attractive woman."

"You're an attractive man."

"But you're not my possession. You're my assistant."

"Yes."

"That's something I need to remember," he says as his fingers brush across my cheek. "But I might forget."

"Okay," I mumble, trying to hide how fast my heart races when he touches me.

"But even if you're not my possession, you can't date those fucks."

"Okay," I reply immediately.

Hoyt stares into my eyes, wanting to say other stuff. I can feel him arguing with himself. The longer he stares at me, the more inclined I am to cross a line and touch him.

"Can I have steak at lunch?" I ask, hoping to break the tension.

Hoyt studies me. "On one condition."

"What?"

"Don't ever say you're ugly again."

"To you or to anyone?"

"Anyone."

"I can't promise that, but I won't say it in front of you."

Hoyt frowns harder, making his handsome face fearsome. Before I can shrink away, he takes my hand and tugs down his loose T-shirt. He presses my fingers against tatted, tanned flesh. My mind swims with arousal, and I feel like I might faint. My heart races painfully in my chest.

Frowning at me, he asks, "Do you think I'm ugly?"

"No," I choke out.

"I got this gunshot scar twelve years go."

Realizing he isn't simply having me touch him, I focus on the feel of his raised flesh under my fingertips. Hoyt lets go of the top of his shirt before lifting the bottom to reveal a long scar across his hard stomach. "Got carved up by a crazy bitch trying to protect her asshole boyfriend."

"I know you're making a point, but I can't think straight when you flash your body at me."

Hoyt offers a small smile, but his gaze remains intense. "I'm not ugly because of my scars, right?"

"Right," I say, covering my mouth to keep from licking my lips like a love-starved nympho.

"Then, how can your scars make you ugly?"

I want to point out a very obvious fact. He's a sexy large rough man whose scars improve his dangerous cred. In contrast, I'm a woman whose entire value has always come down to my beauty. I'm not talented at anything. I'm meek in most situations. I can't make a child. I'm one of those barely average people who survived based on men's desire.

"I can never wear a bikini again," I mumble while my gaze feasts on his chest and my mind imagines the hot skin hiding under his shirt. "But no one would complain if you did."

Nodding slightly at my words, Hoyt remains overly focused on me. His gaze darkens in intensity. I feel him pulling me closer. *How many women have fought their better judgment to claim a taste of this masculine beast?*

"Where did you go?" I ask when he watches me for too long.

"Just drove around with the window down. Pretended I was riding my hog. I think better that way."

"I'm glad you have an outlet for your frustrations. So many people demand things from you. We want you to make our lives better. It must feel oppressive."

"I'm fine most days," he says, exhaling hard as he steps back. "Let's get out of here and eat lunch. I might want the rest of the day off."

"You have two meetings."

"Can I ditch them?"

"If you let me claim you're sick, then yes."

Hoyt walks to the entrance of his office and opens the door for me. I exit and smile up at him. We feel back on the right wavelength. Just in case, I keep my head down when we pass two men entering the building.

HOYT

Selene has me tied up in knots. I doubt she realizes her power. That shit about her being ugly kills me. I want to take her to bed and kiss all over her sexy body until she knows she's a fucking goddess.

And I will. This professional bullshit between us just can't last. Selene is too damn intoxicating. The moment she climbs into my truck in the morning, filling it with her sweet scent, I'm in a state of heat. I spend all day struggling to think straight and pretend I'm not on fire inside.

I can't even keep track of how many times I've nearly kissed Selene. She might smile at me or laugh at some dumb shit I say. Sometimes, I catch her watching me. Our gazes hold tight, and I feel her craving my touch.

Other times, the simplest gesture will set me off. Yesterday, she wiped sauce from my beard, and I nearly pounced on her. Selene felt it, too. Her warm gaze welcomed my attention at first before revealing fear at how I might take the bait.

Eventually, I'll kiss her tempting lips. But not yet. After yesterday, though, I'm not sure how long I can wait. Those men sniffing around Selene set me off. I nearly fucked them up. *How can I keep shit professional when Selene steals my sanity with a mere glance?*

I've got her on my mind later when I'm at the Pigsty for another bitches-and-booze bash. Nash isn't in his usual tomcat mode. Instead, he stands back and watches my club brothers party with the very willing ladies from a nearby girls' college.

"You're here, but not here," Nash says as he hands over a beer.

"I'm here to be seen. That's it."

"A nice fuck might turn that weepy-as-fuck frown upside down, cuz."

"That's not what I need. Not with these chicks, anyway."

Nash's blue eyes flash in my direction. I feel him judging me. I almost laugh at how he considers giving me fucking advice.

"Look, I won't pretend I don't see what you do with Selene," he says after taking a pull on his beer. "She's hot as hell. So is her sister. But you're all worked up in a way that's not healthy. Either fuck her or find a way to shake that shit loose."

"It's not that simple. If it were, I'd have figured everything out myself already."

"Sure, you're the smart one. But you're shitting stress. People are talking."

"Fuck people."

Nash hears the hostility in my voice and shrugs. "Sure."

"It's only been a few weeks."

"Do you think she'll be less hot in a month?"

What I think—but don't share—is how Selene will eventually be in my bed. I can't imagine what happens after she's mine, but I need that woman.

I have never successfully deprived myself. When I wanted to take over McMurdo Valley, I fucked around for a while and tried to avoid conflict. But in the end, I just did what I wanted. Every time I've pushed for something, I've never regretted my choice. Why should I start now?

"Just stay away from her and stop fucking with me, Tomcat."

"Easy on the first part. Selene's hot, but if I'm sniffing around any of Patrice's granddaughters, the other one is more my style. She doesn't laugh at anything I say. I like a challenge."

"You told Patrice you'd stay away from them."

"Yeah, and I will," he says and shrugs. "For a while. No hurry. They're not going anywhere. Patrice also won't be as trigger-happy once her granddaughters move out. Then, I'll swoop in to seduce Yazmin."

"And then dump her."

Nash smirks. "Yeah, that's the part where Patrice's hair-trigger is a concern."

"Just leave her alone."

"Have you even met Yazmin?"

"No."

"Then, you don't know. She's super chill. Not twitchy like your girl."

"Stop fucking with me," I growl at him, and he actually flinches.

Tomcat eyes me warily before a smile warms his face. "I sometimes forget how you won't really hurt me. Your loyalty is a huge weakness," he taunts as I swing at him. "I would pity you if I hadn't wanted that president's patch."

"You suck and would have burned the club to the ground."

"Yeah, but imagine how much fun we would have had first."

I throw my beer bottle at his head, but Nash easily ducks and bats his eyes at me. Around us, people move aside, worried for their safety.

They ought to be concerned, too. I haven't kicked anyone's ass since that first day with Selene when the younger guys got fresh. I nearly yanked out pliers to remove parts of their bodies they would no longer need.

But I don't lose my shit tonight. Tomcat isn't saying or doing anything different than usual. I can't expect everyone to change their thinking just because I'm nursing a crush on a woman.

Instead of throwing punches, I move around the party. The guys watch me, wary of my bad mood. They chill out when I don't shove any of them into a wall.

Of course, the guys get their backs up as soon as I blow off a chick offering me a blowjob. After all, Amber's got zero gag reflex and an energetic tongue. I've seen her blow a line of guys like she's a woman addicted to jizz.

And normally, I'd be fine letting her unleash her obsession on my dick. But I can't enjoy green bean bullshit when I know Selene exists.

She's all I crave now. If that makes me whipped, my club brothers will need to learn to hide their emotions better. Once I claim Selene, I'm not planning on letting her go.

SELENE

Hoyt can't shake what's bothering him since yesterday. This morning, he wears a frown as he picks me up. We barely speak for the first hour. He only finds his voice when we're on our way to the middle school.

"I'm putting you on the pickup list," he mutters as we park in front of the building. "If something happens to me, you can get Joie."

"Okay."

Hoyt's blue eyes flash to me, searching for something on my face. "She doesn't like the dentist."

"I didn't, either."

Hoyt almost smiles, yet he's struggling. Every time he starts to mellow out, something riles him back up.

We walk into the school's front office. When I show my ID, the administrator woman doesn't approve of how it's from out of state.

"It's all I have."

"Get a new one," she mutters.

"What?" Hoyt barks, and the woman flinches.

The other office lady mumbles submissively, "It'd be better if she had one from this state."

When Hoyt stares at her for too long, I sense her fear. I'm agitated, too. He seems bigger right now. His whole body expands. His shoulders and chest widen.

He's like a predator exuding an aggressive stance toward a threat. The small middle-aged women shrink as he grows. Soon, they back away and lower their gazes submissively.

"Who shit the bed?" asks a voice from behind us.

I turn to find a tall, lean blond boy. His short hair hangs loose, giving him an effortlessly jock-handsome quality. His thumbs are hooked into his backpack's straps. His blue eyes flash from Hoyt to me. Then, the boy smiles. Seeing Hoyt looking back at me, I realize this isn't a boy.

"Don't say 'shit' at school," Hoyt mutters with little effort as he walks past his daughter.

"Sure," Joie replies and keeps grinning at me. "I understand everything now."

"What?" I ask and then add, "I'm Selene."

"Oh, I know."

Sharing her grin, I walk to the truck, where Hoyt gets the step stool for me.

"Why not just bring a regular car?" Joie asks her father.

"I need the four-by-four. This is easier."

"Is it, though?"

Faces only inches apart, father and daughter eyeball each other. They're playing a game I bet they enjoy often. Hoyt's demeanor softens, and he shakes his head.

"Stop hassling me," he tells her.

"You started it."

"No."

"I said one bad word, and you got surly."

"I was already surly," he explains and glances at me.

"Oh, yeah," Joie says and climbs into the back seat. "Can we get lunch afterward?"

Hoyt waits until I'm in the truck and then shoves the step stool next to his daughter. "Sure."

"Can I pick where we eat?"

Hoyt joins us in the truck and shrugs. "Don't pick Mexican."

"Does your tummy hurt?" she asks, laughing so hard she snorts.

"I'm glad you're in a good mood," Hoyt says as the truck's engine roars to life. "Normally, you whine about the dentist."

"I never whine. I just complain in a totally normal tone."

Hoyt nods, seeming tense again. "Selene didn't like the dentist."

"I still don't."

"I thought adults didn't go to the dentist," Joie says, leaning forward between our seats.

I look at Hoyt, who shrugs at how he got caught in a lie.

Joie frowns. "Wait, so at eighteen, I don't get to stop going?"

"Well, technically, you don't have to go as an adult," Hoyt explains as he pulls out of the parking lot. "No one will make you. But your teeth might rot like Hobo's."

"Ugh, he's so lazy about hygiene," Joie mutters, sitting back. "Has Selene met him?"

"No, but I gave her the gist. She's only met Nash and a few guys at the Pigsty."

"Did they try to sleep with her?"

When Hoyt immediately tenses, I hear Joie snickering in the back seat.

"Can we have a burger?" I ask when no one speaks for the next minute.

"Do you eat burgers?" Joie asks, suddenly appearing between the seats.

"Sit back," Hoyt grumbles.

"I'm strapped in. If you cause an accident, I won't go through the front window. Now, back to burgers, Selene, are you someone who eats them?"

"Sure."

"A lot?"

"No. But I can now."

Joie frowns and glances at her father. She wants to ask something. I wait for the question, but Hoyt signals for her to zip it.

"Big Bert's Burgers has these amazing **jalapeño** burgers," Joie says, editing herself. "Do you like spicy food?"

"I guess. My grandmother was Cuban. She sometimes cooked. It wasn't spicy, though."

"Granddad Ed loves spicy shit. His doctor said he needs to cut back on spicy shit. Old people aren't supposed to eat spicy shit. But he just won't give up spicy shit."

"Having fun?" Hoyt asks his daughter as we sit at a light.

"Shit," she replies, smiling brightly. "Dad grew up with spicy foods. Right?"

"Yeah," Hoyt says, struggling to remain in a bad mood when his kid keeps grinning at him. "Carolina-style barbecue sauce was a favorite. My dad put it on everything. It's not the spiciest I've tasted. Still, I learned to crave heat as a kid."

"Me, too," Joie says, looking at her dad with such love and pride.

"My father liked mild food," I explain as I admire Hoyt and Joie. "My husband couldn't tolerate most Cajun food despite growing up in Louisiana."

"Husband?" Joie balks. "You're married?"

Hoyt answers immediately, "She's getting a divorce."

"I would think so," Joie replies.

Feeling like I'm disappearing the longer they talk about me, I mumble, "I can't find a lawyer to help me file."

"Can't you get her one?" Joie asks Hoyt.

"Kourtney will probably do it."

Disappearing again, I ask, "Who's that?"

"His ex-girlfriend. She always wears heels. It's annoying."

"We never dated," Hoyt corrects.

I get his meaning. *They fucked.* I have no doubt Hoyt's sampled every attractive woman in the county. I sometimes wish I was the only one to notice Hoyt's attractiveness, leaving me with no competition. He'd settle for a woman like me if he were lonely enough.

"Don't be sad," Joie says and nudges me. "It's just a dick thing."

"Sit back," mutters her father.

104

"Yeah, yeah, read the room, Joie," she grumbles, sounding just like Hoyt when annoyed. "I get it."

When I glance at Hoyt, he frowns at what he sees on my face.

"She's a good lawyer," Hoyt mutters. "Don't know if she does divorce stuff. She normally handles criminal and civil stuff. I'll call her."

"Can she file if she doesn't practice in Louisiana?"

"Don't know. She'll figure something out."

Hoyt pulls into a dental office parking lot. I notice many small children shuffling in and out the door. Already insecure after Hoyt's weird mood, I feel that old longing rise in me.

I'd once wanted a baby so badly. Every month, I felt the sting of disappointment. I tried different diets, positions, meditation, yoga, acupuncture, praying, everything. We finally went to the doctor, but he found nothing wrong. I just never got pregnant. After a year, I gave up, yet secretly hoped not trying would create the magic needed to make a baby.

That was ten years ago. My baby would have been nearly Joie's age. I couldn't imagine what life would be like for the child now. To have LeVoy as a father. To be told I abandoned it by refusing to return to Louisiana. If I tried to take the child with me, LeVoy would have already made another attempt on my life. I think the only reason he lets me live is to enjoy how I suffer. If I were happy, he'd take another shot.

Or maybe he's scared to try in a state where he holds no power. The Bossier City police protected him. I can't prove that, of course. They did their investigation. Wrote down lots of facts. Interviewed many people.

They seemed professional, but I'd seen what they did for LeVoy's brother when he raped a teenage girl. She reported the attack, had physical evidence, and did everything right. Yet, her case remains stagnant despite the authorities having him dead to rights on at least statutory rape. She'll never find justice because she's not rich enough to buy it.

"Where's your head right now?" Hoyt asks when he waits for me to climb out. "Not scared of the dentist, are you?"

Smiling, I shake my head and exit the truck. As usual, I end up standing too close to Hoyt. His rich peppery scent overwhelms me. I remember my fingers against his hot skin yesterday in the office. I recall the way his body felt from his scars to his chest hair. My powerful arousal left me lightheaded.

"I'm fine," I say in a weak voice, betraying my hunger for this man.

Hoyt watches me. His blue eyes reveal lust, affection, and something darker. Anger, maybe. I'm pissing him off, I think.

Standing straighter, I lower my gaze and tug back all my unhinged emotion. I need to stay focused on the job. I'm his assistant. This is his daughter. We are at a dentist's office. Nothing about our situation is sexy. *Snap out of it!*

We enter the office to find it packed with children. Joie rolls her eyes and scowls in Hoyt's direction.

"We have an appointment at eleven," is his response.

Joie and I find a seat while Hoyt gets her checked in. I look around at the moms and their little ones. My chest hurts at how that'll never be me.

However, I'm thankful again for how I didn't create children who would now be trapped with LeVoy. After I ran from the hospital, I never went home. Anything Yazmin couldn't grab before our escape is gone forever. That could have included a child. I'm lucky to be barren. I need to stop pouting.

At eleven, Joie's name is called. She steps around the kids and their annoyed mothers who've been waiting longer. Hoyt takes her empty spot, scoots down in the seat, crosses one long leg over another, and focuses on his phone.

I smile slightly at how Hoyt throws his weight around when necessary. He can be patient when we eat out. I see him wanting to complain, but he'll give the waitstaff some slack. With Joie, though, he doesn't fuck around.

Twenty minutes later, she appears in the doorway, holding a little bag.

"I said you'd call for the next checkup appointment," she tells Hoyt.

Standing up, he shadows everyone around us. I even notice a few kids cringe at the size of him.

"Any issues?" he asks.

Shrugging, Joie walks to the door. I follow Hoyt, who musses up his daughter's hair as they head for the truck.

"Keep up these clean checkups, and you can go once a year when you're eighteen."

"So now it's yearly when I'm an adult?"

"Yeah, but I'm not lying this time."

"Uh-huh," Joie says, yanking down the step stool for me.

I look at her, realizing we're the same height.

"You're going to be tall."

"Good. I might be able to get on the basketball team in high school," she says, holding the step stool for me to climb up. "I'm looking to be good in a sport. So far, I'm okay at baseball and average at soccer."

"I played tennis when I was young."

Joie climbs in behind me and hangs through the seats. "Really? There are courts nearby. We should go play."

"She's still healing," Hoyt says, starting the truck and waiting for her to strap herself in.

"From the shooting," Joie mumbles and holds my gaze. "Did that hurt?"

"Yes," I reply.

"Dad got shot twice."

When I frown at Hoyt, he shrugs. "The other time was in the back. Can't show you that scar as easy."

Thinking of the shooting, I mumble, "I don't remember much from that night or the next week."

"Who took care of you?" Joie asks, leaning between the seats again. "When Dad was hurting, I brought him medicine and food."

Hoyt smirks. "You were my servant."

A grinning Joie asks me, "Were you all alone?"

"I had my sister, Yazmin. She lived in our guesthouse and found me after the shooting. She's why I'm alive."

"I always wanted a sister."

Hoyt looks at me and shakes his head. I smile at how he quietly corrects his daughter. If I didn't already think Hoyt was a beautiful man with a good heart, today would seal the deal. His protective nature with Joie is unbearably charming.

We stop at Big Bert's Burgers for lunch and get a corner booth. Joie sits between us and insists I try her spicy burger to see if I like it.

Hoyt watches us with an overly passive expression plastered across his handsome face.

"Do you like going to the movies?" Joie asks me after we order lunch.

"I haven't gone since I got married."

"Because you couldn't or didn't want to?"

"The first one."

"Do you want to come with us this Friday?"

I look at Hoyt to find him frowning. Assuming he doesn't want me to join them, I shake my head. "No, thank you." When his scowl darkens, I think maybe he *does* want me to come along. "Maybe."

"Just do whatever you want, Selene," Hoyt says, exhaling hard like I'm getting on his nerves.

"Can Yazmin come?"

Hoyt frowns. "Doesn't she work Fridays?"

"No, just the slow nights. Patrice says she can't handle the rush."

"Then bring her," Joie insists before flipping off someone across the restaurant. "No, go away."

I glance toward the entrance to see several men and a woman strutting in our direction. They grin at Joie's middle finger.

The woman looks like a redheaded Joan Jett.

Next to her is a tall, tatted man who keeps winking at anyone who acts irritated by their arrival.

Another man seems like maybe he's homeless, so I assume he's Hobo.

Another man with a humorless expression, short auburn hair, and dark blue eyes brings up the rear with Nash.

Hoyt's cousin is also winking but only at the hot women.

"What's pretty princess doing out of school?" asks the woman.

"I went to the dentist, you troublemaking butthead."

I'm unsure if they're teasing, so I lower my gaze and just hope to disappear.

"Allow me to make the introductions," Nash announces and slides into the booth on my side. "Selene is our president's newest assistant. She's not to be fucked. So, hands off, Goose."

The redheaded woman shrugs. "Not my type. I prefer blond bubba types, but no offense, babe."

"None taken."

Nash grins at my unease while Hoyt gets overly still, like when he was pissed at the school.

"And this dirty fucker is our road captain, Tommy. He won't bathe more than once a week, so don't think begging will change his mind."

The long-haired, shaggy bearded man shrugs. "Soap's got toxins in them, and I'm not looking to get cancer."

The redheaded man glares at Hobo. Suddenly, his gaze flashes to me.

"That's Armor. He's Goose's little brother and our vice president."

"I thought you were."

Nash chuckles. "No, I'm the treasurer. I'm smarter than these fucks."

"Bullshit," Joie mutters, gaining a smirk from her dad and a frown from Nash.

"I exist," the tall, overly tatted man spits out and shoves Nash toward me.

"Watch yourself," Hoyt growls in his scary voice. "Shove him, not her."

I realize he's worried I'll get bumped. My smile doesn't last long when I feel everyone watching me.

"I'm Walla Walla," the guy tells me. "I'm the secretary. Like you but with more guns."

"It's nice to meet you all," I mumble, adding, "I'm not good at remembering names."

"Hot women never are," Goose says.

Hoyt clears his throat loud enough to startle people nearby. "Did you fucks need something?" he asks of his club brothers and sister. "There isn't enough room at our table for all of you."

"We just came in for lunch. Sorry if we're interfering with your vanilla lifestyle," Nash replies mockingly.

"If Selene weren't in the way," Hoyt hisses, "I'd kick you under the table right now, Tomcat."

"I know, but she *is* in the way. So, you know, fuck off."

"I'll kick his ass," Joie says, reaching across me to throw an ice cube from her drink.

"No roughhousing," Armor barks.

Joie ignores him and smirks at Tomcat. "You're in trouble."

"I don't need this bullshit," Nash grumbles, standing up as if angry.

I scan everyone's faces, unable to tell if they're still teasing. Joie's grin makes me think they are, but I feel out of the loop.

"See you around, Selene. Maybe talk our prez into overdosing on chill pills," Nash says and then glares at

Joie. "As for you, pretty princess, suck on an ice cube and go watch 'The Good Dinosaur.'"

Joie bounces in her seat as they leave. "I'm going to be in the club when I'm older. I totally plan to beat up Nash once I'm bigger. He already said I can."

I don't know if Joie is kidding, but her enthusiasm makes me laugh. Between his club people strutting off to another table and me giggling at his daughter's threats, Hoyt settles down and smiles more. He gets a big grin on his handsome face when I try Joie's burger and realize I can handle the heat.

For a moment, I imagine us becoming more than boss and employee. Being professional disappears, and I start viewing the upcoming movie as our first date.

Every sexy gaze from Hoyt is like another shovel for this lust-filled hole I'm digging myself.

HOYT

Today worried me. If Selene acted weird around my daughter, I wouldn't be able to prevent myself from turning on her. No one loves Joie like I do. She must be protected.

However, Selene is mostly amused by Joie. I catch her grinning a lot when my girl gets going on something. They're not fast friends or anything. Selene is too reserved, and Joie rarely lets people close. But they got along better than I assumed they would.

Joie waits until we arrive home before razzing me about Selene. Mainly, she thinks I'm a dork with a crush. My daughter also claims I should kill Selene's husband and marry her.

"Nail that down," she teases.

Smirking at her words, I poke back with, "You just like her because she's easy to push around."

"True. If I'm getting a stepmom, she better be weak. I can't have anyone telling me what to do unless their names are Dad or Tracey."

"Selene is just my assistant."

"Sure," she says and goes to do her homework on the front porch with Tracey.

Later, we throw the ball around the yard and walk with the dog. By the time the sun's down, Joie's crashed on the couch. When she sleeps, my daughter wears the same pouty face as when she was a baby.

Even as a slobbery shit-machine, Joie charmed me quickly and completely. I hope we never lose this connection, not even when she's grown up with her own life, a fella I can't stand, and kids I'll spoil.

Around ten, I hear a motorcycle riding up the long quiet road to the house. Walking outside, I see Wade "Armor" Palmer climbing off his hog. He was clearly on edge at lunch. Unlike Nash or even myself, he never mellows out completely. Plenty of people think he's a heartless fuck.

Armor and I met in elementary school. He's VP because his word is golden. Not once have I caught him lying to me. Though a rough childhood gave him a hard exterior, he isn't cruel. If he calls me out, I know I've done fucked up.

Tonight, he's clearly ready to call me out.

"People are talking," he says rather than hello after climbing off his Fat Boy.

"I've heard."

"Tomcat claimed he mentioned something," Armor says from the darkness. "He also claimed you got your back up."

"Oh, it's up, alright."

"Yet, you're just standing around like a man on vacation."

I storm down the porch steps and face off with Armor. He doesn't flinch. I don't fear him, either.

Hell, we made our first kills together. I was the weapon. He acted as protection. We made a good team. We still do.

However, life's gotten settled. For me, anyway. Armor remains as restless as when we were kids.

"What do you want me to do?" I ask when our staring match gets old.

"People say this new assistant has converted you to the church of pussies and cowards."

"People are saying that, huh?"

Armor steps closer. "I'm saying it right now, Hoyt. People have mouthed off around you in the last few weeks, but you don't do shit."

"I'm easing my assistant into our lifestyle. I can't exactly go berserk on every asshole who looks at me wrong. If that shit happened to you with your mommy around, would you blow up?"

"Yeah, I would. All while my mom sat her ass in the car as I finished making the guy bleed. She understands how holding power can be more difficult than gaining it in the first place. And you know if Joie had been there instead of the new broad, you'd have no trouble laying into any asshole."

Exhaling hard, I think to throw a punch. Armor wants me to stomp on annoyances, and he's currently pissing me off. Except that's not what he's really looking for. My VP wants answers.

"Selene got fucked up by her husband," I mutter and look out at the pond shining under the moonlight.

"I heard."

"Tomcat has a big mouth."

"He's worried the stress of these two chicks will kill Patrice."

"That's fucking stupid."

"He's hearing those worries from Glenn. You know how that shit works."

Exhaling roughly, I grumble, "Selene needs time."

"How is that your problem?"

"I can't fuck up people in front of her. She gets weird when I even raise my voice."

Armor rolls his eyes and steps back. "Hoyt, I get how this chick has problems, and you need an assistant. But it sure feels like you're looking for excuses to puss out."

"Fuck you, Armor. Do you think you'd do better in my slot?"

"If you go down," he says, getting back in my face, "every single person we've fucked over in the last twenty years will ride in here to claim their piece of flesh. Right now, they fear you. The rest of us aren't so much of a concern. So, no, I don't want to shove you aside and take your slot. That puts plenty of targets on me. But you acting like a pussy is also putting targets on us."

I know Armor's right. People fear me. That's why I won the mayoral election over the nice lady who wanted to clean up the parks and that asshole who advocated sticking the town's two homeless people in jail. I defeated them both without promising anything.

Once I showed up, people were too scared to tell me no.

That fear didn't happen overnight. I fucked up many people over the years. Now that I'm no longer a young man, people have started thinking they can shove me aside.

Though the new club guys seem too green to go berserk in the way I did in the old days, they're perfectly capable of spilling blood. If I put out the order, they'll remind everyone why this county fears the Steel Berserkers.

"I'm trying to make something happen here with Selene," I admit to Armor. "You get that, right? She isn't just an employee."

As usual Armor's expression is unreadable. I still sense maybe he didn't know I had a thing for Selene.

"Is this woman worth screwing over the club?" he finally asks.

"I'm not doing shit to the club."

Armor studies me. "Is your inability to get laid why you're so edgy yet passive?"

"Maybe. But mostly, it's what I said about Selene. She's touchy about violence. I can't have her thinking I'm like her husband."

"Is this real?" he asks, kicking at the ground and chuckling. "The words you're saying are so fucking stupid. I can't believe you're not pulling my leg."

"What the fuck are you talking about?"

Shaking his head, Armor backs away as if I can't possibly be serious. "You're Ruin."

"Yeah?"

"So, let's say this lady and you make shit happen. She's in your bed. Hell, you fucking marry her. All happy shit you tried with Nicole. Then what? Do you think you'll hide the part of you capable of sawing off a screaming man's head? Will she think you're a teddy bear while you sneak out to fuck up our enemies? Or are you planning to retire and cuddle with her?"

115

Crossing my arms, I shrug. "Eventually, she'll know the truth."

"What makes you think it'll be easier in six months or whatever time period you've concocted? This chick got fucked up by her husband, right? Didn't she get lit up by a hitman?" When I nod, Armor shakes his head like I'm still too stupid to live. "Motherfucker, that chick isn't getting tougher or calmer. That's the kind of fucked up people don't walk off."

Armor looks up at the moon. "My ma heard a car backfire the other day and hid under the table. Thirty years have passed since those assholes shot up our house, but she's still afraid. Well, that's your girlfriend. Yet you, a man not known for his patience, believe you can wait her out. That's stupid fucking thinking right there."

"I understand how you don't get it. I wouldn't get it if it were you. We're not men who get wound up on this hearts-and-flowers shit. But Selene's special to me. I need to keep her. If that means acting like a fucking pussy or sneaking off to dismember people, I'll do it."

Armor relaxes his arms and exhales deeply. "You're bound to show her the real you eventually. I know your temper. You have a limit. Once you blow, you'll scare the shit out of her. Why not get honest now? Are you planning to wait until you can weigh her down with a baby so she can't run? Because that shit doesn't work. Look at Nomad. His bitch bailed fucking quick once she realized his tats and vest weren't for show."

"You're talking logic, Armor. That's not where my head is at. It's like telling me I shouldn't feel bad for ordering Nicole out of the Valley. Logically, I know the bitch needed to leave my territory. But my heart still feels bad when I see Joie talking about her friends' moms. She knows she's missing out. That kind of hurting isn't something I can just logic away."

"No, maybe not. But if this chick is real for you, you better be willing to be real for her. Nomad thought his bitch loved him. But she was into the *idea* of him. Once she saw the real man, she bailed and never looked back."

Armor glances at Wise Guy barking at the woods. When he returns his gaze to me, he sighs. "You're making things worse by pretending for Selene. By the time she learns the truth, your life might be entangled with hers. Then, her leaving will fuck you up sideways. What then? Are you planning to hide in the woods like Nomad?"

"Enough. I get it."

"Good. Because I'm sick of punching assholes in the back of the head when I catch them calling you soft. That's how damn fast people turn when they're not scared. So, figure your shit out."

"Is this lecture over?"

"Only if I got through your thick fucking skull."

"I know you're right. I have plans to help Selene that won't be as easy if I've been dethroned."

"Being king is fucking hard."

"You have no idea," I mutter and walk back to the porch. "Do you want to stick around for a beer?"

Armor considers whether saying yes makes his earlier argument seem less serious. Like, maybe, he can be bought off with a beer.

But we both know he has nowhere to go. The Pigsty is loud and messy. He's become like a den mom with the guys. The club girls rarely interest him enough for him to even learn their names.

Armor's a man who gave up everything to build the Steel Berserkers Motorcycle Club. Once we reached the top, he looked around and realized he has no one to share his bounty with.

If Nicole knew how to use her birth control, I'd be in the same boat. No oops means no Joie, leaving me where? Would I have built this house if not for my kid?

I imagine I'd be living at the Pigsty with men ten years my junior.

I got lucky while Armor didn't. That's why he joins me in the house for that beer. We have more in common than what separates us. Tonight, we're both men struggling with where we are and what comes next.

SELENE

Yazmin isn't sure she wants to go to the movies. Working has worn her out. She feels on display and judged at the Gin Mill.

However, I know she likes the tips she makes. I see her counting the cash a lot as if reminding herself why she needs to keep going. She told me twice yesterday how she wanted a little dog that would sit in her lap.

In her youth, Yazmin ached for a baby, but Robert forbade her from having children. Most women would scoff at such an order. However, he'd long programmed her to submit.

With no baby in her future, Yazmin wants a dog to cuddle with. I see how much she likes Patrice's cats. That's why she'd much rather stay home with them than go to a noisy theater.

Yet, I'm dying to spend time doing something fun together. We never went anywhere in Bossier City. LeVoy said I needed to be at the estate to oversee things. I spent years stuck on my property, only leaving when LeVoy brought me along to an event.

Now, I can go to the movies with a handsome man, his fun kid, and my best friend and sister.

"We can be normal," I tell Yazmin when she sits passively on the bed. "See an action-packed movie, eat popcorn with that greasy butter, and drink soda."

Yazmin still doesn't want to go. Her gaze reveals how my big dreams of a normal life are too far out of reach for her.

However, we both know we might not have much more time together. Maybe that's why she gets dressed and stands outside with me in the warm evening.

"What do I say?" she asks as we notice an approaching black SUV.

"Nothing if you don't want to. Just enjoy being out."

"Do I have to pay for things?"

"No. Hoyt always pays."

Yazmin nods, looking tired before the SUV pulls up. Joie lowers the passenger window and smiles.

"I convinced Dad to bring a normal-sized car, so you didn't need a ladder to get inside," she says while Hoyt smirks from his spot. "Can I sit up front?"

"Of course," I reply, excited to be out with my favorite people. "This is my sister, Yazmin."

"How come you have such fancy names?" Joie asks as we slide into the back seat.

"Our father thought it made him seem richer."

Joie frowns while Hoyt turns around to smile at us. "Hello, Selene," he says in that voice I feel wrap around my heart.

His gaze flashes to Yazmin. For a moment, I worry he'll go gaga over her beauty. If he fell for my sister, I'd be lying if I claimed to be happy for them. Hoyt is my dream guy. Losing him to anyone would hurt but to my sister would break me.

"Hello, Yazmin."

When their gazes meet, nothing happens. She looks tired. He's just Hoyt. When his gaze flashes back to me, it warms. My relief is palpable.

I exhale softly, admiring how sexy he looks tonight in a buttoned-up black shirt. I don't know if he's hotter in a T-shirt or something a little dressier. Either way, his blue eyes are like tranquilizers, calming my nerves.

We arrive at the movie theater located in the neighboring town of Locust Pines. McMurdo Valley's sister city is nothing more than untouched nature, a few ranches, a trailer park, and this small stretch of businesses. A Walmart, bakery, three bars, one small specialty grocery store, and a theater are flanked by thick woods and a river.

"They had big plans out here a few years back," Hoyt explains while he finds us a parking spot in the back. "We planned to draw businesses into this area."

"What happened?" I ask when he just stops talking.

"It's complicated," he mutters and turns around to look at us. "Is it okay for me to park back here? The locals are notoriously shitty drivers, and they often get drunk during the movies. I don't want my SUV busted up."

Joie sighs. "You're so precious with new things."

Hoyt frowns at her comment before grinning when he realizes she's teasing him. Once Joie climbs out, I follow and tug Yazmin along. My sister drags, seemingly heavily sedated.

Inside the lobby, we stand in line. Though people are rowdy here, they avoid Hoyt. He acts oblivious to their behavior, but I know better.

I hold Yazmin's hand while listening to Joie.

"My favorite movies are 'The Raid' ones," she explains. "I don't mind reading subtitles. I like the choreography. Dad does, too."

Hoyt looks at his daughter with such pride. I never witnessed such love in my father's gaze, not even toward his beloved son.

Of course, my paternal grandparents are cold people, so my father never knew warmth, either.

In contrast, Ed seems like he talks to his son like a friend and also got into rowdy stuff in his youth. I can imagine him taking Hoyt out fishing, just like my boss does with his daughter.

With snacks in hand, we locate our assigned seats. Hoyt wants me to sit next to him. I smile when I realize he can't figure out a lineup where I'm at his side. His frustration is electric. Our gazes meet, and he shrugs.

"I sit next to you most days," he mutters as I take a spot between Joie and Yazmin.

Unable to stop grinning, I only say, "Thank you for inviting us."

Hoyt shares my smile while Joie talks about how she can't eat popcorn unless it's covered in oily butter.

"Home popcorn makes me puke," she explains and then adds, "Right, Dad?"

I admire the easy bond between Hoyt and his daughter. I hadn't been sure what kind of father he might be. On our second day, Hoyt mentioned he had live-in help. I got the sense he might not be hands-on.

For one thing, Hoyt's busy. Plus, he's implied he hadn't wanted to be a family man. He'll say stuff like "I never thought that'd be me" when speaking of attending school functions.

Even if Hoyt hadn't wanted this life, fatherhood suits him. Despite her talking mostly to me, Joie often looks to him for reassurance or agreement.

I feel blessed to share this time with them. As if I'm being let in on a secret. Other than my bond with Yazmin, I've never felt close to anyone. Even my mom could turn indifferent if she felt it improved her status in life.

Yazmin squeezes my hand as the lights dim. I find my sister smiling at me. She knows I'm where I need to be. I've hidden nothing from her.

In Bossier City, I began losing myself. LeVoy picked my clothes, what I ate, who I spoke to, and if I could even leave my room. I'd learned to be the puppet LeVoy craved, losing the ability to react without someone pulling at my strings.

Yazmin's arrival offered me a purpose. She was a ghost like me. They broke her in the hospital. Though I doubt there was much left after Robert was done with her.

I made sure Yazmin showered, ate, and took her meds. I lured her out of her mental prison like her presence did for me. We spent all our free time together. Even if we didn't speak for hours, I felt more alive when she was nearby.

That's why she understands tonight is special. Even if I'm just Hoyt's assistant, I have value to him like I never did with any other man.

The movie proves to be loud and messy. The characters make weird choices. A lot of stuff blows up. Like even objects that shouldn't explode, still do.

Having never watched such a crazy movie, I love every minute. Joie bounces in her seat during the wilder scenes. Hoyt grins at his daughter's reaction. He smiles wider when he catches me watching her. I hear him chuckle at the movie's dumber moments or lame attempts at humor.

As soon as the first action scene occurs, Yazmin seems to want to bail. Everything is so loud and overwhelming. Yet, she soon loosens up on my hand and settles into the fact that nothing's real. Characters get shot and never die. Cars blow up, but no one important gets hurt. The violence is just a game.

I leave the theater overjoyed. At thirty-four years old, I felt like I knew the world. However, this week alone, I've tried a **jalapeño** burger and saw my first wild action movie.

There's so much in the world I've never experienced. For the first time since I arrived in McMurdo Valley, I truly feel what this second chance can provide.

As we walk into the warm evening, Yazmin is smiling at Joie's brutal movie critique. I'm admiring Hoyt as he stretches. He catches me looking and smirks. We share another heated moment. If he weren't my boss and I wasn't his assistant, we'd probably start rubbing against each other. Right then is when I hear a bunch of angry voices.

"You don't deserve this!" shouts an older woman with a big head of white hair.

I noticed her in the theater. Her large group got loud and rowdy. I think some were drinking. I don't know why they're yelling at us.

"This isn't right! You shouldn't be able to smile! You have no right!"

The woman keeps hollering while the men with her get riled up and shout, "Yeah! Fucker! Asshole!"

"What's happening?" Yazmin whispers as we walk faster to the SUV. "Are they yelling at us?"

Joie shrugs while Hoyt's body goes rigid. I notice him crack his neck before slowing his pace enough to fall behind us and act as a shield.

"You murderer!" screams another woman.

One of the men throws a bottle at us.

Another woman hollers, "You have no right to be happy!"

When I glance back at Hoyt, he mutters, "Ignore them and keep moving."

I look into his eyes, needing reassurance. I don't care if I'm being irrational. My mind is overloaded with fear. I can't breathe right. I need Hoyt to do that thing where he stares at me with his sky-blue eyes and makes the world go still. Only he can erase my terror.

Instead, Hoyt hides in his head. He reveals none of the man I've fallen for. He's cold now. Not angry, more like hard and focused.

"You bring your whores to the movies! My boy will never see another fucking movie!" the woman screams while someone else throws a bottle that shatters nearby.

I don't look back. I keep moving despite my building panic making me lightheaded.

We're nearly at the SUV when Yazmin suddenly stops. She squats down and covers her head like she's in a tornado drill. Joie notices her and comes back. I rush to my sister and wrap my arms around her.

"You're in McMurdo Valley. You're with me. Just stand up, and we'll go home and see Patrice. You can pet her cats. Cheryl will put on a funny show."

"I've been bad," Yazmin whimpers and begins rocking. "I can't run. I have to let it happen."

Hugging her tighter, I beg, "Please, Yazmin."

"What's wrong with her?" Joie asks, sounding weirded out.

Hoyt lifts us up to our feet and pushes for us to get moving. "Just go to the SUV."

Another bottle goes flying. Someone screams, "Whore!"

Yazmin crouches again and begins to cry. "I can't run. I have to let it happen."

I wrap her in my arms as more things are thrown. A rock tumbles close to us.

"Dad?" Joie asks, sounding scared.

Tugging Yazmin to her feet, Hoyt tells his daughter, "Go to the SUV."

"You come out with your whores and your weird, ugly little girl and—"

The world goes sideways as I see Joie's expression fall. She looks at her father and seems so ashamed.

"Dad?" she mumbles.

I expect Hoyt to tell us to get moving again. I look into his eyes, desperate for relief from the panic closing in on me. I can barely breathe. Every inhale feels like I'm drowning. The air is too thick. I can't see straight. Joie's expression breaks my heart. Yazmin's old training is dragging me deeper into my panic.

When I look into his eyes, I see something snap. His cold turns hot. His handsome gaze twists into a feral glare. The man I've fallen for is gone. *In his place stands a beast.*

Hoyt turns and runs at the people harassing us. I hear panicked screaming and startled cussing followed by an enraged roar.

The panic swallows me up. I can't think or breathe. The world spins, and I'm nearly on my ass.

The last thing I see is Hoyt picking up a man and throwing him at the others.

Joie somehow gets us moving. Cries of pain fill the night. Yazmin keeps trying to squat down to brace herself for her punishment.

My mind returns to the time I found LeVoy hitting my sister with his belt. She'd gotten upset over something. He yelled for her to stop whining. She squatted like she was trained, so he decided she wanted to be whipped.

I panicked then, too. Running to her, I covered Yazmin with my body and took the spanking. I couldn't think straight. I remained over her long after LeVoy got bored and walked away.

Spiraling into the darkness, I lost myself for a long time after the beating. The panic dragged me further down into the abyss, where living and breathing feel like a lie. I wanted to let go and give into the darkness.

"It's okay," Joie keeps saying as Yazmin and I sit in the back seat with her. She texts into her phone and says the words again. "Dad is handling it. Don't cry."

I can't remain in the present. I'm back in the laundry room when LeVoy cracked my head against the cabinet. Or in the kitchen when he tripped me, and I went sprawling. Or the time on the staircase when he stopped, turned to look at me, and casually pushed me backward.

Every beating returns. I'm again at the mercy of a violent man growing bored of his abuse. LeVoy can't get off on it anymore. I'm no longer the beautiful twenty-one-year-old he married. I'm just this thing always around, flinching and crying.

So, he made a phone call. I can almost see him nonchalantly throwing together the plan. *My life meant so little.*

Every day, I'm thankful he didn't try to kill Yazmin, too. Was he merciful, or did he have plans for her when I was no longer around?

"Selene," Hoyt barks, suddenly at the car door.

"Dad?" Joie mutters and pouts at him.

My panic lets go, springing me back into the present. I'm in the SUV with Joie and Yazmin. My sister is counting to herself. She's lost in her mind. I look at Joie and think of her hurt feelings. She's so lively. I never want her to become an awkward mess like I was at her age.

My gaze finally meets Hoyt's. He doesn't hide his rage now. He's a monster trapped in the body of my crush. He is somehow beautiful yet terrifying. Right now, his anger is directed at me.

Hoyt grumbles, "Just calm down."

"She's scared," Joie tells him.

"I know that."

"But you're scaring her more."

Hoyt looks at me like I'm a fucking loser. I wouldn't be surprised if he fired me on the spot. Maybe that would be best.

We can't go back to our casual flirting. I've seen the monster he hides. He's witnessed the crazy I can barely conceal. Our masks have fallen off. Now, there's only the part where we admit we were lying to ourselves.

HOYT

Selene doesn't say a damn word to me on the way to her place. She mumbles something to Joie and helps her crazy sister out of the SUV. They're both shaking and in tears.

I try to tell her how shit's okay. No one will hurt them. But Selene refuses to even look at me. *I'm the bad guy now.*

Joie pouts on the way to our house. I wait until we're inside before ordering her to spill it.

"You took so long to stand up to them," she mumbles, seeming sad in a way she rarely is. "I thought you agreed with them."

"That I don't deserve to be happy?"

"No, that I'm weird and ugly."

Her expression rips apart my heart. I think back to the parking lot. I knew those fuckers were about to start shit, yet I wanted to keep up my "nice guy" façade for Selene. She's so skittish about violence and my temper. I need to be the guy she wants, even if it's a lie.

If Yazmin hadn't flipped out and squatted down, we'd have gotten away without me showing Selene how I got my road name.

Once they talked shit about Joie, and my baby got that brokenhearted look on her face, I saw red.

What's the fucking point of being the top dog if those losers can throw shit at my kid and call her names? Selene and Yazmin didn't deserve to be threatened, either. But they're fucked up already. Joie's still got a healthy mind. *Why would I ever allow those garbage people to fuck with my kid?*

I can't deny it felt great to go berserk on those assholes. I relished how their bodies broke under my power. The way their voices changed from rage and smug superiority to fear and pain. Every scream fed the monster.

I showed no mercy. They'd crossed a line with me. Everything was fair game. Their women knew it, too. That's why they grabbed their kids and ran while the men broke and bled.

I'm not done, either. I plan to hunt down those assholes—burn down their homes, cars, and businesses. Nothing will survive my wrath.

If me being a nice guy for a few weeks was all it took for them to get cocky, well, I'll need to ruin many people to regain my crown.

Armor was right. About a lot of things. People viewing me as weak made them arrogant and stupid. Plus, Selene needed to see the real me, warts and all.

Of course, going berserk didn't fix the bad feelings in Joie.

"You're the best person I know," I tell her. "The coolest, too. That's why I sent your mom away. She was going to twist you up into someone you're not. She would make you second-guess yourself. Joie, you've got great instincts."

"Then, why didn't you stand up to them?"

"Selene wants me to be soft."

Joie mumbles, "I think she just wants you."

"No, she's afraid of men. Her father and that asshole husband broke her down until she flinches over the smallest shit. You saw how she was after I fucked up those people. She wouldn't even look at me."

Hugging my girl, I exhale hard. "And I want Selene to look at me. That woman's got me all crazy inside. So, I pretended I was this calm motherfucker. But don't let that make you think I didn't want to gut them as soon as they messed with us. Once I felt you were unsafe, I should have reacted faster."

Joie studies me, searching for any lies. She knows she doesn't act like the average girl her age. She isn't interested in boys—or girls for that matter. She never liked dolls or Disney princess crap.

A lot of people thought I made her act like a boy because I really wanted a son. Except I was the guy buying the dolls she wouldn't play with. When her granddad bought her a bunch of matchstick cars, four-year-old Joie went wild. That's when I accepted she was just doing her own thing.

I want her always to be herself. As a kid, I never got twisted up over expectations. My mom was flighty. My dad was a criminal. They let me do whatever I wanted as long as it didn't bounce back at them. I got to become the man I am today. Most days, I like the guy in the mirror. *But Selene leaves me insecure.*

"I am weird," Joie says, revealing her own insecurities. "Everyone wants boyfriends. Mikayla and I made a pact to wait until high school to date. Then, she started acting like all the other girls, obsessing over a stupid dance."

"When I was a kid, I got lucky by finding people like me. But if I hadn't been so lucky, I wouldn't have faked a different personality to fit in. I wasn't changing for anyone."

"But you're trying to be different for Selene."

"The moment I saw her, I got this feeling. Every day it takes over more of me. I don't know what to do with it."

"She's really beautiful."

Smiling softly, I nod. "Yeah, and her heart is soft and sweet. I like when she takes care of me. But that good shit comes at a price. She can't look at me without wanting the guy looking back to be different."

"You'd think she'd want a tough guy," Joie says and kicks off her shoes before taking them to the front closet. "With all those bad men hurting her, she should want to be strong or have someone tough to protect her."

"Maybe she does, but she wants a certain kind of tough."

Joie sits on the couch's arm and watches me. "She really likes you. I see her looking at you all the time. I mean, lots of women do that. It's kinda gross, actually," she says, and we share a grin. "But I like her. She's not nasty about her attraction. She looks at you like you're someone special, not like she wants you naked. It doesn't gross me out."

"I could love her," I admit, testing out the words. "But she was freaked out tonight."

"Her sister acted so weird."

"I don't know Yazmin's story."

"How are they both so fucked up?"

"Bad men broke them."

"That's why I don't want to date. Why rush into that minefield?"

Grinning at her casual wisdom, I explain, "Joie, you never have to do anything you don't want. Look at Patrice. I don't know if she ever liked men. But she got married to an asshole and had kids because that's what people expected. After her husband died and her daughters moved away, she lived alone for a long time. Finally, she met someone she could love for real. Following the flock often means taking a long, hard road to get where you're going."

"But if Patrice didn't marry that asshole, she wouldn't have had her kids. Selene wouldn't exist."

"Yeah, but I wouldn't know what I was missing out on. Patrice finally learned to put her needs first. I want you to do that always. Don't just go along with shit to fit in."

"I want that for you, too."

Crossing my arms, I mumble, "I really liked fucking up those assholes tonight."

"I haven't seen you do that in a long time."

"No, people knew to behave. Except they were still harboring their bullshit. As soon as I seemed nice for a fucking second, they started trouble. Bad people can't be trusted. They'll act reformed, but it's a con."

When Joie nods, I feel her memorizing this advice. She believes one day she'll be a Berserker. I don't know if I want that future for my daughter. Yeah, she's smart and tough enough. But the idea of my kid bleeding doesn't sit well with me.

"Are you okay?" I ask when she watches me.

"Yeah. Tonight was mostly great. Selene and Yazmin liked the movie. I thought they might be too prissy. Instead, they were smiling and seemed into it. I wish that last part hadn't happened."

"Me, too. I figured I had more time before my enemies tested this new softer side of me. When you were born, I got lame for a while," I say, and she grins. "People poked at me a little. Being a dad didn't make me puss out for long. But time's passed. I'm older. They think I've left my best days in the rearview. I learned the hard way what happens when people doubt me."

"So did they," Joie says, and I grin.

"I better shower up. The stink of their tears and blood is on my clothes."

"Can we watch something funny when you get back?"

Messing with her hair, I nod before heading upstairs to my bathroom for a long shower.

My feelings are all over the fucking place. I'm upset over those assholes, thrilled to have pounded them, and worried about Selene.

As the hot water washes off my tension and their blood, I focus only on Selene laughing during the movie. Her beauty blinds me to how we make no damn sense. I can only think of how she's mine. *No other woman makes me feel this way. No other man deserves her.*

By the time I finish jacking off to thoughts of her clingy shirt tonight, I've chosen to dismiss the negative shit. Logic is overrated.

Tonight was great in too many ways. We saw a fun movie. Joie had her buttery popcorn. Yazmin smiled a lot, and Selene mostly looked at me like I was irresistible. The rest of the night was just static.

SELENE

Yazmin keeps trying to squat down. Even after we enter the house to find Patrice and Cheryl watching "On Golden Pond," I need to help my sister focus on walking forward. My grandmother frowns at us, thinking we're nuts.

I don't say anything when she asks what's wrong. A single word will open the floodgates. I'm barely holding on.

I guide Yazmin into our bedroom, where I shut the door. She hides in the corner while I sit on the bed and try to calm down.

The panic still seizes me. I can barely swallow, let alone breathe. I'm stuck in terrified mode.

Thinking I need an outlet, I cry into a pillow. Yet, the tears don't help. I'm still overwhelmed, like I'd been holding back too many emotions for too long. Now, they're raging hot, burning me from the inside out and leaving me feeling as lightweight as ash.

I finally crawl into the corner with Yazmin, who stares at nothing. She's disappeared into her mind, hiding in a safe space or replaying painful memories.

"Everything's okay," I say between sobs. "We're okay."

Cheryl knocks before entering. She is the one to handle our crazy moments. Patrice claims she can't deal with our emotional baggage.

I think of my mom growing up with her tough mom. How did Mariah become so weak? Did Patrice think for her, leaving my mom unable to manage her own life? Is that why she married a controlling man?

"What happened?" Cheryl asks, kneeling and grimacing when her knees don't want to cooperate.

"People attacked us at the theater. Hoyt handled it."

"Then, why are you upset?"

I can't explain to Cheryl about my panic attacks or how my brain repeats bad things when triggered. I'm broken deep inside in a permanent way that no pep talk can fix. LeVoy didn't manage to kill me, but he left me wrecked and useless.

Rather than answer, I hold a limp Yazmin and try to imagine us somewhere safe. *Where would that even be?* Away from people? No, we don't know how to survive on our own. As long as we're dependent on others, we're at their mercy. *Nowhere is safe.*

Cheryl realizes we won't explain anything and returns to the movie.

I sit in the dark room with Yazmin and let time pass. My mind feels beat up. I can't focus on anything. Flashes of the past mix with thoughts of Hoyt and Joie.

Tonight, I believed I could have everything I wanted. I forgot about the scars across my body. LeVoy felt like a bad dream rather than a tangible threat. Yazmin's pain was a faded memory.

My sister and I were enjoying time with vibrant, strong people. I even found myself imagining becoming part of Hoyt's family. He would love me in the way other people get loved. Joie would tell me stories about her school and sports teams. Yazmin would find love, too.

We could enjoy what was stolen from us years ago. We'd get stronger, become tougher like Patrice, and build a real life in McMurdo Valley. No more surviving day by day or waiting for the end. We'd be reborn as better versions of ourselves.

However, the fear dragged us right back to where we've always been. We're still the girls hiding in a closet when our father raged. I remain under LeVoy's thumb. Yazmin must still obey Robert's programming. Once our fear showed up, everything reverted to the natural order of things. *We're weak. Others are strong. Nothing will ever change.*

Hearing noises all night, I can't sleep. I'm sure someone is outside. LeVoy will kill my whole family.

I need to stay up and keep watch. What can I do if a hitman comes? Scream for Patrice and her shotgun? Call the police? Ask Hoyt for help?

I don't know. But I'm exhausted by the time the sun shines. I sit in the living room, staring at the kitchen door. That's where the hitman came from last time. I walked downstairs to get water like I always did. LeVoy never allowed me to bring drinks upstairs. Even with him out of town, I didn't dare disobey. He had the house wired. I'd be punished when he returned.

Like clockwork, I walked into the trap. I nearly didn't notice the masked figure. I only saw darkness where none should be.

Before even realizing I was in danger, I saw the first flash and heard the first pop. The pain hit me immediately. Air gushed from my lungs when the bullet entered my body.

As Cheryl makes coffee, I realize I can't remember where the first shot hit me. Somehow, everything happened in slow motion yet too fast to track.

Like last night when the people started yelling and throwing objects. I can't recall the order of things anymore. I just remember the fear.

For the entire weekend, I can't rest. My mind both races and drags.

Yazmin hides in our room. The weekends are quiet. Patrice works the busier shifts. Cheryl likes to go to the Valley Gin Mill and dance.

With the house ours, Yazmin and I sit silently for most of those two days.

At some point, I remind my sister to eat. At another moment, she tells me to take my medicine. Normally, one of us drags the other from the darkness. But this weekend, we're lost in our own pasts.

On Monday morning at four a.m., I crash hard and can't wake up. When Hoyt arrives, Cheryl explains I'm sick.

I find his messages. He texts twenty times that day. Just asking if I'm okay. If I'll be back tomorrow. Do I remember where the hell he's supposed to go next?

I can't answer his questions. I'm too tired. Picturing the world outside this house terrifies me back into my corner.

As Tuesday arrives, I hide from Patrice standing at the bedroom door.

"If you're quitting, at least tell him."

"He'll be angry."

"Then, tell Wynonna. She'll deal with his bad mood. She can find you something else to do."

I look into Patrice's brown eyes and see my mom. Her disapproval cuts me. Just like when Mariah would ask why I always chose to anger my father. As if his shoulder hurting from swinging the belt was my fault.

Patrice doesn't understand me, but I get how she works. She's a strong woman who doesn't suffer fools. Having built herself a good life, she won't give it up for two mental cases. I heard her say those last words on the second night we arrived.

"I'll call Wynonna," I tell my grandmother who finally leaves the room.

However, I don't dare speak to Hoyt's sister. She'll sound upset, making me feel worse.

I text her instead, explaining how I don't think I can work with her brother. I get too flustered. I space out. I'm a flake. But maybe I can work in a less stressful environment. I heard they need someone to clean houses or run errands. I could do that stuff.

Wynonna tells me not to worry. She'll handle Hoyt. She then asks for me to visit her tomorrow to work out the job situation. She says again not to worry. I feel her talking to me like Cheryl does when I've gone off the deep end.

They're right to worry. Something inside me shut down on Friday night. The panic tore through all my newfound confidence. Whenever I think of Hoyt, I'm afraid.

He won't understand, just like Patrice can't. They're strong people who deal with their problems head on. I don't know how to be like that.

Every time I try to get dressed for work on Tuesday, I freeze up and feel like I might die. The panic chokes me until I back down.

Though Hoyt cares for me, he also thinks being strong is a choice. Like his word alone can make me beautiful and powerful.

In reality, my scars define me. I'll never be what he needs.

So, I'll let Wynonna be the voice of reason while I dig my way out of the depression pit I've found myself inside again.

HOYT

Over the weekend, I try to reach Selene. Just to make sure she and Yazmin were okay after they flipped out. I know they're sensitive to violence. Those Jordan-family assholes called them whores. Shit was thrown in their direction. I likely scared Selene with my excellent beatdown of those fuckers.

Her responses to my texts are short and vague. I figure the violence spooked her. Once she's with me in the truck on Monday, Selene will remember I'm the guy who makes her smile in that special way. She doesn't look at Nash that way. Only me, so we'll be good.

Yet, Selene calls in sick on Monday. That's when my patience switches off. I refuse to have her avoiding me.

However, storming into Patrice's house and making Selene understand isn't an option. I saw how she flinched when I opened her door on Friday night to help her and Yazmin out. She avoided looking at me. Selene is always checking me out, either to admire my looks or just for reassurance. But Friday night, I was the thing scaring her.

Feeling lost, I don't know what the fuck my schedule's supposed to be. I've already gotten used to relying on Selene to tell me where to go and who to deal with. Her answers on Monday are too vague for me to understand. So rather than go wherever the fuck someone expects me, I head over to the Pigsty.

The guys stop goofing around as soon as I burst through the door. They wake up Martin "Walla Walla" Carter sleeping upstairs. Soon, the club sits around the large open living room while I rant.

"Anyone who does business with the Jordan family can't do business with us!" I holler as they dodge and duck whatever I fling around in a rage. "I want them fired from their jobs! I want them burned out of their fucking houses! I want their cars trashed! I want their kids bullied! Nothing is out of bounds!"

Armor listens to my rage, waiting until I finish. He looks around the room at the men and woman we consider family. They know I'm only slightly exaggerating.

The Jordan family once ran this entire county. We took away their power, leaving only the chicks and kids in our territory. But the fuckers breed like cockroaches. The kids also aged up. Now, there are too damn many Jordan shits, making them feel entitled.

"They attacked your president," Armor says in his gravelly voice. "Attacked his kid. They're testing if we're still willing to spill their blood. So, if they work somewhere loyal to us, they get a pink slip. If they rent somewhere loyal to us, their leases aren't renewed. They won't be served at our businesses. If their cars are somewhere easy to boost, you relieve them of that property. If they come at you, end them. No more second chances."

My club family nods in agreement, yet I remain pissed as I walk outside. Armor and Tomcat follow me. I see a few other founding members watching us from the porch.

"I'm not the problem," I bark at Armor when I get the sense of where this lecture is going. "I went to the fucking movies."

"Calm yourself," Armor replies in his usual rough yet almost monotone voice. "We're not the enemy."

Tomcat runs a hand through his brown hair. "What could you do with Joie and those chicks around?"

"This shit isn't me holding my tongue for a few weeks. They were waiting for anything to give them the green light. Anita Jordan's never going to stop wanting blood. We've been too gentle with them for too long."

Crossing his thick arms, Armor nods. "Should have shoved their asses out of the county after we killed their men."

"But we felt bad for their crocodile tears," I growl, pacing back and forth in front of my Fat Boy. "Not one of those bitches felt guilty over the lives their men destroyed. But we gave them pity. No more. That cunt Anita was the first one to yell shit at my kid. Fuck them all."

"We've got this handled," Armor assures me. "The Jordan family hasn't made a move in years without us knowing. That shit at the theater was them popping off thanks to booze and bravado. They'll pay the price. Let's just make sure everyone hears of their suffering. Because I suspect we have enemies who can create more damage for us than the Jordans."

Armor's words calm my rage. Of course, with my temper settling down, I don't know what to do with myself.

Around lunch, I end up at my dad's prairie-style home. I can't go to my regular haunts without Selene. I'm like a lost kid, unable to feed myself now.

"This is a pleasant surprise," Callie says after ushering me inside. The feisty blonde glances behind me before asking, "Where's your assistant?"

"She's sick today."

Callie doesn't ask questions, making me think she knows about the movie theater shit. My dad is less subtle.

"Heard you fucked up those walking dumpster fires," he says as I enter their sunny family room to find him sitting in his favorite chair.

"They were drunk and started something they didn't know how to finish."

"I assume Joie's okay."

"They hurt her feelings, but she'll be fine."

"Scumbags," Callie says and pats me on the shoulder.

My stepmom is a year older than me. If she grew up in McMurdo Valley, I likely would have fucked her in high school. But she met Dad while he was visiting Portland. Somehow, the sneaky son of a bitch wooed a woman half his age to live in our town.

"Staying for lunch?" Ed asks as if that wasn't obvious.

I make chitchat, keeping Selene's name off my lips. Eventually, after we're eating sandwiches, he asks if she's really sick.

"You didn't scare her off, now, did you?"

"Maybe."

"We talked to her about how your club got its name," Callie says.

When I frown, Dad adds, "She seemed a bit spooked."

"Not too spooked," Callie reassures me. "Her eyes got so curious at the mention of you."

"Someone's got a crush," Dad says, and I assume he means me until he winks at Callie. "Ever since Hoyt was twelve, I've had girls showing up and batting their pretty eyes at him."

After enduring their teasing, I listen to details about their planned Barcelona trip. Nodding at whatever they say, I can't get Selene off my mind. I even look over the pictures I've low-key snapped of her. I have one from just a few days ago when she was smiling to herself. I like to believe she was thinking of me.

"You seem so pouty," Callie taunts as she walks me to the front door an hour later. "I hoped lunch would put you in a better mood. Did your dad's teasing get to you?"

Callie's soft blue eyes lull me into blurting out, "Ever since she started working for me, I spend all weekend waiting to see Selene. It's killing me to have to wait another day."

"Aw," she coos and hugs me. "I've never seen you so sappy. It really is a sweet look on you, Hoyt."

141

"I was hoping for words of encouragement."

"Well, those words right there are all you're getting," she replies, offering a shrug. "I don't know jack-shit about Selene, and I won't blow smoke up your ass about her intentions. However, I do know she has the hots for what you're packing. Wait, look, those words right there were encouraging."

Rolling my eyes at her snickering, I mutter, "My father has been a terrible influence on you."

"This is all me, baby boy," she taunts, chuckling at my expression before I walk away.

After leaving Dad's place, I meet up with Nash, Hobo, and Goose. We go riding just to settle me down. I haven't been on my hog much since meeting Selene. She can't handle climbing on back. Not yet, anyway. I bet over time she'll learn to loosen up and enjoy the ride.

No matter what I do or who I'm with, I can't fight the urge to show up at Patrice's house and force Selene to look at me. I need her to prove we're still solid. Yet, I force myself to be patient.

Then, the next morning, before I leave to get Selene, I receive a text from my sister.

"Selene isn't going to work. Come see me. Love always, your dearest sister and most adoring fan."

Already on edge about the Selene thing, Wynonna kissing my ass makes me feel worse. She only lays it on that thick when something's gone wrong.

As soon as I enter her house, Esther attacks my leg. "I yuve you berry much, Unk Hoyt," she says and glances at Wynonna. "Like dat, Mama?"

"Yes, baby, very good," my sister murmurs while Ralph Junior follows close behind.

"The Lord don't approve of lying."

"That's not what the Bible says," Wynonna replies and rubs his head.

"You're fibbing."

"If you want to know for sure, learn to read, kiddo."

Wynonna sends the kids to the next room, where her part-time sitter reads them a book. Once we're alone in her office, she shuts the door and sighs.

"Don't freak out."

"Is she sick again?"

My sister watches me with her dark eyes. "She quit, Hoyt."

"No," I growl in a voice only slightly human.

"I know how you're feeling."

"You really don't," I grumble while pacing. "Why?"

"She says she can't do a good job."

"What the fuck does that mean?"

"This is about the theater thing, right?"

"How the fuck would I know?"

"Don't snap at me," Wynonna growls and shoves me. When I don't budge, she grumbles, "It's like bullying a wall."

"What did Selene say?"

"Not much, but I'm going to talk to her tomorrow."

"Why not now?"

"She's upset, Hoyt. The longer she has to chill, the more agreeable she'll be."

"Agreeable? What's that mean? Is she pissed?"

"Stop being stupid and think, will you? I don't know Selene like you do. Tell me what you think she's feeling right now."

"Fear," I mutter. "She thinks I'm an asshole like her husband."

"But you're not him. She's got her wires crossed. I'll help her fix that," Wynonna says before mumbling, "But it might take a while."

"How long?" I demand.

"Don't go barking at me. You're not a dog, and I don't think it's cute."

"How long?" I say in a quieter voice. "Better?"

"Sure," Wynonna replies and sits on her desk. "She wants another job. I said I would help her." When

I growl with frustration, she adds, "Calm down. You're going to give yourself a fucking heart attack."

I want to tear apart this room and holler until my voice is gone. Mostly, I want to drive over to Patrice's house and shake some sense into Selene. *The woman is making me crazy!*

"If you can't handle this situation, you can't handle Selene in your life," Wynonna explains and waves off the cussing I do under my breath. "She's all fucked up. You know that, and you nod like you get it. But it's like you and your lifestyle. She probably nods about how she gets it, too. Neither one of you gets shit."

I sink into the chair next to the window. "I can't lose Selene."

"As an assistant or is this girlfriend crap?"

I frown at Wynonna. Whatever she sees on my face, she walks over and hugs me to her.

"You've known her for less than a month. You're still strangers. She's upset, but it's temporary. You're riled up now, sure. Soon, you'll get your way. Stop flipping out and just relax."

"You'll fix this?" I ask, wanting reassurance.

"I'll manipulate this situation. Even if I get her a lame new job, it'll only be so she'll miss working with you. Don't you worry."

"What do I do until then?"

"Take a day off, I guess. What were you supposed to do today?"

"I don't know."

"Good Lord, Hoyt. How do you function?"

"This wouldn't have happened if you hadn't met that idiot and had his kids. Then, I'd know where I'm supposed to be today."

"But then Selene never would have been your assistant."

Waving off the scenario she paints, I point out, "Selene would probably work at the Gin Mill. I'd talk her up. We'd date. It'd be easier, actually."

144

"Or more likely, she'd think you were too much man and blow you off. This way, she was stuck with you in that damn truck, eating lunch and hanging out. She can't blow you off."

"Sure feels like she is."

"Give me a chance to work my magic."

Sighing, I rest my head in my hands and picture Selene. Last week, we stopped by the farm where my club's pot grows. She got so excited when offered free tomatoes. I never know what'll make her smile.

However, I'm very fucking aware of what sets her off. That's the real reason I've been miserable for days. Even if Selene chills out, she'll need me to pretend for her. And I will until I can't again.

We're bound to do this dance until one of us changes or walks away. I'm incapable of the first option, and I don't have the heart to do the second.

The question is, what will Selene choose.

SELENE

Arriving at Wynonna's house, I worry she'll bully me about Hoyt. Or he'll appear to do the deed. Yet, I can't tell her no. Just like I won't tell him no if he demands I come back to work. I'm a well-worn doormat.

A light rain leaves me wet as I step onto her porch. Wynonna appears with a towel and a welcoming smile. She brings me into the kitchen while her kids play quietly in their upstairs "chaos room."

"I heard Hoyt freaked you out," she says in a soft voice. "And that's why you're looking for a new job."

"I have a crush on him," I blurt out. Her eyes widen before she smiles knowingly. "But he's not the man in my head. Things would be weird at work."

"Because of your crush or because he scared you?" When I don't answer, she sits at the kitchen table. "He would never hurt you, Selene. I know Hoyt can seem insane when he's in his berserker mode. However, he's never out of control."

When I only stare at her, Wynonna continues, "One time, he went after a guy who was hounding me. I was holding Ralph and pregnant with Esther. Hoyt grabbed the guy without so much as breathing heavily on me. He isn't a blunt instrument. You were never in any danger."

"I can't be around violent men," I mumble, feeling small under her gaze. "I feel swallowed up. It's too much."

"But you were around him for weeks."

"Hoyt's so handsome and sweet. I pretended the other stuff wasn't real. He was a kindhearted, harmless biker who loved kids and the elderly."

Wynonna smirks at my description before replying, "I won't claim Hoyt is a puppy dog in need of a good home to settle him down. He's got a scary side. That's why he's club president. Men fear him, so it makes sense you would, too. But he'll punch a man, and he'll never hit you. So, in a way, he *is* harmless to you."

Realizing she hopes to "logic me" into changing my mind, I mumble, "I've always been weak. It's who I am."

"That's not how you have to be forever."

"People don't change that much."

Wynonna replies, "Patrice did."

"I can't be like her."

"Why not? She was once like you."

Frowning, I shake my head. "No."

"It's true. I've heard the stories."

"I haven't."

"Well, get comfy, then," she says and shuffles her chair closer to me. "When Patrice was in her twenties, she married your grandfather. No one says his name. They just call him 'King Asshole.' I mean, knowing how many assholes live around here, he must have been pretty damn special to win the title."

"I don't know anything about him."

"Well, neither do I really. Don't even know his real name. This was all before our time. But I do know the stories."

"Please share."

Wynonna grins at my curiosity. "So, King Asshole was a manager at the cattle feed store. He made good money for a guy around here. Real catch, too, looks-wise. But he only had eyes for Patrice. She's stunning now, so you can imagine what she looked like in her youth."

I imagine my grandmother's good looks. Though she doesn't hide her quiet beauty, she never wields it, either.

"After King Asshole married Patrice, they moved into a house over on Brass Nickle Road. Nicest house on the block. She had your mom and aunt. What people didn't know was that along with her girls, Patrice suffered two stillborn boys."

147

Wynonna hesitates when I start breathing faster. Accepting my tears are on hold, she speaks again.

"Now, King Asshole was an asshole, obviously. Even before losing his sons. He was the kind of guy to hear someone talk about their parent dying and turn the conversation into his own loss years earlier. Did you go on vacation with the kids? Well, he went on a better vacation with his superior kids. Apparently, he was someone who couldn't wait to belittle those around him."

"And he was that way with Patrice?"

"According to Uncle Glenn, Patrice and King Asshole seemed happy. But I'm sure you know how marital strife can be hidden behind closed doors."

When I nod, she continues, "King Asshole hit a new level after the second stillborn boy. He started mocking Patrice in public. Snide comments about her weight. How he might need to trade up to a newer model. That sort of thing. People were so used to taking his shit that no one said anything. Besides, this was fifty years ago. People weren't so enlightened. Bullies never got called out."

Recalling LeVoy's public treatment of me, I realize not much has changed in fifty years.

"One day, the block threw a party. Kids ran around. Women showed off their best casseroles and baked goods. Men drank beers and talked sports. Real average Americana shit. Now, my uncle doesn't know what set off King Asshole."

Wynonna glances toward the stairs as if she hears her kids. Realizing they're still playing, she lowers her voice.

"When he started bitching about Patrice, she didn't react. He kept on for over an hour. He was also razzing other people. Everyone was on edge. At some point, he said something that went too far, and Patrice yelled at him. That's when he cold-cocked her. Not a slap. Punched her straight in the face."

"Oh," I say, feeling lightheaded as memories flood back to me of LeVoy's hands lashing out.

Wynonna gets Sprite to settle my nerves. "Are you okay?"

"Yes, I just… I never imagined such a painful life for Patrice. Please go on."

"According to the story, she hit the ground hard. Everyone got awkward. Did the men have the balls to stand up for her? The women weren't doing shit. The kids remained oblivious except for your mom and aunt. They screamed over their bloody mom."

Wynonna gestures for me to drink up. Once she figures I'm calm enough, she explains, "King Asshole got embarrassed with everyone looking at him, so he went after the girls. He started slapping and shaking them. People finally told him to calm down. That only pissed him off more. He threw one girl in the street, and she went quiet. Knocked unconscious. The whole block froze. Everyone worried he might have killed his daughter."

I imagine my mom experiencing such fear. Did she believe marrying my father would provide her safety? Or had she assumed men should be so cruel?

"Something switched off in Patrice. Like all her 'good girl' upbringing flipped, and she went feral," Wynonna says and shrugs. "That's what people said anyway. She jumped up and began throwing shit at King Asshole. He went after her, but she brought a casserole dish down on his head. Damn thing knocked him silly. Those old-school casserole dishes are made out of some kind of space-age unbreakable shit. He staggered back, but she wasn't done. She saw a little boy's metal bat on the lawn, grabbed it, and swung like she was trying to win the big game. Crack, crack, crack."

This part is the easiest for me to imagine. Patrice bragged about threatening two people at the bar with her shotgun. The other night at home, she pulled a pistol and warned a drunk off her driveway.

"Fortunately, the girl in the street... I can't remember who it was, but she was okay. Banged up like her mom and sister, but okay. King Asshole was not. He ended up in the hospital. The state cops showed up and wanted details. No one said anything. I doubt many of them would help out King Asshole on an average day, but my uncle and dad made clear how no one was snitching on Patrice."

"What happened to King Asshole?" I ask when Wynonna gets distracted by changing the batteries in Ralph's toy.

"No one knows. Well, of course, *someone* knows. But it's not common knowledge. He got out of the hospital and came to get his shit from the house. The cops wanted to talk to him, but he kept dodging them. Rumor had it he was stealing from the store. That's why when he disappeared, many people figured he ran off. But others assumed a good Samaritan dealt with him. Either way, he was gone for long enough that Patrice got a divorce, sold the house, and moved into something she could afford. She waitressed and worked office jobs before eventually saving up enough to go into business with the Steel Berserkers at the Gin Mill."

Considering Wynonna's story, I mumble, "When I asked my mother where her father was, she said he was living in New York City. As a kid, we visited the city, and I asked if she wanted to see him. She shook her head and never said anything else."

"When he disappeared, everyone was so relieved. That's the problem with being a bad person. No one's bound to look too hard when you go missing."

"The women in my family are cursed to be doormats."

"Patrice isn't."

"Because she gave up men."

Wynonna snorts. "True, but she didn't give up. She rebuilt her life. It wasn't a picnic, but she flipped her script from doormat to ballbuster. You could do that, too."

"She did that for her daughters."

"She needed a trigger to awaken a part of her that already existed. The attack on you could be your trigger."

"But I haven't fought back, and it's been eight months."

"And Patrice didn't change when she was punched in the face, or her daughters were slapped around. It was when one of them might be seriously injured. Everyone hits a point where they lash out. You're there already, but you can't hit your asshole with a bat. That's why it feels different. Nonetheless, you're starting over and sticking up for yourself."

"But you want me to stop standing up for myself and return to work to please Hoyt."

Wynonna pauses when she realizes her logic failed. Shrugging, she says, "Hoyt wants you back. And let's be honest here. He wants you as more than an assistant. So, if you don't go back to work for him, you won't get rid of Hoyt. He's fallen for you, Selene."

My breath catches, and I fight tears. Hoyt Macready is like no man I've ever known. I've craved him since the day we met. In my heart, I suspected he might care for me. But in a superficial way, not deeply. Wynonna's words give me hope while also feeling like something beautiful is now dangled just out of reach.

"I've never seen him so hung up over a woman," Wynonna explains. "Now, maybe you can tell him no forever. You're stronger than you think. But you might also realize there are benefits to telling him yes. And if you're going to say yes eventually, why not say yes now?"

"My body is ruined," I blurt out and fight my nausea. "I can't look at myself in the mirror. I'm disgusting. Hoyt thinks he knows me, but it's like my crush on him. We're fooling ourselves and lying to each other. We're never going to work. So, if I say yes, he will hurt me. Not with his fists but through his rejection."

"I think you're wrong," she says before asking, "Did you love your husband?"

"No."

"Have you loved any man?"

Though I want to believe my face hides the answer, Wynonna gives me a knowing look.

"I dated plenty of guys before Ralph," she says, fidgeting with her shirt seam. "None were good enough. Too tall, too loud, not tough enough, too much bravado. I just couldn't click with any of them. Then, this big dumb asshole comes along and makes me laugh with his terrible pickup lines. I'm ready to write him off, but he gives me this look that says I've hurt his feelings. Ralph just blurts out, 'I really like you.' His friends laughed at him for being lame, but he put himself out there. That was when I saw him differently. I decided to give Ralph a shot. We obviously fell in love. He isn't what I thought I wanted, but I can't let him go. That's how good love works."

"So, Hoyt can think he wants a woman with a nice body, but he'll love me too much to care?"

"When you look at your body, you see the flaws. When he looks at it, he might see the pain you survived. He might see your scars as a reminder of how close he came to losing you before you ever met. He might think your scars mean you can respect his. I don't know if Hoyt is the man I believe him to be. However, I do know he wants you like he's never wanted any other woman."

"Should I date him or work for him?"

"I don't know. He really likes having you as his assistant. Spending time together all day makes him happy. He'd see less of you if you worked somewhere else and dated. I'm not sure what the right answer is. Maybe you should consider if walking away from Hoyt is what you really want."

When I sit silently, she adds, "But if you can't take that step, you and I can still chill together. I won't hold a grudge. If another woman rejected him, I'd likely burn down her house. But I get where you're coming from, so we're cool."

"Thank you," I mumble, choosing to ignore the house-burning-down part. "I got so startled when he lost his temper. I imagined what he could do to me. LeVoy hurt me all the time. Yet, he was never strong like Hoyt. I don't think I could survive your brother's rage if it was focused on me."

"He'll never hit you," Wynonna states like a fact. "I'd kick his ass if he did something so vile. I'm the only one who can beat him in a fight."

"Really?"

"Back in the day, Nash wanted to be president. They would battle each other, but Hoyt always won. He's never lost a fight against a man. But he loses to me."

"Because he loves you?"

"And I cheat."

Laughing at her devious wink, I admit, "I miss Hoyt."

"He's going nuts without you. That's why I meddled today. I hate seeing him feeling so shitty. He's normally a chill guy. It's easy being the top dog once you've kicked aside everyone else. He's been relaxed for years. But the last few days without you around blinded him to all his blessings."

When imagining Hoyt suffering, I instantly lose my nerve. "Can you tell him I'll come back on Friday? That'll give me a day to adjust my thinking."

Wynonna's face lights up. "I convinced you?"

"Hoyt's been so good to me, and I care about him. But I got scared. I worried I was wrong about who he was. Maybe I'm still being naïve, but you did help me remember his sweet side."

"And if he goes berserker, don't think of him hurting you. Instead, try to imagine that beast

153

protecting you from your enemies. Your own sexy attack dog."

Grinning at her excitement, I hang around for a while. She shows me how to cook the casserole she's making for dinner.

By the time I head home, I'm no longer as stressed about seeing Hoyt again.

HOYT

The plan was to see Selene on Friday, but I couldn't wait that fucking long. Besides, we need to hash shit out before we start working together again. Wynonna uses her magic to convince Selene to drop by my place on Thursday.

Selene arrives in Patrice's car just after ten in the morning. Stepping out on my porch, I expect her to approach me.

Instead, Selene lingers next to the car, tugging nervously at her shirt. She looks in my direction but not at me. I'm still a monster in her eyes. No better than the asshole who nearly killed her.

I walk to Selene once I realize she might never move her ass in my direction. She finally forces her gaze to meet mine.

"I talked to Wynonna," she says as if I don't know why she's here. "She helped me realize I overreacted."

"Made it clear, did she?"

"I'm sorry I got spooked."

Selene says these last words with her gaze downward, submissive around the big scary beast. I'm no longer the man she smiled at for weeks.

Sounding angrier than I intend, I ask, "How do I know you won't bail again?"

"You want me to promise I won't get scared again?"

"I was never going to hurt you."

"I know."

"Did you?" I mutter when she looks so beat down just by talking to me.

"I know you don't understand, but I wasn't scared of you. I was just scared."

"That makes no sense."

Selene slowly lifts her gaze to meet mine before whispering, "I know who you are."

Her words leave me unsure what she's saying. *Am I the nice guy from the first few weeks or the monster she ran from after the theater?*

"I can't do this," I mutter and dig the heel of my boot into the soft dirt. "I won't pretend I'm someone I'm not."

"No one is making you."

"That's bullshit. I showed myself to you, and everything fell apart." I notice Selene's lips clasp together to prevent her from speaking. "What? Just say it."

"I'm sorry."

"That's not what you want to say," I grumble as my frustration forces me to push harder. "You think you hide from me, but I see you thinking. I know shit's going on in your head. I can feel you considering words you won't share with me. Instead, I get, 'I'm sorry.' That's not real."

Selene lowers her gaze submissively, but I still feel her refusing to share what's happening in her head.

When she remains silent, I mutter, "I didn't gain power by being nice."

"I know."

"I'm a monster to a lot of people."

"I understand."

"And that scares you."

Selene's golden eyes find me, and she just stares. Her words remain hidden inside her.

"I'm not your husband."

Shrinking in response to my words, Selene doesn't actually move away from me. Yet, I feel the distance now.

Despite her reaction, I'm done holding back. Maybe if we hashed this shit out weeks ago, she wouldn't have run.

"I don't lose control," I state as my gaze waits for hers to stop hiding. "When I fucked up those assholes at the theater, I was running the show. I don't switch

156

off and turn into a beast. I'm always that guy. I choose when to fuck up people and when to let shit go. I'm not your husband."

Selene wants to reply. Instead, she glues her lips together to prevent herself from speaking out.

"What?" I bark, frustrated at how she hides from me. "Just say it."

"You don't understand."

"Then, explain."

Wrapping her arms around herself, she stares at the ground. "LeVoy didn't lash out, either. He knew what he was doing. Picking apart my self-esteem was a slow, deliberate task. If he saw even the smallest glimmer of happiness in me, he'd pick at it. So, you claiming you can control your violence isn't the brag you think it is."

"But I never plan to drag you down. I want you to be strong."

My words don't lift Selene. I'm not the hero. She immediately looks like I've cut her heart open and dug around inside.

"Stop hiding in your head. I'm a big boy. I can handle the real you."

"This *is* the real me," she says, choking on a sob. "I'm not strong underneath all my fears. I'm not a powerful woman broken down by a bad man. I was this person as a child. It's how I was raised to be. This weakness is ingrained into everything I do, think, and say. I'm not secretly sassy. I don't have a steel spine hidden behind my hand wringing. This is me, but that's not what you want."

Hearing such self-hatred in her tone, I nearly wrap her in my arms and hug away the pain. Of course, she wouldn't let me touch her. And I can't stomach her flinching from my every movement.

Instead of touching her, I drop the pretenses and put everything on the table.

"I want you, Selene. The fucked-up stuff and the way you smile at me. I want all the good and the bad. But you hide from me."

Her golden eyes focus on my face. "I just told you that this is the real me. I'm not hiding anything."

"No, but you don't say what you're thinking. When I irritate you, I see the way your mouth gets tight. The same thing happens when you think I'm wrong. Just speak up, even if it's to tell me weak shit. I want to know what's in your head."

"Trust me that nothing happening in there needs to be verbalized."

"It does to me."

"Why?"

"You know why."

Selene watches me with teary eyes before stepping back. "I want you so much."

Her words nearly sending me diving for her. That's why she backed up in the first place. She knows I'm barely holding on to my control. With cool calculation, I can decide who lives or dies. But this woman kills my restraint.

"Why can't you have me?" I ask in a strained voice.

"I promised I wouldn't say it."

"To that asshole?"

"No, to you. At the office that day."

Remembering her promise, I reply, "You're so beautiful, Selene. I can't believe you're real."

"Here," she blurts out in a pained, squeaky voice and waves around her face. "This is all I am. That's it. I look like the old me, but LeVoy ruined my body. It's all stitched up and ugly. I never want anyone to see my scars or touch me. So, while I want you, I don't really want you to want me."

I step forward, just a bit, careful not to spook her. She's wearing the same freaked-out expression as when she climbed out of the SUV last Friday. Tears spill down her face as she watches me approach.

"I showed my scars to you," I whisper, wanting so badly to touch her soft skin.

"That's different, and you know it. You're more than your looks. I'm just beautiful. That's all I've ever been. Now, it's a bunch of smoke and mirrors. My body's disgusting."

"It's a woman thing, right? Goose has her scars. She still runs around in skimpy clothes when it's hot."

"Because she's strong. I'm just beautiful. That's why you want me, but it's a lie, Hoyt. I'm not what you want."

"You're wrong," I say, too greedy to avoid stroking her cheek. "You take care of me."

"That's my job."

"I've had other assistants. You don't just tell me where to go and keep track of shit. You make me feel cared for. Like when you fussed over my steak being tough. You watch out for me. That's not your face, Selene. You're beautiful inside, too."

Her lips tremble as she whispers. "I fantasize about us being together. But it's always the old me. I can't stomach the idea of you touching the real me."

I want to explain how she's fucking crazy. That she's more beautiful than any woman I've known. How I'm in love with her in a way that I didn't think possible. But those words don't prove I hear her.

"You feel ugly," I say, and she begins crying. "It doesn't matter what I see. That's how you feel."

Selene looks into my eyes and nods. My words open her heart again. She's taller now.

"I get how I can't fix the shit broken inside you. That's not how anything works. I do get how you can't see yourself the way I see you. But can you understand what you see isn't what I see? That I look at you and know about your scars but can't hate your body like you do. Is it possible we can both be right?"

Selene glances around as if considering my words. "I guess."

"No guessing about it. I'm not afraid of your scars," I explain softly as I erase a little more space between us. "I'm not afraid of your asshole husband or the sadness you carry with you. I get how it's a package deal if I want you," I say and slide my palm across her jaw. "And I really want you, Selene."

"I'm afraid."

"I know."

Her golden eyes reveal such longing. "But I really want you, too."

"Just focus on that part when I do this," I murmur and cover her lips with mine.

After what's felt like an eternity, I enjoy a taste of this addictive woman. Selene doesn't push me off or back away. Her lips remain soft and willing against mine as her fingers grip the seam of my shirt. I feel her fully with me. Her mind isn't on LeVoy or her shitty father or an overwhelming world. *Selene only feels me.*

When my lips leave hers, I study her expression. I never understood the term "swoon." I've made plenty of women horny. A few blushed. But *swooned* sounded like fainting. And I've never made anyone pass out except from fear.

Yet right now, Selene literally swoons. I feel her sway as if I've turned her bones soft and made standing damn near impossible. Her tender gaze admires me in that special way she has. No chick's ever made me feel as sexy as Selene does with this particular expression.

"I don't know what happens next," she mumbles, staring up at me.

"I kiss you again. Then, you come inside, and we talk."

"Am I still going to be your assistant?"

"Of course. I told you how I like when you take care of me. Fixing my hair, wiping my beard, you make me presentable."

Selene's big smile leaves me hurting inside. I need to know she's mine. This pain in my chest won't ease up until I own every part of her.

SELENE

Hoyt's lips on mine leave me lightheaded. I've fantasized plenty about him kissing me. The reality is so much hotter, sending fire through my body.

Yet, I was exhausted before I arrived. The kiss zaps what remains of my energy. I can barely walk up the wide, stone steps to his front porch. Hoyt ushers me inside the large rustic-style home with a high ceiling and handsome décor. The house suits Hoyt's size and tastes.

The air inside smells of his spicy cologne. My mind swims. My heart struggles between lust and depression. No matter the promises Hoyt makes, I can never have what I want.

He doesn't know what hides under my clothes. He can't imagine how repulsed he'll be. Maybe not right away. His lust blinds him for now. Over time, he'll remember his better options, and things will end.

"Sit down here," Hoyt says when I nearly drop. "What's wrong?"

"I haven't slept well in days."

After I sit on his lush leather coach, Hoyt studies me for a full minute. I don't know what he's thinking. Snapping out of it, he pours us coffee and sits next to me on the couch.

"I missed you," he says after handing me the cup.

"I'm sorry I didn't know where you were supposed to go. When I'm feeling down, I can't concentrate on anything. I couldn't even remember where I put that information. I should have a backup system and be better organized."

"It's fine. People think I've gone soft, apparently. Having me bail on whatever I was supposed to do this week will come off as the right kind of rude. Clearly, I can't go two weeks without being an asshole before the fucking town turns on me."

"I'm sorry."

Hoyt doesn't respond with words. He sets down his cup and slides closer on the couch. I instinctively flinch when his large body moves toward mine.

When his expression darkens, I set down my coffee and scoot sideways to look at him. I very deliberately force my palm to rest on his chest. Hoyt's heartbeat races. On his face, he reveals none of his anxiety. Inside, he's a roiling storm.

"We both hide who we are," I mumble as I force my gaze to meet his. Hoyt's blue eyes expose his lust. "What if the people we're attracted to aren't real?"

"You showed me your true colors on Friday like I did to you. I'm not walking away. Will you?"

I think of Hoyt raging at those people in the parking lot. His violence was so effortless as if he was on autopilot. Brutality is part of his life. I understand how Hoyt became the club's leader. The Steel Berserkers aren't fake tough guys.

"I don't know the right answer," I mumble, causing him to frown. "I just want to be around you. Even if you never kiss me again, I like knowing you're close by. The world feels better that way."

"Because I'll protect you?"

"You can't protect me, Hoyt. Not from the real stuff."

"I think you're underestimating me."

Sighing, I ignore the tension in his voice. "I just want to be around you, hear your voice, and share your smile. I like how I feel when we're together. I wish we could have more. But even if we can't, I like the man I see in you."

Hoyt studies me and smiles slightly. His gaze drops to my lips. I feel the kiss before it happens. The way his heat infects me. My head swims again, and I'm floating.

A moan escapes me when Hoyt's tongue licks at my lips, seeking more. I open up for him, deepening the kiss. Our heat hits another level, setting my nerves on fire.

163

My fingers ache to touch him. I have to force them to move, though. I'm frozen in place. Fear and lust battle for supremacy. The more I crave him, the less sane I feel.

How can I believe we'll build anything real? I'm a failed person. I don't know how to fuck without LeVoy's voice in my head. I can't be open with Hoyt in the way he wants. He can't ever see me naked. I'll never be fearless.

Pushing at his hard chest, I stare Hoyt in the eyes and beg for him to change the world. Make me beautiful again. Turn me into a stronger woman. Transform me into someone worthy of his affections.

But Hoyt can't. *I'm just me.* Hoyt's living in a fantasy I can't embrace.

"Selene," he says as if my name answers all my questions.

"I fell apart over the weekend," I say and lower my gaze. "I'm so tired now. I feel hollowed out. Even when you touch me, and I'm relieved to finally know what you taste like, I can't shake the sense that I'm fooling myself."

Hoyt opens his mouth to insist I'm perfectly capable of being whoever he needs. Before he can share those words, he inhales sharply and silences himself.

His blue eyes survey the room before focusing on me. "How is Yazmin?"

"Lost."

"What was that thing she was doing where she kept trying to sit down?"

"Training her ex-boyfriend programmed in her. When she panics, she isn't allowed to run. She has to squat down and wait for her punishment."

"What kind of bullshit is that?" he mutters, confused by the weakness in others. "Can't she stop? She isn't a computer. What does programming even mean?"

"Conditioning, Hoyt," I say and sink deeper into the corner of the couch. "You can't understand. When people push you, you push back. That's why you get respect."

Hoyt frowns hard at me until I start crying. Suddenly, he looks like someone cut him. He flinches. His body clenches with tension. I feel like he's ready to implode.

Instead, he exhales slowly and scoots closer. I look at how he's stolen all the space between us until I'm pinned between the couch's arm and his body.

"Explain what happened," Hoyt says in a tender voice. "I won't just assume I can fix it."

"You can't."

"I feel like problems have solutions. When someone messes with Joie at school, I show up at the kid's house. I make sure the parents know if my kid cries, I make them cry, too. Nothing is free. But that's not possible here. Killing the asshole who fucked with Yazmin won't fix her, right?"

"No," I say, frowning at how casually he mentions killing Robert. "What if I wanted you to kill LeVoy?"

"I'm already planning to."

"But what if you get hurt or in trouble?" I ask, crying again. "I can't ruin your life when you've made mine better. And what about Joie?"

Hoyt slides his massive arm around my back, tugging me against him until I'm trapped.

"Tell me about Yazmin."

"Why?"

"I need to understand."

"Why her?"

"She's fucked up like you. I think you see her better than you do yourself. This will be practice for when we talk about your problems in the future."

"You can't fix us."

"We'll see."

Frowning at him, I can't believe what a bully he's being. He glances down at me with those relaxed blue

165

eyes, instantly zapping my anger. I want to believe in Hoyt, even if I suspect he's full of shit.

"My father gave Yazmin to Robert when she was nineteen."

"Like a gift?"

"No, more like an arranged marriage."

"But he didn't marry her."

"No. He gifted money to my father before taking Yazmin to live with him. But they were never married."

"Why?"

"I don't know."

"Didn't Yazmin tell you?"

"We didn't speak for years. Robert cut her off from the family. My mother would cry on the phone to me as if I could do something."

"So, Yazmin was trapped with this psycho."

"He was a psychiatrist, and he trained her to behave."

"What's that mean? Behave, how?"

"I don't know."

"But you've been back together for a while, right?"

"She was trained not to talk about it. She never tells me. I just know he conditioned her to be an extension of him. She lost her identity."

Hoyt can't possibly understand. He owns every room he enters. Even when other strong men are nearby, his casual bravado keeps them at bay. Submitting completely to another person makes no sense to a man like him.

"One year, my father pitched a fit, insisting they come home for the holidays. Yazmin arrived, seeming hollowed out. She didn't react to anyone unless Robert told her to. I tried hugging her goodbye. She didn't respond. But when I looked into her eyes, I felt the real Yazmin trapped inside somewhere. Like she was begging me to help her. But I didn't know how."

When I lower my head in shame, Hoyt says, "But you must have helped her since she came to live with you."

"No," I say, sinking deeper into my depression.

I let my fingers trace the tattoo on his arm. His skin is so hot to the touch. I lift my gaze to seek security from his beautiful eyes. The man looking back at me wants everything I can offer. I stare into them and try to see myself the way he does. Instead, I only feel tired.

"How did she move in with you, then?" he asks when I don't continue.

"Can I rest my head against you?"

Hoyt's gaze warms, and I spot a smirk on his lips. He wants me to crave him. If I want him enough, I'll offer him all I have. No barriers will exist between us. I'll never deny him. *He'll own me completely.*

"You can barely keep your eyes open," he murmurs in a gravelly voice. "We'll spend the day here. Tracey can pick up Joie. You can rest."

My left cheek presses against his hard chest. Hoyt's heartbeat is so loud, powerful, and eternal. Nothing can defeat this man. I have to believe our connection won't end him. Otherwise, I'm selfish to draw him closer when I have a target on my back.

"Tell me how she ended up at your house," he says softly as his arm wraps around my body while I close my eyes.

I picture the day I went to the hospital to take Yazmin home. She looked like a ghost. I stared into her eyes and saw no one looking back. The doctor claimed she was doing well. I couldn't imagine what she was like before if this shell of a person was an improvement.

"Robert got bored of Yazmin. After he threw her out, she began stalking him. She lived in her car, sitting outside his office, home, everywhere he went."

"She couldn't function without him," Hoyt mutters. "I bet the asshole got a kick out of that."

Looking at Hoyt, I'm relieved he understands. "Yes," I mumble and stroke his jaw.

His lips brush against mine, testing my response. I sigh at the feel of him. Before I can embrace these feelings, I think of Yazmin.

"Robert had her arrested and committed. She was locked up for a year. Her doctors considered her a threat to herself and others. They gave her medicine and even shock treatment. They said she was dangerous, but she seemed like a drooling mess the one time I was allowed to visit."

"When they let her out, she came to live with you."

"Yes. LeVoy liked seeing her all messed up. He found it funny. But also, if she were at the house with me, I'd be less likely to leave."

"Can Yazmin get normal therapy? Can you?"

"It costs money, and I just started my job."

"You know that's not a thing, right?"

Lifting my gaze to meet his, I frown. "I don't know how anything works. Being your assistant is my first real job."

Hoyt kisses my forehead before tasting my lips. His expression is so patient. Gone is his earlier irritation.

"I'll get you set up with what you need."

"I'm afraid to make the wrong choice here."

"There's only one choice. Let me take care of shit, so your life is easier."

"But I should want to be stronger like how Patrice became after her shitty husband."

"She did it wrong, though."

"How do you know?"

Hoyt smiles at my expression before explaining, "Look at your mom and aunt. They married losers like their dead father. And your mother handed you and Yazmin off to other losers. Patrice messed up by refusing help from my uncle and father. She didn't want to owe Glenn because he wanted her. She decided to stand on her own."

He kisses my forehead again before continuing, "Except working two jobs with two young daughters left her little time to be a mom. Those girls never fixed their thinking about men. They only knew their shitty father, so they married new models of a dead man."

Staring at him, I lost his point. I often get flustered when I focus too long on how handsome he is up close. Hoyt smirks at whatever he sees on my face.

"I'm going to help you."

His warmth and certainty paint a picture of a man sealing his doom. Trying to push him away, I blurt out, "I can't have children."

Hoyt doesn't budge. I can't even squirm free. I'm locked against his hard body.

"How do you know?" he asks after cocking an eyebrow at my failed attempts to flee.

"I never got pregnant."

"So? Maybe he shot blanks."

"No, we got checked out. I'm just barren."

"Did the doctor say that?"

"No. But LeVoy had a son already from an earlier marriage, while I never got pregnant. Even if the doctor couldn't find anything wrong, I was obviously the problem."

"Well, Selene, I'll be honest with you. I am not particularly interested in more kids. I didn't want Joie, either. Once she came along, I think I did right by her."

"She adores you."

Hoyt grins at my praise. "If you wanted a baby, I'd get you one."

"How?"

"Adopt, make one in a test tube. I don't know how that shit works, but I'd figure it out. Assuming you wanted one."

I glance at his dog watching us from the corner. "I've never even had a pet."

"Well, then, we'll start slow. You'll find a doctor for your emotional junk. I'll deal with LeVoy. You'll bond with my dog. The baby question can be down the road."

"But we only just kissed. You shouldn't talk about those things."

Hoyt gives me a little exasperated grin. "You brought it up."

"So you'd know you were getting a clunker with me."

His smile disappears. "Never talk about yourself that way. It pisses me off, and I have nowhere to put that rage. I can only kill LeVoy once."

"Please, don't kill him."

Instantly more irritated, he mutters, "Why?"

"I don't want you to get hurt or in trouble."

Hoyt's frown softens. "I like when you worry about me."

I smile at his words before yawning in an unhealthily loud way. "Sorry."

"Think you could nap?"

"I don't think I should."

"We're taking the day off, remember?" he asks and then kisses me before I can answer.

I go weak in his arms. Once he's done making my heart race and my pussy clench, I'm barely able to hold my head up.

Hoyt slides his arm out from behind me and stands up. He looks toward the large metal and wood staircase leading to the open second floor. Frowning again, he seems to struggle with himself.

Finally, he studies the couch. "Why don't you stretch out here?"

"What about Patrice's car?"

"She can hitch a ride from someone."

"She won't like that."

"I'll send her a fucking limo," he says and grabs a pillow and blanket from a nearby closet. "She'll be fine.

So will you. After your nap, we can hang out and talk more. I like not having to share you with anyone."

Grinning, I know a nap isn't a smart move. However, I'm so tired. Sliding off my sneakers, I crawl over to where he rests the pillow. I watch him cover me with a blanket.

"I like when you take care of me," I whisper.

Hoyt licks his lips like he's thinking about kissing me again. Rather than give in to temptation, he walks over to the large windows and flips a switch to lower the massive shades. The living room goes quickly from bright to dark. Sighing with relief, I sink into the pillow and close my eyes.

For the first time since my panic attack on Friday, I'm free of fear.

HOYT

Today when Selene showed up, I still figured I had enough control to walk away from her if she couldn't adjust to my life. I refused to live a lie, even for the most beautiful woman I've ever met. I figured I could get over her. Keep things professional. A whole bunch of other bullshit to keep myself from admitting I was in too deep.

Once she admitted to wanting me, I stopped denying the truth of our situation. *I'm in love with this woman, and my life can't move forward without her.*

Selene looks sexy cuddled under the blanket. The lids of her hazel eyes can barely remain open. Yet, as I move around the living room, she admires me. I disappear to the kitchen for a few minutes, just so she'll close her eyes and rest.

My plan works. Selene's sound asleep once I return. I settle into a chair and study her tranquil expression. I've never seen her look so relaxed. Selene always holds herself a little off-kilter, like she isn't comfortable in her skin.

I think of her body, damaged from nearly dying less than a year ago. Of course, the scars horrify her. She thinks her beauty is her only quality.

I've met women with that thinking. In high school, I dated a girl who ghosted me for three days when she got a pimple. How could I possibly overlook her acne? I did end up dumping her. One, I don't play games. Two, we never shared conversations that didn't revolve around her beauty or us fucking.

Of course, I get how Selene's head is wired wrong. She won't be able to walk off a lifetime of bullshit. First, her parents sucked. Then, she married a psycho. That's thirty-plus years of garbage shoved into her lovely head.

I can live with her being twitchy, moody, and even self-loathing. If Selene lets me close, I'll love her enough for the both of us. Today, she was all over the place, tugging me closer yet shoving me away.

But she's here. Not knowing how she was the last few days drove me fucking crazy. I can't picture the inside of Patrice's house or what Selene does with herself when she's scared. She's still a stranger. When she isn't around, I feel like she's dropped into an unknown void. Having her close settles me. So, this afternoon is only the beginning of what we'll share.

First things first, I need to eliminate her husband. Killing LeVoy Garry makes sense, but I need more information first. Wynonna texts to say she'll hire someone in Louisiana to sniff around.

When LeVoy dies, the heat will turn to Selene. I want her to look cooperative, doing shit the legal way. So far, she's been in hiding. That's why she needs to file for divorce.

I walk outside to the front porch and look over my land. My life offers so much, but it felt lacking the last few days when I thought I lost Selene. That fragile woman wants to be a tough chick, but she isn't wired for that shit.

Kourtney Clark doesn't have to fake her alpha chick cred. She grew up in McMurdo Valley with her drunk daddy and unhygienic brother.

Hobo has a lot of fucked-up thinking. I think his dad hit him too much and broke the common-sense part of his brain. However, he had a great idea years ago that's paid off tenfold.

Kourtney wanted to be an attorney., so the club sent her to college. Kept her comfortable, made sure she had help with schoolwork, and got her primed for law school.

"I'm the classiest fucking person I know," she explained back then. "It makes sense for me to have a nice office and glossy business cards."

Admittedly, I didn't think the big-mouthed bitch would survive college, let alone law school. I expected her to get knocked up and run off with a stoner.

Kourtney proved me wrong. Not only did she get through school, but she came back to our neck of the woods to set up shop.

Whenever we have legal issues, she irons them out. When one of our younger guys got nailed on a murder charge for kicking some guy's ass in a bar, she worked her magic until the charge was pled down. He was released with time served as soon as the judge accepted the deal.

All those years as a redneck bitch made her aggressive as fuck in legal situations. She's obnoxious. People hate her. They know she's got dangerous clients who will get rough if she isn't happy. Basically, she's a fucking shark, forever swimming in search of her next meal. No one wants to be lunch.

Dialing her up, I ask, "Kourtney, can you talk?"

"Sure, but keep it quick. I'm on holiday."

I roll my eyes at how she uses that term for vacation ever since she dated an English fucker who called me "uncouth."

"You're always on vacation."

"I work hard, so I play hard."

"Where are you currently?"

"The Bahamas with my new boy toy. He has a huge hairy cock. I can give you more details, but we're talking on your dime here."

"Let's skip the hairy cock talk. Instead, tell me if you can file a divorce case in Louisiana?"

"No, since I'm not licensed there. However, have you ever heard of 'pro hac vice'?"

"No."

"It means I can act as an adviser to a local lawyer in a jurisdiction I don't practice in. Why Louisiana?"

"My assistant needs a divorce. Apparently, her husband is a small-town hotshot. Scared off all the local lawyers she contacted."

"I can find someone outside his territory. Only needs to be a lawyer licensed in the state. We'll quickly figure out how far this guy's power stretches."

"I want to make sure you're supervising this."

"Why?"

"You're the only lawyer I trust, and this woman is important to me."

"You can't see it, but I'm tearing up right now, Hoyt. So fucking adorable."

Grinning at her taunt, I explain, "I'll send over Selene's info. She doesn't care about money. This isn't about bleeding the asshole dry."

"No, no, you're a nice guy."

I smirk at how she knows I'll bleed LeVoy in another way. "She just wants her freedom."

"We'll come in hard, though. Ask for fucking everything but seem willing for just half. Then, when we say we'll give up even more if it's quick, he'll be inclined to take it. Or not. Some guys like to see the world burn. Does he want her back? Is that why he's playing hardball?"

"He hired someone to come to his house while he was out of town and kill Selene."

"How close did he get?"

"Six bullets."

"And the law didn't think that was hinky?"

"Local cops, local rich asshole. You can guess how quickly that investigation got scrubbed."

"When was this?"

"Almost nine months ago."

"No other attempts?"

"She ran from the hospital to her parents' place in Naples. Hid out there until a month ago. She moved in with her grandma, Patrice Fuchs. I figure Selene's husband might be leery of pulling shit out of his territory. Or he hasn't gotten the opportunity to take a second shot yet."

"Okay, so I know what I'm dealing with, then. I'll get on this when I return to the office next week. Until then, I'll have my assistant call around to see what Louisiana lawyer we can tag along with. Might need to hire a sleazy ambulance chaser from New Orleans, but we'll find someone. Then, I'll do the heavy lifting."

"Thanks, Kourtney. Enjoy your large hairy cock."

Returning to the quiet house, I find Selene looking exactly like I imagined all those nights when I fantasized about sharing my bed with her. The woman's a goddamn angel.

And she's mine. When she admitted how much she wanted me, I shut down any doubts I had about us.

I don't care how long I need to wait to gain her trust. Or who I need to bully, bleed, or bury. No one, not even Selene, is keeping us apart.

SELENE

I wake up to the sight of a dog's face an inch from mine. Startled, I shrink back. The animal tilts his head as if I'm overreacting. That's a look I've spent a lifetime seeing. The chocolate-brown dog glances back at the sound of Hoyt's voice.

"I know she's fun to look at," he says, running his hand across the large dog's waist, "but give her space."

I smile at Hoyt, admiring his tawny skin in the dark room. The sun moved while I was resting.

"Sleep well?"

Nodding, I sit up and wipe my mouth. Hoyt smirks at what he sees on my face.

"You look beautiful," he says before asking, "Do you want a drink?"

"How long was my nap?"

"Three hours."

"Oh, my, God," I mumble and pet the curious dog. "I'm sorry."

"I'm not. Having you here felt right. Besides, you clearly needed the rest."

"I should get home."

"No," he says from the kitchen on the other side of the ceiling-high fireplace, which acts as a half-wall. "Stick around for dinner. Joie will be home in a few hours. She'll want to see you."

"Patrice's car."

"I already texted someone to give her a ride."

"She'll be angry."

"No, she likes riding on the back of a motorcycle. She used to have her own, but one nasty spill left Cheryl in a panic. Apparently, older people aren't supposed to fall down."

Following his voice, I step into his masculine country-style kitchen with its two-story-high ceiling. The open space is likely good for entertaining. Does

177

Hoyt have his club members over for parties? Was this room designed for his ex-wife?

I'm still wondering about the house when I return from cleaning up. Hoyt stands near the fireplace with two mugs.

"Let's sit on the side patio."

I feel like I should leave. Yazmin wasn't doing well when I left. I'm being selfish. Patrice is likely mad. Cheryl doesn't know how to deal with Yazmin's moods.

Yet, Hoyt's tone doesn't feel like a request as much as an order. I follow him out the side door to a heavy wood-and-stone table.

"I have a club brother who likes to build shit," Hoyt says, settling in the seat next to mine. "Nomad made this table. In fact, he came up with many ideas for the house."

As soon as he finishes speaking, Hoyt's lips find mine. Not a deep kiss but a testing one. Hoyt pauses to study my reaction. When I lick my lips, he smiles and kisses me again.

Hoyt's fingers slide across my cheek and into my hair. With no experience with such lust, I instantly lose control of myself. A moan leaves my lips as I stroke his jaw.

A flick of his tongue, and I let him inside. He tastes like mint and apples. I lean closer, wanting more. But the gesture tugs at my tender muscles.

I back away from Hoyt, both physically and mentally. What am I doing? *How do I think this situation with Hoyt ends?*

"I got you a lawyer," he says as if knowing where my mind went. He drinks from his mug and gestures for me to do the same. "She works for the club. Kourtney will find a Louisiana lawyer to do the legwork, but she'll be running shit."

"How much will that cost?"

"It's part of your employment package," he replies, smirking at his comment. "You're coming back to work for real, right?" When I nod, he adds, "I planned to pay you more in the beginning. But Patrice didn't want you to get used to the money in case shit didn't work out. I went along with that, even though it felt weird to lowball you. Anyway, I'm giving you that raise, so you'll make what I wanted from the beginning."

"Thank you."

"It's not pity money, Selene," he says, cocking his eyebrow. "I need an assistant. You're the best one I've had."

"I bailed on Monday and then quit."

"I knew you had hang-ups when I hired you. We've gotten past that, right?"

Sipping from the mug, I taste a heavy apple cider. I avoid his gaze while considering his words. Finally, I ask him what I'm thinking.

"Am I supposed to promise not to flip out again?"

"No, but next time, you know not to quit. I don't want another assistant. If you flip out again, just take time to get your head on straight. But don't bail on me."

"What if you become a tyrant?" I tease as I sip more cider.

Hoyt chuckles. "Become?"

"To me, you're never that way."

"Well, if I turn nasty, you can rat me out to Wynonna. She'll put me back on track, and we'll keep working together."

Smiling easier now, I remember how Hoyt and I found a work rhythm. When he was tense, I knew to keep my mouth shut. When he was in a good mood, we talked like friends.

I also started keeping his things in my purse. Like when we went out to the RV camp owned by the club. After Hoyt forgot his sunglasses in the truck, he kept squinting. The next day when he did the same thing at the Pigsty, I had them in my bag. The appreciative look he wore left me feeling like the best person ever.

That's the power Hoyt wields. He lifts me so high until I'm not really Selene anymore. I become an extension of Hoyt.

No doubt a therapist would explain I'm exchanging my old master for a new one. That's likely true, but Hoyt doesn't smother me. Even when he pushes for what he wants, like on the couch earlier, I believed he'd have backed down if I really asked. He's a goodhearted bully. At least that's what Nash called him once when Hoyt was out of earshot.

Not wanting to think of LeVoy when my body tingles from Hoyt's kisses, I change the subject away from the divorce.

"Tell me more about Nomad's carpentry."

"Why?"

"I like knowing more about you."

Once Hoyt realizes I'm not hitting up info on his club brother, he settles down. "Nomad's a scary guy to look at. Seems like a sledgehammer. Not like someone with the patience to create anything so intricate. But he's a complex guy. I guess a lot of people are. I have to remind myself of that sometimes. I get to feeling like everyone is what I see. Assholes are just obstacles. Allies are only opportunities."

As Hoyt and I share a smile at how he views people, I ask, "What am I?"

His smile fades as his gaze sharpens. "You're mine, Selene."

"Can you imagine what that sounds like to someone who was literally owned by another person?"

"I don't mean you're an object I bought. You're the person who owns my heart. No woman's ever had such power. Though I don't trust easily, I know you'd never hurt me on purpose. I can't say that about many people in the world. We might still be strangers, but I know you're mine. You should remember that when you worry I'll turn on you."

"But you loved your wife, too, didn't you?"

Hoyt shifts in his chair and mutters, "That's complicated."

"How?"

Hoyt doesn't want to talk about his ex. However, I shared about LeVoy, so he needs to fess up, too. Sensing I won't back down easily, Hoyt shrugs.

"Nicole was a wild chick who didn't mind when I partied with other women. She liked the lifestyle. The whole thing got her off, the motorcycles, parties, money, tattoos, leather, living at the Pigsty. But it was never going to last between her and me. Without Joie, we would have gotten bored and broken up early on."

Hoyt rubs his jaw as usual when on the spot. "I wasn't happy when she got pregnant. I wanted her to be lying about it being mine. Kids aren't my thing. I don't like them, really. Nicole was the kind of girl to fuck around. But my club brothers fear me. I'm the one who kicks their asses. I knew none of them were screwing my girlfriend. Logically, the baby was mine, but I still wasn't happy."

Hoyt glances at me to search for disapproval on my part. While his words seem unsavory, his reluctance toward fatherhood didn't stop him from becoming a man who adores his kid.

Whatever he sees on my face pushes him to continue. "The first time I felt Joie kicking inside Nicole, I got this jolt of energy. That was my kid. I wanted it to have everything. I started working on this house. Got a will written. Did whatever mature men are supposed to do for their kids. By the time Joie was born, I thought I loved Nicole. She was carrying my kid, so I wanted what we had to be real."

Pausing as his mind rewinds to a different time, Hoyt studies me in the early afternoon sun. "Joie was the cutest damn thing I ever saw," he says, smiling at the memory. "I'd never loved anyone like I did my baby girl. She made me think about the future. That's why I stayed with Nicole."

Finishing his cider, Hoyt shrugs. "I don't know if she loved me. I think she was playing along, too. We wanted our kid to be happy. Eventually, though, Nicole grew bored of motherhood and me. Her partying days were over. She needed a new obsession, so she found these crunchy, new age mommy ideas. Though we were living different lives, we shared a bond through Joie. As long as Nicole did right by my girl, I kept the ring on my finger."

"What did she do to Joie?"

Hoyt's gaze grows intimidatingly dark. "Ignored her being sick and treated it with shit she read about on Facebook. If a random fucker nearly killed my kid, I would have wrecked them. With Nicole, I told her to leave my territory. Joie is more important than Nicole or me. I'd rather be the monster who sent away his kid's mom than risk Nicole hurting our girl."

"You're a good man."

"Not really," Hoyt says with utter seriousness. "You know that, too. That's why you were so scared."

Lowering my gaze, I recall how he fearlessly rushed at those people at the theater. His violence felt second nature because that's what it is for Hoyt and his club.

"I still think you're a good man to those you care about."

Hoyt surprises me with a grin. "I'm going to make your life better, Selene. Even if you didn't want me, I'd handle your ex for you. I reward people who improve my life."

"You make too big a deal out of my job."

"No," he says as his thumb strokes my bottom lip. "I miss being a simple biker. Back in the day, I fought and fucked without worrying about consequences. But then I had Joie, and the club grew more powerful. Eventually, I got the bright idea to become mayor."

Hoyt exhales hard as if angry with himself. "My ego keeps pushing me to do more. Soon, I got overwhelmed. I hate all the responsibility, but stepping back would feel like failure. Having you around to organize the chaos allows me to focus on the lifestyle I prefer."

"Well, in that case, I really do deserve that raise."

Hoyt chuckles at my attempt at Wynonna's brand of sassiness. Then, he says in a voice dripping with need, "You deserve everything."

As we sit on his shaded porch, I fully embrace how much I love Hoyt Macready. He isn't only a lustful crush or an unobtainable fantasy. *I love this man.*

I also believe with all my heart that he's bound to be disappointed in me. One day, he'll look at me and realize I don't deserve everything. Accepting I'm unworthy of his heart, he'll regret promising me the world.

Right now, I have to make a choice. *Do I embrace the brief beautiful ride, knowing we face an inescapable and painful ending? Or do I choose the safer route, even if I deprive myself of my one chance at short-lived pleasure?*

HOYT

Selene belongs in my house with me. She feels right here. If I called the shots, she'd move in tonight.

I could wait to fuck. Let her get used to the feel of my body and hers together. She'd learn to embrace my touch. Every kiss leaves her rosy-cheeked and wanting more. Eventually, her feelings for me will override her self-hatred. I suffer no doubt about that.

Unfortunately, I'm not calling the shots. I know she won't leave Yazmin. In theory, I could move her sister into my house, too.

Except I don't know Yazmin like I do Selene. Her behavior on Friday weirded me out. After Selene filled in some blanks about her sister, I understand why Yazmin acted that way. However, I'm still leery about giving her full access to Joie.

Since Selene and Yazmin are a package deal, moving them in can't happen yet. That means I have to let Selene leave at some point tonight. Even so, I talk her into staying for dinner.

"Joie has been worried about you," I explain as we sit on a different patio. "You can meet Tracey, too," I add when Selene seems uneasy about remaining at my house.

"I have to leave after dinner," she says like I'm stressing her out. "And I shouldn't leave when it's too dark."

"Why not?"

"I've never driven in the dark."

Blinking rapidly, I'm once again struck with how fucking infantilized Selene's old life was. She doesn't know how anything works. Joie has more sense and street skills than this adult woman across from me.

"I'll follow you home to make sure you get there safe."

I start worrying about how fragile Selene is in a world where she doesn't know any of the rules. When she grins at me, my stress fades again. She's so beautiful as if a light glows within her. Whenever I make her smile, she shines brighter.

I'm in the process of stealing another kiss from an easily flustered Selene when I hear Tracey's new red Tahoe pull up. Once my lips leave Selene's, I focus my gaze on the side-facing, four-door garage.

Joie isn't accustomed to me bringing women around the house. I'm curious how she'll react to Selene tonight. This house is my daughter's safe space.

"Whose car is that?" Joie asks, walking up to me as I turn the corner of the house.

"Patrice's. Selene is here."

As Joie's blue eyes widen, she leans around me to see Selene approaching.

"You were sick," Joie tells her. "You still look sleepy."

I grin at my daughter's lack of filter. "She's on the mend," I explain while Tracey strolls over.

I make the introductions between Selene and my mother's former best friend. Tracey lost her husband not long before I finished building this house. She couldn't keep their farm going without him, and living alone didn't suit her. Tracey was at that age when many people's lives fall apart after any significant change.

I offered her the house manager job and built a little suite in the back for privacy. Gave Tracey an income, a purpose, and enough free time to enjoy the hobbies she gave up when life got stressful. In exchange, Tracey helps me raise Joie. She's also the one who keeps the house clean and organized.

Nicole and Tracey often rubbed each other wrong. My ex is a flighty, self-absorbed woman. Tracey is a salt of the earth type. Though they never battled, they also stayed out of each other's way. Once Nicole left, Tracey took shit up a notch and became a co-parent.

Right now, her blue eyes study Selene. The older woman glances at me and nods.

"I get it."

"Right?" Joie asks.

I roll my eyes at their taunting. Yes, Selene is beautiful. Of course, I'm hot for her. But it's not like she's just fuckable. I need people to see Selene's other qualities, so she will, too.

"Can I show Selene my room?" Joie asks me.

Rather than answer, I ask Selene, "Is that something you want to do?"

Selene smiles softly at Joie and nods. A part of me immediately gets edgy. Is Selene really interested? Or is she saying what's expected? Is this a fucking game to get into my good graces?

I know the answers, of course. But over the years, I've had too many women try to play the mother role to get close to me. Joie isn't a toy, pet, or tool. Anyone who uses her becomes my enemy. I don't care how well-meaning the person might be.

However, Selene has been curious about Joie since I mentioned I had a daughter. I sense she's starved for those connections I take for granted. When Selene claims to want to see a twelve-year-old's room, she's being square with me.

I watch them enter the house before glancing at Tracey, who's got her comments locked and loaded. The petite woman wears her light brown hair in a wavy pixie cut. Often, she reveals the smile of a mom torn between disappointment and pride. Today, she rests her hands on her narrow hips and sighs.

"So, I finally meet the woman capable of twisting Hoyt Macready into knots."

"What do you think?"

"She's definitely a looker."

"And?"

"I said two words to her. How can I judge anyone with so little to go off?"

"I want her."

"I know."

"I'm going to keep her."

"I'm sure you will." When I don't continue, Tracey steps closer. "What's the problem?"

"Her past left her trashed inside. I worry I'm not patient or tender enough to help her heal."

"You likely aren't."

Exhaling hard, I expected her to lie for my benefit. Tracey just smiles and pats my forearm.

"But you can learn. She's probably smitten enough to overlook your failures. If not, there's no crying over spilled milk."

"I was looking for better advice than that."

"You were looking for lies and promises. Neither will help you in the long run," she says and steps onto the porch. "But if I were going to give you any advice, it would be simple. Enjoy your time with Selene, whether you get a few days or a lifetime. Life moves faster than we expect. It wasn't long ago when Joie was barely walking. Goodness, I can remember when you were just getting the hang of standing on your own."

Grinning at her reminiscing about me as a kid, I enter the house and look up toward the walkway. Joie's bedroom has a connected playroom at one end of the hall. A few guest rooms sit between her space and mine.

When I built the house, I ensured there was space for another accidental child. After I told Nicole to fuck off, I assumed I was done with kids. Now, I've met Selene.

Feeling like I'd lost her tore up something sensible inside me. I'm more primal now. I need to rein in that hunger.

Selene can't handle me going wild. One day, maybe, she'll accept me completely. Right now, she doesn't trust anyone, not even herself.

Unable to keep my ass on the main floor, I head upstairs to find Joie showing Selene her sports trophies.

"I got this in camp," Joie says before noticing me. "Dad sends me away every summer so he can have orgies at the house."

Selene doesn't react immediately. I see her eyes widen slightly when the words hit her. I smile at how her gaze flashes at me. Her expression is so readable when she accepts how Joie is fucking with her.

"He just wants to have fun," Selene tells Joie, who grins. "And without those orgies, you wouldn't have gotten this trophy."

"Did you ever win any competitions?"

"I got fourth place at a tennis competition, but I didn't win a trophy. I did get a ribbon for playing a piano piece one year at school."

"Do you still have the ribbon?"

Selene's gaze shifts as she shakes her head. Assuming something ugly happened to her ribbon, I change the subject.

"The basketball team I was on went to the state championship."

"I'm sorry you didn't win," Selene says softly.

Joie shakes her head. "Dad hurt his knee and couldn't play for most of the game. The rest of his team sucked, apparently."

I grin at how Joie twists the facts to make me sound like a winner. Selene doesn't notice my daughter's lies. Instead, she admires the trophies Joie has won over the years.

In reality, the coaches often gave awards to kids just for showing up. Only in the last few years has Joie won anything for real. Of course, I don't share that info.

"Do you think when you've healed enough," Joie asks Selene, "we could play tennis together?"

Selene's face lights up as she nods. "But I'm unsure when that would be."

Knowing Joie wants to ask about the gunshot wounds, I catch my daughter's gaze and shake my head. She clamps her lips shut as if she can barely control her urge.

Changing the subject, Joie asks Selene, "Do you like stew?"

"Yes."

Unsure if Selene is telling the truth, I follow them downstairs to where Tracey finishes up dinner.

"We often eat dinner after Joie gets home," I explain as we reach the main floor. "We have something lighter before bed."

Joie leans against Selene and whispers loudly, "Tracey goes to bed really early, so she likes eating dinner before it gets too late."

"Did I hear my name?" Tracey asks from the kitchen.

Joie jogs over and hugs the woman she considers a grandmother. "I said you're a great cook."

Tracey smirks before shrugging. "I'm not creative. But what I can make, I make well."

Selene stands awkwardly in the kitchen, unsure what to do. I hand plates to her and gesture toward the dining room. She smiles easily and goes to set the table.

From day one, I noticed how Selene needs prompting. She rarely takes the initiative. But once she's told what to do—and often how to do it—she works hard. After hearing about her asshole husband, I understand why she requires so much hand-holding.

I don't need Selene to take charge. I'm the boss, even with people who aren't my employees. Joie is my second-in-command. We like running the show. Selene's quiet nature fits easily into our groove.

During dinner, she listens to Joie talk about her school schedule and what she wants to do during her next break. Tracey shares a few stories about the local farmer's market. I talk about my motorcycles.

Selene doesn't really add anything to the conversation. Her life before McMurdo Valley was crap. She can't talk about her violent husband or abusive parents. I don't sense Selene has hobbies.

Until a few weeks ago, she was no more than a beautiful empty doll like those fancy kinds kept in display cases.

Now, at thirty-four, Selene has a chance to become a real person and embrace the world she's never truly known.

And I plan to be at her side for every step.

I consider what Wynonna told me about the day Patrice fought back. My grandmother's been pissed for most of her life. Her anger is usually low-key, but having Yazmin and me here has stirred up all her bad memories.

When she looks at us, Patrice sees her failures as a mother. She thinks of how men ruined us. Despite her living in a comfortable house with a woman she loves and owning a piece of a successful business, she still feels cornered by an abusive husband and betrayed by life.

I don't know how to respond to her anger. Patrice's feelings toward me are complicated. I remind her of Mariah—the daughter she loved, failed, and resents.

Patrice wants me to toughen up like she did. Yet, I can see behind her anger now. She fucked up somehow with Mariah and my aunt. Patrice blames herself for them turning out wrong. So, deep down, she blames herself for Yazmin and me ending up as losers, too.

I can't argue with the twisted logic burdening Patrice. It's very unlikely I'll toughen up like she wants. Yazmin and I are permanently broken. That's simply the reality of the situation.

However, I do want to become more self-sufficient like Patrice and Cheryl are. I see how casually confident Wynonna behaves. I'd certainly prefer to be more like them. But even my best will never be enough to impress Patrice.

So, I don't defend myself or offer empty promises. I only nod at her anger and walk to my room. Patrice doesn't need me to fix her bad feelings. She's a strong woman with a support system. Yazmin only has me.

I find my sister on top of the covers in the warm room. I turn on the fan and strip out of my jeans. In the connected bathroom, I wash my face and study myself in the mirror. The woman looking back is beautiful in a lot of ways.

However, she's also past her prime, beat down, and scarred. She had simple goals when she arrived in McMurdo Valley—get a job, find an apartment with Yazmin, and stay alive.

Those dreams felt attainable. Well, maybe not the last one. However, I hoped if my new life was inoffensive enough, LeVoy would ignore me. Not the brightest plan but achievable in the grand scheme of the world.

But then the woman in the mirror met an intoxicatingly handsome man. His rugged charisma surprised and charmed her. Stars formed in her eyes. Her heart begged to make him stay. Her body craved his touch. Her head omitted the truth to allow for the fantasy.

Looking in the mirror, I pity the woman I see. She could have enjoyed a small quiet life in McMurdo Valley. Now, she's dreaming too big and bound to fail. As if her heart didn't get stomped on enough over the last thirty-four years, she's decided to sign up for more abuse.

Hoyt's affections prove to be too tempting. Now, the woman in the mirror is falling fast with no hope of a soft landing. *But what can she really do at this point besides enjoy the ride to her doom?*

I return to the dark bedroom and find Yazmin in the same position. Even without her making a sound, I sense she's awake.

"Yazmin," I whisper. "I'm here."

"I was thinking while you were gone."

"About what?" I whisper while crawling into bed.

"If you have a chance to make things real with Hoyt, don't let me slow you down. Just grab hold of him and be happy."

I rest on my side and cup her face. Pressing my forehead against hers, I sigh. "You are the only person I truly trust."

"He could fall in love with you."

"If he doesn't want you around, he doesn't really love me. It'd be like me saying I love him but wanting to send Joie away."

"She's a child."

"And you're my best friend," I whisper and kiss her forehead. "You're why I'm alive. I would have died that night if not for you. I would have given up in the hospital if you hadn't been at my side. My second chance is thanks to you. No way am I leaving you behind."

Yazmin's wet cheeks reveal her pain, but she sounds calm when she says, "I'll never be free."

"Healing takes time."

"It's been years."

"But you went from Robert to the hospital before joining me in my prison. Then, we were at home with our father. We've only been free of their control for less than a month. And we're still dependent on someone else. Soon, though, we'll have a little house of our own. You'll get a dog. We can buy our own car. We'll truly be free."

"He'll always be in my head."

"It's the quiet," I insist while stroking her forehead. "I hear LeVoy when the silence grabs me. Sometimes, I think I smell his cologne. Or I'm sure I feel him in the room with me. But that doesn't happen when I'm around other people. If we can get the hang of this new life, we can drown out the past with the noise from our present."

"I'm certain you can have a good life, but I never will. I worry you'll miss out if you let me hold you back."

"That's just Robert talking. Or our father. Or that stupid doctor. I'm alone like you, Yazmin. Patrice and Cheryl don't know us. Hoyt cares for me, but we're still strangers. If I left you behind, I'd be alone. You're the only one who knows the real me. I can tell Hoyt about the shooting or share with Cheryl about my therapy. They can hear about my past, but they'll never feel it like you do."

Yazmin exhales deeply. "I worried you wouldn't come home."

"Hoyt kissed me."

Finally, my sister stirs. "What was it like?"

"Like a spicy cocktail," I reply, wearing a smile. "Made me warm all over and a little lightheaded. I immediately wanted more."

I see Yazmin's lips pulling into a little smile. "He looks at you like you're a treasure. I noticed that at the movies. How he was always stealing glances at you. Whenever anything interesting happened in the movie, he checked your reaction."

"I don't know how it'll be to work for him and also kiss and stuff."

"You'll get paid to spend the day with him. That's as cushy a job as we can hope for."

I grin at her teasing. "But he wants everything."

"I know."

"And I can't give him everything."

"He has money, right?"

"Yes. His house is beautiful."

"Then, if he wants to, he could pay for you to get plastic surgery to lessen your scars."

Breath catching, I never considered how I might fix what LeVoy destroyed. "I couldn't ask him to do that. But with my raise, I could save up for it."

"You got a raise?"

"Yes. I'm making twice as much."

"Because you quit?"

"No, because he was always going to increase it after I got past the probationary period," I explain, fudging the facts to avoid Patrice's involvement. "We'll have money for a rental in a month. A car even sooner."

Yazmin tightens her grip on my hand. "I should try working the busier nights. I could make more tips. We could move sooner."

I'm afraid to push Yazmin. She gets overwhelmed so easily, and Patrice isn't a patient boss. When she showed me how to do things, I got flustered, even knowing I wouldn't be waitressing anytime soon. Patrice's annoyance with our presence in her life bleeds into her every interaction with us.

"If you think you can handle more shifts on busier nights, you could try. Callie said there are two houses we could rent soon. One of them is close enough to walk to the Gin Mill. The other has a bigger yard, though."

I feel Yazmin's mood improving. The heavy cloud around her fades until her lips reveal a real smile.

"I want our own place," she whispers. "When I felt bad in Bossier City, I could hide in the guesthouse. But at home with Mom and Dad, and now here, I feel judged. It makes the bad feelings heavier."

"It's only been a few weeks. In a few months, our lives will be completely different."

As Yazmin cuddles closer, I talk about gardening and little dogs. Once I know she's in a better mood, I pretend to be hungry. We get up and find leftovers in the fridge.

Sitting out back, I tell her about my day with Hoyt. Everything from our first argument and kiss to my nap and the apple cider. By the time I reach the end of my day, Yazmin and I can't stop smiling.

The panic attacks last Friday feel like a million years ago. My scars are no longer a barrier. My dreams are once again delusionally hopeful.

HOYT

Selene fits so effortlessly back into my schedule. Between her quitting and us kissing, I worried shit might get awkward. I've never dated one of my assistants. I don't know what Selene even expects.

When she walks to the truck, I'm unsure if I should kiss her. I can already taste her lips. She smiles at me so warmly, but I restrain myself.

Through three morning meetings, I keep my hands off Selene. But when the son of one of the local business owners gives her the once-over, I feel my control slipping.

First, I want to beat him to death. Second, I want to claim her with more than kisses. Finally, I want my devotion to Selene to wipe out every bad memory from her past.

"What's wrong?" Selene asks when we return to the truck.

Unable to censor myself, I grumble, "Men are always looking at you."

"Women are always looking at you."

I smirk at her tone. "Does that bother you?"

"No, I only care when you look back at them."

"Do I, though?"

"Not yet."

"There's only one woman I want to look at," I murmur while running my knuckles across her jaw. "I've never met anyone half as beautiful as you, Selene. I know that sounds like a fucking line. Hell, I think I've used it on a chick before. But I'm being square with you right now."

Staring up at me with her bright hazel eyes, she asks, "Will you kiss me now or wait until our workday is over?"

"I'll let you decide."

Selene goes still. Her gaze lowers. She isn't sure. Am I testing her? What if she chooses wrong?

My fingers slide across her jaw and into her hair. Cupping her neck, I coax her closer so my lips can taste hers.

Selene sighs as I kiss her. My dick thickens immediately. I'm uncomfortably hard by the time my tongue slides across hers. Selene's fingers dance along my chest before gripping my shirt. I feel her opening up to me, craving me closer, wanting more.

However, she still eventually leans away from me, hiding her gaze by looking out at the quiet street.

"Are you thinking of him?" I ask when Selene glues herself to the door.

When her golden eyes return to me, she shakes her head.

"Then, what do you think of when you get spooked like that?"

"How I want things I can't have."

My temper insists I push harder. Why can't I make her open up to me immediately? I could force Selene to explain her reasoning and admit she's wrong to be scared.

I even reassure myself that acting an asshole toward her right now is warranted. Selene will be happier if I take charge and force her to open up.

Before I give in to my intimidation tactics, Selene's gaze flashes to me. I see a woman scarred by other men who knew better than her. They likely also rationalized their bullshit.

No asshole wakes up and thinks, "I'm the bad guy." We all view ourselves as the hero or a victim. I have no doubt LeVoy felt entitled to treat Selene as a possession. She's weak. He's strong. She doesn't know how anything works. He's seemingly successful.

Besides, Selene doesn't fight back. It's so easy to push her, if you ignore the fear in her eyes.

Reaching over, I enjoy the feel of her soft hair against my fingers.

"Telling me no won't kill either of us," I promise as she watches me.

I suspect Selene sees on my face what so many others have in my life. Though I keep my untapped rage chained, it's always right below the surface. I'm not insane. I know right from wrong. Despite remaining in control, the rage lingers around the edges of my every breath.

The fear in Selene's expression drops piece by piece like a puzzle coming apart. Eventually, a smile dances along her pouty lips.

"I have an idea." Grinning, I gesture for her to continue. "What if we added kissing to your schedule? I think I can squeeze it in between meetings and meals. If it's on the schedule, there'll be less uncertainty."

Selene lowers her gaze and grins wider. "Besides, I could use our scheduled kisses as excuses to finish meetings you're bored with. Like when I used lunch as a reason to shut down that long-winded person last week. Derek Mosey figured you were off to an important mayor meeting, but we were really just going to lunch."

"That sounds like a solid plan."

When Selene smiles shyly at me, I realize I'm probably her first real boyfriend. She made it sound like her father picked that shithead for her husband. Though a lot of girls with strict parents would sneak out and go wild, I doubt Selene ever did. It's her nature to please and avoid confrontation.

That's why she comes up with her schedule idea rather than telling me to stop kissing her all day. It's her passive way of taking control of a man she knows won't agree to a leash.

During lunch, I think about how to wrap myself around Selene in every way. She's vulnerable and in need of protection. I've been a weapon for my entire adult life. My money fixes problems or makes them disappear. I need that shit to happen for Selene.

With that in mind, I have one of the club's spare cars delivered to my house. After our last meeting of the day, I drive home with Selene. Despite feeling her wanting to ask questions, she only sinks into that overly quiet place she hides when she's on edge.

"I know you're saving up for a car. Patrice and Cheryl only have their one vehicle," I explain after helping her down from my truck once we're parked in my wide gravel driveway. "This little SUV will give you and Yazmin more flexibility. It'll take pressure off Patrice, too."

Selene looks at the sporty jeep and then at me. I grin at how often I see this expression on her face. She gets it whenever she doesn't understand, but knows she ought to be able to piece something together. Rather than ask what the fuck is happening, she pretends to be thinking hard.

While that move likely worked on her shithead husband, I'm not looking to play games.

"This jeep belongs to the club," I explain softly as my hand slides down her back. "I'm giving this spare vehicle to you. Keep it or just use it until you get something you like better. It's up to you."

Selene takes the key fob and smiles at the car. "And Yazmin can drive it, too?"

Her worried tone makes my chest hurt. She's so used to asking for permission over every fucking thing. Selene never grabs hold of life. She stands back and hopes someone will offer her scraps.

"I'm also going to front you the money for the house you want to rent," I add when she stops looking freaked about the car. "You said at lunch how Yazmin wants to work extra shifts. I could tell that shit worried you. This way, you can leave Patrice's place without doing anything that'll make life worse for Yazmin or you."

"This is a lot," she says, watching me in a weird way.

"Not really."

"It feels like a lot."

"Because you're used to nothing."

When Selene holds my gaze, something unpleasant washes across her expression.

"What are you thinking?"

Selene shakes her head, preferring to hide. I step closer and play detective.

"You think you'll owe me for this, and I'll expect payment."

Eyes filling with tears, Selene shakes her head.

"Then, what?"

Selene swallows hard before looking away. "Every day, I imagine two paths. One is I get to see you, make money for a more independent life, spend time with Yazmin, and go to bed safe. Two is that LeVoy finishes the job."

As my temper instantly roars to life, Selene looks at the car.

"I see a future where Yazmin and I live in a little house. She has a dog and gets more confident with her job. I imagine you and me becoming closer," she says as her lustful gaze flashes to me. "It feels so possible. You pay me well. I can save up. Yazmin and I could go on a vacation. We could be really free."

"I'll never let that fucker hurt you again."

Selene looks at me with tear-filled eyes. "I imagine Yazmin alone in that rental after I'm dead. Can she survive alone? Would she be better off staying with Patrice and Cheryl? And what about you? Whenever I pull you closer, I'm making promises. I feel like I'm wrong to build up all these dreams when I know I won't be around to realize them."

"This is my territory," I say, cupping her face and forcing her gaze to remain on me. "No one fucks with my people here."

"Those people at the theater could have shot us. What would stop them? It's so easy to end a life. How can you protect me?"

"I'll have someone watch your house. You're either with me or at Patrice's. I'll keep you safe."

Selene steps back. "I don't know the right answer. Maybe I shouldn't push LeVoy about the divorce. He doesn't want me to have anything. If I promise to go away quietly, maybe he'll let me live."

"I'm handling that."

"Your tough lawyer won't be quiet."

"Selene, you think like a victim. That's okay, but trust that I know how to deal with men like him."

"No, you don't understand."

"Then enlighten me."

Sighing, Selene wipes her wet eyes. "LeVoy's never been afraid of anyone. He lives in a bubble where he's the meanest motherfucker around. There are never any consequences for his behavior. Even when we weren't in Bossier City, he never got hurt for being an asshole."

Her gaze studies me, revealing desire and fear. "Even though you're powerful, too, he won't think to be afraid. He won't believe he's in danger until you're beating the life out of him. Only then will he realize he fucked up. But I'll be dead, by then. I shouldn't make these plans with Yazmin. Except I don't know how else to give her hope."

Selene pushes away my hands. Stepping back, she stares at me, full of panic. I feel her losing control. She struggles with all these wild emotions wound up inside her. Right now, they spill out.

"Who will take care of Yazmin when I'm gone?" she cries, staring into a dark future. "Without me, she'll kill herself. I love her so much. She's my only friend. The only family I've ever trusted."

Reacting to nothing, Selene backs away and nearly ends up on her ass.

"I never saved her. Not from Robert or the doctors or even LeVoy. I didn't know how. Now, she'll be all alone without me. I didn't come up with a good plan to get away from LeVoy."

I passively watch Selene unraveling before my eyes. I've never known anyone so fragile. She seems too breakable for a man like me to touch, let alone claim.

As her panicked gaze finds me, I see the woman I love. *Selene is mine.* I don't know how to be what she needs. I'm bound to fuck shit up between us. Yet, I can't let her spiral like she is now.

Selene flinches when I move toward her. She shrinks in fear when I wrap her in my arms. I feel her stiffen in my embrace. She's the frightened princess waiting for her gallant prince to save her, but I'm just a monster.

I think of how close Selene came to dying the night she was shot. I never would have known she was gone from the world or what I was missing.

Stroking her head, I try to imagine being Selene. I've never lived in fear. I didn't have abusive parents. I rarely lost a fight.

Though I can't put myself in her head, I do feel her soften in my embrace. Her breathing steadies, and she wraps her arms around my waist. Selene's grip is tight, as if she's dangling over a cliff, and I'm the only thing keeping her from falling.

"I'm going to handle him," I say calmly despite my rage. "I prefer if he doesn't fear me. That way, he won't see me coming. I promise I'll free you from him. That way, you can dream."

Selene looks up at me, seeming exhausted like she did on Friday night when I dropped her off.

I feel her seeking more reassurance. My rage nearly blinds me to the promise she wants most. Finally, I find the words she needs.

"If something happens to you, I'll keep Yazmin safe. Wynonna will help me, so I don't fuck up."

As Selene exhales deeply, a smile washes over her tear-streaked face. "When she came home from the hospital, I promised I would fix things and keep her safe. I don't think I kept that promise. But I believe you'll keep yours."

Though I consider explaining how she did what she could, she won't really hear my words. Selene can't view herself in the way I do.

Rather than use logic, I kiss her lips and hold her fragile body a little longer. Selene feels weak and passive while I'm strong and aggressive.

So, while I might be unable to fix Selene's past, I'm certain how to protect her future.

SELENE

I'm too emotional now. I controlled myself better during the first weeks with Hoyt. Once I cracked in front of him, I haven't been able to stop. More of my façade chips away each minute we're together.

His kisses leave my body on fire. His affection fills my head with wild dreams. I'm full of lust yet feel shame over what sex would reveal about my body. I want him despite knowing we have no future.

Today, I'm drowning in a sea of fear. LeVoy will kill me. Yazmin will kill herself. Hoyt will kill LeVoy, only to find revenge doesn't soothe his rage. I'm not making the world better. I'm just fumbling around.

"Everyone's fucked up," Yazmin whispers that night as I remain restless. "Most just don't know. Their damage hides down deep, sabotaging them from the shadows. Our damage is at the surface for everyone to see. But at least, we know what we're fighting. They're living in denial. We don't have that luxury."

I think of her words before admitting, "When Hoyt kisses me, I want to go wild. I think of sliding my fingers under his shirt to his hot flesh. I'm so curious about how good he can make me feel if I let us push past my fear. But I also know he'll want everything if I open up too much. I can never let him see my scars."

"Because he won't want you anymore?"

Tearing up in the darkness, I nod. "He's in denial. Hoyt showed me his old scar. It was this small flaw on his otherwise flawless body. He refuses to believe he'll see my fresh scars and reject me. But people have their limits. Especially men accustomed to beautiful women."

"Maybe you could be together with your clothes on?" Yazmin says when I begin crying. "Well, not completely on, but you know, like where you could feel pleasure without exposing your scars. Then, you could have what you want without creating a dealbreaker."

I wipe my eyes and ask, "Is that something a person can ask for?"

"I don't know. Maybe not with other men. But those bikers say stuff that others don't. I think Hoyt won't get weird like a normal man might. He wants you. I think he'd be willing to do anything if he could fuck you."

"I'm afraid he might agree and then just make me do whatever he wants."

"But he might do that anyway. It's not like you could stop him."

Yazmin's right about both asking Hoyt and how I'm powerless against his demands. Hoyt said he could handle my truth. I need to trust his words.

I'm thinking about that the next day when we drive toward the Pigsty. Hoyt rarely brings me out to the clubhouse. I'm unsure if he's embarrassed by them or me.

However, the truck doesn't stop at the Pigsty. Instead, we drive past the clubhouse and into the stretch of open land behind it. Hoyt parks the truck and comes around to help me down. He grabs a duffle bag from the back seat.

Watching him silently, I have no idea what we're doing out here. I really don't care, either.

Spending time with Hoyt makes every outing a worthwhile experience. Even when we stopped to grab his dry cleaning, I'd been entranced with how his masculine presence filled up the store.

Right now, he takes my hand and guides me to an area a bit away from the truck. I notice figures placed near the hill wall. They almost look like scarecrows with paper faces.

"Wynonna offered one of her pistols for you to carry," Hoyt explains, pulling the weapon from his duffle bag. "It's lightweight, but don't let that fool you. It can still end a fucker."

My trembling hand takes the weapon. Though I'm afraid to hold the gun, let alone use it, I don't complain to Hoyt.

"Get used to the feel of it," he says, pulling out headphones. "The safety's on. You can't hurt yourself or me. Just get accustomed to its weight."

I do as he instructs while he slides the headphones over my ears. "I want you to think about driving home from work or the store. Just anywhere. You're in your car. Can you see that?" he asks as he turns me toward the targets.

When I nod, he guides my arms up so I can aim.

"You see someone you don't know. He seems to be watching you. Maybe he's a guy admiring a beautiful woman, or possibly he's here to finish the job."

I imagine myself in the kitchen in Bossier City. The man who shot me was hidden behind a ski mask. He could be anyone. I might be looking at him one day without knowing he tried to kill me.

Hands still shaking, I focus on how Hoyt wants me to steady my arms. He talks about how the target seems far off. However, it's better to shoot the guy when he's at a distance rather than waiting until he's closer.

"He might grab your gun if you hesitate for too long. Now imagine your car breaks down. You're on the side of the road. You've called me. I'm coming to get you. But this man stops. And you're afraid. Can you see him?"

I imagine the target is the man from the kitchen. He's aiming at me. I'm not in my nightgown, unarmed and surprised. I'm holding this gun. I can hurt him back.

Hoyt shows me how to take the safety off. His large hands cover mine as he prepares for me to fire.

"There'll be a little kick. Don't hold the gun too tight, but don't be afraid to command control of it. Just use a relaxed grip like you do with the steering wheel.

Show me how you'll hold it when you're aiming at that man."

Hoyt's calm voice sinks into my body, settling my nerves. I feel his wide hand slide across my stomach. He steadies me with his other hand on my right shoulder. I'm safe in his care.

Rather than a mind filled with noise and doubts, I only hear Hoyt's voice.

"You're going to miss the target," he says tenderly. "Probably won't hit it at all today. But that's okay. It's like learning to drive. You need to get used to the feel of the car before you start making maneuvers. That's all you're doing today with the gun. Just learning how it feels when it's quiet and how it kicks when you fire it."

Exhaling deeply, I aim the gun at the target. I don't even think about hitting it. I'm more nervous about the gun flying out of my hands if I'm startled by the gunshot.

I remember the way the sound echoed in the kitchen. The first one seemed like a dream. By the third, I felt trapped in a hell where the sound would never end.

Today, I'm the one pulling the trigger. The first time I fire, I do nearly drop the gun. The sound shoves me back into that night. The way my body opened up for the bullets. The heat and pain shocked me.

Before I panic, I focus on Hoyt's hand across my stomach. His touch is so intoxicating. I feel him stroking me despite how his fingers never move.

Inhaling his spicy scent, I imagine him just out of the shower this morning. He's so handsome and powerful. And his hands own me right now.

I fire again. The sound doesn't startle me so much. I control the weapon's kick. I even clip the edge of the paper.

"Look at that," Hoyt says in a voice laced with pride.

I nearly burst into tears over his words. Hoyt is everything great about the world. If my life was guided by only versions of him, I might have become someone special. He fills me with such confidence.

Though it's too late to be fearless, I can learn to fire this weapon. I don't get cocky and assume I'm a natural. I exhale deeply and inhale Hoyt's scent again. I focus on his hand against my stomach. I return to the same comfort I felt when I fired last time. This shot hits even closer to the bullseye.

"You're a good teacher," I murmur when he chuckles at how my next shot lands center mass.

I feel a smile on Hoyt's face. He must have imagined many scenarios playing out when he devised the plan to train me.

Hysteria would be the most obvious response from me. And I *am* scared. I fear guns. LeVoy used to threaten me with them. Even before the night I was shot, I assumed I would die from a gun.

However, Hoyt's presence keeps me grounded. In my head, I see the man in the kitchen. Yet, I feel Hoyt touching me. I know I'm not back in Bossier City. I'm right here in McMurdo Valley with the man I love.

After the gun is empty, Hoyt patiently teaches me how to reload. He grins when he realizes my gaze is on his face instead of what he's doing. Rather than remind me to pay attention or getting frustrated, he hands me the loaded weapon and has me shoot more.

I'm nearly empty again when Hoyt brushes my hair away from my throat. His lips press against the tender flesh, zapping my energy. I think I'd topple to the ground if he weren't holding me still.

With bated breath, I ask, "Is this a test?"

"I just can't help myself," he replies, sounding like a starving man.

His lips suck at my flesh, setting my body on fire and leaving me lightheaded. Though I want to touch Hoyt, I can't remember how to do the safety feature. So, I take aim at the target and fire until the gun is empty. Setting the weapon on the ground, I tug off the headphones and stare lustfully at Hoyt.

His calloused palms cup my face and draw me closer. I meet his hunger with my own. Hoyt lifts me against him. My legs wrap around his hips. His erection pokes at me through our clothes. I crave him inside my body.

Hoyt must think the same thing since he carries me to the truck. With his lips sucking at mine, he fumbles with the door.

Once I end up in the back seat, Hoyt shadows me. With all the supplies back here, my position is awkward. We couldn't fuck comfortably, even if I were willing to strip down and reveal my every scar to this man.

Kissing Hoyt again, I stroke his erection through his jeans. My fire isn't something that can be satisfied, but his can be. Hoyt is often aroused around me. His erection refuses to be subtle, and our kisses always leave him unsatisfied.

I've never given a man a handjob, let alone through his pants. I fear hurting him. But Hoyt groans at the feel of my fingers across his erection.

He moans my name and sucks harder at my throat. His passion fills the truck, leaving me awash in a lust I never thought possible.

I shiver at the sound of his pleasured moans. His body tenses before going soft when he finds relief. I watch this sexy man in awe.

Hoyt looks awkward over how he turned our gun training into an opportunity to get off. Kissing him quickly, I never want him to feel guilty for his desire.

I need Hoyt to want me. His lust acts as a shield against my past.

"I'm not a selfish man," he says, cocking an eyebrow as he looks over my body. "I'll give as much as I take."

His gaze feasts on my body, imagining me stripped down. I slide closer and force him out of the truck. Hoyt frowns at my gesture.

"Do you like kissing just to kiss, or is it all about the sex?"

Hoyt's frown darkens. "What does that mean?"

"I want to kiss more, but you already got off. Can we still make out?"

His gaze flashes around the empty land before returning to me. I see on his face when he realizes we aren't fucking today, yet I still want to be close. Hoyt's breathing shifts, and a sly grin spreads over his tanned face.

"You're a wild woman, aren't you?" he asks in a teasing voice.

"I'm a gun-toting temptress."

Hoyt grins wider before reaching in to shove the step stool and bags aside. He climbs across me and settles on the seat.

"I haven't made out in the back seat since I was a teenager. And never with a woman even half as beautiful as you."

Grinning, I straddle him and stroke his jaw before our lips reunite. Hoyt wraps his arms around me in a way they can't when we normally kiss in the front seat. This position allows the closeness I've been craving. Based on how long we remain in the truck, I sense Hoyt's been suffering from the same need.

HOYT

Even after Selene agrees to carry the weapon with her, I hire a few local guys and gals in need of extra cash. They follow Selene on her errands or sit outside Patrice's house at night. I'm not sure how realistic the threat from LeVoy actually is considering nearly a year has passed since his first attempt.

"He's a bitch," Armor mutters in his gravelly voice as we sit at the Gin Mill one night. "Men like him are big shots in their territory. Outside of it, their balls shrink up."

"Selene thinks he's unable to fear anything because he's never suffered any consequences."

"Yeah, but she's got victim goggles on. The asshole seems like a super predator to her. I bet she thinks you're a teddy bear who occasionally fucks up people who mess with his cub."

Grinning at his comment, I admit Selene's viewpoint is corrupted by years of abuse.

"I'm going to kill him," I spit out, frowning at the thought of that asshole still breathing.

"Of course."

"I just need to figure out if I should wait until the divorce is over or not."

"What's the point in waiting?"

"What if he's left stuff to Selene, and it draws heat on her?"

"He likely won't leave her shit. Guys like that know how to hide their money. Whether she's the wife or ex-wife, she's getting heat. Cops are lazy, and they look for obvious suspects."

"Kourtney said LeVoy claimed someone tried to murder him and Selene got in the way. When we kill him, the cops can assume the original shooter succeeded."

"Nice of the son of a bitch to give you another suspect to pin shit on."

"So, I should get it done, then?"

"I would," Armor says, falling silent when Yazmin walks over to our table to mumble her question. "I could use another one," he says while I shake my head.

Once she turns away, he lets his gaze linger on her leaving.

"As a favor to me, leave it alone," I say and take a pull of my beer.

Armor cocks his eyebrow. "Are you speaking in code?"

I tilt my jaw at Yazmin behind the bar. "She's not dating material."

"Says who?"

"Me."

"You're the one pursuing a woman who ought to avoid dating for a while."

Exhaling slowly, I can't really argue with Armor about Selene. "I know shit about our waitress that you don't. Trust that she isn't equipped to deal with anyone's dick."

Armor's gaze flashes toward Yazmin returning with his beer. She makes zero eye contact with either of us before leaving again.

"You can't fault me for looking," Armor says once she's gone.

"No, they're beautiful women."

Armor smartly changes the subject. "Has Kourtney gotten anyone lined up to play local lawyer for you?"

"Yeah, and we have a conference call tomorrow at the office. They've filed papers in Louisiana. Apparently, this guy sat down with LeVoy's lawyer. He ought to be able to tell me how drawn out this shit will be."

"What happens when Selene is officially single?"

Side-eyeing Armor, I grunt at his smirk. "Leave me alone."

"Looking to take another walk down the aisle?"

"With Selene, anything's possible."

The next day in my business office, I'm thinking about a future with my sexy assistant. In contrast to my relaxed demeanor, Selene sits across from me, looking ready to cry. I walk over to her chair and lean down to kiss her. I hold nothing back, claiming her fear and leaving her heart racing. She watches me with dazed eyes when I return to my seat.

With her sufficiently focused on the heat between her legs, I dial up Kourtney's assistant. A few minutes later, we link up with Andy Duffer. The sleazy New Orleans personal claims lawyer was willing to take the job. No worries about LeVoy Garry's deep pockets. This guy would likely sue his mom into the poor house if it added even ten dollars to his bank account. I've never been so happy to know how easily people are bought.

"What did the rich fuck say?" Kourtney asks, skipping over formalities and getting down to the brass tacks.

"He's seen the light."

"What the fuck does that mean?" I mutter while holding Selene's gaze.

"He's had a spiritual awakening."

Kourtney barks, "Look, Duffer, if you're trying to be funny, don't think I won't drive to Louisiana and kick you in the ass."

"No, I'm only sharing what was shared with me. LeVoy is claiming to have joined the Jesus party. He's seen the light and is all about peace and love now."

"What does that mean for our filing?" Kourtney asks. "Is he claiming his religion doesn't allow for divorce?"

"No, in fact, he's thrilled to get divorced. He's got a new broad he wants to marry. A real upstanding Christian gold digger, apparently."

Selene's eyes widen. I hate how easily she's conned. If I ever meet her parents, I doubt I can keep myself from wrecking them. They did zero work to prepare this woman for a fucked-up world.

"Then, tell him to agree to our request," Kourtney replies. "We'll give up support payments and have this shit official in a week."

"He wants to speak with his wife first."

"No," I growl immediately. "We're not playing this fucking game. He deals with the lawyers, not Selene."

"But if it makes the process quicker," Duffer says, so accustomed to swimming in shit that he doesn't care about someone blowing chunks of it at him.

"What does he want to tell her?" Kourtney asks. "If he admits to any misdeeds, he'll put his culpability on the record. If he causes any trouble, we'll ask for more money. Where's the payoff for him?"

"He claims he wants closure."

Kourtney instantly replies, "Tell him to film an apology, and we'll show it to her. They're not speaking to each other. Even if they stand feet apart in court, she will never speak to him. Make that clear, Duffer."

Smirking, I can tell Kourtney's losing her temper. "I'm flying in next week to sit down with the asshole's lawyers. He better be prepared for what happens when I get there. If LeVoy Garry acts like you didn't make this clear, I've got four other ambulance chasers willing to take your place."

"No reason to be hostile."

"This is how I talk to my parents, asshole," Kourtney snarls at him. "Do you think you deserve better treatment than the people who brought me into this fucking world?"

"Good Lord," Duffer mutters. "Fine, I'll make your feelings clear."

"Don't arrange these meetings again unless you have real news. I don't give a shit about LeVoy discovering Jesus in a bitch's snatch. Facts only. Get it?"

After we end the call, I study Selene. Is she worried LeVoy's screwing with her? Does she think he's really into this other woman? I can't read her expression as she watches me.

"Do you wish I was more like Kourtney?" she asks, proving I really don't know what's going on in her head.

"Not even the smallest fucking bit."

"She's tough like Wynonna. You like them both."

Frowning, I cross my arms. Selene notices my irritation and shrinks into the chair. She's so easy to intimidate. I want to wrap her in my arms, where the world can't hurt her. Of course, I'm the one currently causing her stress.

"Do you think I only want you because of your looks?" I ask and lower my arms, so she feels less threatened. "That I wish I could take your outside and fill it with a different inside?"

"I don't know," she says, lowering her gaze submissively. "But I wish I could fill myself with a better person."

"I don't know if I'd love another version of you, Selene."

Eyes widening with surprise, she looks at me. "Oh."

"I like that you're soft. I wish you weren't scared, sure. But I like how tender you are with me. Even though other chicks are soft, it's better when you are. That's why I love you."

Selene's surprised expression shifts into a silly grin. "I love you, too."

Sharing her smile, I nod. "I know. I see it in your eyes every time you look at me lately. I can't get enough of it."

When she gets to thinking too much, I pull up a medical report on my phone. "Just for your records," I say and show her the results. "My dick is clean."

Selene's cheeks turn a rosy red as she imagines my cock. In her golden eyes, I see a blizzard of emotions—lust, longing, fear, and self-loathing. I hate that last one.

A few times, I've considered having her over for dinner and giving her a few drinks. Then, when Joie's asleep and Selene's defenses are down, I'd take her to bed and prove I'm not a shallow fuck.

However, I fear pushing her too fast. I grew up believing people were stronger than they thought. They just needed a good push. I don't even sugarcoat most shit for Joie. She's got to know the truth if she wants to face a harsh world.

Selene and her sister have made me reconsider that view. When she's in my arms, kissing me with the wild abandon of a woman swept away by lust, I believe I can take everything without her minding. Selene's getting stronger and healthier every day.

Yet, if my fingers slide over her right thigh, Selene immediately flinches. She stares at me with the kind of fear I can barely stomach. I see her teetering on the edge of a cliff.

The day I gave her the jeep, she danced far too fucking close to the brink. I don't know what happens if she falls off. Will she hide for a few days, like after the theater before returning to me? Or will her reaction be what she fears Yazmin will do if left alone?

I hate to think of Selene as broken. But she often feels like a beautiful doll shattered and rebuilt. How strong is the glue keeping her in one piece? Am I capable of rebuilding her again if she shatters?

Rather than risk ruining this woman, I force myself to hold back. I don't take what I want but enjoy what she offers. It's only been a month. I'm still a stranger. She remains a mystery. We have time.

And I'll wait for the rest of my life to ensure I never lose Selene for good.

SELENE

Hoyt and I have a daily routine. Today, though, he texts before I'm even awake to say he's working on something and I need to cancel all his other activities. He also suggests I take the company credit card he gave me and go shopping for an upcoming wedding.

"I'm expected to attend this crap, and I need a hot date," he told me the day before.

With my day off, Yazmin and I plan to meet Callie for lunch. She wants to show us two rental houses coming on the market.

Despite missing Hoyt, I'm excited to be able to enjoy a fun day with Yazmin. Back in Bossier City, we often talked about shopping and getting a late lunch.

"Drink Bellinis like decadent bitches," Yazmin would say as we sat by the pool and dreamed of life outside the estate's gates.

Our first stop today is at the small mall on the outskirts of McMurdo Valley.

I'm unsure what kind of dress to wear to this wedding. LeVoy always chose skimpy outfits for me. He wanted to show off his hot wife to his friends and enemies. The more revealing, the better.

"I need something that'll hide my scars without looking like a grandma dress," I tell Yazmin when everything attractive we find is too short or sleeveless.

"Think classy rather than sexy," she replies while checking through the dress racks. "An elegant dress can be long without looking frumpy."

We find so many beautiful dresses. I'm in love with one until I try it on and realize one of my chest scars is visible. When I cover it with my hand, I look like the old me. But there's no way to wear this dress without everyone seeing what is best hidden.

Yazmin joins me in the dressing room and wipes my tears. "We'll find something beautiful."

"Living in McMurdo Valley and being around Hoyt makes me forget. When I avoid looking at them, they disappear. Then, I'm shocked when his hand brushes over one of the scars. Or startled when I try wearing something too lowcut or short."

Yazmin slides my hair from my shoulders and fans my flushed face. "I found a few others you might like. They're higher cut. The sleeves are sheer, but the color might be dark enough to hide your arm. Or you could wear a slick pantsuit if the dresses won't work."

"No," I whisper and hold her gaze. "I need it to be a dress."

Yazmin frowns at how insistent I am. "Did Hoyt say you had to wear one?"

I look around, feeling exposed even in the dressing room. I lean closer and whisper, "I'm hoping to be with him after the wedding."

Yazmin doesn't understand at first. Her gaze shifts when she recalls how Hoyt and I fool around in his truck. Understanding how a dress allows access without me getting naked, she smiles softly.

"We'll find something beautiful, even if we have to go to ten stores."

Our search doesn't take nearly that long. Yazmin and I enter a store with prom dresses. Most are too heavy or revealing. But a pale-yellow dress with a sweet floral design covers all my scars and looks softly beautiful without being showy.

"He's going to have trouble keeping his hands off you," Yazmin says when I try on the dress.

Grinning like a lovesick fool, I imagine his lips on my bare neck. After the wedding will be the perfect time to share my body with Hoyt.

With the dress chosen, Yazmin and I travel to McMurdo Gorge Dining. The restaurant overlooks a breathtaking drop into untouched beauty. I recall how small I thought McMurdo Valley was when I arrived. The town felt like a speck next to Bossier City.

However, there's more to the area than I imagined. Everything is simply spread out. McMurdo Valley offers everything from fine dining to greasy dives.

Callie Macready arrives full of energy. She smiles and waves at people, both customers and employees. Everyone recognizes her. Callie's face is printed on a billboard just outside of town along with many bus stops.

She slides into her chair and smiles at us. We order quickly since she's hoping for us to see both houses before she needs to be home at four.

"The town's on fire," she says and smiles brightly. "Ed wants me home when the streetlights come on."

Though I don't know what she's talking about, I keep my mouth shut. Yazmin is likely thinking the same thing.

"Both houses are around eighteen hundred square feet," Callie explains of the rentals. "Neither have enclosed parking. One is closer to the Gin Mill. They both have fenced yards. One yard's just bigger."

"And the cost?"

"Fifteen hundred each, but I think I can get them down a little. Rentals are hard to come by. With the nearby women's college, there'll be interested parties. But Hoyt's the mayor, and you're his assistant. I expect the owners would like for him to think positively toward them."

Callie offers this threat so casually that I nearly miss its meaning.

When our lunch arrives, Yazmin and I share a Bellini.

"Can't hold your liquor, huh?" she asks, and I realize she lacks a filter like Wynonna and Joie.

"We take medication for our, um, emotions," I explain while Yazmin eats her pesto pasta. "We didn't know if it would be safe for us to drink much."

Nodding, Callie cuts into her scallop. "Are you two close out of necessity, or do you actually get along?"

221

After glancing at each other, Yazmin and I look at a grinning Callie.

"We're best friends," Yazmin mumbles.

"I think that's just peachy. I'd probably murder my sister if I had to spend so much time with her. But she's a twat."

Grinning at Callie's comment, I admire Yazmin. "I trust my sister more than anyone."

Once Yazmin's gaze finds mine, she grins. Callie stares like we're weird, but I need my sister to know she has value.

That's why we pick the Spanish-style cottage as soon as my sister's eyes glow at the sight of it. The white house speaks to her with its dark-stained front pergola and red-tiled steps.

Inside is compact but stylish. The yard is smaller, but I like the high white security fence. We can sit out back without anyone peeking in at us.

Yazmin stands in the kitchen with the terra-cotta tile and white countertop. She trembles, allowing herself to hope for a better future.

"She really likes the house," Callie says, as if my sister's being overly dramatic.

"We've lived in beautiful homes before. Large ones with pools and excellent views, but they were prisons. This is the first place where we're the ones holding the keys."

Callie's blue eyes study me. I don't think she understands. She probably can't really grasp what this little house means to Yazmin and me.

Even so, she smiles softly and nods, maybe understanding how powerful a second chance can feel.

HOYT

As a young man, I'd go berserk over the smallest shit. A snotty comment from the wrong person could send me into a violent rage. I trashed plenty of bars and wrecked more than a few people.

Age helped me pick and choose my battles better. However, my temper remains volatile. *And today it's on a fucking roll.*

I'm awakened just before sunrise by Armor. "Hobo caught a Jordan fucker on our land. He was carrying a duffle bag full of Molotov cocktails and several guns."

I order the club to the Pigsty for a nine o'clock meeting. If the Jordan family wants a war, we're giving them one.

Texting Selene, I tell her to enjoy a day with Yazmin. She agrees to join me at my house for dinner.

Next, I take Joie to school. Tracey stays behind to check our security. My dad drives over to help her out. After what the Jordan family pulled at the theater, we can't assume they won't target my kid.

I head to the Pigsty with killing on my mind. Despite being more impulsive, the younger version of me hadn't driven the Jordan family from the state. I figured the assholes would be harmless without their men around.

For decades, they held their tongue and stayed out of our way. All while breeding new pieces of shit to cause us trouble.

I arrive at the Pigsty to find the founding members on the porch, except for Nomad.

"Where is he?" I ask my VP.

"He wouldn't come in," Armor mutters, dragging a hand through his reddish-brown hair. "Claims he's got an important errand today that can't be rescheduled."

"What the fuck?"

223

"I don't know," Armor says, rubbing the back of his neck. "He's cracked, man."

I know now isn't the time to rant about Nomad's priorities. Having bigger issues, I look over the other founding members.

"Why are they doing this now?" Hobo asks as he squats on the stairs. "You being nice for a few weeks isn't any reason to try and burn down the Pigsty or harass your girl at the movies."

"It's Anita," Armor mutters. "She used to run shit before her man and sons died. Now, those little boys left behind have aged up. The asshole in the shed is no more than twenty-one."

"Anita needs to die," I mutter and look over the quiet land we've owned for decades. "Shit, I'd say they all do. It's the only way it ends."

Goose frowns fearlessly at me. "So, we're killing their runts, too, now?"

"Of course not. But these people are poor. If we move the surviving women and kids somewhere else, they'll struggle getting back here. That's what we should have done years ago."

Walla Walla shakes his head. "Anita was a fucking fool to send her grandson here."

"Maybe she didn't know," Nash suggests, always falling for old ladies' lies.

"Oh, she fucking knew," Armor growls. "That old bitch has been planning her payback for twenty damn years. Now, she's got men old enough to do her bidding. She filled their heads with big dreams of stealing from us what we stole from them. That's why a man with a baby on the way signed his own death warrant. None of the Jordans have any sense. Anita has always been the brains."

Thinking back to when we claimed McMurdo Valley, I remember considering whether to add Anita's body to the pile. I knew she was the mastermind behind her violent sons' enterprise. Except I liked the idea of her suffering on top of the ashes of her dead children. Something about seeing her around town, broken in body and spirit filled me with smug satisfaction.

As decades passed, I got comfortable and lowered my guard. So busy living, I'd forgotten about the bodies I stepped on to reach my throne. Now, those decisions are back to haunt me.

We walk to the shed where Jasyn Jordan struggles against the ropes binding him. I look at one of his Molotov cocktails cradled in my hand.

"You planned to burn my people alive, huh?" I ask, and he glares at me. "I heard you've got a baby on the way. Has your woman picked out a name? If not, she can name the baby after its dead daddy."

As Armor lights the cloth on the bottle, I grin at the guy mumbling behind his gag. "Your grandma fucked you, kid."

With that, I toss the bottle at him. I don't shut the door and walk away. My father taught me if I was man enough to take a life, I ought to be man enough to feel the price of a light snuffed out.

So I watch Jasyn Jordan burn alive. I listen to his screams. I think of his woman at home with their kid inside her. I imagine her tears. None of that makes me smile.

No, I save my grin for when I arrive at Anita's little house on the south side. My club remains on their rides while I walk through a muddy yard unfit for growing anything.

This entire area gets too much water, leaving the land forever shifting. The Jordans built shanty houses on top of cinderblocks to keep their homes from sliding away.

For twenty years, they've had nothing—shitty jobs and crappy homes. Hell, the only reason they could afford to go to the movies was one of them works at the theater and sneaked them inside.

The family's current misery stands in contrast to when McMurdo Valley bowed to them.

On the front porch, Anita rocks in her chair like everyone's favorite grammy. Her thick white hair is wrapped up on her head. She was never an attractive woman, and time hasn't been good to her.

"Jasyn failed, but it's not all bad news," I announce, holding Anita's gaze.

Her shitty family begins filling the porch. I notice one of the young men holding a rifle. If Lawsyn ends me right now, my club will burn his family to the ground.

"Jasyn realized he wasn't able to make a good life in McMurdo Valley. Too much bad blood between my club and your family. So, he's gone ahead and relocated to Texas where it's toasty warm."

Anita grits her teeth and glares at me. Back in the day, whenever the Jordan family killed someone, they'd claim the person moved to Texas. I remember how Anita's father, Teddy, would laugh whenever he heard someone was relocated to the "devil's balls."

That's what Lil Danny said about his baby mama after he shot her in the head by the lake. When I killed him and his family, I didn't use a euphemism. I just flat-out said they were dead. There's nothing cute about talking around an issue. But for today, I'll make an exception for Anita Jordan.

Nearby, Jasyn's baby mama rubs her belly and gets all teary-eyed. The other young mothers pick up their kids and move them into the house. The men linger while I grin at Anita.

"I think it's past time for the Jordan family to leave McMurdo Valley. The Steel Berserkers are more than willing to pay relocation costs. Get you settled in a new place with people who aren't looking to burn you out."

"You son of a bitch!" Anita hollers, losing that sweet grandma vibe. "You stole our town!"

"Killed your sons, too. It was real kind of you to raise their kids. Got yourself an audience for your grieving old bitch performances. Bet that's how you convinced Jasyn to move to Texas when he was just starting life with his pretty gal and their baby."

"You better leave," Lawsyn tells me while gripping his rifle.

Smirking at his attempt to play the man of the family, I point out, "Anita's going to cry when you die, kid. Weep to the heavens. When she's bored of that act, she'll send the next dipshit to die. Anita's got, what, six grandsons left?"

"I'm going to kill all of you!" Anita hollers and stands up. "I'm going to kill your weird kid and that slut you have following you around."

Smiling wider, I cross my arms. "I figure one of us will be very happy in a week. The other will be dead in a pit with their kids. I'm feeling good about my odds."

"Shoot the son of a bitch," Anita growls at Lawsyn.

"Maybe he doesn't want to die," I say when the guy hesitates. "Did you ever consider some of these assholes might want to get old? Hell, I bet a couple wish they could have known their daddies. But instead, everyone lined up to die for your cause. These young men might not mind starting off somewhere fresh with their women and kids. No one treating them different for having the last name Jordan. Man, that sounds pretty golden. But maybe they've got a taste for dying like your sons did."

Still busted up from the theater brawl, Jacksyn cracks first. I know he was closest to Jasyn. They were Irish twins, born to a mama who got stuck raising five kids alone when Anita sent her man after the club.

That's one reason Jacksyn isn't looking to die young. He's also got a pretty ginger wife and a dumb-looking son who probably laughs at his dad's farts. They're just starting out in life. So was Jasyn, but he'll never return home to be with his crying woman.

"How do we know you won't do to us what you did to my brother?" Jacksyn asks while Anita orders him to shut up.

"We didn't come at you at the theater. It wasn't us showing up with Molotov cocktails and weapons. We had a truce. She broke it," I say and gesture at the pissed woman.

The more I talk, the bigger the discord I sense in the Jordans. So, I keep bullshitting to see where this family feud goes.

"If Anita wasn't a bitter bitch, she'd have offered your family to act as muscle for the club. Gotten in nice with us. It's been twenty fucking years since we went to war. But she couldn't let it go. Now, your brother's, well, in Texas forever instead of waiting for his kid to be born. That's on her, not us. She's an old woman, having lived her life. Now, she's using your generation as cannon fodder."

Justyn steps up and frowns. "My baby girl is doing real good in school. She's got a lot of tight friendships, too. I don't wanna move."

"Are you asking me if your family can stay if the troublemaker ends up in Texas?"

"Wait, Texas means dead, right?" Justyn asks Jacksyn.

"Yeah."

That gets Jasyn's woman crying harder. Yep, she got screwed by having her man take the first step in this fresh war. Whether he volunteered or was pushed into it, the motherfucker is dead while apparently these others assholes are looking to grow old.

"I like the Valley," Jacksyn says. "This land is covered in our family's blood. It's what we know. I don't want to leave."

Anita sits back in her chair, plotting again. She's lost the narrative. Probably told them how easily they could take back what was once their family's birthright. Now, Jasyn's dead and the others are weighing their options.

I rub my chin. "After what happened today, I can't trust you to keep your word. Anita's burned too many bridges. She got you to come at my baby girl. Sent your brother to kill my people. I can't imagine what you could do to earn the club's trust."

Jacksyn looks around the porch at his people. He gets a sense of them in a way I can't. They all look hostile and dumb.

"What if we gave you a sign that we weren't gonna stir up shit anymore? Something to prove you wouldn't have any trouble at the theater or your clubhouse. Then, could we stay here?"

"It'd have to be a pretty big fucking sign," I reply.

Jacksyn nods before pulling a pistol from his back holster and firing once into Anita's head.

Though the old woman never knows what hits her, I sense she had a feeling for what was coming. She raised her grandchildren to be bitter and selfish. They think shit is owed them. What they want now is a good life in McMurdo Valley. Her death might offer just that.

I watch Anita's body slump out of the chair and roll off the porch. Gravity takes her right into a puddle of mud. Once she finishes traveling, I look at Jacksyn. Behind me, the Steel Berserkers wait for trouble. But I sense Jacksyn is done losing family members.

"That took balls," I tell him while the women inside the house cry louder.

"I killed my grandma for you."

"No, you killed her for yourself and your kin here," I say and gesture at his brothers, cousins, and Jasyn's baby mama. "For twenty years, you've lived in these shacks because of her. We offered your family deal after deal during the war. She always told her boys to reject us. Once they were dead, she kept fighting a losing battle."

I step back and sigh. "With her out of the way, the Jordan family can get a second chance. While it won't bring back your brother, it'll offer his kid a better future."

Jacksyn isn't a bright man. None of the Jordans are. Even back in the day, they were mostly muscled morons wielded by Anita against her enemies. Now, maybe these dumb fucks will act as muscle for the club. If they don't do right by us, well, I'm not against killing their men and shipping off the women and kids.

However, Jacksyn's big play flipped the script. While his family remains dangerous, they might be more useful under our control than packing them up and hoping they don't come back. One thing I've learned over the years is people who get comfortable will put up with a lot of shit to avoid returning to poverty.

"I'll let you deal with your grandmother's unfortunate heart attack," I say and gesture for my people to get ready to ride. "The town will mourn her. When you're done putting her in the ground, come around the Gin Mill. We'll see if we can't find a way to get you boys better paying jobs."

Jacksyn glances at his sweaty woman and their dirty kid. He's already picturing what they can spend the extra money on around this shithole.

Yeah, soon, they'll be comfortable which will hopefully make them loyal. Maybe then the Steel Berserkers won't need to deal with this shit again in another twenty years.

SELENE

The wedding is an outdoor affair with a sunflower theme. My dress feels even more appropriate with all the earthy colors.

Hoyt looks magnificent in a simple russet-colored suit with a beige buttoned shirt and no tie. For days, I've wondered if dressing up would hide his natural masculinity. Instead, he's just a gussied-up Hoyt.

Arriving in one of his SUVs, Hoyt's gaze warms, and his breathing shifts when I emerge from the house in my dress. I can't express how powerful I feel knowing a man like him finds me beautiful.

Hoyt kisses me several times on the drive over. Once at the wedding, his behavior becomes more professional. No kissing, but his hand is often pressed against my back or near my forearm. He never lets me forget his presence.

When a man gets too friendly toward me, Hoyt threateningly expands his stance. Through the wedding and reception, he walks the line between my boss and boyfriend.

As I slide back into the SUV to return home, Hoyt's control cracks. His lips are quickly on mine, stealing my breath and leaving me dazed.

"Can we go somewhere quiet?" I mumble when he stands at the open door and admires me.

Hoyt gives me a knowing smirk before coming around to his side.

I slip off my heels as Hoyt pulls the SUV into a quiet patch of land near his home. We come here often to kiss in private. I sense Hoyt hopes we can move the fun into his house and bed. I'm not sure that'll ever happen. However, I know what I want to happen today as the sun shines bright at the horizon.

Hoyt gives me a kiss, sealing my decision. He climbs out and comes around to help me out. The SUV is lower than the truck, so I don't really need any assistance. Yet, he's gotten in the habit, and I'll never ask him to stop.

When our lips meet again, Hoyt breathes me in. I moan at how his fingers dance down my spine.

Inside me, a battle rages between my cold dread and the fire this man ignites. I'm terrified of messing up our first time.

Before I climb into the back seat, I carefully slide down my panties. Hoyt cocks an eyebrow at my gesture. He wants to speak. I see the words on his lips. He's not a man who edits himself. For me, though, he considers his words.

I practiced a little speech for this moment. Yet, when I look up at Hoyt, I tumble into the lust in his blue eyes. Unable to speak, I look at my panties and wonder if I'm doing this right.

Hoyt's fingers slide across mine before he steals my underwear and presses them against his lips. Inhaling my scent, he looks at me like a man breaking free of his restraints.

Once he slips them into his pants' pocket, I reach up to slide off his suit jacket. I fold it neatly and rest it on the seat. Before he can speak and break the spell, I climb into the back seat.

Hoyt joins me. I reach across him and close the door. The open windows allow a soothing warm breeze to fill the vehicle.

I straddle Hoyt's lap like I have so many times in the last week. His gaze studies my features, making me feel beautiful. *In his eyes, I'm a goddess.*

Resting on his lap, I kiss Hoyt and let his flavor intoxicate me. My fingers glide through his thick blond hair. Hoyt feels more real than anything in my life.

His hands move down my back, leaving behind overheated skin. Between my legs, I feel his erection and imagine it filling me.

I've never wanted any other man inside me. Embracing the way my body feels when against his, I break into a smile.

"I love you," Hoyt says, sounding pained. "I never thought I was capable of this feeling."

Exhaling softly, I let his words erase my past. I only see Hoyt.

"I never knew men like you existed. Couldn't even dream you up," I whisper and kiss his throat. "I can't believe you're real."

Hoyt cups my cheek with his palm before leaning me back enough to taste my throat. Leaving kisses along my tender neck, he groans when my hips roll against his. His free hand cups my breast. A simple graze of his thumb against my hard nipple sends my hips rolling again.

Leaning me back, Hoyt kisses at my shoulders before his lips move lower. When his fingers tug at the top seam of my dress, I go still. My fingers remain in his hair, tugging him closer even while I stretch to move out of reach.

Hoyt lifts his gaze to meet mine. I force myself to explain rather than hide in my head.

"I can't do this if my dress comes off."

"I'm not a shallow fuck, Selene. There are no dealbreakers."

"You don't know that. It's something you believe, but it hasn't been tested. What if you're wrong?"

"I'm not," Hoyt insists as his gaze studies my face and his hands wrap possessively around my butt to keep me from fleeing. "I love you."

"This is magic," I say, panicking over how he refuses to understand. "A spell can be broken."

"It won't."

"Have you been with a woman with a scarred body?"

"No, but—"

"You think you know yourself, but you never expected to feel this way for me. Do you have control over your heart?" I ask in a squeaky, terrified voice. "If you're wrong, everything we have could end. Maybe not instantly. But it could ruin us. I'd rather have less than nothing at all."

Hoyt wears a stubborn frown, refusing to believe he's too shallow to love me, scars and all. However, he can't be sure how he'll feel.

Hoyt studies my face for maybe a minute, leaving me unsure if I've destroyed us by being honest.

"This is what you need," Hoyt says before nodding. "This is how you feel comfortable."

I realize he isn't asking. He knows me. What I want matters more than his need to prove himself.

"I feel beautiful when you touch me," I say and stroke his jaw. "But I don't know if I can feel that way if you see me."

Though Hoyt wants to talk sense into me, he chooses to edit himself to keep me happy. I wish he didn't need to do so. In an ideal world, I'd be a fearless woman.

However, Hoyt said after the phone call with the lawyers that he loved me for me. And I'm not fearless.

Today, giving myself to Hoyt like this, is the boldest thing I've done in my life.

Hoyt rewards my brashness with a raw kiss filled with all the need he's kept hidden for weeks. His arms wrap around my body, trapping me against him where the world is safe and glorious.

HOYT

Selene's a twister of emotions. She wants me to claim her body. I feel the heat radiating off her. She's as horny as I am. We've been dancing around this moment since we met. Yet, she fears I'll view her body with the same hatred as she does.

I've imagined fucking Selene a hundred times. I'm constantly imagining her pussy wrapped around my cock. She's all I think about when we're apart. Joie's even gotten to teasing me with how I'm always spaced out lately.

However, this isn't how I wanted our first time to be. I planned to kiss her every scar, proving nothing about Selene repulsed me. Every inch of her is beautiful and mine.

Yet, she gets this heartbroken panic when I attempt to push for more.

I have a choice—wait until she trusts me enough to reveal herself completely or enjoy only a sample of what I truly want.

How can I deny her or myself? She fucking glowed at the wedding. I couldn't take my eyes off her.

My patience is gone. We're here in this private place with a relaxing breeze flowing around us. Selene is gorgeous with her flowered dress and flushed cheeks. She smells like a goddamn peach orchard. My dick is rock hard. Her bare pussy is hidden under her skirt, begging to be filled by me.

No way can I take a principled stance against fucking right here and now. Selene's clearly planned out today. She wants me inside her body. Telling her no would be cruel to us both.

I'm not the bad guy for saying yes.

And I do say yes.

I'll make Selene come apart even if I never get her dress off.

My lips tease her hard nipples through the soft fabric. Selene's whimpers make my dick twitch. I love how limp she is in my embrace. The trust she has in me is intoxicating.

"Baby," I say when she stares with dazed arousal. "I've got to free my dick. I don't know if I can last long with you. I'm so hard. But if you're patient, I'll get hard again quick."

Staring at me, Selene doesn't understand. Like taxes and health insurance, fucking is a mystery to her. She does what she's told and walks away when dismissed. She doesn't really understand a man's body, let alone her own. I wonder if she ever plays with the hot pussy I feel against my slacks.

"Trust me," I murmur when she watches me like I'm a damn godsend.

Reaching between us, I undo my pants and shove them down enough to give my cock space to breathe.

For nearly a month, my cock's been desperate for a taste of Selene. I don't usually make it suffer this long. But Selene's a prize we need to earn. And the wait was worth it.

I slide my cock against her slick pussy, eliciting a moan from us both. Selene's breathing quickens. Her hands rest on my shoulders. When my hand slides under her ass and taps ever so gently, she lifts up as if understanding on some primal level how our bodies will come together.

I swim in her golden eyes as my wet cock teases her hot flesh. I tease her hard nipple, winning a heated gasp from Selene. She's so damn wet. Her pussy sucks at the head of my cock as I enter her. Each inch is more incredible than the last.

Selene makes a pained groan when I stretch her wider. Her back arches and my cock drills deeper. I love how her eyes flutter as my erection tickles the back of her pussy.

"Are you full, baby?" I ask, drawing her attention to my face.

Selene tightens her pussy around my cock and moans approvingly. I worried she'd be afraid. Or unresponsive. I didn't know how a woman like her would react to being fucked.

Selene's painfully aroused. Every little movement gains a smile and moan from her.

Her hips begin to move. My cock feels incredible inside her tight, wet pussy. She tugs at my flesh, drinking every drop of my precum.

Selene moves slow and deliberate, taking me as deep as she can before tightening her pussy and lifting up. Every thrust is addictive.

I can't hold out after waiting for so long. I'm going to come in the first three minutes.

My fingers slide inside her skirt, past her scarred thigh she doesn't want me to know about, and to her sweet pussy. I slip past her soft wet hairs to her clit.

Selene flinches when my finger taps the tender flesh. Yet, she can't stop riding my cock. I feel her struggling between fear and arousal. The need to fuck overwhelms her worries.

I know I'm close. My balls are humming, ready to let loose. I need to make Selene come first. I want to feel her pussy grip hold of my cock and thank it for a job well done.

My thumb makes loving little circles against her clit while my free hand teases her hard nipple. Selene gasps as her head drops back and she grinds harder on my cock. She's as close as I am. A little pinch of her nipple and increased pressure on her clit sends her past her control.

My name fills the SUV. She moans it while bouncing wildly on my cock. My balls let loose, filling her with my jizz.

Despite the powerful orgasm, I keep my eyes open and watch Selene come hard. She's never more gorgeous than when she loses control. Right this moment, she doesn't feel anything beyond our bodies.

SELENE

Hoyt winds up my body, inspiring an orgasm capable of stealing my breath and leaving me spinning. I've never felt so incredible. I can't see past the magnificent man holding me.

I wish I could rip every stitch of clothing from Hoyt's hard body. I want to feel his bare chest. Kiss his belly. Admire his tight ass. Taste his cock.

Of course, my hang-ups are why our first time is in the back seat with us mostly dressed. I'm sure Hoyt would prefer to stretch out in bed and get creative. He isn't a virgin, happy for a quickie. I'm sure he has many wild fantasies about us together.

"Selene," he murmurs, drawing my gaze to his face. "Say you love me."

"I love you, Hoyt Macready," I whisper and admire this passionate man. "You are everything."

Hoyt watches me, seeming vulnerable. I don't understand the look on his face. I've never seen him watch me like this before.

Exhaling softly, he doesn't explain his feelings. Instead, his lips find mine. For the next few hours, we speak with our bodies. I stroke his bare flesh. He kisses mine. His cock remains firmly planted inside me, even in between fucks.

Our second time is slower, more intense. I'm not so overwhelmed by the pleasure. I feel every thrust. My gaze holds Hoyt's. Despite our clothes, I feel no barriers between us.

I don't dare retreat into my mind during sex. No going on autopilot or feigning my pleasure. I only offer Hoyt the truth.

His fingers under my dress and between my legs leave me wild and overstimulated. I grip my nipples, nearly tearing my clothes off. I can't get enough. My pussy is so full of his heat. I whimper Hoyt's name as another orgasm rips through me.

When he comes, Hoyt wraps me so tightly in his arms. He doesn't let me go once our bodies are spent. I rest my cheek on his shoulder, feeling at peace.

"Selene," he says, and I lift my head. Hoyt studies my face. "I don't want to take you to Patrice's place."

"I'm sorry."

"Can't you hang out with me tonight?"

"And go home later?"

"Why not stay and submit to my needs?" he asks, smirking as his hips nudge his dick deeper.

"Um, I can't be naked."

Hoyt wants to argue this point. He's certain he'll still crave me after witnessing my scars. He might be right. If he isn't, things end between us. Why risk everything on a hunch?

"I want to go home and talk to Yazmin," I explain as I slowly lift myself off him.

Hoyt grips my dress, silently threatening to keep me pinned. He relents once the option is losing the battle or tearing the fabric.

"To brag about how good I made you feel?" he asks, sounding insecure.

"She's very curious about if you're a hot lay. She often mentions how you might offer many orgasms."

"Really?"

Shaking my head, I grin. "She knows I love you."

"Of course," he says, sliding his spent cock into his trousers. "She knows all your important stuff."

"Are you okay?"

Hoyt runs his hands through his hair and shakes his head. "I really want to take you home and keep you there for a while."

"I'm sorry, but this is like dating. I've never had a boyfriend."

"I don't want to date you, Selene. That's what people do when they're testing someone out. I know I want you."

"I could come over," I mumble as I fix my dress to ensure everything important is covered. "I like spending time with you and Joie."

Hoyt watches me in that weird way again. Sighing, he rests his head against the window and closes his eyes.

"I don't know the right move here."

Sliding my hand across his, I ask, "What are your options?"

"Bully you into spending the night or allow you to go home with the assumption that you'll return willingly tomorrow for lunch and dinner."

"Can I wear a skirt tomorrow so we can do this again?"

"In the truck?"

"In the living room on the couch would be fine."

Hoyt chuckles at the idea of him fucking me in the family room on a Sunday with his daughter and Tracey in the house. As I scoot closer to him, his arm wraps around me.

"You made a mistake by letting me fuck you," he says, nuzzling my head. "Now, I'm obsessed in a whole new way. I'll need all your free time."

"I'm moving into my rental house soon. You can come over and have sex with me on the couch in my living room. Yazmin can take her dog for a really long walk."

Hoyt grunts, literally making an animal noise to reveal his displeasure.

"Is that a happy sound?" I ask as my hand caresses his chest.

"Yes," he lies.

"Do you support me getting my rental?"

"Of course," he lies.

"Will you fuck me in each room of the rental house?"

"Yes," he replies, finally telling the truth.

"I'll fuck you in all the rooms not belonging to your daughter and Tracey." When Hoyt doesn't respond, I find him frowning. "What's wrong?"

"I don't want to take you home."

"Can't we sit out here for a while? We could listen to music."

Hoyt watches me for a moment before offering a soft smile. "I'm keeping your panties."

Laughing at his expression, I giggle harder when I realize he's serious.

I return home hours later, bare-assed like a wild woman. Hoyt kisses me goodbye before making me promise to come over for lunch tomorrow.

Entering Patrice's house, I feel like a new person. Hoyt got under my skin so quickly. I've craved him from day one. Even when I feared him after the theater, I couldn't deny his pull on my heart.

Now, I've shared myself with him in a way I haven't with anyone else. I held nothing back. My lust was on full display. "Lust" always sounded like such a negative word, implying weakness. However, the desire I feel for Hoyt empowers me.

Patrice and Cheryl ask about the wedding. I tell them about the food served, since I know that'll satisfy their curiosity.

"Had fun, did you?" Patrice asks while Cheryl smirks.

"The reception was fun, yes."

Nearby, Yazmin sits in a chair, petting one of the cats. Once I announce I need to change, she slides out from under the animal and follows me.

Rather than showering, I rest on the bed and enjoy how my body feels.

Yazmin shuts our door, watching me in a strange way. Suddenly, she begins to giggle. She has such a throaty laugh, and I love the sound. I can't remember the last time she got so animated.

"What?"

Still giggling, Yazmin tugs me to my feet and walks me to the bathroom. In the reflection, I witness what Hoyt's hot kisses left behind on my throat. When I gasp, Yazmin laughs harder.

"You're a giant hickey," she says, hugging me from behind. "He marked you good."

"I should have known. I've had a hickey since Thursday. But I only looked in the truck's visor mirror. No wonder Patrice and Cheryl were so amused."

"I'm sorry," Yazmin says, still laughing. "You look beautiful, though."

Turning to her, I exhale softly. "It was amazing. Hoyt made me so hot, even though we were still mostly dressed."

"Was he happy to get laid?"

"Yes, but he wanted more."

"Oral?"

"No," I say, smiling at her teasing. "He wanted me to stay over at his house."

Yazmin's smile fades. "Why can't you?"

"How would I hide my scars if we were in the same bed?"

"Wear a nightgown," she says, playing with the poof on my dress. "He only needs access to the one spot."

"I don't usually sleep in nightgowns," I explain despite Yazmin knowing my every little secret.

"Because you think of that night in the kitchen. At Hoyt's house, you'll think of him. It won't be the same as if you wore it here."

Nodding, I wrap my arms around my body and glance at the shower. "I don't want to clean him off me."

"Then don't."

"Do I smell?"

Yazmin sniffs me and shrugs. "I smell him and you and the goo, but it's not stinky bad. Like I won't gag when we're trying to sleep."

"What about Patrice and Cheryl?"

"Don't hug them, and you'll be fine."

Grinning at the thought of hugging Patrice, I relent to reality and have Yazmin unzip my dress.

"I don't want the day to end," I admit as I hug the dress once I stand in my bra.

"Where are your panties?" Yazmin asks before laughing again. "Why would he want them?"

"I don't know."

Yazmin looks at me as if my boss/boyfriend/lover/dream man is a weirdo.

"Hoyt's a different kind of man," she says, nodding at the thought. "More visceral, less about image. If he wants something, he just takes it. We're used to fake men, so he seems odd."

I smile at her way of describing Hoyt's panty thing. I don't know if that behavior is normal. I just want him to have whatever he desires.

Once I'm changed into sweats and a T-shirt, Yazmin and I sit on the bed. I share about the wedding and what happened afterward. I hold nothing back.

How incredible it felt. How I wanted more. How I felt safer with Hoyt than I have in my entire life. How I wish I could cuddle with him all night and see what kind of bedhead he has in the morning. Yet, I'm still afraid to reveal my ugly body to him and ruin this amazing thing I stumbled on with Hoyt.

Yazmin seems more alert today. Is she inspired by how I stepped out of my comfort zone and didn't fall into a bottomless pit? We might not be the most capable women in this house, let alone the world. However, we're stronger than we suspected.

Today was just the beginning.

HOYT

Selene's been mine in a small way since the beginning. There's an inevitability to our relationship as if we're on a single path with no possible detours.

This fact ought to offer me comfort as I return home and change out of my fancy wedding clothes into my usual blue jeans and a T-shirt. The sun will be out for a while, and Joie seems restless. I should accept Selene will be in my house full time soon, and stop pouting over how she isn't here now.

Once outside, Joie and I enjoy the mild evening weather. Wise Guy runs around, sniffing everything. Tracey sits out back, listening to Crystal Gayle.

My mind imagines Selene at Patrice's house before very deliberately picking her up and moving her like a chess piece to my place. I see her sitting on the front porch, watching Joie and me. She smiles at me like I'm everything. Yeah, that image settles my edginess for now.

"You're so hooked on Selene," Joie teases as she throws the ball.

"You have no idea."

"Are you going to marry her?"

"Yes."

Joie catches the ball and frowns at me. "Really?"

"Yeah. I thought that was obvious."

"I was only teasing."

"Well, I'm not. I don't know jack-shit about romance. You see how our family is about marriage. But I know Selene is it for me. I can't imagine ever caring for any other woman like I do her."

Giving me a wary glance, Joie throws back the ball. "I don't know."

"About what?"

"The whole thing."

"Tell me what your sticking points are. We can figure out solutions. Maybe you'll tell me something I haven't seen."

"She's not like us," Joie says, catching the ball. "Her being around will change a lot of stuff."

"She's already changed things. But I'm still me. You're still you. We'll still like the same shit we do now."

"She won't want to watch Kung Fu movies or go fishing."

"No, maybe not. But she doesn't have to do everything we're doing. She has her own stuff. It's like with Tracey. She's part of the family, but she isn't with us every minute."

Joie's stubborn pout appears. "You're going to want to be with Selene all the time. That's why you want to get married and move her in."

"Joie, don't be a dumbass," I say and she throws the ball hard. Grinning at her temper, I point out, "I never want to spend all my time with anyone. Not you or the club. Sometimes, I want to be alone. Why would that shit change?"

"Women change stuff."

"You sound like Nash."

"No, I sound like Granddad."

"Well, he didn't change his life for anyone. That's why women left him. But Callie likes boating. She enjoys Mexican restaurants and going to the movies on week nights. They have enough in common that she doesn't leave him. But they don't spend all their time together, either. So, no, women didn't change stuff for him. But, yeah, I'll need to include Selene. I thought you liked her."

"I do, but I want stuff to stay the way it is."

"I do, too, but Selene makes me happy. I'm not giving that up."

"Even for me?"

"Especially not for you."

Joie throws the ball hard enough to hurt my hand. I frown at how much she reminds me of me.

"One day, you're going to do your own shit," I explain as I rub my throbbing palm against my jeans. "Whether you move away or stick around, you'll be your own person. So, if I wrap my life around you, I'll end up with nothing when you're gone."

"I'm going to be a Berserker."

"I know," I say despite praying she changes her mind. "But I don't spend all my time with my club family. They don't spend all their time with each other. We have our own shit. You do now, and you will more then. For fuck's sake, a grown woman won't want to ride with her dad all the time."

"I might."

"No, you won't," I insist and throw her the ball. "I liked riding with Ed, but I preferred riding with my friends. You won't be any different. And while you're enjoying your youth, I'll be alone as an old man. You should want me to land a great wife, so I won't cling to you later."

Joie snort-laughs and tosses the ball. "I don't want her changing stuff too much. Like, the way the house looks or what we watch on TV or how we eat. None of that should change," she says, sounding unreasonable and again reminding me of myself. "But Selene's a wuss. I bet she'll go along with whatever we want."

"You've got to treat her nice, though."

"I will. But no babies."

"She can't have any," I say and add, "But we'll probably adopt one."

"Why?"

"Because she might want a baby, and I want her to be happy."

"But she can't have one. That's a sign."

"Joie," I grumble, sighing deeply at how obnoxious the Macready family can be when we want our way. "That woman's suffered a whole lot in her life. Not just the shooting, either. She's went through plenty of hardship. If she wants a houseful of kids, I'll give it to her. That's what people do when they love each other."

Likely noticing how she's pissing me off, Joie considers my words. "I'll allow two kids. That's it. They can be extra loud, though. That way, she'll think the house is full."

I roll my eyes at her attempt at negotiation. Catching the ball, I glance at our home.

"We've got space for a few more without needing to change anything."

"Think of all that poop and the crying. I might have to live with Mikayla or Granddad for a while."

"I'll miss you," I reply, making her snort-laugh again. "But that baby thing isn't happening yet."

"When will she move in?"

"I don't know. I'm not pushing anything. She's still planning on getting a rental house. I hope to talk her into moving in here instead. Why move twice?"

"But if she moves in, what about Yazmin?"

"She'll come, too, I guess."

"Is that what you really want?"

"I don't know. Yazmin is weird to me."

Joie frowns like she gets what I mean. We're not people who bring outsiders into our circle. Adding Selene is a big deal. Yazmin feels like too much. Except Selene can't be happy without her sister.

"This thing I'm feeling is new," I say, and Joie watches me with a new seriousness. "I've never wanted a woman. It's not something I've longed for or whatever. But Selene owns me right here," I say and pat my chest. "I need her. If I have to change some shit to make her happy, I'll do it. I hope you can understand that."

Joie's blue eyes scan our property. She's always lived here. Besides Nicole leaving, nothing has changed in a long time. We have a solid routine. Tracey is the grandmother my own mom never wants to be. Ed and Callie visit regularly. We have Steel Berserkers showing up all the time. We're not lonely people, searching for our missing piece. From Joie's point of view, Selene is unnecessary.

However, my daughter also got excited when Selene agreed to watch her next Little League game. Joie likes the attention. She's curious about Selene, too. More than anything, Joie understands how my woman accepts her. Selene never wonders why Joie doesn't wear dresses or obsess over boys.

I don't know what exactly clicks for my kid. Maybe she understands what my heart needs or she's open to Selene's brand of warmth. Either way, she smiles and accepts how our life is about to change.

SELENE

The last week has been wonderful yet exhausting. Hoyt and I spend our days together followed by dinners with Joie and Tracey. Yazmin joins us on her nights off.

By the end of each day, I'm fatigued. Yet, on the nights Yazmin works, I set my alarm for twelve-thirty so I'll be up when she gets home.

The shifts she shares with Patrice leave her depressed. The nights she works with the other manager or by herself leave her agitated. Either way, she settles down when I listen to her. By two, we're always in bed.

Tonight, I sit in the living room and wait for Yazmin to arrive. The sound of the jeep on the quiet road alerts me. I hurry to the door with my little gun in hand. I'm wary of anyone waiting to cause trouble during her walk from the car to the door.

Hoyt promises I'm safe, but paranoia seems smarter than complacency. Even if I'm certain he has people watching the house at night, I won't stop worrying.

Yazmin shuffles inside, radiating a weird silence. She's a quiet woman. We were trained to keep our mouths shut. Yet, I can feel when she's actually calm rather than hiding in her head.

Tonight, her silence feels oppressive.

Yazmin moves past me and into the bedroom. I follow her, afraid to speak until the door is shut.

"What happened?" I ask when she stands near the closet.

Yazmin rips her hair from its ponytail and shoves herself into the corner. Her eyes stare at me and then through me. She's looking into her past, digging around in what can't be changed.

Joining her in the corner, I squeeze her hand enough for her to see me again.

"Whatever happened, I love you. We're a team. We survived our father. We survived LeVoy. We're in this together."

Yazmin's panic deflates, leaving her depressed.

"Nash fucked me," she whispers, seeming so tired. "I'm in trouble."

"In trouble, how?"

"Patrice will be angry. People will get mad."

"Go back to how that happened. I didn't know you were interested in him."

Yazmin can barely keep her head up. Just as we used to do as kids, she uses my shoulder as a pillow.

"He comes in a lot during my shifts. Not many people do since I take the quiet nights. It's him and Wade and a few others who drop by regularly. Tonight, it was basically empty, but I still felt comfortable working alone. I've closed by myself twice now."

Yazmin sounds so proud when she says those last words. Then, she sinks deeper into her dark place.

"During my first closing, Wade stayed until I locked the bar and got into my car. I thought maybe Hoyt or Patrice asked him to. Tonight, Wade and Glenn weren't around. It was just this one guy and Nash. I was a little nervous because the one regular always asks if I want to see a movie. I explained how I couldn't date customers. That's the lie Patrice told me to say if anyone flirted too much. But this guy Paul wouldn't accept that."

"Why didn't you tell me about him?"

"Patrice says we complain too much. I also wasn't sure he was really a problem. How can I know? Glenn is always around, flirting with Patrice even though she won't ever want him. They have this familiar way of talking. I thought maybe that's what the guy was like with me."

"Did he hassle you?"

"No, but Paul didn't leave when I warned the bar was closing soon. I made the announcement at the last hour mark and then thirty minutes out. He just ordered another drink. I felt something coming off him. Like the way men will stew silently when they're plotting. You can feel them getting angry and talking themselves into something bad."

"Like Dad before he punished us?"

"Yes," Yazmin whispers. "I got nervous. But Nash was there. He's kinda pretty, you know? Not handsome like Hoyt or Wade. Softer like a sweet guy in a romantic comedy."

Yazmin frowns as if her words are wrong. Once I stroke her hand, she sighs.

"I got nervous that Nash couldn't deal with Paul who is a burly guy. I never worried about that with Wade. He's scarier, I guess. I didn't like Wade in the beginning. He has a growly voice, like he's always mad. And his expression is hard."

Yazmin flinches at an unseen threat before continuing, "But Wade's never mean to me. I realized that hardness is just how he is with everyone. I'm not scared of him, but others are. When Wade's around, I don't worry about anyone starting trouble. I wasn't sure Paul was scared of Nash, though."

"Did Paul start trouble?"

Yazmin shakes her head. "Nash walked over and leaned down to whisper to Paul. I don't know what he said. I got nervous about them both hurting me. I started thinking about calling for help."

Cradling her hand, I try to steady my heart. I've considered teaching Yazmin to shoot a gun. However, a part of me fears giving her a weapon.

I know how quickly the darkness can grip a person. Guns offer too fast of a final solution. Though I'm also afraid to have one with me, Hoyt asked me to carry it. I always struggle to tell him no.

"What happened next?" I ask rather than suggest fixes to her situation.

"Paul finished his beer and left. I was still nervous. What if he was waiting for me? Then, Nash came over and said Paul just had a crush. Could I blame him?

251

Nash said I was the prettiest girl in town. Men were bound to get crushes. But Paul knew to leave me alone."

I close my eyes and imagine how Yazmin saw the situation. How vulnerable she'd feel. The way the darkness outside the bar would oppressively bear down on her. How long the drive home might seem. The way her mind is trained to become submissive when afraid. And now, there's a handsome man smiling at her.

"He kissed me," Yazmin whispers. "He asked if I wanted him to stop."

Tears prick at my eyes as I know the answer. Yazmin was trained never to say no or stop. No matter how many years have passed since Robert grew bored of her, she still can't escape his programming.

"It's not your fault," I tell her, adjusting so I can cradle her in my arms. "You get swept up in that old thinking."

"I don't know what I want."

"Nash shouldn't have messed with you. He doesn't understand how your mind works. Hoyt told him to leave you alone."

"I haven't had a man touch me in a soft way in so long. I didn't want Nash, but I'm not sure how I feel now."

Stroking her head, I whisper how everything will be okay. *What else can I do except lie?* I don't know what will happen.

Yazmin's head is wrecked with old programming from our father, Robert, and the doctors. What rules will win out?

I do know Nash doesn't care about her in a real way. Hoyt made his cousin sound damaged with women. "Mommy issues" is how Hoyt put it.

"Nash is forever chasing something he lost when his mom abandoned him," Hoyt explained weeks ago. "But he doesn't actually want to catch these women. He wants to know he can have them. That way, he does the rejecting rather than having them leave him. The guy's mental."

Nash's problems collided with Yazmin's tonight. She's bound to react to what happened with him in a wholly unhealthy way. She stalked Robert. She tried to kill herself after the gardener forced himself on her. She hid in a closet for three days after the security detail tried to rape her.

I don't know what Nash's lust has stirred up inside Yazmin. She's not much stronger than when we arrived.

Hoyt helped me grow, but I'm not healthy by any means. However, I'll be ready to help Yazmin through whatever reaction her broken mind conjures up to deal with this latest trauma.

HOYT

Selene bails on work with a cryptic message about Yazmin suffering from an illness. I ask if she's also sick. Selene says no.

However, she's oddly unresponsive to my questions. The last time she acted this way, she quit. I was forced to call in my greatest weapon. I do the same today.

"She said Yazmin is sick," Wynonna texts after I ask for help deciphering lady-speak.

"What does that mean?"

"Maybe they're on their periods."

Remembering how heavily Wynonna would bleed before she had her kids, I can imagine Selene and Yazmin remaining hunkered down at their house for the day.

Except Selene likely had her period a short time before the wedding. I remember her using the bathroom a lot and ordering different foods those days. We were still getting to know each other, so I didn't think to press the issue.

Even after we've fucked several times, I'm still unsure about asking questions. That's why I send Wynonna back for more info.

"I think you pissed her off," my sister texts.

I dial up Wynonna and grumble, "Why?"

"She sounds weird. Like when you scared her. I asked if you did something wrong. She said no, but I felt like she was lying. So, you know, stop fucking up, Hoyt, and I won't have to keep saving your ass."

"I didn't do shit."

I think about yesterday. Selene was in a great mood. We mostly drove around, looking at property for sale in the next county. We ate lunch at a steak place in the town over. Selene loved the lobster mac and cheese. I couldn't take my eyes off her as she moaned approvingly about lunch.

Before the end of the day, we found a quiet spot. Selene has an entire routine she goes through to get her pants off and cover up with a blanket before she sits on my lap. It's ridiculous how paranoid she is about me seeing her scars.

Yet, the fucking is incredible, and I need her close. If she wanted to screw in a dark cave, I'd agree.

When I dropped Selene off, she smiled at me like she was in awe of her good luck. She seemed so damn happy.

"I didn't fuck up," I tell Wynonna.

"Okay, lie to yourself. Whatever. See you later," she says and hangs up on me.

My day sucks without Selene. Thanks to her messages, I know where to go, complete with instructions about what I'm doing and why. But I miss her being next to me. Feeling grumpy, I grab lunch with my dad and Callie to avoid hanging out alone.

"He isn't getting any loving," Ed tells his wife. "You can always tell when a man's junk has shriveled up."

I ignore their teasing and message Selene. She says she's eating sandwiches with Yazmin in the backyard.

"I miss you," she adds, soothing some of my irritation.

Unable to help myself, I push, "Will you be around tomorrow?"

"Probably, yes," she says, irritating me before adding, "I hope so. I miss you."

Smiling at her words, I accept how Selene might not actually be upset with me. For one fucking thing, there's no reason for her to be pissed. So, maybe Yazmin really is sick. I'm reading too much into shit.

Yet, I find myself wary of stopping by Patrice's house to check on Selene. As if the truth might only ruin my day, so I best stick with her sweet lies.

I still drive by, just to feel like I've been close to her today.

This shit is ridiculous, though. I'm a grown man. Selene's my woman. I should show up and talk to her.

However, Selene's weird little rules have me tied up in knots. I'm afraid to set her off. Worse, I'm terrified of losing her. Selene owns me down deep. If she walks away, I won't bounce back.

That's why I'll continue playing everything overly careful despite my natural habit of bulldozing problems and making them work out for me.

Slow and steady has panned out with Selene. On day one, I wanted to kiss her. I held off but eventually got that kiss. Now, we're lovers. She didn't only submit to me fucking her. Instead, Selene instigated our first time after the wedding.

She *wants* to be with me. If I don't push too hard, I have no doubt she'll give me everything.

Hell, missing me might be good for her. I'm hoping to get her to spend the night soon. A little time apart could help her move faster in that direction.

With my head on straight again, I start riding home. Except the place is empty tonight. Joie plans to sleep over at Mikayla's house and Tracey is at a cooking class. Too restless to be alone, I consider heading to the Pigsty or the Gin Mill.

Before I decide, I receive a text from Goose telling me that shit's going down between her brother and my cousin.

"We pried them apart at the Mill," she explains. "Better come over and talk sense into them."

Looping around on my Fat Boy, I race to the bar. The parking lot is full of hogs. Were they having a fucking party and forgot to invite their president? Or did Goose call in reinforcements who were closer by? Either way, I enter the fray late.

"What's this shit?" I ask Goose and gesture at her bloodied brother seething with one group of Berserkers while a banged-up Nash stands with another cluster.

"It's chick shit," she mutters and throws up her hands. "They're fighting over a fucking woman. I don't know what's wrong with you twats."

Grinning at her exasperation, I walk toward Nash. Based on his expression and busted face, he wasn't the aggressor. I change directions and join Armor.

"What woman are you two fighting over?" I ask, squatting down where Armor's nursing his wounds.

Armor flashes a glare at his sister, who shrugs and says, "I don't lie to our president."

My VP focuses his anger at Tomcat nearby before asking me, "Don't you know?"

"If I did, I wouldn't be asking you."

"No, you would. You love to pull that 'just asking a question' bullshit when you already know all the answers."

"Well, this time, I'm actually clueless."

Goose grunts her disapproval while Armor can barely avoid running at Tomcat again. His rage fills the air before he finally focuses on me.

"He fucked Yazmin."

I glance at Tomcat, who is explaining shit to Hobo. My mind returns to Selene's weird behavior today. Yazmin's illness suddenly makes sense.

"How do you know?"

"He bragged about it."

"Tell me exactly what he said."

Armor sees something on my face. Probably my rage seeping out from behind my calm exterior. His glare returns to Tomcat.

"I asked why Gitty was working Yazmin's shift. She said Yazmin was sick. Tomcat acts all put out like it wasn't his fault. Claimed she was going to make a big deal out of shit. I didn't know what the fuck he was talking about," Armor mutters.

Again, I feel him ready to take a run at our club brother. He glares at the other man while continuing, "I should have known what he did since he's a fucking skank bitch. But you made clear how Yazmin was off-limits. That's when he claimed she was sad and lonely, so he threw her a bone. Now, he was worried she would get clingy."

"That's when you busted him up?"

"What the fuck else was I supposed to do?" Armor hollers at me. "Talk to him about his fucking feelings?"

I glance at Tomcat sulking at how he got hammered by Armor. I'm sure he fought back. But between them, it was never going to be an even fight.

Walking toward my cousin, I think of his insatiable need to fuck women and then complain about their clinginess. His parents wired his brain wrong with all their weird romantic choices. Glenn spent years vocally in love with Patrice. Mattie drank too much, screamed constantly, and liked to throw shit. I never liked visiting their house.

Tomcat's no longer a boy. He's got his own damn kids to raise. He shouldn't still be pulling this crap.

In the past, I never got involved. I let him bang every girl in the Valley. Never rode his ass to do better by his kids. Just allowed him the space to succeed or fail. Now, my leniency has come back to bite me in the ass.

I grab Tomcat by the scruff of his neck and yank him away from the others. When they try following, I glare back at them until they catch a fucking hint.

"I told you to stay away from her," I growl into his ear.

"She was lonely. You could see that shit a mile away."

"She's fucked in the head," I mutter and slap him upside his head. "She was a piece of shit's toy. She's been in the nuthouse. They cranked her brain with electroshock. Yazmin needs therapy, not your dick."

Tomcat immediately turns the blame on me. "You never told me that."

"I shouldn't have to give you someone's fucking medical records to get you to listen. I said she was screwed in the head. Patrice warned you to stay the fuck away. Armor clearly has a thing for her. You knew all that shit, yet you fucked her anyway. What the hell is wrong with you?"

"She was looking in that way women do when they need someone close. You know that look."

"Yeah, I know it. But I also know you weren't helping her out. You were fucking the new chick in town. Don't act like you did her a favor."

Remembering Yazmin squatting down in the theater parking lot, I can't even fucking guess what goes on in her head.

My rage takes over, and I shove him. "Maybe you did it to mess with Armor. Or you wanted to push my buttons since you're so fucking sure I won't hurt you. Or maybe you saw that broken woman and got a thrill by messing with her."

"I like her, okay?" he hisses at me. "Why is Armor sniffing around her fine while I'm a sick freak for doing the same thing?"

"Did you already forget where your dick ended up, asshole?"

"You act like you own the two of them," Tomcat growls, trying to make me the bad guy. "Like you've got a two-for-one deal. But you weren't there. I know how she looked at me. She didn't want Armor. She wanted me. And I wanted her. So we fucked. He can shove his hurt feelings up his ass instead of coming at me like I'm the fucking enemy."

Exhaling hard, I mutter, "I hope the fuck was worth it. You've pissed me off. You've cut your club brother off at the knees rather than hashing out what's what. And you fucked with that poor woman's mental state. I hope it was the best screw of your life because you won't live this shit down quietly."

Tomcat refuses to admit he messed up. He's like his damn mom. They're always the victim. They can't be at fault because then they might need to change. And nothing scares them more than facing the monster in the mirror.

Of course, Mattie means nothing to me. However, Tomcat is my club brother. He's also blood. Cutting him loose isn't an option. Crushing him under my boot might work, though.

I hear the pop a second before the gunshot rips through Tomcat's chest and into my arm. He topples against me while I bring us both to the ground.

Glancing at Armor, I find him with his gun out. For a split second, I think his temper got away from him.

Except the shot came from the other side of the road. The same direction Armor is aiming at now.

Gunshots ring out like they did in the old days in McMurdo Valley. Our battles with the Jordans were followed by a war with moonshiners. Next was the drug-running Edwards family.

One battle after another for years. Our people got out lucky. We rarely lost anyone. Our shots were better, our revenge swifter.

I turn Tomcat over to find him stunned by the blood rushing out of him. I press my hand over his chest wound and whistle for Goose to get her ass over here.

She scrambles toward us and rips off her shirt. Using it to hold back the blood, she gives me a terse nod. As a young woman, Goose worked as an EMT. She's been our medic for years. Right now, I need her here rather than chasing down the shooter.

Ignoring my arm wound, I rush past a few cars as my guys fire into the woods. They're obviously not aiming at anyone, just trying to rattle the sniper. I quickly hook up with Armor behind a truck.

"One asshole, high-powered rifle," Armor explains and points at the dense woods. "He's being careful with his shots. Most of this noise is from us. But I hear him, too."

Glancing back at Tomcat, I feel myself worrying. What if this is an attack by the Jordan family? Was I too soft on them? Has Selene neutered the berserker inside me? Is she in danger? How about Joie?

I'm tempted to pull my phone and call for a lockdown. Make sure everyone's protected. Patrice and Cheryl are handy with their weapons but how will they know to lock down?

"Ruin," Armor growls at me and pokes my bleeding arm.

I glare at him, finding his gaze as cold as ever.

"Do you need to talk to a fucking therapist?" he spits out, never offering a bit of pity. "I could try asking the shooter to give you a breather to figure shit out."

I get his point. My head's screwed on wrong. Someone came to the club's bar and shot my people. I imagine Joie and Selene dead. My world is over. I have nothing to lose. There's only violence and death now.

My berserker's heart takes control, pushing me to stop hiding. I run out from behind the truck. Zigzagging from one vehicle shield to another, I get closer to my target. Armor follows while the others offer cover fire.

I lose the part of me softened by fatherhood and romance. The lavish house, the mayor's job, and a decade of quiet living peel away until I'm a beast in search of its prey.

Inhaling rage, exhaling vengeance, I'm in the zone now. I fear nothing. I can't picture Joie or Selene in my head. Everyone falls into the darkness. I just see my target as he realizes we're on his tail.

The asshole makes the mistake of moving south rather than north. The woods he retreats toward are thick and thorny. The rocky ground makes movement dicey. One wrong footstep might slide his ass right down into a stony creek.

His mistake allows me to move faster. I know this land like the back of my fucking hand. I grew up in the Valley, exploring it day and night. As a restless child, I never wanted to go home. This land was my playground.

I separate from Armor. We crouch low and move faster through the thorny brush. The gunman occasionally shoots, unsure where we are in the dark woods. These primeval trees block out the sun. Getting lost in here would be easy for someone in a panic.

In contrast, Armor and I aren't in a hurry. We move with purpose. I can picture the gunman's steps. I hear him grunting at times as the thorns grip his clothes. He lets out a curse when he slips, sending his ass hard on the ground.

Closer, we prowl. Our every step remains deliberate. He becomes more frantic, feeling us catching up to him. His shots go wild. A bullet flies close to my head. I don't hesitate, still herding my prey to its doom.

This part of the Valley is full of random creeks and shallow caves. The land isn't safe for hiking. No one but crazy fucks traverse this area.

Armor and I played here as kids. We trained here as young men. Today, we recognize how the shooter's frantic bad choices have corralled him right into Hawk's Gorge.

The asshole stumbles back and down the embankment. Holding the high ground, we can wait him out. Whether he runs right or left, we'll easily track him.

I peer through the overgrowth as a thorn slices my cheek. The gunman tries to climb up the other side of the gorge. The rock breaks away under his fingertips. Last night's rain left the dirt soft and muddy. He can't gain a footing.

Panicked now, the man fires wildly in our direction. His fearful face is hidden behind a mask. His heavy black boots grow muddy in the shallow creek. I watch him glance to his right and then his left. He could run. But he won't get far. The gorge will keep him pinned for at least half a mile.

I aim my gun and fire into his gut. No reason he should get off easy. Let him suffer before bleeding out.

The guy falls back, still holding his rifle. He fires again toward the ridge where we watch. Armor's shot rips off the asshole's fingers. The rifle drops to the ground. I whistle for Armor to watch me while I descend the gorge.

Once the shooter reaches for a holstered pistol with his left hand, Armor takes those fingers, too.

Groaning, the asshole knows he's fucked. I walk toward him, kicking away his weapons. My big boot lands on his crotch first. I hear air gush from his lungs at the shock of my foot moving to his open wound.

I lean down and rip off his mask. I fear one of the Jordans will be looking back at me. Hell, I half expect to find Jacksyn seeking revenge for his brother.

Instead, I frown at an unknown man.

"Who the fuck are you?" I ask as I ease my foot off his gut.

"Just kill me."

"No, I'm not doing that."

While he holds his guts in place, I rifle through his nearby bag. I find weapons and ammo but no ID. Makes sense for him not to bring his life story with him on a job. Based on his supplies, the guy's a pro.

"Ruin," Armor says when he joins me in the gorge, and Hobo keeps watch up top. "He got you."

I look at where Armor gestures to find a new wound on my side. Between all the thorns and my arm, I hadn't really noticed the bullet taking a chunk from right above my hip.

The gunman chuckles. "I did get you, motherfucker."

Armor snarls immediately. Not over my second wound. He hears the asshole's accent. I lift the shooter off the ground and shove my hand in his open wound.

"Who sent you?"

The asshole nearly passes out from the pain. He tries to hit me where I took the second bullet.

I slam him against the soft dirt wall and ask my question again. After the third time, he's gone limp and stares with glazed eyes.

"I didn't get a name," he mumbles in that sticky Louisiana accent. "A big shit back home had someone hire me. I never met the main fuck."

"Are you here alone?" Armor asks, texting into his phone.

"I was supposed to kill you," the guy says. "Once you were out of the way, I could finally finish off the bitch."

Logically, I should keep this fuck alive longer and tear more info from him. However, his words imply he was Selene's gunman. This sick motherfucker looked at that fragile woman and filled her body with bullets. My restraint cracks under the weight of the image of her bleeding on the ground.

I yank the guy's intestines from his body and throw him into the mud. He flops around, making gurgling noises while I turn to Armor still on his phone.

"Who the fuck are you texting?"

"Patrice. She's got them locked down. I guess someone already called her."

I look at the dead guy and then up at Hobo. My head swims from the rage. I want to kill LeVoy this very fucking second. Just jump on my hog and keep riding until I get to his shitty town. I'll tear the son of a bitch limb from limb.

"He'll know you're coming," Armor says as he gestures at the incoming hog riding from the gorge's entrance half a mile up.

"What?"

"You're bleeding out, asshole," Armor says as if I'm an obnoxious kid he's ready to spank. "Stop talking and thinking. Just go quiet. I'll lock down our people. We'll deal with LeVoy later."

I don't feel out of it. My mind seems sharp. Yet, I climb on the hog, unsure how it got down the embankment. Walla Walla's voice sounds weird as he tells me to hold on. When he says we're headed to the hospital, I assume we're checking on Tomcat.

I don't feel fucked up until the nurse starts asking my name. That's when I realize I'm on a damn bed.

My father appears above me and smiles casually. "Getting slower in your old age," Ed taunts and places a hand on my forehead. "But still a lucky fucker. Neither shot hit anything important."

"How's Nash?"

"He'll survive. Too bad the shot didn't blow off his dick and make his life easier."

I look around the room. In the hallway, I spot the familiar stance of a man who's always had my back.

"Is Selene okay?" I ask Armor. "Where's Joie?"

Ed answers instead of my VP. "The first one is on her way over. The other one thinks you fell off your hog. She'll do better without knowing the truth until you're home. Everyone you care about is okay."

"For now."

"Worry about the asshole later," Armor insists, finally walking over to my bed.

Running a hand over his bald head, Ed nods. "Focus on looking okay for when your skittish woman arrives and feels like the world is ending."

Ed is right. Selene struggles with her emotions on even the best day. Last Wednesday, she nearly cried when a young woman showed off her baby. On Friday, she got spooked by a car backfiring and nearly ran off.

Seeing me in the hospital will leave her fucked up.

"I need to get home."

Ed shakes his head. "You need to rest."

"Am I dying? Am I bleeding out? Why do I need to stay?"

"So the nice nurses can baby you overnight. The doctor stitched you up when you got in. Don't you remember that?" When I don't answer, Ed nods. "That's why you're staying overnight."

"Do I look fucked up? I can't have Selene see me weak. She can't process that crap right."

Ed grins at me while he takes a seat. "You're kinda cute all stupid in love like this, Hoyt. I'm glad this woman clicked for you."

"She's fragile."

"No doubt."

"She needs me to fix her world."

"No, I think she needs what most women do," my dad says and pulls out his little bag of peanuts that he's always eating. "Just love her. Tell her how pretty she looks. Give her something sweet for those special days the ladies go gaga over. Make her come in bed. Doesn't take much."

I think to mention how he's on wife number four, so maybe he isn't the best man to give me advice. Except I don't know many happily married people. Not in my family or within the club.

Though I don't trust Ed's wisdom, I do value my gut instinct. It's never done me wrong. Today, I worried I'd fucked up with the Jordan family. So far, though, my gut was right about them.

It was also correct about LeVoy. I should have killed him right off. None of this legal shit. He was only biding his time while digging around into the people protecting Selene. Once he got his shot, he took it. His assassin missed.

Unfortunately for LeVoy Garry, my guy won't be so sloppy.

SELENE

Patrice rarely explains anything. She believes she's right and we're stupid. So, she tells us what needs to happen and expects us to follow. It's her way or the highway. Patrice isn't so different from LeVoy or my father in that way. At least she seems smarter than them and less likely to get us killed.

Tonight, when she barks for us to get down to the ground and stay away from the windows, I don't ask why. I never consider pushing for details or taking control. I just do what I'm told. Yazmin grips my hand as we sit in a corner and wait for our next instructions.

For sixty minutes, I don't even consider what might be happening. As my mind wanders, I imagine Yazmin and Nash. Next, I picture myself at Joie's next baseball game. I fantasize about Hoyt's expression when he orgasms inside me.

Not once do I come up with a plan to escape or fight back. If the threat gets through Patrice, no way will I be able to stop it.

That's why I'm pleasantly calm when Goose walks through the door and toward me.

Her words are filled with lies. I feel her editing herself. I don't know Goose well, but she's like Patrice and Wynonna. They don't hold back normally. Today, she is careful with her words. However, I force myself to read between the lines.

Hoyt's hurt but not dead. He's at the hospital. Nash is, too. Hoyt wants to see me. I need to help him. Goose brought a car and an escort.

I should leave Yazmin at home. She doesn't need to be on display. Yet, once trouble hits, I reach for her. From childhood through LeVoy and now in McMurdo Valley, we fall into our patterns.

Unable to think straight, I hold on to her hand as I push my feet to take the next step. Cheryl reminds us to put on shoes. She also hands my purse to me, understanding how I'm not in control of myself. I don't want to leave the house. If it were up to me, I'd rather hide.

Except an injured Hoyt wants to see me.

As Goose drives the SUV, I don't ask questions. Two motorcycles flank the vehicle. Goose hums along to Joe Walsh on the radio. I only know who the singer is because of Hoyt. He listens to this music when we're driving. I often ask who someone is, just to hear him speak. I love Hoyt's voice.

We arrive at the recently built midsize county hospital with its shiny new signs. Hoyt said he nearly lost his mind going to all the meetings necessary to get this place up and running.

"Being responsible fucking sucks," he muttered one day when we drove past the building.

Hoyt only wants to play. He's happiest when the mayor's responsibilities are off his shoulders, leaving him to be a wild man.

"Why don't you quit? I asked once.

"And give my enemies a win?" he replied, frowning hard at the thought. "No, my suffering is worth knowing I hold power over them."

Though Hoyt loves to play, he also knows the downside of being weak and lazy. If he were like me, the club would have been stomped on by their enemies long ago. McMurdo Valley and the Steel Berserkers Motorcycle Club need Hoyt to suffer for them.

The emergency room is filled with bikers whose names escape me. I hold Yazmin's hand as we follow Goose through the crowd of men. Several non-Steel Berserkers cower in the corners of the large room, afraid of what happens if the club starts spilling blood.

Feeling like I'm walking in mud, each step becomes a chore. Yet, I must keep moving forward. I don't focus on the journey, only on the destination.

We arrive at a doorway where Wade stands watch. His gaze flashes to Yazmin before focusing on me.

"Hoyt is doped up," Wade explains. "He acts like he's fine. The doctors stitched him up. The shots went through. Nothing major damaged. Just blood loss. He'll want to leave in a few hours."

I stare into Wade's blue eyes and think to ask what happened. Except I probably don't want to know the details.

"Nash is still in surgery," he says more to Yazmin than me. When she doesn't react to his words, he reaches over to open Hoyt's door.

Before I enter, I remember to ask, "Where's Joie?"

"At her friend's house. We've got someone guarding her, just in case."

Exhaling softly, I think of Hoyt's complicated daughter, both confident and insecure. Hoyt does a great job helping Joie through this tricky time in her life. He has to be okay for her.

I start to enter the room, still attached to Yazmin.

"Best for you to go alone," Wade says, and his tone leaves little room to argue.

I look at my sister, who stares at me emotionlessly. I wish she would cry or get angry. Instead, she's lost in her head.

Wade yanks a chair from an empty room and drops it near Hoyt's door. "She can wait here."

Yazmin studies me with her blank expression before saying, "Hoyt Biker Man wants to see you."

Smiling at her wording, I force my fingers to release hers. I turn toward Hoyt, resting quietly. Once I enter, the door shuts behind me.

Hoyt's shirtless torso is bandaged just below his rib cage. His right bicep is also dressed. An IV gives him fluids. A silent monitor reveals his strong vitals.

I stand next to his bed and struggle with how he nearly died. Today, Hoyt felt the burn of bullets tearing through his beautiful body.

My breath catches, and I recall the night in the kitchen. I'd fallen hard on the ground. I couldn't breathe. Remaining motionless in a pool of blood on the white marble floor is probably what saved me. The gunman thought he finished the job.

He was probably also startled by the sound of Yazmin approaching the house. I'd cried out once after the second shot. She heard the gunshots, too, no doubt.

My sister had been fearless in the face of danger when she thought I might be in trouble. Her love for me is why I'm here now. Would I have been as brave?

"Selene," Hoyt says, breaking through my panic.

My tears block my view. He feels so far away. Someone hurt him today. He could have died. I would have lost my love.

I see Wynonna crying over her brother and friend. I hear Joie calling for her dad.

Hoyt's hand wraps around mine, tugging me closer. I wipe my eyes and see him clearer.

"You're here with me," he says as I cry. "We're okay."

Nodding, I don't feel his words. I remember the pain and fear I felt as I lay dying. I'm back in that world. Hoyt feels too far away.

His calloused fingers wipe tears from my cheeks. Though wanting to tell him how much I love him, I choke on the words.

"I'm going home soon," Hoyt says as I lean my cheek against his palm. "I want you to stay with me at my place."

My head swims. I think about who hurt him today. Was it that evil old man with the rough sons? Or those people from the movie theater? Hoyt has so many enemies.

"You can bring Yazmin," he continues when I only cry. "I'll have you go to Patrice's and pack up enough for a few days."

Shaking my head, I don't know what's right.

"Selene," Hoyt says, and I force my gaze to meet his. "I know about Nash and Yazmin. She shouldn't be alone, but I need you to help me as my assistant and my girlfriend."

Nodding, I wipe my eyes again. "I'm sorry."

"About what?"

"I don't know. Crying, I guess."

"If you came in here and acted normal, I'd get my feelings hurt."

Grinning at his words, I take his hand and ask, "Who hurt you?"

"It doesn't matter."

"Was it because of me?"

"No, baby. It was just an evil fuck. He's dead. But I still need you close. I can't rest if I don't know where you are. Do you understand?"

Exhaling deeply, I squeeze his hand and nod. Despite my insecurities, I believe Hoyt loves me. While I don't trust his interest long term, I know his heart wants me right this moment.

"Are you in pain?" I ask and stroke his forehead.

"Naw, they've got me flying on these meds."

Smiling at his expression, I kiss him softly and hope he knows how important he is to this town, his club, his family, and me.

After I sit on the edge of the bed, Hoyt wraps his hand around my waist and rests it against my back. I realize he's pinning me to him, so I can't flee.

Hoyt struggles to stay awake. The medicine pulls him toward sleep. Yet, he opens his eyes as if startled. Finding me still at his side, Hoyt breathes easier and offers a small smile.

I can't believe I own the power to soothe someone as powerful as him. He's a virile creature, capable of great destruction when his temper breaks loose. Right now, though, he seems soft and fragile.

As Hoyt dozes off, his large frame claims most of the bed. His muscled chest lifts and drops with every deep breath. I admire him while forcing my gaze away from his covered wounds. Every time I imagine his blood spilled today, my panic returns.

271

So, I picture Hoyt at home. He's in his bed. I can't really picture the room, but I imagine it's filled with dark wood.

The ceiling is likely high. Hoyt prefers large areas. He's a wide-shouldered man topping out over six-four. The world gets too small sometimes. I see him ducking when we visit Miss Millie Miller's house with the tight doorways and low-hanging plants.

Hoyt's home breathes different from hers. The high ceilings allow light to fill the space.

In my mind, I imagine helping him into clean clothes once we get to his house. He'll rest in bed. I can clean the blood from his skin. I see specks in his beard. Once he's safely at home, I'll wash away as much of today's violence as possible.

I keep that hope in mind when Hoyt wakes and asks Goose to escort me to Patrice's.

"Get her packed up for a few days and bring her home. I'll meet you there."

I don't want to leave Hoyt's side. He smiles at how I refuse to budge despite my butt going numb an hour ago.

"I need you at my place," Hoyt says, giving me a goal to focus on. "I'm not sticking around here much longer. I want you at my house when I get there."

Nodding, I fall back into my easy habit of obeying. Hoyt suffered today. The least I can do is give him what he needs to feel like himself. I kiss him goodbye before walking into the hallway, where Yazmin stares at the floor.

I take her hand and follow Goose. We walk past the same people as when we arrived. The songs on the SUV's radio are similar to the ones when we drove to the hospital. Time feels stuck.

Patrice struggles with the plan of Yazmin and me going to Hoyt's. She fears I'll mess up things, get fired, and end up at her house forever. I explain how Hoyt needs me to take care of him.

"I'm his assistant," I say, and she cocks an eyebrow.

"You're more than that."

Shrugging, I fill half of the suitcase with my belongings. Yazmin adds her own.

"Why does she have to go?"

"Hoyt wants me to have help taking care of him."

Patrice considers my words. "Well, he is a big baby when in pain. Makes sense."

Nodding at her agreement, I carry the suitcase and walk back outside with Yazmin. Goose waits at the SUV. The two bikers idle next to her. None of them are talking. The club remains on edge, making me wonder if the threat is truly over.

Rather than worry, I imagine Hoyt in a different SUV on his way home. Can he walk on his own? His house has so many steps. Even with upper body wounds, the pain, blood loss, and medicine can weaken his body. I remember how much difficulty I had moving, even months after my shooting.

I'll take care of him. Help Tracey with whatever she needs. Make sure Joie is okay. Yazmin will be at my side.

Weakness might be how I'm wired, but I'm not useless. I'll pull myself together to make life easier for the man I love.

HOYT

The ride home nearly kills the chill I'm riding on my pain meds. I'm in a rush to leave the hospital. My enemies are watching for signs of weakness. Nash won't be going anywhere soon. That means I need to make a show of heading home.

The ride is a motherfucker. I swear Armor hits every damn bump. When I bark at him to be careful, he growls for me to stop whining.

"Maybe the mayor should have paved this fucking road," he adds as we near my house.

I probably call him several choice names. I can't be sure since the pain and meds work together to leave my head screwed on wrong.

Tracey is waiting for me on the porch. When I arrive, she pretends she isn't worried. However, I can tell she's been crying.

"You're like my mom," I say, unable to edit myself when the pain meds fuzz up my brain. "But loyal."

Tracey smiles at my praise as she guides me into the house. I stop before entering. Turning back, I eye the road and frown.

"Where's Selene?"

Armor checks his phone. "A few minutes out."

"We'll wait."

"Hoyt, you should rest," Tracey insists.

Ignoring her reasonable suggestion, I stare out at the road and wait for the woman I never knew I needed. Selene was so scared at the hospital, crying over my bloodied body. I need to see her calm again.

As I use the doorframe to keep me upright, Tracey asks Armor, "Was today an isolated incident?"

"Seems that way. But we'll need to cut the head off the snake."

"I'm going to tear that fucking head off," I growl as my anger zaps more of my energy.

Tracey and Armor chuckle at my slurred threat.

"Yeah, about that," Armor says and crosses his arms. "This asshole knows you. He might have people looking for you. Meaning you riding into that Louisiana shithole makes no sense. Plus, you won't be ready to handle this problem right away. While you heal up, he could hire other gunmen. Makes more sense for you to send someone else to rip off his scummy fucking head."

"Like who? Are you gonna do it?"

"I was thinking Nomad."

"He didn't even care enough to come to our mandatory meeting," I mutter, sounding like I'm about to cry. "I'm not actually sad. It's the Norco shit they gave me."

"Sure," Armor replies while Tracey glances toward the road as the sound of motorcycles gets louder. "I'll track down Nomad and get his ass here tomorrow. He could have Selene's husband in the morgue by the weekend."

Nodding, I turn to Tracey. "Is Joie okay?"

"She's none the wiser. She'll be home tomorrow after school."

"What if someone tries to hurt her?"

Armor frowns as if I'm stupid to ask. "Hobo is parked out in the woods near her friend's house. He won't let anyone hurt your baby."

Exhaling deeply, I feel weak. If I weren't out of it, I'd punch someone to prove my power. Instead, I wobble and wait for Selene.

My woman has such a deliberate way of moving. As if she spent a lifetime worrying that one false step might lead to a painful punishment. When we go anywhere, she acts the same way. Tonight, though, she darts from the SUV's back seat as soon as the car stops.

"You should lie down," she says, rushing to my side.

"I was waiting for you."

Selene smiles at my words before her gaze focuses on my bandaged arm. I know she wants to cry again.

275

She's got no stomach for violence, having built up zero resistance to it over the years.

Yazmin exits the SUV in the passive way Selene normally moves. She takes a bag while Goose grabs the other.

I catch Armor frowning at her. His ego is bruised. I think he hoped to seduce the broken woman. He's got far more patience than I would. Clearly, more than Nash. That's a shitstorm waiting for me when I'm better.

For now, I wrap an arm around Selene and slowly march my ass into the house. By the time we arrive upstairs, I'm exhausted and Selene's crying. She heard me wince during a middle stair and got riled up emotionally.

Selene and Tracey strip me down to my boxers before I ease into my comfortable bed. That's when the realization hits me. I'm finally about to get Selene into my bed.

"I'll be downstairs," Tracey says, backing away as if afraid to take her eyes off me. "I'll help get Yazmin settled in a guest room. Fix you up dinner, too."

As Selene watches Tracey leave, I'm relieved to see her tears lessen.

"Do you love me?" I ask, and her tired gaze locks on to mine as she nods. "Then, come cuddle up. I'm feeling weird. Weak, I guess. I have no control of myself. I hate that shit. It's why I rarely drink heavily or get stoned. I want to know where I am and who to punch at all times."

Selene doesn't hesitate. Dressed in light gray sweatpants and a loose half-sleeved shirt, she looks more casual than I'm used to. I can imagine her soft flesh hiding underneath those comfy clothes.

Of course, fucking isn't an option right now. I doubt my dick will work when I'm flying so damn high.

Resting against my uninjured side, Selene asks if I need anything to get comfortable. I'm not lying when I say no. Between the meds and Selene at my side, I don't even feel myself crash.

Later in the night, Selene helps me piss and eat the food Tracey brought. At some point, she changes into a red-flowered, long-sleeved, calf-length white nightgown. I can't imagine this getup is more comfortable than her sweats.

Except after Selene turns off the lights, her lips find mine. I swim in the heat of her kisses. Her hand slides into my boxers, finding me at half-staff. With a bit of stroking, she has my cock rock hard.

"You said fucking relaxes you," she whispers as she tugs down my boxers and straddles my lap. "It relaxes me, too. This way, we can sleep better."

Smiling at the way her pussy slides across my erection, I wish I could strip her bare and enjoy every inch of her body. Of course, I'm too weak to do much of anything tonight, even if Selene didn't have her hang-ups.

We still enjoy a great fuck. Afterward, I rest on my good side and wrap my injured arm around the back of her. She fits perfectly against my body.

Though I already knew I loved Selene, I feared she'd bail at the first sign of trouble. Violence tears apart the thin armor she wraps herself in. She might not be able to survive in my life.

Despite her fear, Selene doesn't look away from what happened today. She takes care of me all night. In the morning, when I'm in pain but too stubborn to use the hard meds, she massages my scalp and helps me relax. Regular Tylenol takes enough of the edge off to get me through the morning.

"I'm glad you're here," I tell her more than once. "For weeks, I've wanted to wake up next to you."

Selene smiles so sweetly as if I'm the nicest man she's ever met.

All morning, I feel pretty damn chill. I don't even mind how Yazmin startles me more than once. The woman's like a ghost, moving soundlessly around the house. I never hear her coming. Then, bam, she's suddenly at my side to see if I need a coffee refill.

"You're not at the Gin Mill," I finally tell her. "You don't need to serve me."

"Why am I here, then?"

"To serve her," I say and gesture at Selene.

The sisters eyeball each other for the longest time. I wonder if they're speaking telepathically. Maybe so, since they break into a smile at the same time.

Yazmin still gets me a refill, but she isn't so present for the rest of the morning.

As the sisters help Tracey with lunch, I sit on the front porch. Wise Guy rests at my feet. I tell myself he's clingy out of concern for his master.

Of course, I'm usually gone during the day. Maybe the dog's weirded out by me breaking into his private time.

Though I'm chill all morning, I haven't forgotten why I called for Nomad. He shows up by walking out of the woods. I have no fucking idea where he parked his hog.

The club's enforcer is a massive man with a wide chest and shoulders. His legs are like tree trunks. Many of his clothes are made for fat guys, meaning they're usually tight across his chest and too loose around his waist. He wears his dark, wavy hair long. Silas Bennings is all muscle, hair, and rage.

Nomad stalks up to the house, looking wild-eyed and exhausted. He's always been reclusive and a little off. Since his wife ran off, he's been downright weird.

Nomad ignores Wise Guy growling at him and glares at me. I only smile since I'm surprised Armor got Nomad to leave the woods.

My enforcer drops into the nearby seat and rubs his hands together. "What is it that you need?"

"What have you been up to lately?"

"Got me a new woman," Nomad announces as his gray eyes size up the day. "Really pretty one."

"Who's this?"

"Her name's Landry. Real beautiful. I'm just waiting for her husband to die of natural causes. If that doesn't pan out, I'm putting him down."

"Did this Landry ask you to handle her old man?"

"No. She doesn't know me yet. I'm waiting until she pops out her latest kid. Women never feel sexy when they're so far along. I know that because your sister yelled the information at me when she was huge with Ralph Junior."

"I feel like this is a topic we should explore more."

"Why?"

"Oh, I don't know," I say, scratching at my beard while I study him. "I think you killing a Shmoe so you can have his wife might be crossing a line."

"Outlaw bikers shouldn't have lines."

"I thought you didn't kill kids."

"I don't."

"Then, you have a line. And maybe killing this guy ought to be one you don't cross."

"He isn't good to her," Nomad explains, shrugging his big shoulders. "Cheats. I think he might be hitting her. I know he yells plenty. I hear him when I'm hiding in their backyard."

"Well, seeing as you've put so much thought into this plan, I'm not interfering."

Nomad cocks one of his thick eyebrows. "What could you do?"

"Organize the entire club to jump on you at the same time. I bet we could take you down that way."

Nomad's rough face smirks. "You're in a funny mood. Did they give you good meds at the hospital?"

"Only the best, but I'm not on them. Don't want to feel slow if there's trouble."

Nomad glances around the property. His gaze lingers on Eagle's hog parked nearby. Finally, he focuses on me.

"So, what did you want from me?"

I glance back into the house to see if Selene might overhear. Lowering my voice, I say, "The guy that shot Nash and me."

"The dead one?"

"Yeah. He wasn't here to fuck with the club. My woman—"

"Since when do you have a woman?"

"Since a few weeks back. If you were around more, you'd know that."

"I can't babysit you, Hoyt," he says and sighs while dragging a hand through his wild hair. "Glad you're getting quality pussy, though."

"Selene's a good woman with a nasty ex. He tried killing her before. Put six bullets in her beautiful body. I wanted him dead before he sent someone here. Now, I have nothing holding me back."

"What was doing that before?"

"I sometimes forget being a member of the Steel Berserkers means I'm above the law."

Nomad smirks. "You spend too much time avoiding those lines you can't cross."

"Exactly, but this guy came to my fucking town to kill my fucking woman. He put bullets in my fucking body. Nash will be in the hospital for days to get over the hole in his chest. So, now, I've got no more lines regarding the asshole."

"I'll kill him," Nomad says and glances at Wise Guy who now sits at my feet. "Just tell me who and where. I got nothing I can do around here anyway. Not until Landry has her baby. I'll get your problem iced and be back by the time her new one comes along."

"How many does she have?"

"This will be number five. He likes her barefoot and pregnant. Keeps her from running off when he's on a long haul."

"What makes you think she doesn't want the same things he does?"

"I hear her crying on the phone in the backyard when her kids are asleep. Landry isn't happy. Soon, she'll be rid of him, and I'll make her life better."

"What do you want with raising another man's kids?"

"I was already going to do that, wasn't I?" he snarls at me. "Had little booties picked out and everything."

Nomad's ex-wife wanted a bad boy. She sure got one with him. Quickly, though, she realized his secrets weren't fun. Neither was cleaning the blood out of his clothes. That led a bored Kati to sniff around other men.

Nomad saw none of it. He suffered from tunnel vision, focused only on her youth and beauty. When their kid was born, he was fucking thrilled. I'd never seen anyone happier.

Well, the celebration ended when the real daddy showed up. Nomad nearly killed him. Kati ran off with what was left of the guy. She took the kid—the one Nomad had fallen head over heels in fucking love with—and moved to the other side of the country. The bitch even took the booties he carried around all the time for his soon-to-be-born kid.

If I wasn't worried about Selene's safety and nursing bullet wounds, I'd talk shit out with Nomad about this new woman. He might have officially cracked. Or maybe he's right about doing this Landry chick a favor.

Since he isn't making any moves until she pops, I've got time to sort that shit out. For now, I need him to focus on ending LeVoy.

That's why I give him the info and let him disappear back into the woods. Soon, Selene can enjoy the fresh start she deserves.

SELENE

All day, Hoyt struggles with his pain. He claims the more powerful pills make him loopy. An edgy Hoyt sits in a leather chair, staring at the front door and waiting for Joie to arrive. I linger nearby, worried about agitating him. Eventually, I can't deal with the tension filling the room.

I stand behind him and massage his scalp. Hoyt's expression turns feral when I first touch him. I see the berserker wanting to break his enemies.

Knowing the real Hoyt underneath, I don't shrink away. My nails stroke his scalp as he watches warily. Then, as if a switch flips inside him, Hoyt smiles at me.

"You're going to give me a boner."

"There's no time to deal with that," I reply like I'm his assistant, keeping him on schedule.

"I bet we could hurry."

I glance at the staircase before shaking my head. "Is there somewhere we can go downstairs?"

Hoyt holds my gaze, considering his options. I see something in his eyes. He almost pouts when he shakes his head.

"The office might work, but there'll be too much maneuvering."

I understand his meaning. I can't just yank down my pants and let him inside me. I have a routine to get ready. Sex will never be carefree with me.

Hoyt sees something on my face. His fingers curl around the back of my neck and tug me down for a kiss. I swim in his affections.

"I wish I could give you everything," I whisper against his cheek.

"I wish I could erase your past and give you a fresh start. But life doesn't work like that. We can only work with what we've got now."

"I'm still sorry."

Hoyt's blue eyes study my face before he smiles. "I'm glad you're here. The last time I got hurt, I had Nicole around. It's not at all comparable. I'd wanted to be alone rather than having her bugging me. With you, I'm annoyed when you're away from me. Love is its own kind of addiction."

Smiling at his words, I cup his face and kiss him softly. Soon, my fingers are back massaging his scalp as we wait for Tracey to arrive with Joie.

I sense Hoyt is afraid of Joie's reaction. I've never seen her "roid rage," as he calls it. Hoyt's mentioned her temper before. Usually, he sounds proud. Today, though, he seems wary.

The twelve-year-old comes running into the house. Her blue-eyed gaze takes in the sight of Yazmin and me before focusing on her dad. Joie sizes him up as she hurries over.

"You fell off your bike?" she asks like the story doesn't pass the smell test.

"I got shot."

Joie goes still before narrowing her eyes. "Why did you lie?"

"I wanted you to have fun at Mikayla's house while I got stitched up."

Joie gives him a dirty look. She notices me smiling and frowns harder.

"What?" she mutters at me.

Nervous under her temper, I stammer, "Your angry face reminds me of Hoyt."

Joie smirks. "I don't look like Nicole. Don't even have her boobs."

Still seeming overly tense, Hoyt lets Joie inspect his injuries. She sits on the table in front of him and shakes her head.

"I'm not a baby."

"I felt like one last night," he says, and her eyes widen. "The meds the doctor gave me were too strong. I was nearly crying. It was pathetic."

"Gross."

"Armor kept picking on me, too."

"He's an asshole," she says, grinning at his exaggerated whining. "But you're okay, right?"

"Yeah. Mostly. There's pain but no tears."

Joie frowns and exhales hard. "You can't keep lying to me. I'm not a little kid. I need to know what's happening. When you lie, I don't trust you."

"Well, we can't have that."

"I'm not weak," Joie says and flashes a glance at me. "I can hear the truth."

"When I was your age," Hoyt replies, "my mom said she was going to visit her sick friend. She was gone for two months. I spent that time thinking she was helping a dying lady. Like her friend had cancer or some shit. It made me think my mom was a nice person. When I found out she was separated from my dad and spending her time partying, I wished she'd kept up the lie."

"Grandma's a dipshit," Joie says and kicks off her shoes. "You're not. I want you to tell me the truth."

Hoyt smiles at his daughter. I watch them in awe of how open they are with each other. Even when Hoyt hides the truth, he eventually fesses up. My parents never told me anything. Not because they were trying to protect me, either. They just figured I didn't deserve to know.

Yazmin and I spent our childhoods going places without knowing the destinations. We had visitors who came and went without explanation. Our lives felt out of control.

Joie knows her place. She feels awkward at times since she's unique. People trying to put her in a box makes her edgy. When she's in her element, she's fearless.

Hoyt gave her that power. I watch them as he explains what happened. I sense he holds back. Joie must get the same vibe because she looks at me whenever he shifts gears to omit information.

"Selene and Yazmin are staying for a few days," he says after he explains the gunman "mysteriously died of unspecified injuries." "Is that okay?"

"Are you moving into my house?" Joie asks me.

"No," I say.

Hoyt shrugs. "Eventually."

When I frown at him, he only smirks. Joie takes the Gatorade given to her by Tracey.

"Dad and I talked," she tells me. "I told him I don't mind if you want to live here."

Wearing a silly grin, I mumble, "Okay."

Hoyt and Joie notice my reaction and smile at each other.

"So, you got shot, and we might be under attack, but you didn't even have me protected?" Joie asks in a grumpy tone.

"Hobo was hiding in Mikayla's yard all night. You were safe."

"Really?" Joie asks, grinning now. "I had a Berserker playing bodyguard. Huh, I should have noticed him."

"He's very good at hiding."

"But he has all that wild hair. You'd think I would have looked out the window and seen his big head in the bushes."

They laugh at Hoyt's club brother. Just like that, Joie seems fine. Or maybe she's putting on an act for me.

As Hoyt walks outside with Joie to play with the dog, I consider following. Except I sense they need time alone.

I join Tracey and Yazmin in the kitchen, where we put together honey mustard chicken tacos for dinner. Though my sister says nothing, she's often curious about food and cooking. When I catch her gaze, Yazmin smiles softly.

In a weird twist of fate, Hoyt's injuries offer Yazmin a new path. Rather than us hiding at Patrice's while our grandmother wonders about our new dilemma, we're in this wonderfully warm house. Hoyt, Joie, and Tracey have such a welcoming vibe.

After dinner, we sit outside and enjoy the nice weather. Eventually, Tracey heads to bed early, leaving us to watch a movie. I sit next to Hoyt. Joie takes the other spot next to him. At the movies, she wanted my attention. Tonight, she's all about making sure her dad is okay.

Yazmin sits in a chair, casually petting the dog who has taken a liking to her. I don't pay much attention to the movie. I'm mostly overwhelmed by the last few days.

Once Joie and Yazmin are in bed, I follow Hoyt into his bedroom. In the handsome stone-and-dark wood bathroom, I help him redress his wounds. The shock of his injuries lessens every time I see them. I teach myself to focus on helping him. If that doesn't work, I admire his shirtless chest.

Tonight, I cover his wounds with waterproof bandages so he can take a shower.

"I need help in the water," Hoyt says and wraps his wide hand behind my back to prevent me from escaping.

"How?" I ask, choking on the word.

Still keeping me close, Hoyt flips off the light. The moon brightens only the room's edges, leaving Hoyt and me shadowed. Hoyt believes the darkness will hide my scars and allow me to be free.

"I can't," I mumble.

"Selene, I can't lose you," he says as he tugs off his T-shirt before waiting for me to help with his injured arm. "I can't go back to my life before I met you. Even if you remained my assistant after we broke up, I'd know what I lost. I can't accept that emptiness."

"I don't understand."

"You think I'll reject you because of your scars. That's why you hide from me, right?"

"Hoyt, you can't be sure."

"We're still strangers. You aren't sure you can trust me. You're smart to be careful. But I know my heart like you don't. Selene, you must feel how I love you. I'm not a man who gives up what he wants. I need all of you."

"Not yet."

His hand cups my trembling jaw. "You think there's a point where my love will be strong enough to overlook your scars. Except I knew about your shooting before I knew I loved you. I've always accepted how your body suffered. That's what the scars are to me. Rather than flaws, they're reminders of how you suffered before we met."

I hear something in Hoyt's voice. That tone he uses when he isn't asking. He uses it with his club brothers or when speaking to a local. It's not his hostile, "I'll fuck you up" tone. But there's no denying he's putting down his foot.

"I'm afraid."

"I know. But you should focus on my wounds. I'm supposed to be careful in the shower. You can make sure I am. By the time we get out of the shower, you'll realize the world didn't end."

"I don't care about the world," I whimper, feeling like I'm dancing on the abyss's edge. "I just don't want to lose you."

"Why do you think I'm so shallow?" he asks, sounding hurt enough for me to back away.

"You're so handsome, Hoyt. You could have any woman."

"And I want you," he says as the need in his voice wraps around my body and tugs me closer. "No one's ever owned my heart like you do. I thought I knew love. I felt something for Nicole. I obviously love Joie and my family. But this thing with you is powerful in a way I didn't think I was capable of. I want you to feel the same way. Except you view my love as weak as a teen crush."

"No," I mumble, wanting him to understand. "It's just I would never want me if I were you."

"So, you're shallow?" he asks.

Nodding, I run my fingers over his chest. "I wish you could have seen the old me. I was beautiful."

"You still are. And those scars will always remind me of how strong you are. I know you're a timid woman in a hundred ways. But when you could have given up, you fought to survive."

My body craves his touch. So many nights, I've imagined our naked bodies moving together. To feel his hot skin against mine would be incredible. Except my lust can't overcome my self-loathing.

However, my love proves stronger. Right now, Hoyt needs me to help him in the shower. I want to show I can handle his life. I might not be tough like Patrice or sassy like Wynonna. Yet, I can face the danger Hoyt lives with every day.

"Promise you'll keep the lights off," I whisper as I help him tug down his sweatpants. "Do you swear on everything that matters to you?"

"Yes," he says, exhaling softly as my lips slide across his bare erection. "I love you, Selene. Losing you would kill me."

Feeling lightheaded, I kiss the head of his cock before forcing myself to stand.

"Can you turn on the water to the temperature you like?" I ask, choking on each word as I struggle to breathe.

As the panic tries to suffocate me, I force my hands to remove my shirt. I focus on Hoyt's bandaged arm. He's in more pain than he lets on. Weakness scares him. He won't allow anyone to see him defeated. But he still needs help.

I slide off my bra and rest it on the sink next to my shirt. Soon, my sweatpants and panties are piled on top of them. The steam turns the bathroom pleasantly warm. I don't look at Hoyt before stepping into the shower. I check the temperature and reach my hand out to him.

Even with so little light, I catch him smiling. Hoyt really does love getting his way.

Soon, I help him wash off under the hot water. He regularly sighs at the feel of my soapy hands against his skin. Once he's finished, Hoyt turns around. Now, I'm under the main showerhead. I lean back to allow the water to wash away my tears. With his good hand, he soaps up my hair. I smile at how careful his touch remains.

The shifting moonlight allows me to see his face better. I smile at how beautiful he is, not only on the outside. No matter his dominating nature, Hoyt is perfectly kind to me.

Gently wrapping my arms around him, I soak in my luck over winning the heart of such an incredible man. His fingers slide down my back, passing over a scar. I tense for a moment before his heartbeat lulls me.

"This isn't so bad, right?" Hoyt asks as his warm voice bounces off the stone and echoes in my head.

Lifting my gaze, I smile and shake my head. "You kept your promise."

"What if we dried off and moved this party to bed? No lights. Before the sun comes up, you can get dressed."

Breathing easier, I nod again. "We can explore more in bed than in the truck," I whisper as my hand gives his cock a loving stroke.

Hoyt kisses me possessively. Our lips barely part as he turns off the water. After drying us off, I redress his wounds before taking his hand and walking to the bedroom.

Once he rests on his back, I climb over him and sprinkle kisses on his lips, cheeks, and forehead. Hoyt smiles at my excitement.

"I finally get to enjoy you going wild in my bed, yet I can barely fucking move."

"Just relax," I whisper, wrapping my hand around his erection as I kiss his throat.

"Let me feel your tits, Selene," he says in a voice laced with desire. "I need to taste your nipples."

I don't hesitate. My lust bulldozes through my fears. In the shower, I quickly became addicted to our naked bodies pressed together. As long as I'm hidden in the dark, I need him to touch me in ways we couldn't in the truck.

Hoyt's beard tickles the soft flesh around my nipple as he sucks the hard flesh into his hot mouth. I squirm at the new round of heat consuming me. I've never been more aroused. Exposing my body to Hoyt has released something in me. I want this powerful man to claim everything I am.

Propped over him, I moan as he at first kisses, then sucks, and finally nibbles at my sensitive nipples. I can't believe how incredible his mouth feels on my skin. Why am I so surprised? Hoyt's an amazing kisser. Now, my nipples reap the benefits of his talented lips.

Hoyt's fingers slide along my hips, nearly touching my thigh wound before dipping between my legs to where I'm blazing hot. I buck when his thumb grazes my clit. Moaning louder, I forget to censor myself. In the truck, we have a wide-open space to fuck. I never worry over making noise.

After a moment of concern over Joie, I remember she's on the other end of the hall. With the approaching storm whipping up the wind outside, I doubt she'd hear me if I screamed in joy.

I come hard around Hoyt's fingers. He plucks at my clit and nipples at the same rhythm, leaving me panting with pleasure. I wish I could ride this feeling forever.

My mind recalls his abandoned erection. I imagine the precum needing to be licked. I picture the feel of his thick cock filling my mouth and pressing against the back of my throat.

Wanting to taste him, I climb off Hoyt and turn around. My hand tenderly wraps around his cock, winning a groan from this sexy man. I lick the slit, tasting his hot seed.

Sucking him deep, I want Hoyt to own my throat like he does my pussy. I love how his size stretches me wide. I'm so full, like when he fucks me in the truck. I can't imagine a sexier man than the one groaning my name as he fills my mouth with his pleasure.

The moonlight reveals his gaze on me. He says my name in a rough whisper. I move closer and kiss his lips.

"I need you to help me get hard again," he insists, and I stroke him again. "No, I want you to sit on my face and let me feast on your sweet pussy."

"I don't know how to do that."

"Use your imagination," he murmurs and scoots lower on the bed. "Straddle my face like you do my hips. Let me taste you."

When I hesitate, Hoyt kisses me while his fingers tease my nipples. My fears of messing up in bed zap my confidence. I've never done this with any other man. What if I lose control and hurt Hoyt?

"Selene," he says when our lips separate. "If you let me eat you out, my cock will get rock hard. Then, you can ride it until we're both tired and ready to sleep. Where's the downside to that plan?"

"I'm scared."

"Not of me. You know it'll feel good."

"What if I do something wrong?"

"Baby, someone shot me yesterday. I'm not afraid of you grinding your pussy on my face."

Laughing at his teasing, I kiss him again before crawling over him. I tremble with fear as I lower my pussy over his waiting lips. I pray I don't do anything gross or stupid.

Hoyt's tongue against my hot flesh overrides every bit of brain power inside me. I'm a live wire of pleasure as he licks and sucks at my wet flesh.

Gripping the headboard, I rest my forehead against the wall and moan deep in my chest. I can't believe how quickly he works me into a frenzy. His tongue makes wicked circles around my tender clit. His drenched thumb teases my asshole as his other fingers pump into me. I whimper as the orgasm twists me into knots. Hoyt laps up my waves of pleasure, sending me over the edge again.

My body goes loose, leaving me wanting to collapse for a few hours while I regain my senses.

I picture his cock, thick against his thigh, waiting to fill me. I love how my body offers Hoyt pleasure. Not just a quickie. He can get that kind of pleasure from his hand. Yet, when we're together, Hoyt opens up in a way that startles even him.

That's why I don't drop next to him in bed and ask for a break. Instead, I carefully climb off his face, kiss his wet lips, and stroke his drenched beard.

"Did I make you hard enough?" I ask, knowing the answer as I reach for his cock.

"Do you remember the day in the truck when we fucked four times?" he asks while I kiss his jaw.

"Of course. I could barely walk straight afterward."

Chuckling, he groans at the feel of my fingers teasing his balls. "I couldn't come that last time. Or maybe I didn't want to. We just kept fucking and fucking. That's how I feel now. You'll need patience until my balls agree to give up this party."

"I have nowhere else I want to be."

Hoyt cups my face. "Once I heal, I'm going to fuck you every which way. But for now, I'll need you to do most of the work."

"I distinctly recall long fucks in the dark being part of my job description," I murmur before kissing his chest.

I move carefully down his body, teasing his nipples and nibbling at his unharmed rib cage. I smile at how he flinches as if ticklish. He sighs when I lick his belly button and suck at his pelvic bone before cleaning his wet cock.

Climbing over him, I feel so free in the darkness. I can be the old Selene. Though she was a timid victim, she had an incredible body. That's the woman Hoyt deserves. I pretend I'm her again as my pussy welcomes his cock.

I ride his dick with abandon. No worries over Hoyt touching in the wrong place or if the moonlight reveals my scars.

In my head, I'm the flawless Selene. The night of the shooting is just a bad dream. I was never on my deathbed. I've always been this wild woman with a sexy biker's dick stretching me wide.

HOYT

Patience never interested me. I've bullied my way through life, never seeing the point of being any other way.

However, taking my time with Selene proved some things are worth the wait. Now, I'm sharing a bed with my woman. During the last two nights, we explored as much as possible with me basically immobile.

Around two a.m. this morning, we found ourselves together again. A trip to the bathroom with her help led me to take advantage of her nudity. As long as my fingers don't linger for long on her scars, Selene is fearless in the dark.

I wake in a sun-filled room to find a glorious sight. Selene rests on her back, sound asleep and uncovered. My gaze feasts on her delicate, gorgeous body revealed for my inspection.

I admire her perfect round tits, lifting and falling with every soft breath. Her dark pink nipples hardened under my kisses last night. Now, the soft nubs look as fragile as the rest of her.

Over the last few weeks, I've caught sight of Selene's chest scar whenever she bent forward. The mark is just above the curve of her right tit.

On her arm next to me, I see a small scar from a shallow wound. The bullet likely only clipped her.

The one on her stomach was nearly fatal. I can imagine the damage it left behind. Another stomach scar is closer to where I was shot days ago. Painful but mostly harmless.

I hate to think of Selene suffering. She must have been heavily sedated early into her recovery. I understand why she hesitates to push her body. Though the skin has healed, the damaged muscles still tug and pinch when she tries to move.

My fingers are dying to stroke her scarred flesh and claim it as mine. Rather than touch a sleeping Selene, I let my gaze dip lower, past her belly button and pelvic bone. A tidy bush of dark hair begs to be stroked. I recall going down on Selene. Those soft hairs smelled of her chocolate-scented body wash. The memory makes my dick twitch.

I finally see the scar on her right thigh. My fingers have grazed it for weeks, first during our clothed make-out sessions and later when she was hidden under a blanket in the truck. Now, I can see the red puckered skin.

Another scar on her right inner thigh answers why she often limps slightly on that side.

I study the six scars. Exit wounds hide on her other side. In the shower, my fingers slid against her back scars. Selene flinched often during our first time in the darkness. She worried I was pulling a trick on her. That I'd turn on the light and inspect her like she was a product I was considering buying.

Last night, she trusted me more. I wasn't a man using her. I was her man loving her. Selene desperately wants to be accepted and cherished.

That's why I don't wake her gently and reveal how I've seen her naked. I could prove my honor by embracing her scars. But that would only help my ego.

Selene would be so rattled by how she exposed her flaws to a man she still wants to impress. I can imagine her expression. How hurt she'd be. How much she'd hate herself for forgetting to slide into her nightgown after our last fuck.

Would she trust me again with her body? Sure, but there'd always be a hesitation. She's so certain I'll reject her.

I gently tug the blanket over her body like she'd want. Resting on my side, I admire her peaceful expression.

On the day we met, I'd been hornier than hell. Selene just seemed terrified. But even then, she revealed the way I awoke something inside her.

A month ago, we were strangers. Two weeks ago, she pushed me away out of fear and self-loathing. For most of that time, I thought I was in control of myself and the situation.

Now, I accept I'm a slave to this feeling. Losing control scares me, but losing her is more fucking terrifying.

Her eyes open at the sound of Wise Guy barking. I wait for her to notice me. Sleepy and unsure, Selene wears a confused look. She's still getting used to my house.

I think Selene got lost yesterday around the gym. She became turned around and wasn't sure which direction led to the kitchen. I hate when she's too nervous to ask questions.

Her golden-brown eyes find my face. I love the look of recognition filling her worried gaze. She soon rewards me with a gorgeous smile.

Her love-filled gaze is what patience won me.

SELENE

Hoyt is especially cuddly looking when he first wakes up. His hair and beard seem softer. His eyes lack their usual quiet intensity.

I find him watching me in the sunlit room. Smiling at his expression, I breathe in the way my body feels after another night of incredible sex.

Hoyt hates how he can't take charge in bed yet. I'm a little afraid of the beast waiting to break free. If a subdued Hoyt can wreck my self-control, I can't imagine what the unleashed version will do.

Waking more, I admire the sun-kissed room. The light warms Hoyt's tanned skin. He's completely naked, unashamedly uncovered.

Moving my legs under the blanket, I realize I never put on my nightgown. I stare into Hoyt's eyes and know I wasn't covered up when he woke. That's why he's just watching me now. The day before, he woke me up with his kisses. Today, he feels different.

"I'm sorry."

"I barely saw anything," he murmurs. "Just enough for a boner. Then, I covered you right up."

Hiding my face behind my hands, I feel the world drop out from under me. I'd been so comfortable last night. Hoyt's body intoxicates me, leaving me joyful and reckless.

Why wasn't I more careful when my future depends on keeping Hoyt's affections? Can I return to the woman I was before I met him? Can I survive without his love?

"Selene, I'm going to give you a harsh truth now. Can you handle that?"

Still hiding behind my hands, I shake my head and try to steady my breathing. Hoyt exhales hard.

"Well, I'm still telling it to you anyway," he says and slides his hand under the blanket to my stomach. "I don't want to just fuck in the truck. I need you to live here with me. For us to be together in a real way, like we are in the dark. I think that's what you need, too. We have this connection that must be fed. Can you see that?"

Whimpering behind my hands, I know the last two nights have been incredibly freeing. To be able to touch Hoyt in the darkness and explore his body turned me into another woman. Less timid, more self-assured.

Except it was based on the lie of me being my old self. Now, I've been revealed as the woman chewed up and spat out by LeVoy.

"It's not realistic to think we can live together and hide you from me. We're not a weird religious couple, ashamed of fucking. We want to touch each other. I can barely keep my hands off you when we're working."

Hoyt scoots closer and whispers, "We're going to share a bed every night. That's what you want, too, right?"

Still hiding, I nod at his question. I've slept so well the last two nights. Hoyt's presence erases my fears about someone hiding in the house. I've stopped flinching at every shadow.

"We're going to be together every day. How can you hope to hide from me?"

"I want you to want me."

"I do."

"What did you see?" I ask, peeking through my fingers and watching his reaction.

"You really don't like blankets," is his answer.

"Yours is too heavy and hot."

"I hope you say that about my cock one day."

Laughing behind my hands, I shake my head. "I want you to find me beautiful."

"I wasn't kidding about my boner, Selene."

"That's just a physical thing. I want you to find me beautiful in your head. I want you to see the old me."

"That isn't the woman I fell in love with. She was still back in her prison. She hadn't gotten her second chance. She isn't the one who takes care of me when I'm a slob or keeps me organized when I'm lazy. That's not my Selene. This right here," he says as his fingers slide across my stomach scar, "is the woman I want to marry and grow old with."

Crying, I wish I could see myself like he does. My hands move to his on my stomach. I don't push him away. I only hold him touching my scarred flesh.

"I was going to see you eventually," he whispers against my ear. "And you were glorious, baby. So peaceful and well-fucked. I've never seen anyone more beautiful."

Still teary-eyed, I fight a pout. "You saw everything?"

"Well, I didn't flip you over and look at your back, but I saw your sexy tits and that sweet muff I tasted last night. The soft curve of your hips and your ticklish thighs."

Wiping my eyes, I try to embrace the picture he paints for me. Hoyt kisses my temple and breathes softly.

"You were waiting for a perfect time to show me your scars. Like it'd be easier one day. But you'd only be wasting time and effort with all your attempts to hide. Now, you can get more comfortable with yourself. Better today than tomorrow or a year from now."

I breathe easier when Hoyt talks about the future. He's not the most sensitive man. He can't lie as well as he thinks. I see his reaction to people giving him gifts he doesn't want or offering gross food. He hides little, even when he tries his best.

Right now, I search for disgust in his expression. Does he regret making promises? Is he rethinking the future he's describing?

Hoyt notices me studying him. A grin warms his face. I can't help mimicking the gesture.

"The first shot was right here," I say and force the blanket down enough to reveal the chest scar.

Hoyt's gaze hides nothing—rage, love, fear, and lust. I don't look away. Despite my panic trying to drown me, I hold his gaze and offer him everything.

His lips cover mine for a brief moment before kissing my scar. I gasp, struggling between the urge to hide and the desire to reveal myself to the man I love.

"When I turned, the second shot was in my arm," I say, remembering that night clearer when Hoyt's gaze holds me.

I twist to make it easier for him to kiss my arm wound. His lips return to mine, filling me with more confidence.

"I tried to run. The next shots were in my legs. I fell and rolled on my back. That's when he shot me in the stomach."

I use my feet to help tug the heavy blanket off until I'm exposed. My panic returns.

The first time I saw my body, I nearly threw up. I even considered taking my life.

However, I stumbled back from that abyss for two reasons. One, Yazmin needed me to live. And two, surviving the gunman was my one "fuck you" to LeVoy after a dozen years together. I couldn't give up.

Right now, I hold onto Hoyt to steady my racing heart. The panic threatens to swallow me up. I hear all my flaws recited back to me by my treacherous mind. Yet, Hoyt rests his cheek on my stomach and holds me.

He acts as my anchor. The stormy seas of panic can't send me off course. I have this powerful man to keep me safe.

The panic releases its grip on my heart. I breathe easier, matching Hoyt's pace as he kisses the scar. I exhale deeply, pushing away all the ugliness until I only see the man I love.

His gaze finds mine before he kisses me. When our lips separate, I whisper, "I'll always feel ugly."

"And I'll always find you beautiful."

Studying his face, I smile softy. "I love you."

His smile breaks through the last part of my worries. I can't deny the acceptance I find in his gaze. As he kisses me, I don't hold back. I meet his hunger with my own.

In the sun-kissed room, I straddle his gorgeous body and admire his every line of ink, scar, and toned muscle. Somehow, he becomes more striking every moment we're together.

Hoyt's gaze feasts on my body as I take his cock inside me. His hand reaches for my breast, stroking my nipple.

When we fuck, I feel like an extension of Hoyt—powerful, sexy, and bold. The world isn't a minefield. I'm not a victim. There's more beauty than suffering. My future can be beautiful if I look at it as fearlessly as Hoyt looks at me right now.

HOYT

Selene's mood is all over the place this morning. She glows with pleasure. I catch her watching me as if I'm a miracle. But then, I'll notice her falling back into her habit of worrying over my rejection.

During breakfast, she nearly starts crying. At another point, she gets the worst giggles. I can almost feel her thinking about me eating her out at that moment. Her silly grin at Yazmin makes me chuckle. I doubt there's anyone in this world as perfectly odd as Selene.

Just after lunch, we move outside to the side porch. I plan to relax in the sun to distract from the nagging pain from my side wound.

"You pulled something when we were together today," Selene whispers as she helps organize the pillow on my chair. "I need to baby you more."

I can't tell if she's serious or not. Either way, I smile at how much she loves me. Selene shares my grin as she settles into a chair next to mine.

Yasmin sits off in the yard with Wise Guy. Joie is playing video games inside. Tracey gardens. The property feels calm despite my club brother, Eagle, still lingering in the woods, keeping watch.

I think about Nomad on his way to Bossier City. My thoughts then turn to Nash. I haven't texted my cousin since the shooting. Ed checked on him. Glenn is hunkered down with Nash, playing nursemaid. Armor said he's got guys watching the hospital. Shit is handled.

However, I can't yet find the words to deal with Nash. He crossed a line, and I'm not ready to decide what that means.

"Were you going to tell me about Yazmin and Nash?" I ask Selene when she digs my sunglasses out of her bag.

Looking startled by the question, she mumbles, "Yes."

"When?"

"When I came back to work. But then, you got hurt, and I didn't think it mattered."

Rubbing my jaw, I glance at her sister. "I didn't realize Yazmin liked Nash. I know chicks can't help finding him appealing. Of course, I don't see it. But I hear he's irresistible."

"He's handsome in a pretty way."

I study her in the afternoon sun and ask, "If I hadn't made my move, would you have dated him?"

"No. I had a crush on you immediately. Nash would have been a step-down."

Grinning at her wording, I know she isn't blowing smoke up my ass. Selene's never shown any interest in my cousin.

Sure, I'd worried in the beginning. Nash has a way of sweeping women into the fantasy he builds of himself as a loving partner. That's why my assistants always quit. Believing so fully in Nash's lies, they broke a little when they realized the truth.

However, Selene never got swept up in his bullshit. Yazmin wasn't so lucky.

"Why was she upset?" I ask as Selene glances at her sister. "Did he make promises?"

Selene's gaze avoids mine. "It's difficult to explain."

"You've thought that way about plenty of shit. Yet, I always catch onto whatever you're explaining."

Selene takes my hand and stares at it. "She can't tell men no. About anything. If you told her to clean the floor with her tongue, she'd do it. She can't help herself."

Frowning, I ask, "So, she didn't want Nash to fuck her?"

"I don't think so. I sense she likes Wade. But, when someone pushes Yazmin, their will overrides hers."

I'd been pissed enough at my cousin when I thought he wooed a broken woman into sex. I figured she wasn't savvy enough to see through his bullshit.

Except even if she saw him for the asshole he is, Yazmin couldn't deny him. A little part of me hopes Nash is hurting today. Fuck him and his insatiable need to use women to fix what his mommy broke.

"Yazmin shouldn't be working around the public," I tell Selene.

"She needs a job."

"I can get her something else. Working around others allows them to bully her."

"What kind of job?" Selene asks, looking worried she messed up by telling me the truth.

"She can be Hoyt's assistant," Wynonna announces as she appears from around the house.

"Where the fuck have you been?" I bark at my sister.

Flinching, Selene stares wide-eyed when thinking I'm really fighting with Wynonna. My sister just flips me off.

"I couldn't deal with you whining," Wynonna explains as she strolls over. "I stayed away until you were past the wimp phase of your injury."

I grin at my sister, knowing she gets weak if I bleed. When we were kids, she literally fainted after I cut open my leg while we were playing in the rocky gorge by our old house. I ended up dragging her back home, where our dad and uncle were drinking beers on the back deck.

"He's finally killed her," Ed said and sucked on his beer.

Glenn hadn't missed a beat before replying, "Always assumed it would be the other way around."

While my leg got stitched, Wynonna swore up and down how she hadn't fainted.

Yet, she's never been able to stomach me in pain. Anyone else can get fucked up without her dramatics.

She doesn't even freak out when her kids scrape themselves. If I get an owie, though, she goes weak.

"I won't lie," I mutter, frowning at my sister. "You hurt my feelings, butthead. I nearly died, and you took two fucking days to show up."

"I texted."

"I was too injured to respond."

"Yet, you still did."

"That was Selene," I lie, and my sweet assistant stares blankly, neither confirming nor denying my bullshit. "What do you want, Wynonna?"

"Just came by to see if you were finished whining and whimpering?"

"No."

Shuffling closer, she looks me over. "Heard you got flesh wounds. Barely a scratch."

"I nearly died from the pain alone. You'd have missed saying goodbye."

Resting her hands on her hips, Wynonna mutters, "Are you done making me feel guilty?"

"Tell Selene why you were a no-show," I insist, smirking at my sister.

Wynonna sighs deeply. "I can't see Hoyt suffer. It's my one weakness. Well, that and olives. I can't stand them."

"Selene took good care of me when you were too busy hiding."

"I bet she did," Wynonna replies and settles in a chair. "Got you all these women serving your every need. So much debauchery."

"I've earned it."

Wynonna smiles at Selene. "I've never seen my brother in love before. It's so cute. Like a big-eyed cartoon squirrel farting animated hearts."

Selene grins at me and nods. "I see that."

"What's that crap you were saying about Yazmin?" I ask my sister while admiring Selene.

"Stick her in the business office. Have her file shit, be in charge of certain projects. I've often said you had

305

too much crap for one assistant to do," Wynonna explains before focusing on Selene. "Do you think Yazmin would like to work alone? Or is she better around people?"

"Probably alone."

"Then, she'll do well in the office. It's quiet. There are restaurants nearby for lunch. Of course, Hoyt will need to stop using the office for midday fucking. It's a small sacrifice to make for family, though."

Selene opens her mouth to correct my sister regarding where our midday fucks occur. Catching herself, she smiles at me.

"Do you think Yazmin would like sitting around that office all day, taking calls and filing paperwork?" I ask her.

"I don't know," Selene says, nervous about agreeing to anything. "Can I go ask Yazmin?"

Wynonna smirks at how Selene requests permission for the most basic things.

I wait until we're alone before asking, "Did you check on Nash?"

"Yeah. I got there right after his kids visited. He looked ready to cry. Apparently, getting shot in the chest makes you sensitive to noise."

Still pissed about Yazmin, I mutter, "He's an asshole. I hope those brats blew out his eardrums."

"Are you okay?" Wynonna asks, suddenly serious.

"Yeah. Solid. Was in pain. Now, I'm in less pain. Got to fuck Selene in bed. That's the definite highlight of my week."

Wynonna glances at where the sisters talk. "Do they know about the shooter?"

"No."

"That's probably best."

"Nomad's taking care of the guy's boss. Selene will be safe soon."

"Is she sticking around?"

"I hope so. Having her here has got me flying," I say, and my sister grins at my enthusiasm. "She's lowering her guard with me, too."

"Is that a sex thing?" Wynonna taunts.

"Yes. Selene has a lot of hang-ups, but I'm making quick work of most of them."

"I want you to be happy."

"I am."

"I see that."

"What?"

"Nothing. This is my *proud sister* expression. You don't witness it often since you rarely do anything worthy of my pride."

"Well, I'm bummed I can't be the one to do LeVoy. I wish I could tear him apart slowly. Maybe keep him tied up somewhere and let him die slow for the shit he put Selene through. But dead will need to be the prize if torture isn't on the menu."

"The police might come calling."

"I know."

"Think Nomad's clearheaded enough to get the job done and return home unscathed?"

"I think killing is what he does right. It's everything else that's gone wonky."

While Selene talks to her sister, I explain to mine about Nomad's new obsession. This openness is what I hope for with Selene one day. I want to be able to tell her anything. Until then, I'm glad my sister overcame her squeamishness to act as my confidant again.

SELENE

Today has been a dream. My good fortune continues when Hoyt doesn't judge Yazmin harshly for how she reacted to Nash. He even offered her a better job.

Hurrying over to where she sits in the grass, I plop on my butt and grin.

"Hoyt wants you to be his assistant, too," I share, fighting a wild grin.

"Why?"

"He thinks having you work at the Valley Gin Mill is dangerous. People might bully you."

"Because Nash fucked me?"

"Waitressing puts you on display, and you're beautiful. Remember how nervous you were with Paul not wanting to leave the bar?"

A frowning Yazmin glances at Hoyt. "How can I be his assistant?"

"You'd work in his office."

"In the back of the Valley Gin Mill?"

"I think mostly at the nice office in the business campus. You'd answer phones and file papers. Organize things."

Rather than seem relieved by this news, Yazmin deflates. "I was just starting to make tips."

"My pay is better than your waitressing one."

"But he's dating you."

"If you don't want the job, you can just say no. You don't have to look for reasons."

Yazmin mumbles in a small voice, "I want to rent that house. Can I do that if I'm his assistant?"

Hesitating, I feel like Yazmin and I are suddenly on different paths. "Hoyt's talking about us moving in here."

Yazmin's face clenches as if I've slapped her. Just as quickly, her expression goes blank.

"We can't have the rental house."

I grip her hand. "I want to live with Hoyt."

Shoulders sagging, she gets smaller. "We'll live here."

"Is it safe for you to live alone?"

Yazmin stares at me with her blank eyes, revealing a decade of programming. "Did he ask you to move in?"

"After breakfast, Hoyt asked if I would be happy living in his house. I said yes." Seeing a growing panic in her usually blank expression, I add, "Maybe I should wait. We could live in that house for a while first."

"Why move in there if you'll need to move soon anyway? I can't afford to rent alone."

Yazmin startles me by bursting into tears. I wrap her in my arms as she grabs hold as if she's drowning.

"I wanted that house," she whimpers in my ear. "I saw us there. I was going to have my own place. I wanted it so bad, but I can't keep you from having this life."

"I'll talk to Hoyt. He'll help us figure it out."

Yazmin doesn't want to let me go. She assumes the worst will happen when I talk to Hoyt. Despite still crying, she finally releases me and pets Wise Guy. I step away from her, unsure what to do.

I end up rushing over to Hoyt, who is chuckling at whatever Wynonna told him. His smile falls when he sees my expression.

"She didn't want the job?" he asks.

"Will I need to pay rent to live in your house?"

Hoyt gives me that look he gets when people say something stupid. "That's not a real question, right?"

I look at him and then at Wynonna. Unsure what I said wrong, I shake my head. Hoyt sees something on my face and sighs.

"No, baby, if you move in with me, you won't have to pay rent. That's not how it works."

"Will I still get paid to be your assistant?"

"Yes," he replies as if suspicious now. "Why?"

"Yazmin wants to live in that Spanish rental, but she can't afford it alone. If I lived here, would I be able to help her pay the rent?"

Hoyt stares at me for too long. He does that sometimes when I say really dumb things. Wynonna offers me the same look.

I've never noticed the physical resemblance between them until this moment. Now, they're both watching me like I might be the dumbest person they've ever met.

"Is it safe for her to live alone?" Wynonna asks while Hoyt stares at me.

"I lived alone in the guest house," Yazmin answers from behind me.

Looking at her, I can't say the words I really want. She walks to me and whispers in my ear.

"I could have killed myself in the guest house just as easily as I can in the Spanish house. Besides, if you think I'm so close to the edge, why would you want me around Joie?"

Gripping her now, I whisper back, "I can't lose you."

"Not to interrupt," Hoyt says, standing up and watching us. "But there's no issue with the rental. If you want it, it's yours. If you want to own it, I'll buy it for you. You'll both have salaries for your jobs. The world isn't ending. Everything is fine."

We look at him like maybe he's the one making no sense. I wipe Yazmin's wet cheeks. She does the same to me. We watch each other for a moment before smiling.

"It's a really nice house," I tell her. "I can picture you happy there."

"This is a really nice house, too," she replies. "I can picture you happy here."

"Wait, so I'm getting what I want?" Hoyt asks, sliding his uninjured arm around my shoulders. "I wasn't sure that's where this conversation was headed."

I frown at him. "I don't understand how things work."

"I know, baby."

"I want to be with you, but I must protect my sister."

"I know that, too."

"You looked like maybe you didn't."

"I was just confused. You were so upset, like something bad was happening. Why wouldn't I pay you to be my assistant?"

"I don't know. I've never had a job before. Or a boyfriend. Or moved in with a man I loved. It's new stuff."

"Well, everything is fine," he says, sounding smug.

"I don't know how you stand him," Wynonna announces, shaking her head. "He's insufferable. A brat. I've been saying that since we were kids."

"No, you were the brat. I was the long-suffering older brother."

"Maybe you hit your head too many times," she mocks. "There's no other explanation for your delusional thinking."

"Want to see my wound?"

Wynonna narrows her eyes. "You're fine. Bet there was no blood. I should leave."

"No, help me change my dressing," he taunts, following after her. "It's starting to get smelly."

"Leave me alone!" she screams as they disappear into the house.

"I think they're messing around," I tell Yazmin. "But I'm not sure."

"I think she would probably sound angrier if it were real."

"Are you okay?"

"I really want that house."

"I did, too. I kept thinking of us moving in and how we'd hang out at night. But then, I thought of that happening here."

"You want Hoyt more than the house."

311

"But not more than you."

"It's okay to want him more than me. I'm picking a house over you."

Laughing at her smirk, I nod. "Are you messing with me?"

"A little. Though I'm sad you're not moving with me, I also knew this might happen. Hoyt's so obviously in love with you. Why would he let you live apart?"

"Despite how he likes me around, I figured he might not want a woman in his house full time."

"He had Joie's mom here."

"But with Selene," Hoyt announces, returning with his sister stuck in a headlock, "I won't have to pretend to be sleeping whenever she wants to talk."

"You were a terrible husband," Wynonna mutters. "I want it noted that I'm choosing to remain trapped. If I were willing to harm his injured body, I'd have this motherfucker on the ground by now."

"She isn't lying," Hoyt says and releases her. His gaze studies me before he asks, "Are you okay?" When I nod, he looks at Yazmin, "Are you okay?" After she nods, he sighs. "I'm going to sit down inside, put my feet up, and watch sports. You chicks can do your chick things. I need to be alone with my thoughts."

"Can I sit with you and watch sports, too?" I ask, just to mess with him.

Hoyt gives me a great smile and nods. "I was hoping you'd ask."

Wynonna laughs and points at me. "Screwed yourself there, chickpea."

While I join Hoyt inside the family room, our sisters discuss work and houses.

I can't believe how comfortable I feel in this home with these people. Soon, Joie joins her dad and me, watching tennis. An hour later, Tracey finishes lunch with Yazmin's help. Wynonna bails to get back to her kids.

"I'll bring them around when Uncle Hoyt isn't such a whiny baby," she says before messing with her brother's hair. "I can't have them see you so pathetic."

Hoyt grins at her teasing. I never had such a fun relationship with my brother. He didn't even visit me when I came to stay with our parents after the shooting.

Yazmin, though, will always be a part of my life. Those years, when she was with Robert and in the hospital, I lost something vital inside me. She was the one person I trusted. Even a hollowed-out Yazmin was better than anyone else.

Now, we have a new family. I hope their warmth and fun antics rub off on us. Yazmin living alone terrifies me. I don't know how she'll react to what happened with Nash. Or if she'll do well with her new job.

However, Hoyt's calm steals my fears, replacing them with the comfort only he provides.

HOYT

While putting Wynonna in a headlock, I make her promise to protect Selene and Yazmin if anything ever happens to me. She doesn't ask why, obviously. I was nearly killed days ago. My life isn't as safe as I'd led myself to believe.

More than anything, Wynonna understands how ill-equipped Selene and Yazmin are for the world. I can't imagine what fuckery they might have fallen for if Patrice hadn't taken them in. They're so beautiful and clueless about how anything works. Some jackass would quickly pick up on their weaknesses and take advantage.

Later, I'm thinking about them while we watch a movie. Selene is more confident now than a month ago. In a year, she'll be smarter about many things.

Neither woman is dumb. Selene and Yazmin absorb new information fine. Yet, they'll always be easy to manipulate. I've come to accept how their old programming won't wash away with time.

That's why Selene is nervous about getting naked in front of me when we head to bed.

After fooling around in the shower, though, she jumps right back into the fun.

However, sometimes, her frailty comes in handy. That's why I never warn Selene about LeVoy's death.

She has no clue anything's happened until two detectives show up in McMurdo Valley to speak with her. We meet Kourtney and them at my business office.

Selene's shocked reaction definitely helps sell her innocence. She also seems so confused about how he could be dead and why anyone would kill him.

"Did he have enemies?" asks the man detective.

Kourtney doesn't wait for a stunned Selene to answer. "Mister Garry claimed his enemies were

314

behind the attack on his wife. Are you claiming that wasn't true?"

"We're not claiming anything," the woman detective replies. "We're asking Missus Garry a question."

Selene mumbles, "LeVoy told my parents I'd startled the gunman who came for him."

"What did he tell you?" asks the man detective.

"Nothing. I was in the hospital before going to stay with my parents."

"You didn't speak to your husband in all that time?"

"He came to the hospital once," she says, seeming lost until I take her hand. "LeVoy said I looked like shit. He also mentioned my stomach wounds would have been more bothersome if I weren't barren."

"Good Lord," Kourtney growls so I don't have to. "Is anyone genuinely upset over this piece of shit's death? I'm certainly not. Well," she says, tapping her manicured red nails against her jaw, "actually, if he were alive, we likely would have gotten far more money than with his death."

"How do you figure?" asks the woman detective.

"He lost a lot of money halfway through their marriage and made a whole lot back during their marriage. I planned to get half of that."

Kourtney sighs deeply while glancing at a weepy Selene. "Now that he's dead, there's likely a will with others named as his main beneficiaries. According to his lawyers, LeVoy had a young girlfriend he was planning to marry. There's also an adult son who will no doubt be named. Can't imagine Miss Norris will be in the will, but you'd know that better than I."

The detectives decide they aren't getting what they want from Selene and choose to focus on me instead. I assume they don't know about my recent run-in with a gunman.

"Did you have any dealings with Mister Garry?" the man detective asks me.

"I'll be square with you. I always figured he was the one who sent the gunman to kill Selene. So having him get killed sort of messes with my blame game. I guess a different person could have sent the one who offed LeVoy. Unlikely, but I guess I could be wrong. It's happened from time to time."

"Did he suffer?" Selene asks, teary-eyed like a grieving widow.

"It was a rifle shot. Witnesses say the first shot missed. The second was nonfatal. The third killed him."

Selene squeezes my hand and wears a pout. Does she wish he suffered more? I know I do. Most likely, she's trying to accept her boogeyman is dead.

"Look, I get the routine," Kourtney tells the detectives while sounding annoyed as usual. "You have to interview the wife. But she was here when LeVoy died. You must know she didn't sneak off and shoot him, right? And if you know Bossier City, you likely already have a few suspects with better skills than the asshole's abused ex-wife."

"Abused?"

"Now, I'm sure you're screwing with me," Kourtney gripes, tapping her nails on the table. "As Bossier City locals, you know all this shit. LeVoy Garry was hinky. He might not have been mobbed up, but he ran in those circles. I learned that shit just from the divorce investigation."

Kourtney leans forward. "You know the same shit. But here you are, hassling the wife he might have attempted to kill. Because that's the deal, isn't it? He either tried to kill her, so you think she has a reason to murder him. Or you think she was collateral damage, so you know he had enemies."

"But those enemies aren't easy to railroad into a conviction," I mutter. "So, you try to pin this shit on my woman."

"We're just asking questions to get a full picture."

"You know we have access to TV, right?" Kourtney says, and I nearly roll my eyes at her bullshit. "We've seen movies. Good cop, bad cop, just asking questions, it's always the wife or husband. We've seen your tricks. We know what this is. You're here to harass this poor woman over her evil fucking ex. A man so selfish he couldn't even wait to get murdered until I'd taken half his shit."

By the time the detectives leave my office, they really hate Kourtney. I can feel their disgust without them saying a damn word. Kourtney's excellent at drawing attention where she wants it.

"They have nothing," she tells Selene and me. "I've seen the basic file from the shooting. Witnesses scattered when the shots happened. No one saw the gunman. Some of the cops' notes indicate LeVoy was with shady fucks when he was killed. They're not even sure he was the target. Another guy got hit. Yeah, those detectives aren't coming back."

"Wait, you knew that's why they were here?" Selene asks me.

Cupping her face, I stare into her gorgeous eyes and love how she still hasn't considered that I'm the one who sent the killer. Maybe that's for the best. She seems genuinely bothered by LeVoy's death.

"Baby, I kept an eye on him because of the divorce," I lie as my thumb strokes her lips. "I wanted to know if he was planning to screw you over."

Selene stares at me with overly emotional eyes. I can't tell what she's thinking.

"I wasn't kidding about how you'll lose out financially from his death," Kourtney tells Selene while typing into her phone. "You're likely not in his will. I'll get something from his estate, but it would have been better if he died after the divorce."

"Well, shit happens," I say, and Kourtney finally catches on to how Selene hasn't caught on.

Hobo's sister exhales deeply. "Well, I'll get you something."

317

"I don't need anything. I have a job here, and Hoyt pays well."

When I grin at Selene's praise, Kourtney rolls her eyes. "Oh, she's precious, but I'll still get what I can. You deserve way more. I don't care if you keep the money or donate it. I'm not letting his estate cut you out completely."

For the ride home, Selene remains overly quiet. We haven't been working since my shooting. I'm taking my time, testing the resolve of my enemies, feeling out my allies, and enjoying time with Selene.

We arrive home to find Yazmin alone in the living room. She's stretched out on the couch, flipping channels while eating Doritos. Wise Guy sniffs around for crumbs, having learned that trick from Joie.

"What's wrong?" Yazmin asks, sitting up and frowning at the expression on her sister's face. "Did they tell you anything about your shooting?"

"LeVoy was murdered."

"How?"

"Someone shot him."

Standing, Yazmin asks, "Are you sure it's not a trick?"

"They seemed like real detectives."

Watching their conversation unfold, I wonder again if these two would crash and burn without supervision. Their naivete makes me want to hide them from the world.

"He's dead?" Yazmin asks, taking Selene's hands.

I stand nearby, struggling with how to respond if they start crying. I don't think I have it in me to pretend to care about that motherfucker's death.

Instead, Selene and Yazmin startle me by squealing. They begin jumping up and down.

Rather than have to fake empathy, I stand back and grin at their reaction.

"He can't ruin your life anymore," Yazmin says as Selene squeals again.

They hug each other, laughing and crying. I've never been happier to have ended a life than I am right now.

One day, I might explain shit to Selene about the gunman who shot me and how Nomad did LeVoy. Or maybe she doesn't need to know anything more than she's free.

Her fear of LeVoy kept Selene from making long-term plans. Now, she can look at her future without worrying about that piece of shit ruining any more of her life.

SELENE

Ding, dong, the dickhead's dead! That's what Patrice says when she hears LeVoy was murdered. She even dances with Cheryl as Yazmin and I watch.

My grandmother was already thrilled when I texted to say we were moving out. She really did fear Yazmin and I would never leave.

Her worries weren't farfetched. We didn't know how to do anything when we arrived. She couldn't be certain if we'd squat in her place until she was in the ground. But less than two months after we arrived, she's getting her house back.

"Don't be strangers," she says and startles me with a hug. "You've got a second chance. Don't blow it."

As she hugs Yazmin, Cheryl suggests we make a habit of joining them for dinner. I hope I can find a way to build something real with Patrice. She's resented my mother for decades, but I'm not Mariah. Maybe she can learn to trust the woman I've become.

Yazmin and I move our scant belongings into Hoyt's house. She'll stay with us until her lease starts.

Those next weeks are wild. Yazmin and I organize the Valley Gorge office. Hoyt has a few guys move most of the paperwork from the Gin Mill to the business campus. We fill file cabinets and buy proper office furniture along with a fridge for the kitchenette.

One weekend, at the farmer's market, Yazmin and I discover old photos of McMurdo Valley. One taken during a parade reveals Patrice and her two young daughters in the crowd. In another town celebration, we spot Glenn with Nash on his shoulders. We buy them for the office to give the space a warmer feel.

Before Yazmin starts, Hoyt has a security feature installed. Now, she'll need to buzz people in rather than letting anyone walk through the door. I bet he's thinking about those suited men who leered me. I'm relieved she'll have more security.

I keep waiting for Yazmin to react to the Nash thing. For weeks, she's busy setting up the office and then her house. During that time, she never seems bothered by what happened. However, I'm not naïve enough to believe her messed-up brain will allow her to walk away from trauma unscathed.

Living with Hoyt is easier than I expect. Patrice warns we'll be at each other's throats after spending all day and night together. She's wrong for two reasons.

First, Hoyt is endlessly entertaining to me, so I rarely get annoyed by him.

Second, we actually do spend time apart. A few nights a week, Hoyt hangs out with his club. He needs to be present for them. They aren't work buddies but his second family.

I use that time to hang out with Yazmin at her place. Or she'll come over and spend the night at the house.

We're learning to cook. So far, Joie's liked everything we made. Though she insists Tracey makes better mashed potatoes.

I love Joie's honesty, even if her words sometimes hurt my feelings. Hoyt's working on her learning a little more tact. He's also trying to avoid his dumbfounded stare whenever I ask stupid questions. I'm working on not taking everything so personally.

Though Joie's a great kid, we take a while to get used to each other on a deeper level. Mostly, I struggle with acting like a parent.

After a while, I come to realize I'll never be a good disciplinarian. I'm afraid of responding like my parents did. If I get angry, I'm turning into my father. If I shut down my emotions, I'm becoming my mother.

"I want to help more," I tell Hoyt one night. "But I get stuck."

321

"You just met Joie," he assures me. "I'm her dad. Let me handle her bullshit. You can enjoy the fun stuff."

I do like the cool part of parenting. Her baseball games are exciting. She has so much hustle and stops many runs. I probably clap too much. I'm just so proud of her, even if her team usually loses.

After one loss, we attend the usual pizza party. Joie remains irritated throughout, keeping her distance from the other players. Hoyt whispers a warning about Joie's upcoming "roid rage."

We arrive home, where she paces before focusing too hard on me.

"I want to swim," she announces.

"Go swim, then," Hoyt says as he checks his phone. "Or we can work out in the gym."

"I want Selene to swim, too."

Hoyt frowns at his daughter and then at me. Though he tries to protect me, I agree to swim.

I've felt so confident lately. I walk around naked all the time in front of Hoyt.

Wearing Tracey's one-piece swimsuit, I'm relieved my ugliest scars are hidden. I insist to myself that I'm capable of swimming with Hoyt and Joie. There's no reason to be afraid.

Yet, I stand at the edge of the indoor pool and refuse to remove my towel. The panic grips me tighter than I do the fabric.

Joie swims around, calling out to me in her fearless way. I was never so confident, especially not at twelve. My father was terribly annoyed when I hit puberty. Hoyt simply treats his daughter like she's the same person he's always loved.

I want to be open like that with Joie. She's my family. I don't need to hide.

However, I can barely pry my fingers from the towel before I force it to drop at my feet. I step into the water, trying to pep-talk myself out of a panic attack.

322

Except I'm exposed in a way I rarely am. This pool room is large with many windows. I'm not alone with Hoyt or Yazmin. The entire world can see and judge me.

I start gulping air as if I'm drowning. Joie's blue eyes turn concerned. She looks so much like her father. I hope she grows up to be strong like him.

Hoyt joins us in the pool. Standing behind me, he slides his wide hand across my stomach and rests the other against my shoulder. Similar to the first day we went target shooting, he gently guides me past my panic. I lean back against him and inhale easier. The world stops spinning. I can see straight again.

Feeling guilty now, Joie reaches out her hand and says, "Don't be afraid. You look beautiful in Tracey's old lady swimsuit."

Chuckling at her wording, I fight through the exhaustion brought on by these panic attacks. I take her hand and walk forward. Hoyt joins us in the deep end.

His gaze says everything. I'm safe with Joie and him. Family works differently for them than it did for mine. If I find myself dancing too close to the edge, they'll be there to bring me back rather than shove me over the side.

I know I'm not magically healthy. Love didn't fix a lifetime of submission and pain. LeVoy's death hasn't ripped away the terror of our life together. Shooting hoops in the pool with Hoyt and Joie can't turn me confident.

Yet, I'm stronger than I was two months ago when I arrived in McMurdo Valley and met a handsome biker president in need of an assistant.

HOYT'S EPILOGUE

Out of morbid curiosity, I get a copy of LeVoy Garry's autopsy record. My focus goes to the gnarly pictures of what remained of his head. Wynonna is more interested in something mentioned in passing in the file.

"He had a vasectomy," she mutters, tapping that part of the page. "What a piece of shit."

The asshole must have loved getting Selene's hopes up over a baby, all while knowing he was fixed.

"Selene will be so excited," Wynonna says.

"No, I can't tell her."

My sister frowns. "Why?"

"Remember when it took you a few months to get pregnant? You got upset like you were defective."

"Yeah, and this guy ensured Selene went through that shit for years. She told me how much she wanted a child."

"Exactly, but what if she can't get pregnant now? I shouldn't raise her hopes."

Wynonna smiles at my concern. "You're so sweet to worry about her heart. Especially when you had all those ball injuries and probably can't knock her up anyway."

"You're the only one who's ever nailed me in the balls."

"What about Joie or my kids? Babies love to stomp on testicles. It's written into their programming."

Ignoring Wynonna's teasing, I make her promise to keep her flappy mouth shut about a possible baby. If it happens, it'll be a fun surprise for Selene. If it doesn't, she won't suffer another disappointment.

With LeVoy dead, I'm free to make things legal between Selene and me. Our wedding is small with only our closest family. My club is there. Her parents aren't.

I never plan to let them near Selene or any kids we might have. They broke my woman and deserve none of her blessings.

Marriage to Selene suits me. I enjoy her company. We don't get bored spending time together. She's easily entertained by my stories and interests while I find her endlessly fascinating.

We fall into an easy routine. Target shooting becomes a family affair with Joie and Yazmin joining us. We often go to lunch together afterward.

Tennis is another regular activity. At first, Selene struggles to keep up. Her body doesn't always cooperate when wants to exercise it. We've started training in the home gym to build up our muscles fucked sideways by our shootings.

After a few times at the tennis court, Selene realizes she doesn't need to work very hard to beat Joie and me. We're terrible at hitting the balls.

I don't know why my hand-eye coordination is so damn bad at sports. I can time shit just fine when I'm fighting or doing just about anything else. Yet, Joie and I miss half the balls flying toward us.

Joie still likes tennis. She often practices her swing with Selene during the weekends.

They're so funny together. Joie dominates their relationship, making Selene seem like the younger sibling.

However, my woman doesn't sit on her ass and watch me parent. She engages with Joie, playing video games and holding the punching bag when our kid is pissed.

Selene is desperate to connect with people. When Joie comes to her after school to share, I see how much my wife's face lights up.

One day, while Joie practices karate moves on her stepmom, Selene gets dizzy and ends up on her ass.

"I didn't even touch her," Joie says as we help Selene up.

Still seeming spaced out, Selene mumbles, "I just got dizzy."

When her vertigo continues for a week, I insist we see a doctor. That's when he announces her pregnancy.

"No," Selene says in a strained voice.

"Yes," the doctor replies.

"How?" she whimpers.

When the doctor gives her a weird look, I answer, "It's probably from all the fucking."

The doctor hears the tension in my voice and backs off. Oblivious to my temper, Selene starts crying. She remains teary-eyed until we get home.

"It won't stick," she tells me when I ask again what's wrong. "My body is messed up."

"I think you didn't get pregnant with LeVoy because he was old and shitty. Let's assume that's why and focus on how I'm hot and powerful."

Selene smiles at my wording. "I won't believe it until I feel the baby move. It seems like a cruel joke."

No longer sure about keeping my secret, I admit, "LeVoy had a vasectomy. Maybe he did that after you left him. But it also might be why you couldn't get pregnant."

Selene's expressive face reveals her working out little signs from the past that she missed. When her gaze meets mine, she allows a hopeful smile.

"So, this baby might stick?"

Grinning, I kneel and nuzzle her belly. "Hopefully. If not, we can try again and again. Fucking you is a fantastic way to spend my day."

Selene chills out after we cuddle for a while, but she still insists we keep the news quiet. Secrecy might work easier if she wasn't constantly dizzy. Her vertigo ends tennis games, shooting, and even walking around the property. Selene feels like she's spinning when just sitting down.

By the time she's showing, everyone pretty much figured out she's pregnant.

"Name the baby Walker," Joie announces one night while we watch "Walker, Texas Ranger."

"Okay," Selene says, resting with her eyes closed to deal with a bad case of vertigo.

"We'll see," I add.

"No, she already agreed," Joie replies. "You've been outvoted."

I throw a pillow at my laughing daughter who announces, "If it's a girl named her Svetlana."

"No," I answer before Selene can agree. "And why that name?"

"There was a girl in my class with that name. She smelled like chocolate."

I grin at Joie's teasing. "She still smells like white chocolate," I explain while rubbing Selene's feet. "My beautiful dessert. But no to Svetlana."

Fortunately, we never need to negotiate a girl's name. Walker Macready is born after a long, painful labor, followed by an emergency C-section.

I've never been as scared in my life as when I hold Selene's hand during the surgery. Her blood pressure drops as she stares at me with blank eyes. The doctor gets that anxious tone when he speaks to the nurses.

I feel myself losing her. Beyond the panic, I'm pissed. Selene fought so hard to survive. My love offered her a second chance. Yet, I'm also why her body is failing.

My large son is born screaming. He says what I can't. *The world is ending. Nothing will be okay again if Selene doesn't survive.*

Five days later, our family returns home. Tracey attaches herself to Selene. I barely leave my woman's side. The club rallies around, ensuring everything runs smoothly while I focus on Selene and the baby.

Over time, life settles back down. Selene gets stronger. She spends every waking moment in awe of the son we created together. I don't think she trusted Walker would be okay until she held him in her arms.

LeVoy might be dead, but his cruelty burned scars deep inside Selene.

"I love you," I say one night while we listen to Walker gurgling in his nearby crib.

Selene presses against my body and whispers, "I love you, too. Every day and in every way."

Smiling at her certainty, I force myself to say the words. "You can't get pregnant again. It's too dangerous."

"I know. I should have gotten fixed when I was cut open."

"We had no time to think of any of that. And I don't want you cut open again. I'll get fixed to be sure. Walker is a gift, Selene, but losing you isn't an option."

I was so worried Selene wouldn't understand. She gets ideas in her head about how things ought to work. She's also used to sacrificing her safety and happiness to please others. I suspect she'd carry more kids if I insisted.

Except nearly losing her broke something in me. My life was too fucking golden for too long. When I thought Selene would die, I looked into the abyss and realized I didn't have the stomach for that kind of pain.

Give me a fistfight or a shootout. I'll go berserk until I'm triumphant. Yet, the day in the hospital, I'd been completely helpless. I never want to feel that way again.

However, my fear helped me understand my wife's mental scars better. Logic alone can't defeat raw panic. When I can't find her in the house, I get paranoid despite my common sense saying she's probably upstairs. Hell, I've gotten agitated when she spends too long in the restroom. That isn't rational behavior. Despite knowing I'm overreacting, I can't control the feeling.

For most of her life, Selene lived gripped by fear. That's why she still struggles every day with her past trauma. I see her hesitating at times. Her eyes might fill with absolute terror over the smallest shit.

Thanks to our routine, we both move past our fears. All of those good days patch over the damage from the bad ones.

Once I stop being so paranoid about Selene's safety, I take her riding with me. I've long wanted to feel her arms wrapped around my waist while I ride my Fat Boy on the roads I've known since I was a kid.

Sure, I insist on her wearing a helmet, and I go slow enough to get outpaced by an old timer on a bicycle. Still, Selene feels great on my hog. She also smiles like a goddess when we return home.

"Next time, maybe we can go fast," she suggests and strokes my chest.

Grinning, I think back to the day we met. An overly nervous Selene could barely get out a full sentence. She remained shy even after moving into the house.

Every day, Selene finds her voice easier. When she does stumble, she'll look to me for strength. I'm no longer the scary stranger she couldn't deny. These days, I'm the complicated man she can't live without.

SELENE'S EPILOGUE

With my habit of missing super obvious things, I often feel like a moron. Like how I never once considered LeVoy was killed by Hoyt.

"I assumed you suspected," Yazmin tells me when I mention my revelation.

"He was paying Kourtney to get my divorce. I figured he had things handled, so why kill LeVoy?"

"Because LeVoy sent the man who shot Hoyt," she says like everything was very obvious.

"How did you figure that out?"

"The way they acted after Hoyt was shot. It seemed like they knew who had attacked them. Then, LeVoy died less than a week later."

"Why wouldn't he tell me?"

"Do you feel bad knowing LeVoy nearly killed Hoyt?" Teary-eyed, I nod when I consider how my problems might have ended the man I love. "Well, that's why he kept it a secret. Hoyt likes protecting you."

I think of her words later when I'm in bed with Hoyt.

"Did you kill LeVoy?"

"Nomad did. I was too busy getting babied by you."

Cuddling closer, I whisper, "Thank you."

That's the last we ever speak about LeVoy's death. I'd already split the money from my ex's estate between Yazmin and Patrice. They both saved my life—one by keeping me alive and the other by providing a second chance.

Though Patrice claims she doesn't need the money, I remind her how she promised to take Cheryl on vacation.

They do travel more after my gift. I'm glad I could give her a little relaxation after she spent her life fighting so hard.

Tracey also starts taking more little trips. She knows Joie is in good hands with me, so she's comfortable about going away.

My preteen daughter learns to trust me as a real mom rather than just as her dad's girlfriend. Joie's going through a wild time in her life, needing a woman's advice. I'll never be the parent to lay down the law. However, I can offer her hugs and a shoulder to cry on when the world makes no sense.

After Hoyt and I started dating, he talked about getting me a baby. Like we could pick one up at the store. It sounded silly, but I let myself dream.

Yet, I was still shocked when I got pregnant. LeVoy fucking with me all those years was less of a surprise.

Pregnancy zaps my energy, and constant vertigo makes me feel trapped for seven months. Despite my Lamaze classes, I'm unprepared for how my labor goes on and on. The C-section leaves one more scar on my body. During surgery, Hoyt is so afraid I'll die. Throughout the pregnancy and delivery, I kept worrying my son would prove to be a mirage.

Once Walker is born and I trust in this blessing, I promise myself to be the best mom I can. If I'm unsure, I'll ask questions. If I need help, I'll reach out to those who love me.

My son is so beautiful. Walker reminds me of Hoyt, from his blond hair and blue eyes to how he bulldozes his way into every room.

I love holding his little body against me and soaking in all his cuddles. Walker loves riding around on his dad's big shoulders, but he's also a sucker for his mama's lap. When he gets hurt, only I can soothe his tears. He thinks I'm funny, even though I'm not.

Often, Hoyt will catch Walker watching me like I'm the coolest thing ever.

"I know how he feels," Hoyt says, building up my confidence as he has from day one.

Walker's mostly a calm kid, though he goes wild at Joie's games. My little berserker will holler and stomp his feet whenever she does anything remotely cool.

By the end of junior high, Joie starts hitting the ball more often. Walker goes absolutely berserk when she gets her first homerun. He runs back and forth, hollering and waving his arms like the world is on fire.

Wynonna asks me if I mind being the only girly girl in a house full of butch bullies.

"Hoyt's my favorite person," I tell her. "Having two smaller versions of him is a dream. Besides, I get my girly-girl fix with Yazmin."

Even after Walker is born and I'm home more, I still love riding around in Hoyt's big truck. Though I'm past needing a step stool to get up into the passenger seat, Hoyt never stops helping me down. I use his assistance as an excuse to feel him up. Sometimes, we fondle each other so much, we're late to our destinations.

Over the years, I've learned to accept my scarred body. I wear shorts and tank tops, revealing what I survived. I'll never sport a bikini at a club pool party, but I've learned to love myself more thanks to Hoyt.

I've also gotten past some of the hurt I felt toward my parents. Even after Walker's born, Hoyt refuses to allow them in McMurdo Valley. Patrice approves of his anger. She long felt excluded. Now, she's the one on the inside.

A part of me still wishes my mom and I could get closer. When I was healing at her house, she treated me kindly. She also gave Yazmin and me money to come here rather than forcing us back to Bossier City.

Yet, when I tell her Hoyt doesn't want them to visit and meet Walker, she reminds me why we'll never enjoy a real relationship.

"If that's what he wants, you should listen to him," she replies, forever submitting even to men she doesn't know.

One day, I admit to Yazmin, "I sometimes wish our father would die, and Mom would come here. She could find closure with Patrice and be free."

"She'd probably just marry another man like him," Yazmin says and sighs. "But you never know."

The longer I live in McMurdo Valley, the more I let go of my past. I'd been long defined by my father's cruelty, my mother's submission, and LeVoy's abuse. I wasn't really a person as much as a possession.

Now, I'm a woman filled with hopes rather than just fears. I'm passionately in love with my husband and our kids. Yazmin isn't my only friend, though she remains the person who knows me best. I have hobbies from tennis to photography to riding on Hoyt's motorcycle.

My life was once a prison. I nearly lost everything one dark night when an evil man sent his hired gun. Even with my second chance, I felt like a discarded object unworthy of a future. I nearly talked myself out of the interview for the assistant job.

Everything changed after I met a sexy biker who would become my boss. Once Hoyt Macready took the helm, my life's been on a very specific path to an extremely blessed destination.

THE END

Made in the USA
Monee, IL
13 September 2022

13925281R00184